Praise for Gerry Boyle

Straw Man

Winner, Crime Fiction, 2017 Maine Literary Award

"Deftly drawn characters and a strong sense of place add texture and depth to this gritty tale of rural crime and vigilante justice."
—*Publishers Weekly*

"Gerry Boyle is a rare author—a true grandmaster of suspense. It's no wonder his latest, *Straw Man*, is unforgettable . . . This hypnotically suspenseful, beautifully written novel is impossible to put down."
—Gayle Lynds, *New York Times* bestselling author of *The Assassins*

Once Burned

"Plot, characterization, atmosphere—everything works in Boyle's excellent 10th Jack McMorrow mystery."
—*Publisher's Weekly*

"A truly riveting read from first page to last, *Once Burned* continues to document novelist Gerry Boyle as a master of the mystery/suspense genre."
—*Midwest Book Review*

"The details a   1 observational
skills come a

tery Magazine

RANDOM ACT

A JACK McMORROW MYSTERY

Other books by Gerry Boyle

RANDOM ACT

A JACK McMORROW MYSTERY

GERRY BOYLE

ISLANDPORT PRESS

This is a work of fiction. Names, characters, places, and incidents either are the product of the author's imagination or are used fictitiously. Any resemblance to actual events or persons, living or dead, is entirely coincidental.

Random Act
A Jack McMorrow Mystery

First Islandport Edition / June 2019

ISBN: 978-1-944762-68-1
ISBN: 978-1-944762-69-8 (ebook)
Library of Congress Control Number: 2019931592

Islandport Press
P.O. Box 10
Yarmouth, Maine 04096
www.islandportpress.com
books@islandportpress.com

Publisher: Dean Lunt
Book Design: Teresa Lagrange, Islandport Press
Cover image courtesy of iStock.com/sanjeri

Printed in the USA

For Vic. Onward.

If you cry about a nickel, you'll die 'bout a dime.
—Robert Johnson, "Last Fair Deal Gone Down"

1

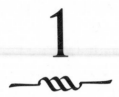

It was December 5, a Wednesday. The snow had come in wet at midday, fat, sticky flakes giving way to rain. And then the temperature had plummeted and the rain had frozen into a shell of hard crust.

That was the last day we'd seen Louis.

We were all supposed to work in the woods the next morning, cutting for our old friend Mrs. Hodding. The usual plan: Meet at Clair's barn at 6:15, have coffee, load the saws and tools, ride up to Hyde in his truck. The skidder and trailer were parked in the woodyard.

Louis didn't show up. He didn't answer his phone or our texts, sent when Clair and I were leaving in the morning, when we broke for lunch, when we loaded up the gear to drive home.

Friday afternoon we packed up early, got in my truck, and headed south for Sanctuary.

"It's not like he's never gone silent," I said, as we turned off Route 3, headed for Liberty.

Clair didn't reply at first, just looked out at the woods, the black-trunked leafless trees looking like a fire had swept through. I waited. More woods, a right at 220, the light falling fast as the sun slid lower behind us.

"I know," Clair said finally, knowing I'd hold my last thought. "But when he starts to sink, he holes up. Just want to make sure he isn't sinking too deep."

For Louis, deep was a very dark place. Ramadi, 3/5 Marines. House to house. Insurgents firing from around every corner. Screaming women and children. A sniper killing Louis's best friend, Paco, his brains spattered on Louis's face. Kicking in doors and killing the armed men inside. Killing all of them, no prisoners. Just killing, killing, killing. Not a fight to the death. A fight immersed in death, as Louis once put it, in a whiskey-driven talk in Clair's barn, "blood as thick as mud."

We knew this about Louis, Clair more than me. Vietnam, Iraq, Afghanistan. Different wars, same story. They'd been there, had both fought hard, with great skill and a dose of luck. And survived. And then they'd retreated to their refuges in the Maine woods—in Clair's case, to marry and raise a family. In Louis's case, to be alone.

Clair took a long breath, added, "Just want to know he's okay, that's all."

We rattled along, the Toyota pickup jouncing over bumps and potholes. The sun had lapsed behind the ridges to our west, leaving the road in a side-shadowed darkness. I flicked the lights on, concentrated. Saw red glowing eyes on the roadside to my right.

"Deer," I said.

I gripped the wheel.

"He's probably fine," I said. "Lost his phone. Got absorbed in a good book. Decided to go backpacking someplace, sleep out."

"He only does that when things aren't good," Clair said.

"And he always comes back," I said.

We were quiet as we swung east on two-lane 105, zigzagged our way through the six-house settlement of Washington, crested rises over streams, twisted down steep grades, then hurtled back up. And then we were in the town of Sanctuary, where there was more woods, more darkness. For Louis it lived up to its name.

I slowed and waited for the turnoff, then drove north for three miles, eased up on the gas as the entrance to Louis's long driveway drew closer. And then I spotted the single red reflector nailed to a tree. The same tree held one end of a steel cable that Louis sometimes slung across the drive, padlocking it in place. He did that when he wanted to make sure he was going to be alone.

The cable was down.

"Interesting," Clair said. "Stop here."

I did, just short of the turnoff. With the lights on and the engine running, Clair got out and I followed. He stopped and stared at the gravel driveway, where tracks showed a car had turned off and driven down the driveway.

"Not his Jeep," I said.

"No," Clair said. "And they were here for a minute. Can see where the exhaust melted the snow."

He squatted.

"That was Thursday," he said, "the way the tracks are frozen in. And they don't come back out."

We climbed back into the truck and I started down the driveway, the tire tracks leading the way. The single lane continued for about a mile, the trees close on both sides. We crossed a black-running stream on a wooden bridge, hemlock timbers that Louis had cut and milled. We swung to the left and climbed a short rise. Another jog to the right and we could see the vague shadow of the cabin.

No lights.

Drawing closer, we could see Louis's jacked-up Cherokee parked in the dooryard by the pole barn. Beside it was an SUV. The truck lights swept past it. A new Audi. Vermont plates. A numbered sticker on the back window, lower right.

"Rental," I said.

"Huh," Clair said.

"Tourists and criminals," I said.

He reached under his Carhartt, made an adjustment. His gun.

"These little Glock forty-threes," Clair said. "Hardly know it's there. Nine millimeter's a sign of my advancing age, I suppose, not wanting to lug the forty or forty-five." A little patter to cover up his concern for Louis.

We got out and looked toward the house. There was smoke coming from the chimney, thick and puffy like the fire was damped down.

Clair slipped a flashlight from his jacket pocket and turned it on. The blue-white beam swept the Audi, the Jeep, the yard behind them. We turned and crossed the dooryard side by side, stepped up onto the porch, and stood.

Footsteps. Inside.

The flashlight beam swiveled and swept the floorboards of the porch. There was a fine dusting of snow. No footprints.

"Might have gone out the back," Clair said.

"Yeah," I said. "Dog must be with him."

"Clearly," Clair said.

Louis's dog was named Friend—130 pounds of shepherd and hound—and he protected the perimeter here. If he pegged you as a bad guy, only a bullet would slow him. A big one.

Clair stepped to the big plank door and leaned close. Listened. He motioned to me to come closer, and I leaned in. A woman's voice from the right said, "Who is it? Is somebody there?"

An accent. Faintly Eastern European.

"Friends of Louis," I said.

"He's not here," the woman said, still to the right of the door.

"Is he out back?" I said.

There was no reply.

Instead there were two footsteps, from the direction of her voice. I reached out and knocked again. Then said, "Hello," lifted the latch, gave the plank door a push. It swung open, no creak.

I stepped in. Clair followed, swept the light across the floor. There were two L.L.Bean boots off to the right, nobody in them. I was starting to turn to the left when the woman spoke.

"Freeze," she said. "Or I'll blow your fucking head off."

A white light blazed on, wavering in the darkness.

"Arms above your head," she barked. The same accent. Agitated. We raised them, half turned toward the light.

"We're Louis's friends," I said.

"I don't know that," she said.

"Where's Louis?" Clair said. An ominous tone.

"Keep your hands up." A tremor in the voice. Fear? Anger?

Clair looked at the light. My eyes were adjusting. I could see a woman's shape behind the glare. Not old. Athletic.

"Lie down on the floor," she said. More accent. "Hands straight out above your head."

"Where's Louis?" I said.

"Get down," she shouted, and the light moved to her right, behind us, in front of the open door. The cold air rushed in.

"You a cop?" I said. "Or do you just watch a lot of television?"

"I won't say it again. And I mean that. Last chance."

We eased to our knees, then to our bellies. The floor was cold. The light on the gun illuminated the room in rapid flicks. I saw a woman's handbag on the island that separated the big open room from the kitchen. It was brown. On the next sweep I saw a small leather duffel. Matching.

I turned my head and saw her, peripherally. A shadow. Dark hair, jeans and a cream-colored jersey. The gun in the ready position. Tan grips and a flashlight under the barrel. Louis's new Sig. Had he given it to her, or had she used it on him?

"Arms out," the woman said. "Stay flat."

I saw red socks. Another gust of cold wind blew through the door, snow scattering like fairy dust.

The woman moved closer, training the gun on Clair's back, then swinging it toward me. A beep and the woman said, "Where are you?"

"Right here," Louis said.

He was behind us, had come through the door.

"Hey, Louis," I said.

"Hey," Louis said, like this was all normal. And then to the woman, "It's okay."

"Okay. Sure. But how was I supposed to know that?" the woman said. "They just walked right in."

The light dimmed, the gun trained on the floor behind us. And then there was the clicking of dog claws on wood as Friend trotted inside, sniffed Clair, then me. He wagged his tail and we stood. The woman slipped her finger out of the trigger guard, her nails the color of pink pearls. She smiled, but not apologetically.

"This is Marta," Louis said. "Friend of mine. We go back to high school."

"I had no way of knowing," Marta said. "Who you were."

"Marta has been through some stuff," Louis said. "Bad guys came to her house."

"Too bad for them," I said.

"Not really," Louis said. "They caught her asleep."

A momentary vision of that, its implications. It all made more sense.

We nodded. She passed the gun to her left hand and stepped over, shook Clair's hand, then mine. Looked us in the eye. Hers were big and dark, with a hyperalertness, like an animal that navigates in the dark.

"Louis's friends. Wonderful to meet you," Marta said.

"Likewise," I said. "Sort of."

"I'm sorry. But you understand?"

"They killed her boyfriend," Louis said.

A pause as that sunk in, too.

"I'm sorry," Clair said.

Marta nodded. Smiled. She was very attractive. High cheekbones. Full lips. Hair pulled back in a short stub at the nape of her neck.

"So you can understand why I may have overreacted," she said.

"Didn't overreact at all," Clair said. "But what was next, if Louis hadn't come in?"

She looked to him, like suddenly it had turned into a competition. Twenty questions on home defense.

"Search you," she said. "My boyfriend, Nigel, he used to tell me what to do."

"Search both of us?" Clair said. "How?"

"Start with you. Put my left hand on your back, keep the gun in my right."

"And then you do him?"

"Yes. Switch hands."

"We were too close together. As soon as you shift your attention to Jack, I kick a leg out from under you. You start to fall, I roll over and fire with the weapon still in my shoulder holster. It swivels."

"But I still can shoot you, right?" Marta said.

"Low percentage, because you're falling, gun pointing up. You're dead before you get off a second shot."

He opened his jacket and pivoted the holster and the little Glock. "Word to the wise. For a friend of Louis."

Marta seemed to be running the sequence through her mind, then she said, "That's good to know," like he'd told her how to change a tire. "Louis told me you were very—how did he say it?—resourceful."

The dog flopped on the floor and sighed, bored with all the talk.

Louis moved closer to Marta, put a hand on her shoulder and leaned close, mouthed the words, "Good job." Gave her a quick kiss on the cheek.

Two things from that: His instructions. If somebody comes in . . . And she wasn't his long-lost sister.

"Did all this happen recently?" I said.

"Three months," Louis said.

"In some ways it seems like yesterday," Marta said. "Other ways, like from a different life."

"You survived," I said.

"Yes, I ran, hid in the wine cellar," Marta said.

"I'm sorry," I said.

"It was hard, in many ways," she said, but in a flat tone that said she'd moved on.

"So what brings you here?" Clair said.

They looked at each other, held the glance.

"We were friends," Louis said. "In high school."

"He makes it sound like the two of us, we were in the chess club," Marta said, smiling at me.

"You weren't?" I said.

"No, we—"

She looked back at Louis.

"Dated," she said.

She leaned into him with her hip and pressed. He gave her a squeeze and smiled back. It was as surprising as the gun. Almost.

2

We stood there for a moment, adjusting to this new world order. Louis with a woman. The woman with a gun pointed at our heads.

Then we moved to the kitchen part of the big room, and Louis threw a log into the woodstove.

"Sorry to barge in," I began. "But you didn't answer your phone, and—"

"We got worried," Clair said.

"I think my phone went dead," Louis said.

He went to the refrigerator, took out a growler of his home-brewed ale, and put it on the counter. Then he took down four canning jars and filled them one by one, handed them around. "English-style black," he said. "Got a little bored, all this IPA."

It was Marta who first raised a glass. "To old friends," she said. "And making new ones."

Off to such a good start.

We clinked jars and drank. Marta lowered hers and said, "Very nice. If I'd known Louis had all these talents, I would have tracked him down sooner."

The accent was fainter, like it came out in stress.

"Been a long time?" Clair said.

"Since before Iraq," Louis said.

"Our last night was in a motel outside Camp Pendleton. The Best Western in Oceanside, eleven years ago now. It's hard to believe. But we took up right where we left off."

She smiled at Louis. There was a lot of that going on.

"Like we started up the same conversation," she said. "Right, babe?"

Babe.

Marta moved to him, put her arm around his waist, in case we didn't get it.

"Heard a lot about you guys," she said. "Wish Louis had shown me pictures."

She put a hand on her left hip, kept her right on Louis's waist, stretched her right leg out as though she expected us to admire it. Then she glanced at Clair's chest, the lump under the jacket.

"Vietnam, right? I saw it on TV. Ken Burns."

Clair nodded. "A long time ago."

"Louis says you're—what do they call it? The real deal?" she said. Turned to me. "And you're a reporter."

Wariness in her tone.

"Somebody has to take notes," I said.

"Oh, Jack pulls his weight," Louis said. He went to the refrigerator and took out another brown jug, opened it, and topped off our jars.

"We should sit," Marta said, back in control.

We had the couch. Louis had his big chair. Marta sat on the arm of the chair, her arm still around his shoulders. He looked content, sated. Conjugal bliss, well-armed.

"Marta was here way back when. When it was just the little cabin down by the stream in all these woods," Louis said.

"Eleven years ago," I said. "A long time."

We smiled and sipped. She leaned closer to Louis and took his hand in hers.

"All that time deployed," Louis said. "I kinda lost my way, I guess."

"Me, too," Marta said. "The bright lights blinded me. But when we were together we were in love, or at least as in love as you can be at seventeen. But you know, I think that can be a lot."

She squeezed his hand.

"Marta and I were at Pelfrey at the same time."

"It's a boarding school in Pennsylvania," she said. "I was the new foreign student. My uncle in New York sent me there after my parents died."

"Died where?" I said.

"Kiev," she said. "Ukraine. Their car hit a bus."

"I'm sorry," I said.

She shrugged.

"I met Louis the first day at the school. He was the one who stuck up for me, everyone looking at me like I was nothing and nobody, some foreign freak. The only one had my back was Louis."

Louis the Good Samaritan. That I could picture. Never met a rescue mission he didn't like.

"To the girls there I was a target. They were awful. Made fun of my clothes, my shoes, my hair."

"Didn't like you because you were prettier than them," Louis said.

"The guys were different," she said. "I was their prey."

I'm sure you were, I thought. Waited as Marta drank, lowered the jar.

"At my first party, I'd been there, like, three weeks. Everyone drinking, somebody's parents' house, the mom and dad away. All these Americans with their big smiles and shiny white teeth. What do I know? They decide they get me drunk and have some fun with me. I went to use the bathroom upstairs and I can still remember the feeling, being swept along, you know? Out of control, not knowing what was happening, two of them pushing me down the hall and through a door, and the rest were waiting."

She glanced at Louis.

"But Louis was watching, had followed them upstairs. He bangs the door open as they're pushing me onto the bed. He pulls them off, throws them across the room. It was so great."

She grinned at the memory.

"One boy tries to punch him and Louis smashes his nose. Another one attacks him and Louis just hits him. *Kapow.*"

"Poochie Halloway," Louis said. "Always hated that guy."

All of this I could picture.

"There's blood all over the place and they're all yelling, but none of them dares to come close to us. After that they stayed away from me. Far away. They were all afraid of Louis."

She looked at him.

"Weren't they, babe."

We looked at him and back at her.

"So you started dating," Clair said.

"That whole year," Marta said. "Together all the time. Then the year ended and this counselor at the school got me into Bryn Mawr. The poor orphan girl. We decided we'd break it off for a bit, not do the long-distance thing. We thought we were being very mature. Louis was supposed to do a gap year. But he just disappears, like off the earth."

"Not totally off. Just Fallujah and Ramadi," Louis said.

"His mom and dad, they practically had heart attacks. They had no idea he was going to join up."

She looked to Louis.

"Remember your mother? Oh my God."

He nodded.

"I was so worried, but I always supposed he was still alive," Marta said. "I mean, I would have heard if he'd been killed or something, right? But still, maybe not. Maybe he's missing in battle, whatever they call it. Then, after how many years?"

"Eleven," Louis said.

"Where does Louis pop up?" she said.

She looked at us. We didn't answer.

"Facebook."

We looked at him. Louis? Facebook?

He shrugged. "Buddy wrote me a postcard. General Delivery, Sanctuary, Maine. Said the Three-Five had a Facebook page. Pictures of everybody back in Iraq."

"Good to reconnect," Clair said. "Those guys know you like nobody knows you. Or maybe ever will."

He looked at Marta.

"Somebody from school shared his picture," she said. "It was like, 'Louis Longfellow is back from the dead!' I cannot believe it. I message him, say, 'WTF, Louis? Where are you?' He said he was living in a cabin on the family land in Maine. I said, 'Are you with somebody?' I mean, I didn't want to visit him and his wife and kids, right? He said, 'Me and the dog.' I was on my way. Didn't even tell him."

Make sure he'd still be there, I thought.

"Surprised you found it," I said.

"Oh, I remembered. One school break we drove up and stayed in the little cabin and—"

She looked over at him and smiled, eyebrows twitching almost imperceptibly.

"Hung out," Louis said. I felt like I should blush.

"And that's what we've been doing," Marta said, looking at me, then Clair, making sure we knew what she meant. "Hanging out."

Clair looked at her and smiled, said, "I'm sure there's a lot to talk about."

There was a pause in the conversation while we all drank. The dog watched from the floor, his eyes flicking from person to person, coming to rest on Marta. When was she leaving?

"Sorry I didn't show on Thursday," Louis said. "Marta rolled in middle of the night. Then I couldn't find my phone. When I did, it was dead. Didn't see your texts until this morning."

"No problem," I said. "Good to get out of the house, go for a ride in the country."

"What else is there around here?" Marta said. "There's woods, and then there's more woods."

"After you've been here a while, it's more complicated," Clair said. "There's woods—and then there's different woods."

Marta looked at him, smiled. "Right. Maple trees, pine trees, some other kind of trees?"

Clair let it roll off.

"So where have you been, Marta?" I said.

"Oh, you can Google me. Marta Kovac. New York, Florida, London. Last stop, the Caribbean. My partner, Nigel, he had a place on Virgin Gorda."

I gave her a blank look. Nobody talks to reporters like somebody who feels the need to educate them.

"BVI?" Marta said. "It's the third-largest island."

Clair watched her, listened the way he does, taking it all in, not showing anything. The dog got up and circled the room, his claws clicking. Louis got up from his chair and went to the woodstove, put in two sticks. The dog followed him. Louis stood in front of the stove with his back to us and scratched Friend behind the ear.

"What happened? I said. "If you don't mind . . ."

Louis came back and sat. Marta looked at him, as if for encouragement. He nodded and she started in.

"Four men. An inflatable off a bigger boat offshore. Three of them came up from the path from the beach. Fourth one was a lookout. Somehow they disabled the alarms and surprised us in bed."

We waited.

"Nigel fought with them, of course. He was very tough."

"SAS," Louis put in. "But three on one . . ."

"Tough odds," Clair said. "But only if they're professionals."

For someone like Clair or Louis, amateurs weren't a problem.

"What did they want?" I said.

"Passwords. Account information. They were Russians."

"Huh," I said.

"Nigel didn't give up anything. He was trained for that sort of thing, they tell me."

"Yes," Clair said. "We all were."

"So, what . . . ?" I said.

"When Nigel was fighting them, I ran. There's a place in the wine cellar, a wall board that lifts off, with a space behind. It was a hiding place for jewelry, cash. I stayed in there."

She swallowed, took a long breath.

"To try to get the numbers, they tortured him," Louis said.

"Yes, left him tied to a chair in the bedroom. For hours."

"He bled out," Louis said.

"A couple of the accounts, they were emptied that night, like *whoosh*," Marta said. "Later the police told me the money went to a bank in the Philippines and then just disappeared."

"And they weren't caught?"

"No."

"How long ago?" I said.

"Three months and four days."

A pause, out of respect. I could see why Louis would want to be hospitable.

"I'm very sorry," I said.

Marta clasped her knees to her chest. We all watched the flames, Friend crouching close to Louis. Marta looked over at them and smiled like it was sweet, a man and his dog. Louis pulled on leather slippers that had been in front of the fire, picked up a canvas wood carrier, crossed the room, and went out through the side door to the woodshed. The dog followed.

Marta looked back at us.

"You're probably wondering what we have in common, Louis and I, after all these years."

A country song shot into my head. Willie Nelson. *If you've got the money, honey, I've got the time.*

"That year in school, we were both outsiders," she said. "Louis, by choice. He was the quiet rebel type; his parents had, like, all this money, but he didn't care. He thought it was all bullshit—Pelfrey, the social stuff. Me, I was always on the fringe. From a different place.

No parents. My uncle having nothing to do with me except to pay the bills."

"What did he do in the US?" I said.

"Parking lots," she said. "Those ones with the person in the little building, takes your money. He had, like, forty of them. New York. DC. Philly. He had girlfriends, fancy cars. When I finished at Pelfrey, he was in some sort of trouble. I was on my own."

"So, Bryn Mawr. What did you study?" Clair said.

"Art history."

"You like art?" I said.

"It's fine, but it was an investment. Art history majors come from money, generally. My girlfriends—and I made sure I had some—had brothers. I ran up a bunch of credit cards going to weddings."

"And weddings led to—?"

"I met Nigel at this fancy wedding in London. The bride's charming uncle. He was forty-one, I was twenty-three. Handsome in a British sort of way. I mean, think Daniel Craig, but better-looking."

"With money," I said.

"Some from his grandparents. His grandfather was Baron Toddington. An ancestor supposedly was at the signing of the Magna Carta. That gave them time to save up a pile of cash, I guess. Nigel added a bunch of his own."

"No Mrs. Nigel?" I said.

"He was separated. The divorce was like negotiating a nuclear arms treaty."

"But you weren't married?"

"We were going to do it as soon as the divorce went through, and then he wasn't sure. 'Why do we need government to make our relationship real?' and all that. Eight years in, still no ring. And then he goes and gets himself killed."

I hesitated, then said, "And the estate?"

"Ah, the reporter," Marta said. "No, a good question. The short answer is, his kids got everything. I guess he never changed the will. But hey, that's okay. Because I can say it now. For Nigel I was just another possession. The plane, the boats, the houses, the cars, the much-younger girlfriend."

In that order?

"And there were other things," Marta said.

She paused, like she was deciding whether to confide in two guys she's just held at gunpoint.

"Nigel was a domineering, abusive man. Psychologically, mostly, except for the hard squeezes. He'd get your upper arm and just crush it. At first it was okay, even if it was sort of paternal, him being older, it being his money, his world. So I thought it would get better, me being more equal. But more and more, I had no say over anything. If I didn't have everything the way he liked, told the cook to make his shepherd's pie, he shouted and pounded his fist. And then he left. Leaving me alone, that was his punishment for me. I was alone a lot. It was like they do with little kids who misbehave."

"Timeout," I said.

"Yes," Marta said.

She drank, a quick nervous gulp, then took a breath like she was readying herself for something.

"I'm sorry about what happened to him, but in a way, I'm glad to be rid of him," Marta said. "Oh my God, I can't believe I'm saying this. Isn't that awful?"

"No," Clair said. "It's not awful at all."

There was a rattle at the side door, Louis coming back with a load of firewood. She got herself together in an instant, looked at him adoringly. He knelt to stack the wood, and she said, "Babe, I'll get the door."

Marta put her jar down, padded over in her socks, glancing back at us to make sure we got it, this new world order and her place in it.

Not the help. Not alone anymore.

3

We rattled out of the drive, tracing our tire tracks in the snow. After we swung onto the road and I got the truck up to speed, Clair let out a long sigh.

"I know," I said.

"Pretty girl."

"His first real romance. Maybe his only."

"That sort of thing can stick," Clair said. He and Mary had been together since they were high school sweethearts.

"She drove all the way to Maine to see him," I said. "She's been through all of this traumatic stuff with this robbery, this abusive guy. Kind of like Louis and the wars."

"And she needs him," Clair said. "Don't underestimate that—not with Louis."

We looked out the windshield, the pickup slicing through the billowing snow like a plane through clouds.

"Isn't grieving much for old Nigel," Clair said.

"If he was abusive, I can see why."

"Sure. First rule for survivors like her: You move on, don't look back."

I nodded, and then we drove in silence all the way up to Route 105, took the left, and headed northwest, headlights flailing at the darkness. It was snowing harder, the flakes streaking in front of the truck like shooting stars. The snow was picking up and I slowed, then turned the dial to put the truck in four-wheel.

"How much money do you think Louis has?" I said.

Clair shrugged.

"Few months back, he told me he gave a couple of hundred thousand to the hospital in San Antonio for wounded vets," Clair said. "The one he was in."

"Not small change," I said.

"Last week, he sent twenty thousand to a buddy from his unit. Saw on the Facebook there that the guy's baby was sick, they had expenses. I get the feeling he does that kind of thing fairly regularly."

"Generous."

"I said that. He said, 'Whatever. Just spending the interest.' "

"And the grandfather made wire?" I said.

"A lot of wire in the world."

"Means a lot of money."

"She didn't come all the way up here to commune with nature."

We pondered that as the truck plunged through the snow squalls, leaving a swirling white cloud in its wake. We were at the crossroads at Liberty when I said, "Home invasions—most of the time the victims are known to the crooks in some way. Drug dealers have a falling-out. Somebody hears there's a stash of cash."

"Russian gangsters," Clair said.

"He's been in London," I said. "Swarming with them there, from what I understand."

"And she's Eastern European. Maybe she's got connections. Wonder who this Ukrainian uncle was."

We drove. The snow was sticking, the roadway turning into a white blanket.

"The longtime girlfriend gets wind she's left out of the will," I said.

"Probably knows vaguely where the money is parked, and how much," Clair said.

"Maybe she tips off somebody connected with criminal elements, as they say. Maybe the uncle."

"Have to be somebody tough, if he was SAS. Unless they were just gonna shoot him. But that doesn't get them anywhere."

"Had to move fast from the second they got in the door."

"Which maybe was left unlocked."

"The alarm system turned off."

We watched as dim taillights appeared in the swirling whiteness ahead of us, then the vague shape of a semi. I backed off.

"Listen to us," I said.

"Yes."

"Stranger things have happened."

"Much," Clair said.

4

I dropped Clair in his dooryard and drove on to my house, past the next stretch of woods. The lights were on in Sophie's bedroom, my girl waiting up.

I went in through the shed, grabbed a Ballantine ale from the fridge, and headed upstairs. Sophie was in bed, books piled around her like she'd dug her way out of a library. Roxanne was sitting beside her, listening to her read. *Blueberries for Sal.* There was a contest in the second grade. The student who read the most books got a gift certificate to the bookstore in Belfast. Sophie said she was in the lead.

"Dad," she said, and she kicked the covers off, took two hops, and gave me a hug around the waist. "Did you see it's snowing again?"

"I sure did."

"Can we get the toboggan out?"

"Tomorrow," Roxanne said. "After Daddy picks up the new toilet."

"Can we get one that has heat? Cilla's grammy has one that gets warm so when you sit down you don't freeze your buns."

"Wow," I said. "Cilla's grammy is living large."

"She lives in New York," Sophie said. "They go to visit her."

"Be worth it," I said. "A toilet like that."

Roxanne smiled, patted the bed beside her. "Bedtime," she said.

Sophie sprang back onto the bed and crawled back to her place and read.

Sal made friends with the bear cub in the blueberry barren. All was well with the world, his and ours.

When she was done, we gave her hugs and kisses and then Roxanne turned out the light and we left the room, the door ajar.

Downstairs Roxanne got a bottle of white out of the refrigerator and a glass from the cupboard. She poured and we sat down at the kitchen table. Touched glass and can.

"To love," I said.

She looked at me.

"What?"

"I'm hoping that's what Louis is in."

Roxanne froze in mid-sip, swallowed. "He found someone?"

"More like she found him."

I told her about Marta from high school.

"Louis is on Facebook?" Roxanne said.

I nodded.

"So all weekend they were—"

"Making up for lost time," I said. I raised my eyebrows up and down. "If you catch my drift."

"Huh," Roxanne said. "So what does she look like?"

"Very attractive. Dark hair sort of to here." I touched my shoulder blades. "A good figure, as they say."

"Was she nice?"

I hesitated.

"Once she put the gun away."

I told her about the Sig. The explanation for why Marta might be jumpy.

"My God," Roxanne said. "That's awful."

"Yeah. But it wasn't like she was devastated with grief."

I went through it—the parents dying in Ukraine. Brought to the US by her uncle. Goes to college mostly so she can latch on to a rich guy.

"Very 1950s," Roxanne said.

"It worked," I said.

I told her about how Nigel turns out to be domineering and abusive. And he won't tie the knot. And he's in some shady business that gets him killed by Russians. Marta not sorry to see him gone, but feels guilty for thinking it. In the end she gets screwed out of the money.

Roxanne was reaching for the bottle. I got up and took a box of stoned-wheat crackers from the cupboard, a block of Irish cheddar from the fridge. Sat back down and took out a stack of crackers. Sliced a piece of cheese with my Swiss Army knife. Offered it to Roxanne, who took it and held it. I made one of my own. We crunched.

"How much does Louis have?" Roxanne said. "Millions?"

"Several, be my guess."

"And she knows that?"

"Knew his family fifteen years ago," I said, "and clearly he hasn't spent it. I'll bet she can do the appreciation in her head."

"Huh," Roxanne said.

"Yup."

"You worried about him?"

"A little," I said. "But mostly that's Clair's job."

"Right," Roxanne said. "And remember what we decided."

"Compartmentalize," I said.

"Right. Nobody's gonna get past the firewall."

"No way, no how," I said.

She smiled, reached across the table, and touched my hand. She was beautiful, her hair mussed from the pillow at Sophie's bedtime, her sweater rumpled. Our eyes locked.

"The toilets are on sale at Home Department," she said. "Kohler Classic, two-piece. I considered beige but I think we should stick to white. The new ones use way less water, which even with a well—"

"I love you," I said.

Roxanne paused.

"I know," she said. "I love you, too."

"You never know what's coming."

"No," she said.

"One day you're lying by the pool and the next day you're running for your life."

"And you end up in the wilds of Maine."

"With a guy you haven't seen or talked to in ten years," I said.

"But he makes you feel safe."

"Even if you aren't."

We sipped our drinks.

"You think somebody could find her up here?" Roxanne said.

"Depends."

"On what?" she said.

"On how hard they want to look."

We stood there for a moment, thinking about it.

"Maybe they had masks on," Roxanne said.

"Yeah," I said. "We can only hope."

At 5:10 a.m. Saturday, I heard the clunk of Clair's plow dropping, then the scrape of metal on gravel and the rumble of his big Ford as he cleared the driveway. Home Department was in Riverport on Stillwater Avenue, out with the rest of the big-box stores. The store opened at six a.m. My plan was to be on the road by 5:30. I eased out of bed, took clothes from the bureau, went downstairs, and found my boots. I put them on in the kitchen, grabbed my parka off the hook.

And then I turned back, dropped the parka on the table. Went to the study, tapped the laptop on. In the blue glow I typed in *Nigel . . . home invasion . . . Virgin Gorda.*

Several hits: *BVI News* said his name was Nigel Dean. He was forty-nine. He died from injuries "sustained at the hands of unidentified intruders." Burglars broke in after staff had left for their weekly night off. It was the first murder on Virgin Gorda in thirteen years.

And this from the *Telegraph:* Multimillionaire investor Nigel Dean died in a burglary gone wrong at his estate. Dean was a former SAS officer who ran the private equity firm of Tortola Quay. He had three children and was divorced from Tabitha Wrigglesworth, the fashion magazine editor and daughter of Sir Roger Wrigglesworth, the MP. The crime was under investigation by the Royal Virgin Islands Police.

Nothing about Russians. Nothing about money being drained from accounts. Nothing about torture. Nothing about a witness. Nothing about the woman who had parachuted into our Maine woods from another world.

I sat in the cab and pondered as the truck warmed up, thought how my stories had changed over the years. I'd done drownings, women killed by their abusive husbands, hippie marijuana growers who got in too deep. Lately it had been gangs moving north from Boston, drug dealers trading dope for guns. Shootings where there used to be fistfights. Now someone on the run from the Russian mob holed up in Sanctuary, Maine.

The walls between us and the outside world had been breached. Waldo County didn't seem so much of a hideaway anymore.

I pushed it all back and pulled out of the drive, flicking the lights on as I turned onto the road. Felt myself sour, pressed the gas and tried to fight it off. But the questions wormed their way back in. Was there an accomplice in Louis's bed? Had she left a trail of crumbs behind her?

They'd plowed Route 7 northbound out of Brooks, but the west wind was blowing across the stubbly cornfields, pushing the snow back onto the road like waves against a beach. I drove through, the truck hitting the drifts with a *whump*.

I swung east on Route 202 at Dixmont, climbed the hills, and looked out at the broken clouds racing past from the western mountains, the last remnant of the snowstorm. The road passed collapsed dairy barns, crushed by time, double-wides parked next to sinking farmhouses. Ordinarily this would prompt me to consider mortality, the fleeting nature of our accomplishments. But I kept thinking of Louis and Marta, all the way to Newburgh, then north on the interstate.

He was a big boy, as Clair said. He knew what he was doing. They were close, by all appearances, certainly attracted to each other. And why should Louis sleep alone? Or was alone a much safer place?

My gut kept saying Marta was trouble, that she was using sex and their past relationship to work Louis, wrap him around her, take what she wanted. And what did a woman like Marta want? Right now? A place to hide. Long run? Security. Status. Money.

I pulled off the highway and flipped the radio on. BBC News, the usual reports from the yawing deck of the *Titanic* that is our world. Politicians lying to your face. The planet wrapped in a smoky, ever-warming shroud. Refugees—men, women, children—drowning in the Mediterranean within sight of land. Countries arguing over who should fish out the bodies.

I turned the radio off. Sighed. Thought maybe I should think of Marta's arrival as a needed bit of good news. Woman escapes murdering thieves and her abusive boyfriend. Comes to the Maine woods and finds true love.

"Yeah, right," I said.

The parking lot was nearly empty at seven a.m., a few retired guys looking to get out of the house. A couple of them had women along, and I thought of Louis. Would Marta go everywhere with him? Would he ride in the passenger seat of her Audi? How long had she rented it for? How confident had she been that she'd be able to hook right back up with an old boyfriend after a dozen years?

Very, I thought.

I caught myself. But what if he was just a port in the storm? What if she'd hooked him again, rekindled his feelings for her. And when she'd laid low long enough, she'd be gone. He'd wake up to an empty bed.

Or was I just jealous of this woman muscling in on our territory?

I got out of the truck, grabbed a dolly. A toilet would have some weight to it. As I wheeled the dolly toward the store, a blue SUV cut me off and pulled into a parking spot in front of me. I stopped and the woman behind the wheel gave me a wave.

She buzzed the window down, said, "Sorry." She was fiftyish, attractive, with an upturned nose and short silver-blonde hair. A small, similarly blonde dog hopped up on her lap and yapped at me furiously.

"Harry, *shush*," she told the dog, and pushed him back. She turned back to me and smiled and said, "Sorry. He's all bark."

I thought of Louis's dog, all bite.

"He's just excitable, I'm sure."

I paused and reached toward the window. Harry paused from his barking to sniff my fingers.

"He likes you," the woman said, easing him across her lap and back into the car. She was wearing a white sweater with holly on the front. Christmas.

"He smells pony," I said.

She stroked the dog. "Harry, the nice man has a pony," she said.

The woman lifted him into the backseat and he sprang to the front. She gave him another push, and backed out of the door, saying, "I'll be right back." I pushed the dolly around the car and heard the door *thunk* shut, another door open. She was getting her bag out of the backseat as I passed. Black leggings, knee-high wine-red leather boots.

The boots looked expensive.

I heard her call out behind me, "Aren't we the early birds," wanting to talk.

I considered waiting for her to catch up but I was rolling along, on schedule. In and out, grab the toilet, have it hooked up by ten. If I stopped to chat with everyone along the way, I'd be an hour behind. I pretended not to hear her, pushed the dolly through the automatic doors.

Inside, the employees were standing in front of the registers like carnival hawkers, smiling and making groggy eye contact with the shoppers, who walked right past. I did, too, down the plumbing aisle, across to the toilets, lined up on a head-high shelf. The toilets looked pretty much the same, so I asked a worker to point me to the Kohler Classic. In white.

She pointed to it and I saw the tattoos on her forearms. Somebody or other, RIP. If you write it on your arm, does that make it happen?

I thanked her and walked over and looked up and established that the toilet looked perfectly usable. There were cartons of them below the display model, and I dragged the first one off the shelf and wrestled it onto the dolly. I pushed the dolly down the toilet aisle, crossed to paint and varnish, took a left by the artificial Christmas trees. They were green, white, and pink, and an inflated Santa looked down on them proudly like he'd grown them from seed. I rolled up to the first register and a guy said, "Find what you need?" I said yes, and he leaned across the counter and pointed a gizmo at the toilet until the gizmo beeped. He was tapping at the register and I was digging for my wallet—

When someone screamed.

We looked up.

It was a woman's voice. Again. Then again.

5

People started to run toward the sound, from the direction of the side door, the one that led to the nursery. There were workers in red shirts and aprons, the guy ahead of me trying to get his phone out. The automatic door to the nursery was sliding back and forth like it had short-circuited, people dodging through.

I was right with them, heard a woman crying now, sobbing, someone saying, "It's okay, buddy. Just stay right there."

A woman was on the floor, her legs splayed open, an arm outstretched. A guy was standing beside her. He was wearing a black knit mask and a black hooded sweatshirt. There was a red V hanging from a cord around his neck, like the scarlet letter upside down. He had a black tomahawk raised over his head and he was shouting, "She has left her mortal body. I assure you, people of Lintukoto, she is no longer a threat."

It was like they were staging a play, some sort of weird performance art. Four guys in red uniforms were circled around the guy with the hatchet, close to a display of Christmas wreaths. The woman who had directed me to the toilet was on her phone. "Home Department.

Oh my God, he chopped this lady! By the Christmas trees. You gotta get here."

And then the four employees rushed the guy and he swung the tomahawk, hit one guy in the shoulder, and said something like "Hakata" and "Show thy power." The other three gang-tackled him and he went down, arms above his head, legs kicking. One of the guys pulled at the hatchet, but the guy wouldn't let go until one of them punched him in the face and another kicked him hard in the groin.

He gasped and dropped the hatchet and the worker who was standing kicked it across the floor toward me, where it skidded to a stop. It was black except for the cutting edge of the blade, which was silver. The reverse side was a metal point like something on a weathervane and on the grip, USA, in small silver letters. The hatchet side was streaked with blood.

I looked toward the woman. She was on her face and a dark pool was spreading from underneath her head. The back of her skull was slashed, her silver-blonde hair matted.

Blood spatter on her white sweater. Embroidered holly, green leaves and red berries, up near the collar.

Wine-colored boots.

"Oh, no," I said.

It was her.

The woman from the toilet aisle said, "They're coming," and moved closer to the woman on the ground, then crouched and scooped up the woman's bag. It was brown leather and stuff had come out of it.

A phone. Lipstick. Her wallet.

The worker woman stuffed the things back in the bag, carefully placed it on the floor, like she was neatening things up for company. I was thinking, But I just talked to her. She has a dog in the car.

The guy in black was wearing dark red boots, tall rubber ones like a fisherman would wear, the soles wrapped in bands of silver duct tape. Head pressed to the concrete floor, he shouted something like "Hakata" and "You don't know!" and "Mortals desist!"

And then two cops ran in from the parking lot, a man and a woman, the woman with her gun drawn. She shouted, "Everybody back the hell off," and the three guys rolled away. The cop said, "Put your hands out over your head. Now."

People had phones out, shooting video, which made it seem like a movie set, that somebody would shout, "Cut," and everybody would get up.

But they didn't. The ax guy extended his hands over his head, and the closer cop dropped down hard on the guy's back and grabbed for one of his arms. The guy fought back and the second cop moved in close, screaming, "Stop resisting!" He did, lying still. She hesitated, then holstered her gun. Started toward him. He started shouting again at the cop on his back, twisting to look at him. She yanked her orange Taser loose and leaned in. There was a rattle and the dart sank into the guy's leg. The guy started thrashing and screaming and still the cop couldn't get the cuffs on.

The three workers jumped back in, two of them holding the guy down while the other helped the cop pull the guy's arms to the center of his back. The cop snapped the cuffs on, and the guy started to roll over and the woman cop pepper-sprayed him in the face.

"Your power is nothing," he screamed, spittle flying.

"Put the fucking phones away," the guy cop shouted, but nobody did.

The woman cop moved to the woman on the floor and touched her neck. Her head flopped to the side, showing her face. The cop turned to me and said, "You know this person?"

"No," I said. "I just passed her in the parking lot. She was driving a Honda CR-V. Blue. There's a little dog inside."

The woman cop turned back, touched the woman's neck again. She reached for her shoulder mic, said, "Eleven-three, Home Department victim, severe head injury. I mean, really serious. Severe wound. Hit with an ax."

There was an unintelligible response and the cop put her hand on the injured woman's shoulder. A worker came up with a blanket, the kind you move furniture with. He flapped it open and the cop helped him cover the woman, all but her head. The blanket smeared the blood across the floor.

Two more uniforms arrived, an older sergeant and a patrolman. The patrolman helped the first cop yank the hatchet guy to his feet. They hustled him out of the sliding doors, weaving with him as he struggled. He was shouting and they drove him into the side of a cruiser, sprayed him again. The guy screamed, "Your power is nothing!"

Rescue rolled up and two paramedics swung out of the truck and trotted inside. I could see them crouching beside the woman, the woman cop standing there with her arms folded across her flak vest. The paramedics were reaching in, touching the woman's neck, then her head.

She was on her side, her mouth open, her face pale. The blanket was pulled down and her right hand lay in the pool of blood. Next to her hand was a gold-painted pinecone. It was bloody, too. Behind her there was a bin of them and I pictured her picking one up, wondering if the gold would look tacky.

"Jesus," I said.

I felt myself sinking. I should have stopped to talk to her. I'd walked away. *"Harry, the nice man has a pony."*

They slid the woman onto a board, still facedown, and lifted the board onto the gurney. The pool of blood showed black on the floor, like a car had leaked its oil.

The sergeant, a balding guy with a gut, said, "Everybody out," and started waving his arms like he was herding sheep. The woman cop looked at me and said, "Sir, come with me."

As the cops unrolled crime tape, she led the way to her cruiser and turned. She was young, early twenties, right out of the academy. Her hair was pulled back tight and she had a military posture with broad shoulders, strong like a gym rat. Her name tag said Hernandez.

"You spoke to the woman here. Can you point out her car?"

I turned. It was maybe fifty feet away. The yappy dog was sitting quietly in the driver's seat, waiting for his mistress to return.

"Right there."

"Was there anyone else with her?"

I shook my head.

"Just the dog. His name is Harry."

I added, "She's dead, isn't she."

Hernandez hesitated.

"It's a very serious injury."

"Right," I said. "You know, she was really nice. Friendly. Cheerful." I looked toward the wreaths and bows. "She said we were early birds."

My mind raced. Maybe if I'd stopped to chat he would have picked somebody else. Maybe he would have been discouraged and left. Maybe I could have stopped him, grabbed him before he could get in a swing.

I said, "You all know the hatchet guy?"

A beat of hesitation. "We're familiar with him."

"What's with the talk about gods and mortals? Is that his shtick? Mentally ill?"

Hernandez looked away, then said, "I really can't go into that."

"I understand," I said. "And you should know I'm a reporter."

She turned to look at me.

"From around here?"

"I live in Prosperity."

"Reporter for who?"

"Myself. Freelance," I said. "*The Globe. New York Times.*"

"Christ. All we need."

"What's that mean?"

"Nothing. Just hard enough without the media making stuff up."

"I'm not making up anything. I'm just telling you what happened."

She shifted back to business, said, "So you witnessed the assault?"

"No, just heard screams. From the register."

"I doubt it was her who was screaming," Hernandez said, then caught herself.

The sergeant came to the gate and waved her over and she said, "Just wait here," and hurried away. I watched the cops and then walked to the woman's car. The dog started to bark, and when I got close he started jumping up and down, clawing at the glass.

"Easy boy," I said. "Easy."

I turned and glanced back to the cops, then walked around the car to the passenger side. The dog leapt across, slammed against that window. I stood close and peered in. The dog was jumping on a stack of mail. I leaned down, saw the name on the top envelope, *Lindy Hines.* The envelope had been forwarded. The new address was 112

Franklin Street, Riverport. The old address was a P.O. Box, Bernard, Maine. Mount Desert Island, the backside.

A summer house on MDI? Just moved to Riverport?

I looked the car over, the dog still barking tirelessly. The Honda was no more than a year old, barely any snow on it. Garaged. The seats were leather, a top-of-the-line model. She'd had some money. A plan. Spend the winter in the city, head back to Mount Desert for the summer. Or maybe she'd moved to Riverport for a new job. I pictured her—a friendly person, confident, at least on the surface. Was there a Mr. Hines waiting at home? Maybe they were supposed to meet for lunch. Maybe they had kids to visit. Which cop was going to be the one to break the unfathomable, impossible news? "Your wife was buying a Christmas wreath and a stranger walked up and killed her with a hatchet. We're very sorry for your loss."

And I kept on walking. Jesus.

I went to my truck, grabbed a notebook from the console. Leaning over the seat, I scribbled the name and addresses. Glancing back, I took the plate number of the car, stuck the notebook in my jacket pocket, and started back toward the cruiser. With my phone, I took a shot of the Honda and the crime scene in the background. And as I walked past, a shot of the dog sitting in the driver's seat. He looked at me and mustered a halfhearted bark.

Maybe he remembered me—the guy he'd barked at, that his mistress tried to make small talk with . . . the one who went right through the automatic doors and was gone.

So she went out to the garden shop, maybe with the guy in the boots and the black hood following her. Maybe she'd smiled at him, made eye contact. Maybe he'd noticed she was alone, that if somebody was going to be sacrificed, she'd be an easy mark. And she never saw it coming, her time on this planet ended in the most violent, random way.

The dog yipped again.

"It's okay, boy," I said.

But it wasn't.

6

I was back in my designated spot when the detectives rolled up in an unmarked silver Malibu. They were out of the car—a man and a woman, the woman striding ahead. The lead detective, literally. She was tall, slender, had short-cropped reddish hair. He was shorter, chunky with a barrel chest, shaved head, and a goatee. She was wearing a fleece vest; he was wearing a short jacket. I watched as they bent under the crime tape, holding the tape up so it cleared the guns on their hips. They walked to the sergeant, who was standing by the blood. The three of them looked down at it like it might hold a clue, then walked to where the hatchet still lay on the pavement.

This time the detectives crouched. The woman detective stood and the guy followed her lead. The sergeant led them to the clerk, the woman who had screamed. The woman detective shook her hand and the guy held back. They led her to the Malibu and she sat in the front seat with the woman detective. The guy shut the car door for the clerk and then walked over to me.

"Detective Tingley," he said. No small talk. Abrupt. I got it. This was a murder scene.

"Jack McMorrow," I said.

He looked at me and said, "The reporter? *New York Times?*"

"Stringer," I said.

"Huh," he said. "What are the chances?"

"Of being killed by a stranger while you're buying a Christmas wreath?"

"Of a reporter standing there when somebody gets killed by a stranger while she's buying a Christmas wreath."

"I wasn't exactly right there. I was at the register. I ran over when I heard somebody screaming. Like everybody else. Have we met?"

"Not until now," he said. "But I know guys in ATF. The thing in Waldo County."

"Ah," I said. "The guns."

"And I know a guy in the fire marshal's office. The arsons down in—where was it?"

"Sanctuary," I said.

"Right."

He looked at me with distaste.

"I don't need you getting in the way."

"I didn't mean to be, believe me."

"Your rep. You ask a million questions, don't take our word for anything. Then you go off and do your own investigation, step all over evidence, witnesses, turn things into a freaking cluster."

"I like to think of it as being thorough."

He gave me a close look.

"And that was when you were just a reporter. Now you're a witness."

"More like a bystander," I said.

He looked at me, shook his head.

"Go ahead."

I told him how I'd interacted with the victim. He wrote it down, and said, without looking up, "She say anything lead you to think she was in danger?"

"No. She was cheerful. Making small talk. It's really unbelievable. That this happened."

Tingley shrugged.

"Hey, off the record—and if you burn me, I'll cut your balls off—streets of this city are crawling with freakin' whack jobs. Every once in a while, one of them goes totally off his nut. We come in and pick up the pieces. Tell me what you said to the deceased."

I did. The dolly. The barking dog. The friendly smile. I didn't tell him I knew her name and where she lived. I didn't tell him she wanted to chat and I kept on going.

"You know this guy with the hatchet, don't you. He a regular."

"We haven't released his name," Tingley said.

"I know that. Just thinking he must be a frequent flyer."

He looked over toward the Malibu, where his partner was still questioning the woman, hesitated.

"Come on, off the record. Background," I said. "I'm just wondering. I mean, if he's a transient, you've never seen him before, it's a very different story. There'd be a very different feel to all of this. Am I right? This is way too, I don't know, calm."

Tingley looked at me, shook his head, and said, "Nope."

"Okay, tell me if this is way off. He's a local guy, probably homeless, at least some of the time. PD has been dealing with him for years. When he's on his meds, he's harmless, maybe even productive. When he's off them, he wigs out and gets in trouble. But nothing like this before."

He hesitated, then shook his head again.

"I just wonder what he was thinking?" I said. "Why this poor lady? And how did he get here? Can't imagine he drives, so what did he do? Take the bus with his mask and cape under his jacket? Seems like that would take some planning and premeditation. Who's Hakata? If this was his big fixation, I wonder if he had other hatchets. Do police take them away, reports of him raving on some street corner, waving the thing around? To come all the way out here—ax central—and pick one up and immediately kill somebody, the first stranger he sees, practically . . ."

I paused. He didn't butt in. I figured I had the green light.

"Was he getting sicker? Maybe the meds weren't working. I wonder if he had a guardian or anything. A mental health worker? Did anybody have an inkling he was going off the deep end? And why this lady? Did this woman remind him of somebody? His mother? A teacher? She sure didn't look like a comic book character. And he looks like he's what, late twenties? If he's attacked people before, did he get off because he's sick? Is this an escalation but not something entirely new? Should somebody have seen this coming?"

He shook his head. "Like I said, McMorrow."

"That your partner?" I said, looking toward the Malibu.

"Detective Bates. She's senior, does the bigger homicides. Don't play games with her."

"Bad cop, badder cop?"

"She'll rip you a new one."

Detective Bates was talking to the store manager, who was pointing to the girders under the roof of the nursery. They both stared upward. Surveillance camera.

Tingley looked over at me, said, "Off the record. Slam dunk."

We stood for a minute, feet getting cold on the frozen pavement. The sky was a new shade of gray, with dark billowing clouds off to the west. It felt like another snowstorm, like we were locked in some black orbit. Cold. Snow. Death.

Tingley looked behind me where customers were pulling in, looking to buy wooden planters filled with balsam fir boughs and holly berries. A woman got out of a minivan, slid a door open, and kids tumbled out. Tingley started toward them, hands up in front of him.

A red VW pulled in, a snowboard on a rack on top. A young guy got out, tucked a notebook in his back pocket, and headed for the cops. He looked vaguely familiar. I figured the *Riverport Broadcast*.

I moved toward the main entrance, where a group of workers was standing all in a row, like coaches on a sideline. Some were smoking. One was off to the side, fifteen feet away. She was on her phone, pacing as she talked.

The woman from the toilet aisle. She'd been headed through the sliding door to the nursery when the guy attacked the woman. The primary witness.

I walked slowly, stayed close to the concrete blocks and the snow throwers. When I got close, I stopped. Looked across the lot and waited.

"It's just totally fucking insane," she was saying to somebody. "He just took this big ax thing and walked up behind the lady and lifted it up and smashed it down. Like he was splitting wood . . . I was right there, like twenty feet away. I couldn't fucking believe it. I'm saying, 'Oh my God. This can't be happening.' I mean, it's on TV all the time, people getting mowed down by some nut job. And here it is, happening right here in front of me. Unbelievable."

She held her phone up.

"I got some video. People had phones out all over the place."

I scribbled in my notebook. *Like he was splitting wood.*

The woman said, "No, just after, the crazy bastard ranting, No, not when he killed her. What do you think I am? Listen, I gotta go. No, they said I can't go anywhere until I talk to the detective lady . . . Right . . . I'll text you. No, we're closed. It's friggin' unbelievable."

She slipped the phone in the back pocket of her jeans, pulled a pack of cigarettes from her jacket pocket, and lit one. Put her head back and blew the smoke skyward, like a whale spouting. The smoke started to drift away and she pulled the phone out again, stared at it, put it back in her pocket.

I moved alongside her. Heard the sound of shouting. She was replaying the video.

She looked at me.

"Oh, the toilet," she said. "Sorry you didn't get it. We don't have no say over them closing us down."

"That's okay," I said.

I surveyed the scene.

"Unbelievable, huh."

"God almighty, did you see it?" she said.

"No. I was behind you. She was down when I came through the door."

"Unfreakin' real. The sound. I'll never forget that fucking sound."

She took a pull on the cigarette, said, "I don't know if I can go back in there."

I smiled. "Give it a day."

"I won't sleep for a freakin' week. That poor lady. That poor, poor lady. Splattered her like a bug. Just standing there looking at the wreaths. I mean, what the hell? And she gets killed. What kind of whacked-out world is this, you know what I'm saying?"

I stood for a moment while she smoked, took her phone out, put it back.

"I'm Jack," I said.

She hesitated, like maybe I was hitting on her. And if I were, was that good or bad? She gave me a quick once-over.

"Hey," she said. "I'm Sheila."

She was forty, maybe much younger. Her eyes were puffy from crying, or maybe from cigarettes. Or both. A decent, weathered face. She pulled her red Home Department fleece tight around her.

"I should tell you, Sheila," I said. "I'm a newspaper reporter."

Her head jerked sideways toward me. "Buying a toilet? You working?"

"I wasn't when I got here. I am now."

"This gonna be in the paper tomorrow?"

I shook my head—reassuringly, I hoped.

"No, I don't write for Maine papers. I write for other papers. New York. Boston. Magazines."

I said it like they were very far away.

"I write longer stories. Sometimes they take weeks to put together."

Weeks. As in, no worries.

"Why are you here? In Riverport?"

"I live here," I said. "Down in Waldo County."

She processed that, finished her cigarette and dropped it to the ground, ground it out with her Nike. Took a ChapStick out of the pocket of her jacket and lathered that on. "What a fucking nightmare," Sheila said. "I'm telling ya."

"I'm sure."

I slipped my notebook out, said, "Mind if I take a few notes? I mean, you were right there, right?"

"Freakin' right behind them. They're just walking along. Everything was fine and then, boom."

"He was carrying the hatchet?"

"Yeah. Tomahawk ax. Thirty-nine ninety-eight. They're, like, super high-quality. They use 'em in the military."

"Tomahawk," I said.

"I know. Like the Indians. Jesus."

"Had he bought it?"

"I don't think so," she said. "I think he picked it up over in Tools and was just walking around with it."

"What did he say?"

"Some crazy shit. Gods and mortals, and he's shaking the hatchet up at the ceiling and talking about his power. Christ, I knew he was kinda nuts but—"

I looked at her.

"You knew him?"

"Not really knew him. Just knew him as this guy who'd come in. We called him Taxi Man, 'cause he'd buy something—some pine boards, a half-sheet of drywall, some screws or something. And then he'd call a cab and load the stuff in the trunk."

"Where'd he go?"

"Downtown. They said he did work for people. I mean, he knew what he wanted. Never had any questions. Seemed to know what he was doing, unlike some of the customers come in here. People said they'd see him walking around town."

"Know his name?"

Sheila had finished her cigarette, was digging for another. She held up her hands.

"Look at me. I'm freakin' shaking."

"I'm sure," I said. "Pretty upsetting experience."

"I'm gonna have nightmares, sure as shit."

She got the cigarette lit, took a deep drag. Shook her head.

"You know his name? Other than Taxi Man?"

Sheila looked at me. "I don't want to get involved, no more than I have to be. The cops took my statement."

"As well they should," I said. "You're the eyewitness."

"Christ, why me? I was about to go on break, too. I only stayed 'cause Robert was late covering, helping some lady in Hardware with drawer pulls. You wouldn't believe how some of these people need their hand held."

I waited, then said, "You know his name then?"

Sheila looked at me. "Robert?"

"No, the Taxi Man."

"Oh, not really. One time, though, I was walking by him, I go, 'Hey, Taxi Man. How you doin'?' He goes, 'That ain't my name.' I go, 'Okay.' 'Cause I can see he's a little upset. Don't want to upset customers. A couple of those get reported, you're history. CIIs, they call them. Customer Interaction Incidents."

"So you said—"

"I go, 'What should I call you, then?' I knew he was a little nuts. His eyes, the way they kind of darted all around."

"And he said—?"

"He goes, 'My name's Teak. Like the wood.' We don't sell it. People come in once in a while. Usually they're working on a boat or something. We send them to a place in Old Town. Mahogany and all that shit."

"Teak what?" I said. "Did he say?"

"No, and I didn't push him. I go, 'Okay, Mr. Teak. Let me know if I can help you with anything.' And I kept on truckin'."

She pushed at her bangs. Another suck on the cigarette.

"Guess that was a good freakin' call, huh?" she said, blowing smoke. "Get in an argument with the guy, he stoves your head in. Unfriggin' believable."

I took a last note. *Teak, like the wood.* Slipped the notebook into the back pocket of my jeans.

"Thanks, Sheila," I said. "Sorry to meet you like this."

"I guess to hell."

"I'm Jack McMorrow. Could I ask your last name, Sheila?" I said. "In case I need to get in touch later?"

She hesitated, looked at me, then away.

"Bard," she said.

"You from Riverport?"

"Orrington," Sheila said. "But mostly you can find me on Facebook."

She looked over my shoulder, toward the scene. I turned, saw the detectives headed my way, Bates taking long strides, Tingley, hurrying to keep up.

"Hey," Bates said, coming up on me. "No press. We'll be releasing a statement later," she said.

"Right," I said.

Beyond them I could see a TV crew waiting patiently, a blonde woman in black high-heeled boots, a camera guy in a watch cap, ready to be spoon-fed.

"Besides, you're a witness," she said.

"Like I said, more of a bystander," I said.

"But you talked to the victim," she said.

"She wasn't a victim yet," I said.

7

I peeled off when the *Broadcast's* reporter came up and Bates turned
to herd him away. I walked to the truck, tossed my notebook on the
passenger seat, and climbed in. Roxanne was going to be disappointed
about the toilet.

It was snowing again, dry fine flakes that speckled the parking
lot like road salt. Customers were driving up, eyeing the flashing blue
lights, the police cars blocking the main entrance. Some customers
drove away. Most parked and watched. Nothing like somebody else's
tragedy to start the day.

I sat back in the seat for a minute, took a deep breath. Closed my
eyes and saw the woman on the ground, Teak standing over her. His
arms were raised over his head, the black hatchet pointed toward the
roof. Only the blood moving.

And then I heard her voice. "Aren't we the early birds?"

"God almighty," I said.

It was 8:10, too early to call Vanessa at the *Times*, but I needed
to pitch the story. I also needed to begin the process of making sense
of it, to dig and dig until something emerged that could explain what
had happened, and why, so we could file it away in the appropriate

folder on our collective desktop. The world—more and more filled with craven greed and brazen liars—would be restored to its sad but ultimately righteous self.

Lindy Hines dead and Teak in a cell? There had been times when that would have been enough for me. File the story and move on. But this time it wasn't going to be that easy. After almost twenty years of covering murder and mayhem, crimes of passion and crimes of calculation, this one had sunk its barbs deep inside me, had torn at something that had been festering.

I didn't want to accept that this was normal. I didn't want to accept that violent death was doled out randomly, like the number on a scratch ticket. I didn't want to accept that this nice person had simply been in the wrong place at the wrong time.

Because if she had, I'd helped put her there.

Franklin Street was across from City Hall, just up from the post office. Lindy Hines's building was a rehabbed three-story brick factory with parking on the ground floor. The units on the south end overlooked a little park that in turn overlooked a slow-moving stream.

I parked on the bridge and walked back. The edges of the stream were frozen but the part that had current was open, and ducks were swimming in the black, rippling water. There was a bench, and in front of it some bread was frozen into the snow. I wondered if Lindy Hines had sat on that bench and fed the ducks. Not if she took her dog.

The entrance to the condo building was a glass door under a green awning. I walked up and stood, put my hand out to shade the glass and peer in. There was a fake rubber tree to the left, mailboxes to the right. The door was locked.

I turned away and waited. The street was busy, a steady stream of people tapping in a security code at a side door at the bank across the street. Back on this side, a garage door rumbled open and a car pulled out and drove away, the guy at the wheel giving me a wary glance as he passed.

I waited five long minutes, watched three more cars pull away. Finally there was a rattle inside—a mailbox being opened—and I turned as a thirtyish guy approached the door. I smiled. He went to poker face, the expression people save for panhandlers on a dark street.

He pushed the door open. Scruff of beard, very tight jeans, neat lace-up leather boots, black waffled parka.

"Hi there," I said, and gave him my pitch. Reporter. *New York Times*. Did he know Lindy Hines?

"I don't live here. My girlfriend does."

"Is she here?"

He started to sidle by me. I moved with him.

"She doesn't know anybody here, either," he said. "And I gotta say, I'm not big on mainstream media. One step above scumbag lawyers."

I was tired. I'd just seen an innocent woman killed in a gruesome way. I'd had to leave my toilet on the cart. The world was getting more insane by the minute, and I was supposed to smile and tell this dipshit to have a nice day?

"Screw you," I said.

He stopped, turned to me. Our eyes locked.

"What did you say?"

He leaned close. I said it again.

"I oughta—"

"Make my day," I said, smiling. He didn't get it.

"Clint Eastwood. Before your time, chump."

He tried to hold the pose but then his eyes backed down and the rest of him followed. He scowled, tucked his pasty dumpling of a fist into the crevice of his pocket, and hurried off.

With a deep breath, I looked at my reflection in the glass of the door. I looked rattled and I knew why. Lindy Hines, executed in broad daylight. A strange woman with a weird, violent past moving in on Louis. The world turned on its head.

I knew what I had to do.

Write a story. Find some sort of order in the chaos, make sense of the nonsensical. Because if it made sense, the world wasn't entirely lost. There was a way back to life as we had known it, where crimes were rooted in passion and greed, and good and evil was more than just an empty, meaningless phrase.

Don't give up, people. The world may be spinning out of control, but not here. There was a method to this madness, folks. All of us are not depraved animals. We just have to keep pushing back. Dig deep and feel the outrage. Don't just look away, hope that the next ax that falls doesn't hit you. Don't lose what humanity we have left.

I took another deep breath. Felt for my notebook. Saw a man and woman come into the lobby and walk toward the door.

They were sixtyish and silver-haired, tanned and trim, wearing track suits and down vests, carrying matching water bottles—on the way to the gym. I backed up a couple of steps as they came out the door, the guy holding it for the woman. I smiled.

"Good morning," I said, and they looked at me suspiciously. But didn't run.

"I'm Jack McMorrow. I'm a reporter, and I'm writing a story for the *New York Times*."

They took a step back.

"It's about someone who lived in this building, and I'm wondering if you knew her."

They stopped. Thank goodness for nosiness.

"Who's that?" the woman said.

"We've only lived here a year," the guy put in.

I smiled, ruefully this time.

"Her name is Lindy Hines."

"Lindy?" the woman said, searching my face for a clue. "Why are you doing a story about Lindy?"

"I'm afraid I have some bad news," I said, the words forming. Why I got paid the big bucks. "Lindy's dead. She was killed this morning."

The woman blanched. The guy frowned.

"Oh my God," the woman said.

"I'm sorry," I said.

"Are you sure?" the guy said. "Silver hair. Kind of medium height?"

I took a breath, then told them the story. Home Department. Christmas wreaths. After a deeper breath, I added the hatchet.

"Oh my God," the woman said again, and she clutched at her husband's arm. He put the other arm around her protectively.

"They caught the bastard?" he said.

"He didn't run," I said.

"Oh, poor Lindy," his wife said. "My God, I just saw her."

"And where was that?" I said, and when she hesitated, I added the yes-or-no part. "Was it here?"

"Yes," she said. "Right here."

I slipped my notebook out and the guy said, "You don't write that political crap, do you?"

"No."

"Oughta let the president do his job."

"I write Maine stuff. But not politics."

He looked at me like he might be able to sniff something out.

"What's your name again?"

I told him, took a card out of my other pocket. He peered at it, then looked at me and said, "When did you say this happened?"

"This morning."

"*New York Times.* Johnny on the spot, aren't you?"

"I'm based in Maine. I just happened to hear about it."

"What? A police scanner in your car?"

"Something like that," I said.

He looked at my card again and said, "This piece of crap in custody?"

"Very much so. I watched them take him away."

"Ought to have a goddamn death penalty in this state," he said. "Law-abiding people, minding their own business, some lowlife—"

"She was lovely," the woman said. "Just the sweetest person."

"She just moved here in—what was it?—end of October?"

The guy nodded.

"She was in our book club," the woman said in disbelief, as if that should have protected Lindy Hines somehow. "There's a group of us gals, we were reading Oprah's book. The new one. It's about taking time for you. Lindy was in the midst of a divorce, and there's this part about how Oprah, she forced herself to make new friends, even when she was fifty. Oprah is really an introvert, and Lindy was sort of shy deep down, so she had to really try to meet people."

I nodded. Thought of the parking lot.

The woman said, "Lindy told us, 'If it's hard for Oprah, then it's okay for it to be hard for me.' And everybody liked her once they got to know her."

"Real nice lady," her husband confirmed.

"Where did she live before?" I said.

"Mount Desert," the husband said. "Her ex was some big building contractor."

"Don't put this in the paper," his wife said, "but her husband had an affair. Ran off with a younger woman, a fitness trainer person. I told Hal, 'I'm gonna keep an eye on you when we're at the gym.' "

I looked to the husband. The guy seemed to swell at that, the idea that a younger woman might find him attractive in his gym shorts.

"So you're Hal?" I said.

"And I'm Fran. We're the Lofgrens."

I nodded and wrote that down.

"Oh, this is so horrible," Fran said. "I mean, it's crazy. She was just getting her new life together."

"Family? Kids?"

"A son."

"He's gay," Hal said, like that was a significant detail.

"Uh-huh," I said.

"Lives with his husband in Orrington, I think it is," Fran said. "I've met him. Very nice young man. Handsome. But you know, Lindy was a very attractive woman."

"And his name?"

"Barrett. He's a high school teacher. Math, I think."

"Right. Last name? Same as hers?"

"Well, it is now. Used to be same as his stepdad's, but he changed it after the marriage fell apart. I mean, he was really angry at his stepdad. Lindy said it was the last straw for Barrett. He never felt that his father approved of his—"

"Sexual preference," Hal said. "Her ex was a jerk."

"I see," I said. "And her ex's name?"

"Rod," Fran said. "Except they weren't divorced yet. Still hashing out the details."

"The money," Hal said. "She had him by the—"

He paused.

"Last name for Rod?" I said.

"I don't know. I don't think she ever said."

"That's fine. Seems like you knew Lindy pretty well."

"Lindy just needed someone to talk to," Fran said. "She said this was such a friendly city. And it is. Riverport, I mean. How could something like this happen here?"

As opposed to a place filled with hatchet-swinging crazy people? They walked off, Fran clinging to her husband as she processed this new reality.

I moved through the open door after they left. The mailboxes had names, and I found L. HINES, top row, all the way to right. It was empty—the mail was on the seat of Lindy Hines's Honda. I pressed the button and waited. Nobody came on the intercom, nobody buzzed me in. The empty apartment of a murder victim, filled with the stuff of her abruptly ended life.

There was a bench along the far wall of the foyer, and I sat down, went through my notes, underlining the quotes. The story was becoming sadder still: A woman's marriage falls apart, she musters the strength to start over, and then she's picked out at random and killed.

Try explaining that one as God's plan.

I was flipping through the pages when I heard elevator doors open somewhere behind an inner door. I waited and the door started to push open. I stood. A guy came through carrying a plastic bucket full of tools, looked at me, said, "Can I help you?"

He was in his sixties, stocky and wide, salt-and-pepper hair and matching beard. His baseball cap said PATRIOTS. I told him who I was and what I did.

"Sorry, but you can't just walk in here. This is a secure building, right? And this foyer is for the condo owners only. You know what would happen if we let people loiter in here? Homeless and druggies and every other thing. So I'm going to have to ask you to—"

"I was talking with the Lofgrens," I said.

"I don't care who you were talking with. This is my building, and you can't be in here."

He walked across the foyer, pushed the door open, and held it.

"Don't you want to know what the *New York Times* was talking with the Lofgrens about?"

"That's their business, what they talk about. I'm just telling you, sir—you can't be here. I don't care who you are. I answer to the residents, not the *New York Times*. If you'll just—"

I crossed the room, stopped in front of him.

"You had a condo owner named Lindy Hines."

He looked at me, his eyes narrowing.

"What do you mean, *had?*" he said.

He was officious but he wasn't dumb. And there was something else, a new hint of concern in his tone, like he cared about Lindy Hines in some way. I decided to temper it.

"I'm sorry to be the bearer of bad news, sir, but Ms. Hines died this morning."

His mouth dropped open and I could see silver fillings in his teeth, like fish in a shallow pond.

"What do you mean, died?"

"She was murdered."

"Oh my God."

He dropped the bucket to the floor and sagged and stumbled inside, the door closing behind him. After stepping past me, he bent and put his hands on his knees, like he might be sick.

"I'm sorry," I said.

He turned toward me, still bent over, his face gray as the snow in the gutter.

"What happened?"

I told him.

"Oh, Jesus," he moaned. He was stricken, still couldn't gather himself. I waited, and after a half-minute he pulled himself upright.

"You were friends, then," I said.

He took a breath, said, "Well, not really. I mean, I just worked here, and she was a tenant, but she was real nice. Always had a smile, you know. We're both divorced, so, I mean it wasn't anything. We just talked; she told me how she was doing."

A crush. Maybe he thought they'd get together someday. And now she was gone.

"She hadn't lived here long?" I said.

He took deep breaths, then spoke.

"Two and half months. I showed her the place."

He seemed to be picturing it.

"The agent was late so I let her in. She had the end unit, nice view of the stream. Said she wanted some water 'cause she came from the coast. Was used to seeing the ocean."

"I see. Her estranged husband still down there?"

"Yeah," he said, disdain dripping through. "Guy was a contractor. Built those mega houses for the rich people around."

"Money in that, I'll bet," I said. "You know his name?"

"No. Well, maybe. Rob, or Rod. But she said the company was something like Rock Spruce Construction. Black Spruce? Spruce Rock? Something like that, one of those towns around Bar Harbor. She built it with him, she said. Went to school for accounting. Had a head for numbers."

"So what happened? Did she say?"

"He got full of himself, ran off with a younger woman. Happens. Guys don't want to grow up. Don't know it's only their money has these young babes even looking at them."

I thought of my reporting days in New York City, gray-haired Wall Street guys and their blonde third wives. Marta cruising the weddings.

"And sometimes they know and they don't care," I said.

"Right."

The guy who hadn't wanted to talk to me was back. He was holding a Starbucks coffee and his phone. The super went over and opened the door for him. He scurried to the stairwell, no eye contact, and my guy came back.

"Good person," he said, running his hand through thinning, gray-streaked hair.

"Tragic," I said.

"Well, you know where they say nice guys finish. I guess it's the same for nice ladies."

I nodded. He shook his head and said, "Couldn't be some kinda mistake? Mistaken identity?"

I shook my head.

"Christ almighty."

I waited.

"What was her life like here? What did she do?"

"Well," he said, and then paused, pulling a tin of mints from the pocket of his jeans. He opened it, popped one into his mouth, then held the tin out to me. I took one, popped it into my mouth. Cardinal rule of street reporting. Take whatever's offered, unless it might kill you.

"She had money. She was no dope. I think she was sticking it to old Rod—good for her. So she didn't work. She told me she had to be useful, didn't want to just sit around."

"Really."

"Oh, yeah. Lindy was wicked smart. I mean, you could just tell. My ex, only numbers she did was what she blew at the casino. Lindy, I mean, she said she could help these nonprofit outfits with their books. She said it would keep her out of the bars."

He smiled, seemed to be losing himself in memories. Maybe they'd gotten together in more than the hallway.

I was about to get his name when he said, "She'd just started doing stuff for the homeless shelter."

I looked up, smiled encouragingly.

"Really," I said.

"Not the place where the people sleep and all that. The office part. You know, where they go around raising money."

God, I thought. Killed by one of the very people she was trying to help. There was my hook.

"How did she like that?" I said.

"Okay, I guess," he said. "Except they didn't know what they were doing. Last week she said she'd spent the whole morning looking at papers stuffed in shoeboxes. She goes, 'Haven't these people ever heard of a computer?' "

I asked him if she said anything else about that and he said he couldn't recall anything. He said his name was Leroy Larkin, but people called him Roy. I thanked him, said I was very sorry for his loss.

When I left the building, he was sitting on a bench in the foyer with his head in his hands. Lindy Hines had stolen his heart, and Teak Like the Wood had stolen Lindy Hines.

What were the chances?

8

I was climbing a snowbank to the street headed for my truck when the silver Malibu rolled past. Tingley's head swiveled. I kept going, had the motor started and was putting the truck in gear when his car backed up and stopped beside me.

I shut off the motor. Tingley got out, came around the car wearing a cop's tough-guy scowl. I buzzed the window down. He said, "Outta the truck, over here."

He crossed in front of the truck, stepped up onto the snowbank. His leading leg went through and he swore and jumped onto the sidewalk and shook the snow off his trousers. Waited for me with his hands on his hips. I walked up to him and took out my notebook.

"Any more information on the perp?" I said.

"You tell me," Tingley said.

"What do you mean, Detective?"

"First employee on the scene, lady works the register. She says she told you she knew the guy."

"Goes by Teak," I said. "Employees call him Taxi Man."

"I know, I know. She told us, too. But after she spilled her guts to you."

"Some people get chatty. It's a nervous reaction."

"And some people get stuff wheedled out of them. But that's not the bone I'm picking," Tingley said, poking the air in front of my chest.

"Oh, yeah? Then which bone is it?"

"The one that has you here."

I waited.

"We haven't released the name of the deceased."

"Gotta do next of kin, right?"

"We're looking into that."

"I can help you. People here told me there's only one, a son. His name is Barrett and he lives with his husband in Orrington, teaches high school math. Barrett, not the husband. Lindy Hines was separated from her husband, in the process of getting a divorce. He's a contractor somewhere around Bar Harbor. Successful. Builds big houses for wealthy summer people. I was told the son blamed the stepdad for breaking up the family."

"Been busy," Tingley said.

"Yup."

"Holding out information."

"Just told you what I know," I said.

"Didn't say anything this morning about knowing the victim's name."

I shook my head.

"Nope. I've got a job to do too. You get over here, spook everybody, I've got nothing."

"I don't want you trampling on our investigation," Tingley said.

"I didn't trample," I said. Well, maybe the hipster guy. "I picked my way very carefully."

"Don't go near the son," Tingley said.

"When are you going out there?"

"None of your fucking business. This is a homicide investigation. When we do have something to say, I guess I know who we'll be talking to."

"Local press? TV? I'm not worried."

Tingley turned and watched the traffic roll by. Reached down and shook more snow off his trouser leg.

"What else?" he said.

"What else what?" I said.

"What else did the people in the building tell you?"

"Not much. The divorce. Lindy Hines was in a book club and they were reading Oprah. Super was carrying a torch for her."

"What?"

"Had a thing for her. He's divorced, too. She expected to do well financially in her divorce settlement and didn't have to work. That's about it, except for some young guy who told me he doesn't like reporters."

"Good for him."

I shrugged. He looked over at his idling car, traffic edging around it. A guy in a pickup buzzed his window down and shouted, "Get that thing out of the road." Tingley pulled his jacket to the side to flash the badge on his belt.

"Going to a lot of work for a slam dunk," I said.

He looked at me.

"Off the record," Tingley said, "real sympathetic victim will help keep this wingnut in a real jail."

"Insanity defense?"

"If he has any sort of lawyer."

"He seemed pretty nuts to me," I said.

"Well, let him be nuts for the next fifty years in maximum security. Off the record."

"Or they could adjust his medication."

Tingley turned to the street, said, "Is it that lady's fault this fucking asshole decided to stop taking his meds?" and walked back to his car and pulled away.

I got back in the truck, called Roxanne's cell. She was at the school, and ed techs didn't have their phones on. It went to voice mail. I left a message, said I was sorry I couldn't get the toilet, but there was a murder at the store. It would be on the news. No need to worry; I'd be home to for dinner.

Put the phone down, Took a deep breath. Kept going while I still could, before it all hit me.

The homeless shelter was on the shabby end of the main drag out of town, in an old two-story brick building across from a small, scuffed-up park. Both the park and the shelter were flanked by rows of tenements that rose up a steep hill like tombstones. The shelter looked like it might have been a small manufacturing shop at one time, but now there were bedraggled curtains in the second-floor windows and a hand-painted sign that said LOAVES & FISHES. The sign had a couple of each, the fish looking like largemouth bass and not something you'd drag out of the sea in Galilee. I parked out front, shut off the motor, and sat.

There were no cops showing, a couple of beat-up minivans parked beside the place, one black, one red. Two guys came out of a side door and walked toward the black one. The older guy was wearing a bandanna, pirate style, and walked with a limp. The other had on a blaze-orange knit hat and a hooded sweatshirt, like he'd rather be hunting, except this was downtown Riverport. Both were aged by the street, faces drawn and pocked by booze or drugs or both.

Drugs and hopelessness, not always in that order.

The two guys lifted boxes out of the van, then Orange Hat reached back and slid the door shut. They crossed the lot and went back into the building. I got out of the truck, pocketed my notebook, and followed.

It was a big open room, a counter in front of the door like the place used to sell hardware or auto parts. The counter was stacked with cartons and plastic grocery bags, a sneaker sticking out of one, a bunch of bananas from another. The two guys had disappeared, but I heard a thump to the right. The boxes being dumped on the floor.

"Come on," a woman's voice barked. "Go easy with that."

There was a door to the right, and the two guys came back out. They looked at me and I returned their gaze, said, "Hey. How you doing?" They looked away, moved past me and back outside. I walked to the inner door, stepped through. A woman was bending over one of the cartons, pulling stuff out and setting it on the floor.

"Aftershave? Are you freakin' kidding me?" she said.

She started scooping the bottles up, dumping them back into the box, and shouted, "What the hell is the matter with you guys? Didn't I tell you to screen this crap first? Now we have to haul it all the way—"

She turned and saw me, said, "Oh."

"Can't get good help?"

"No, it's just that now we're stuck with stuff we can't use and it takes up space and we have to dispose of it and—"

She mustered a half-smile and moved to the next carton. I moved with her, stood as she yanked things out. Toothpaste, bar soap, shampoo. "More like it," she said.

I bent and crouched beside her.

"Donations?"

"Church did a drive, everybody bringing something in. Some get it more than others. Most of our guys don't care about smelling pretty."

I nodded, glanced over. She was in her forties, five foot six, chunky and solid. Short hair dyed pale blue, work-weathered hands. Her sweatshirt said MAINE and had a red lobster on the front. She was wearing pink Converse high tops.

"I'm Jack McMorrow," I said.

She handed me a tube of hand lotion. "Now that's useful. People outside in the weather, their hands get wicked dry."

She took the hand lotion back.

"I'm from the *New York Times*," I said.

She looked at me sideways. I had her attention.

"Yeah?"

"And you are?"

She considered it.

"Harriet Strand," she said. "I'm the director. And most of the staff. And the chief cook and bottle washer."

Still crouching, she held out her hand and we shook. Her grip was strong and her skin was rough. When she looked at me straight on she showed a missing front tooth. I must have reacted.

"I know. Just happened. Sometimes there are misunderstandings, you get caught in the crossfire. You know they want three thousand for an implant? I said, 'You shitting me? That's a lotta pasta.' "

I smiled.

"So what? *New York Times* is doing a story on Riverport?" Harriet said.

I was about to reply when the two men from the van came back in, Pirate Guy saying, "Last ones, Miss H."

He dropped a carton beside me with a booming thud.

"Freakin' books," he said.

"You get everything from the back?" Harriet said to him.

"Yup," he said.

"You're sure. Because if I go out there and there's stuff left in that van, there'll be hell to pay."

They let it roll off, stood there smelling like cigarettes and alcohol. Pirate Guy dug in his ear. His buddy took his orange hat off and scratched his head, put the hat back on. They all looked at me and waited.

"I'm writing a story," I said.

They waited more.

"About a guy you might know. I'm told he's here a lot."

"Who's that?" Harriet said, wary now, like this wasn't necessarily a good thing.

"His name is Teak," I said.

"Oh, we know Teak," she said, relaxing. "Full name is T. K. Barney."

"Shit, yeah," Pirate Guy said.

"We put him to work," Harriet said. "Carpentry and plumbing—"

"And electrical," Orange Hat said. "But he ain't got no license."

"Where did you run into Teak?" Harriet said. "Did he talk your ear off?"

"About comics?" Pirate Guy said.

"Oh, jeez," Orange Hat said.

Harriet said, "He can go on for hours. Sometimes I have to—"

"I'm doing a story because Teak's in jail," I said. "He killed someone at Home Department."

Her mouth froze open in mid-sentence. The two guys were looking at me with no expression at all. Tough nuts.

"Are you sure?" Harriet said. "I just talked to him—what was it? Last week. Wednesday. I mean, he seemed okay."

"This was a couple of hours ago. He killed a woman with a hatchet."

"Oh, no," she said.

"Off his meds," Pirate Guy said, shaking his head.

I looked to him and said, "Does he go off his meds?"

"I guess," he said.

"What's your name?"

"I'm Dolph. Like Randolph, without the first part. Is this gonna be in the paper? 'Cause I don't want to be in the paper."

"Me neither," said Orange Hat.

"Who are you?"

"Arthur. But I don't want to be in the paper either."

"That's fine," I said. "I'll leave your last names totally out."

They didn't protest. Harriet didn't either.

"How well do you guys know Teak?"

"See him around," Arthur said. "Good shit, mostly."

"And when he's not?"

"Thinks everybody's from one of his comic books," Dolph said. "Like we're all flying around and being superheroes and whatnot."

"Does Teak think he's from the comic book? When he's off his meds?"

"I guess," Arthur said. "Puffs out his chest and walks like this."

He put his arms out to the side like he was a weightlifter. Dolph did it, too, both of them holding the pose like they were in a bodybuilding contest.

"Teak was talking about something called Hakata. So what's that about?"

"He invented him," Harriet said. "It's his superhero."

"The ax man," Dolph said.

"Teak is Hakata?"

"No," Harriet said. "He answers to him. When Teak's in a bad way, he thinks he works for Hakata. Does his bidding, or however they say it."

"Kills people?" I said.

"Oh my God, no," she said. "I mean, until now. He just goes off on missions. To protect people from evil or whatever."

The guys nodded.

"Goes on patrol," Arthur said.

"With an ax?" I said.

"Smaller," Dolph said. "More like a hatchet."

"But he never did anything like this before," Harriet said.

"He isn't normally violent?" I said.

"Gets in your face," Arthur said, as Dolph nodded. "Punched Doogie in the ear. Wicked hard. Miss H. had to call the cops."

"If I can't calm him down," Harriet said. "He's just fine most of the time."

"One time he told the cops he couldn't be killed by bullets," Dolph said.

"How'd that work out?" I said.

"They pepper-sprayed the shit out of him," Arthur said.

"Three of them had to sit on him," Dolph said.

"Strong?"

"Oh, yeah," Arthur said. "One time I seen him pick this guy up and throw him over—"

"Listen, guys," Harriet said. "I don't think he needs to hear all that. Jack—it's Jack, right?—let's go in the office and talk."

Arthur and Dolph looked disappointed for two guys who didn't want to be in the paper.

Harriet took me by the arm and guided me back out around the counter and off to the left side of the main room. There were cots lined up and we slipped between them, then up a flight of stairs, where the walls were marred and dented. When we emerged on the second floor, there were more cots. Some parts of the room were partitioned with sheets hung from a steel cable.

"We get a lot of families now," Harriet said, repeating a practiced line. "It's the economy. People get evicted, or there's domestic abuse and they have to flee the home. It's not just guys like Arthur and Dolph."

She led the way to a door that she opened with a key from a pink coiled key ring that was looped around her wrist. Harriet stepped in and I followed. There were piles of stuff and a desk and two metal folding chairs. I took one and Harriet took the other. I had my notebook on my lap. She sat with her legs splayed, her high tops flat on the floor, like a basketball player on the bench.

"So what happened?" she said. "I didn't want to get the guys all riled up."

I recounted it for her. She listened, closed her eyes when I came to the killing part.

"One of the workers there said it was like he was splitting wood," I said.

"Oh my God," Harriet said, putting both hands over her face. "That poor woman."

"Yeah. By all accounts she was a nice person."

She shook her head. "I just can't believe it. Teak. What was he thinking?"

I hesitated.

"I don't know. But I think you may have known her. The victim."

Harriet froze. "How would I—was she a client of—"

"I'm told she'd started to volunteer here. Maybe the administrative side? Her name was Lindy Hines."

Harriet gasped like someone had squeezed the air out of her. Notebook in hand, I waited for her to start breathing again.

9

—m—

"But I just met her a couple of weeks ago, at our administrative office," Harriet said, like that would make the murder less likely. "She was going to come and help out at the shelter, do our books. She was an accountant. Are you sure? A very pretty lady? Sort of small? She said she just moved here from—"

"MDI?" I said. "Yeah. Tell me about her."

Harriet shifted in her chair, looked away. "I don't know much. I mean, we just talked at the office a couple of times. And not for long. One of our board members knew her. Said she moved to town, was looking for a place to volunteer. And she was good with money and books."

"Had she started yet?"

"No. I mean, sort of. I gave her some stuff when we met. She looked at it and said there were better ways to keep track of our donations, with spreadsheets and all that. She took the stuff with her and I never heard back. She hadn't come to the shelter yet."

"How long ago was that?"

"A couple of weeks. Maybe a little more. She was very nice. I mean, I can't believe it."

She looked back at me.

"Where is he now?"

"County jail," I said. "So he had problems here?"

"Sure," Harriet said. "I mean, some of our clients—no, actually many of them—have some kind of mental illness."

"What's his diagnosis?"

Harriet looked away from me, said, "I'm really not supposed to—"

"Background. I won't say it came from you. I really need to put a name on it. It tells people that it's a real illness. So they can't just dismiss him as nuts."

That seemed to make sense to her, the stigma part.

"Okay. It's something called schizo—schizo something. Affected? Anyway, it's a disorder. That's what the lady from the State said."

"What are the symptoms?"

"With Teak? Manic. Just wired. You've got to understand, when he's on a mission for this Hakata, it's all very real to him. One time I tried to say it was all made up and he got right in my face."

"That thing with the cops. Was that here?"

"We couldn't calm him down so we had to call. He wouldn't settle down for them, either. Like I said, that was a bad day for him. Maybe the worst I've seen."

"How long ago?"

"I don't know. Six months? But most of the time he's fine. Better than fine. I mean, he's a huge help around here. He can do anything, like the guys said. He put in a new light receptacle for me. Built the back stairs himself. He's happiest when he has a job to do."

Still scrawling, I said, "Where's he from?"

"Somewhere Down East—Ledge Harbor, maybe? I think his father is a lobsterman."

"Single?"

"Oh, yeah. I mean, I don't think Teak could maintain a relationship."

"But he had one with you," I said.

She looked at me sharply.

"A working one, I mean. He was your Mister Fix-It."

"Yeah, but that's different from living with somebody."

"These comic-book delusions. Did he talk to you about that stuff?"

Harriet smiled.

"He tried to. This god and that god. It had something to do with Sweden or Norway or something. I couldn't figure it all out. Who's fighting who, which prince is related to which princess, this bad guy from some other planet who was banished by somebody a thousand years ago. It's complicated, like the Bible or something"

"And he invented it all himself?"

"Yeah, but he really thinks it's real. For him, it isn't just something made up. He thinks this world is out there someplace."

Harriet waved toward the ceiling, like there was this other world beyond the stained ceiling tiles. I wrote in the notebook, catching up. Harriet waited, saying, "Oh, Lindy Hines. This is unbelievable."

I finished and looked up, said, "So nothing told you Teak was capable of doing something like this?"

"My God, no. Like I said, he works here with me. I mean, he comes in here and I give him a to-do list. He comes back with everything checked off. Literally. With a pencil. Never a pen, for some reason. But last time I saw him, he was fine."

"Who makes sure people like him are taking their meds?"

"State has case managers. They come here. But they go out and find the people, too. It's called the Community Action Team. CAT. They pick the people up, take them to the clinic. If they can find them."

"Where does Teak live? When he isn't here?"

"He has a room. Somewhere on the hill up past the courthouse. But somebody like Teak, he'd just decide he wanted to roam. He'd be gone for a month, come back and I'd say, 'Where you been?' He'd say, 'Here and there, Miss H.' And he'd give me this sort of cagey smile. Sometimes he'd say something about being on an assignment. I'm like, 'Glad you're back, Teak.' He'd go, 'Whatcha got for me to do?'"

Harriet smiled. The good old days, before this morning.

"Does he have anyone here he's especially close to?"

She thought, shook her head. I wondered if she did her hair herself, how long it had been blue. Was the idea to fit in with the clientele, position herself somewhere on the fringe?

"No, not really. You have to see the way things work here. The ones with more serious mental illnesses, they interact but not like you're interacting with me. They kind of have this parallel thing going, you know?"

"Teak did that?"

"Yeah, but Teak's different. He kind of sits back and observes. Like he knows what's really going on and the rest of us are just, I don't know—"

"Mere mortals?" I said.

"Yeah, and he's been sent here to keep us from getting into too much trouble."

"Huh."

We both sat for a moment in silence. I was wondering what role Lindy Hines had played in the movie in Teak's head. An impostor? An evil sorcerer disguised as a fifty-year-old woman?

"Did Teak ever go to these other offices, the administrative place?" I said.

Harriet shook her head.

"It's just one office, really. A reception space. A room where the board meets," she said. "I mean, he'd have no reason. There are no clients, no beds, no food. Nothing to fix."

"And Lindy Hines, she never came here," I said.

"No," Harriet said. "She never had a chance."

I sat in the truck out front. It was spitting snow, the showers that come with the squalls on the tail end of a storm front. Dolph and Arthur banged out of the side door of the shelter and trudged out to the sidewalk, then past my truck. They walked slowly and stared at me as they passed. I nodded. They looked away.

Tapping my phone, I looked up "schizo affected disorder." The web sent me to *schizoaffective disorder*. The medical websites said it's a combo of schizophrenia and a mood disorder, like mania and depression. Hallucinations, delusions, disorganized thinking, depression, and manic behavior. Treatment is meds and therapy. People who have it should be monitored closely, the online experts said, as the symptoms can be severe.

Got that right.

I called the *Times* and Vanessa was just getting out of a meeting. I waited, adjusted the rearview mirror so I could watch Dolph and

Arthur as they walked up the street. They were twenty feet apart now, Dolph taking point.

Vanessa came on and I told her the story. She was silent until I got to the part about Lindy Hines volunteering to sort out the shelter's finances.

"There it is," Vanessa said. "Good Samaritan killed by the very people she was trying to help."

"Yup," I said.

"I can pitch it for section front," she said. "When will you have it?"

"Say, late afternoon tomorrow."

"Who else is on it?"

"Locals, but mostly they're just following the cops' lead. I'm two steps ahead."

"Fifteen hundred words?"

"Give or take," I said.

She waited. After five years as my editor, Vanessa could sense that there was something else coming.

"What's the matter, Jack?"

I hesitated.

"I don't know. This one has gotten to me. So totally random and bizarre. I feel like I have to at least explain the delusion, the cause of it. Maybe then, in some weird way it won't be quite so senseless."

"People die randomly all the time, Jack," Vanessa said. "Wars. Floods. Earthquakes. All the murders you've covered. That kid in Bed-Stuy who stopped to let the guy in the wheelchair cross the street."

"And got hit in the head by a stray bullet fired from a block away, I know. But in some way it's getting harder and harder for me to accept that life is nothing but a friggin' crapshoot."

I heard Lindy's voice: *Aren't we the early birds?*

Early enough to die a violent, meaningless death.

"I want to tell the whole story of this one. If this was the last domino, I want to trace it back to the first one."

Another few moments of newsroom murmur and then Vanessa said, "Give me two hundred for the New England digest by two or so."

"Sounds good."

"And I don't know why I still bother to say this, but you be careful. And don't get me into trouble."

"As always."

"Try to do better than that, Jack," she said.

The snow had covered the windshield as we talked, and I sat in the half-darkness for a minute, the story running through my mind, the places I had to go. The office of these case managers, to ask about Teak and his meds. Jail, if I could persuade Teak to talk to me, and get past his lawyer. Lindy Hines's son. The contractor on Mount Desert. The forensic psych people—get a sense of whether Teak would stand trial at all. His family Down East. Other homeless, like Dolph and Arthur.

I looked in the side mirror. The two guys were sitting in the park on separate benches in front of a big monument. There was someone on a third bench with a shopping cart full of belongings, and a fourth person, a woman in a camo parka, talking to the guy with the cart.

I'd grabbed my notebook and was reaching for the door when my phone buzzed. I looked at it. A text. Roxanne.

—YOU OK?
YES. YOU GET MY MESSAGE?
—YEAH. IT'S ON THE BROADCAST WEBSITE. YOU COMING HOME SOON?

PRETTY SOON. WHY?

—LOUIS IS HERE. HE BROUGHT HIS GIRLFRIEND. SHE
SAYS SHE WANTED TO MEET ME, NEEDS SOME GIRL TIME,
WHAT WITH ALL THESE MACHO MEN.

I sighed, put my notebook on the passenger seat.

ON MY WAY.

I made it home to Prosperity in fifty-three minutes, driving south
to Unity and then across and up to the ridge through the swirling
snow, down the other side to home. Louis's Jeep was parked beside
Roxanne's Subaru. I pulled in and hurried inside, heard Sophie saying,
"Sit, Friendy, sit."

It was early release at Prosperity Primary, something about state
testing, and the younger kids and ed techs got sent home. Sophie was
feeding the dog bits of cheese from a chunk of orange cheddar. Marta
and Louis were sitting at the kitchen table, and Roxanne was pouring
Marta another cup of coffee. The zucchini bread was half gone.

"Daddy," Sophie said. "Friend's almost as big as Pokey. I think we
should get Pokey's old saddle and see if I can ride him."

"I don't think dogs like to be ridden," I said. "Maybe we could
get him to pull you in your sled."

"A sled dog, like the Eskimos."

Sophie ran out of the room. Friend trotted after her and I looked
to the company. Marta had her hair pulled back and was wearing a
cream-colored fisherman's knit sweater under a bright green down
vest. That and the jeans and Bean boots.

"Hey," I said.

I moved to the table and Marta got half out of her chair. I leaned
down and she clasped my shoulder and did the Euro double-kiss

thing. Her lipstick was blood red and looked like it had been applied with a paintbrush.

"Welcome to Prosperity, Maine," I said. "Sorry I was held up."

"We heard," Marta said. "What on earth happened?"

Sophie was out of the room, a brief window. I went to the counter, reached for a tea bag. Barry's. Poured a cup and came back to the table and gave them the thirty-second version. Lindy Hines. The ax. Teak. The police.

"How horrible," Marta said, her hand on her chest as if to still her heart.

"Awful," Roxanne said. "I wonder whether his caseworker dropped the ball. I mean, the people I knew, they didn't snap in an instant, or even a day. It took time to build."

Marta looked at her.

"I worked for the State—Child Protective Services," Roxanne said. "Before I started working at the school. With the state, sometimes it was abuse. Sometimes it was neglect. Sometimes all of it was because a parent wasn't mentally stable."

I dabbed the tea bag, listened to the voice of experience.

"It's a cycle," Roxanne said. "If you know somebody who's sick, you can usually see it coming. Sometimes we did home visits, watched to see how the adults were doing. Were they stable? Showing signs of anxiety?"

"Nobody saw this guy coming," I said.

"Then somebody wasn't paying attention. Do you think they knew each other?" Roxanne said.

I shook my head. "It looks like wrong place, very wrong time. Just totally random. Just executed her, like ISIS or something."

"America, it's so violent now," Marta said. "Crime in BVI, what little there is, is almost always economic. Burglaries, the occasional tourist held up for their iPhone. Things like what happened to Nigel were unheard of. Never anything like this."

I turned to Roxanne and said, "I told you about Marta's partner."

"Marta," Roxanne said. "I'm so sorry for your loss."

"You know, you can read about this sort of thing every day online, but it's like it's always in some other world, you know?" Marta said. "You don't ever think one of those stories could be you."

"And they have no idea who did it?" Roxanne said.

Marta shook her head. "You have to remember: It's a small island with not much for police. And there are all these other islands with boats and private planes. In three hours you could be just about anywhere. Mexico City, Miami—next flight out, you're gone."

"Do they know you're in Maine?" I said.

Marta looked at me.

"Who?"

"The investigators. Anybody," I said.

"Did you pay for gas with a credit card?" I said. "That's the easiest trace."

"Prepaid Visa cards," she said. "Buy them at Walmart for cash."

We looked at her and she caught herself.

"Nigel," Marta said. "He liked to stay under the radar."

There was an awkward moment, Roxanne shooting me a look. And then a slam, the door to the mudroom. Sophie came in with her boots and jacket on, leading Friend by his thick, leather collar. The dog padded along patiently.

"We're ready," she said.

"Oh, fun," Marta said. "I wish I was back on Instagram. My boyfriend and his sled dog in the deep north woods."

We trooped outside and around to the backyard, where trails led through woods and eventually to Clair's barn. I grabbed Sophie's toboggan on the way out, tied a rope to the loop on the front. Louis tied the end of the rope to Friend's collar and led him away to take out the slack. Sophie climbed onto the toboggan, arranged her feet, and grabbed the line tightly.

"Go, Friendy, go," she said, and Louis gave Friend a whistle and started to trot away. The dog followed, pulling the toboggan easily. Sophie whooped and Marta clapped and the team started down the wide part of the trail to Clair's barn, disappeared beyond the first bend. Marta started walking slowly and we walked with her, one on each side. She was quiet, eyes on the trail in front of her.

"Are you okay?" Roxanne said.

"Yes," Marta said. "It's funny, but I sort of am. It's like I escaped from this glittering sort of prison and I'm free now, with you guys and Louis and all this nature."

Trees, trees, and more trees. Maybe Maine was growing on her.

"It was bad for a long time?" Roxanne said.

"Oh, God. A good six months, but there were signs. And then for years I was berated and belittled."

"Was it physical?" I said.

"He never struck me. But he squeezed so hard it left bruises, purple spots, one for each fingertip."

"I'm so sorry," Roxanne said.

"And when he wasn't hurting you, you were supposed to adore him because he bought you all of this. And you had to have sex when he wanted because that's what you bring to the party, you know? And he was so angry if he didn't get it."

"It's all about power," Roxanne said. "And control."

"Why didn't you leave?" I said.

"Always the first question," Marta said. "Because after a while I believed him. I'm nothing. He's everything. I should be grateful for everything he gives me. Without the great Nigel Dean, I'm nothing and nobody."

We walked, boots crunching in the snow. Suddenly Marta said, "Can I tell you something? I've only told Louis this. When they came in the house—the Russians, I mean—part of me was ready to run. But the other part wanted to stay and see him lose. See him beaten. See him put down. And when I did run, partly it was because I was afraid. But another part was because I wanted to escape."

"From them or him?" Roxanne said.

"Both," Marta said. "It's messed up, I know, but in this very weird way it was like I'd been rescued."

We introduced Marta to Pokey, who came to the door of his stall and took a carrot from Sophie. Marta fed him an apple, after Louis sliced it into pieces with the five-inch knife on his belt. The dog sniffed the barn and eyed the pony face-to-face, and then we hitched Friend back up and he pulled Sophie home.

Everyone came inside and Roxanne made cocoa. Marta and Louis each had a cup, Marta sitting next to Sophie at the table and talking horses. Marta's pony when she was a little girl in Ukraine was named

Snowflake and she was white. They kept her at their country house. Sophie said it was too bad Snowflake and Pokey couldn't be friends, because Pokey's only friends were Mary's chickens.

Louis stepped outside through the shed and I followed. We watched a gaggle of blue jays land in the line of spruce trees beside the house. They squawked and squabbled and three crows flew in, and then a great-horned owl launched out of a tree on wide stiff wings, jays and crows in pursuit.

"You okay?"

"Actually, yeah," Louis said. "I'm good. It's kind of like being deployed again."

I glanced at him. He was staring out at the trees. I figured the bulge under his sweater at the hip was his Kimber .45—if Marta still had the Sig.

"You picturing it as permanent?" I said.

Louis shrugged.

"Who knows? I've seen her three days in eleven years."

"But you had a good thing at one time."

"We were kids," Louis said. "But yeah. It was special. Still is. She is."

We stood for a moment and listened to the sound of the distant birds.

"You worried about somebody coming looking for her?" I said.

"Wouldn't say worried. More like aware."

I knew what that meant for Louis. Walking the perimeter around the cabin. The guns locked and loaded. When he did that, the dog went on high alert.

"Can she shoot?"

"Okay with a handgun," Louis said. "But the best weapon for her is the Benelli. We spent some time with it."

I pictured their last couple of days at the cabin. Hop out of bed and grab the tactical shotgun. Not your typical love nest.

We could hear the crows still mobbing the owl in the distance. I was feeling guilty about thinking that Marta had way more downside than upside, that without her we never had to worry about Russian gangsters at all. And then she was behind us, said, "Hey, Lou. We gotta run. Let this beautiful little family get back to their day."

They started for their car, Marta taking Louis's hand in hers. Sophie and I waved and walked back to the house, in the shed door and through to the kitchen. Roxanne was at the sink, rinsing the carafe from the coffeemaker.

"You have to get ready," she said to Sophie, and Sophie bounded out of the kitchen and up the stairs. Roxanne cranked the faucet tighter and turned back to me.

"You okay?" she said.

I took a breath, closed my eyes. Opened them.

"It was really horrible."

She took my hand.

"I'm sorry."

"I mean, an ax. It's . . . it's not anything you want to see."

"I know, Jack. Maybe you shouldn't write anything."

"It's a story," I said.

Roxanne squeezed my hand, touched my shoulder.

"Having just talked to her. That makes it even more awful. It's just surreal. And now this Marta here, and Louis with her. It's just a lot."

"I know," she said. "But Marta seems okay. A little lost, like she's trying to re-create herself."

"Who knows what she really is?"

"You don't believe her?" Roxanne said.

"I don't know. Why should I?"

"Because Louis does," Roxanne said. "And we know Louis."

"Do we? Sometimes I think we just know what he wants us to know."

"That seems harsh. Because if you think that about him, then Marta—"

"—is a complete unknown," I said. "We don't know jack."

10

—◦m◦—

Gymnastics was Sunday mornings at the community center in Belfast, twelve miles to the east. Sophie would fling herself around on the mats with her buddies and Roxanne would make a quick stop at the co-op. I waved good-bye and stood until the Subaru was out of sight.

They were on their own.

I walked into the house, filled the electric kettle, and stood as it hissed and rumbled. It steamed and I made a fresh cup of tea and took it into the study, flipped open my notebook.

The digest story was done and gone:

> RIVERPORT, MAINE—*In a bizarre daytime attack, a woman in a crowded big-box store was killed by an ax-wielding man who was then subdued by store workers.*
>
> *Lindy Hines, who had recently moved to the city from nearby Mount Desert Island, was attacked by T. K. "Teak" Barney, 27, while she was shopping for Christmas decorations at the Home Department store in Riverport, police said. Ms. Hines suffered a single blow to the head. She was transported to Eastern Maine Medical Center where she was pronounced dead.*
>
> *Her alleged assailant was taken into custody at the scene. He remained in the Penobscot County jail late Saturday. Bail*

had not been set.

Mr. Barney is known in the community as a street person who frequents a local homeless shelter. According to one close acquaintance, he has suffered from a mental illness for several years and was being treated with medication. Police said they did not know what triggered the attack.

Hines had just started volunteering with the administrative office of the same shelter where Barney was a client and pitched in as a handyman, said Harriet Strand, manager of Loaves & Fishes.

She said Hines, who was trained as an accountant, had volunteered to organize the shelter's finances, but had yet to visit the actual facility. "She never had the chance," Ms. Strand said.

The bigger story awaited.

I opened the laptop and started to type out an outline. Sheila at Home Department, Detective Tingley, the neighbors at the condo, Harriet at the shelter. Arthur and Dolph.

Then I sat back and paused. Leaned in and opened the browser and googled BVI news. The website had a stream of stories: an American tourist kicked out for bad behavior; the under-fourteen football squad headed for a tournament in Puerto Rico; a local guy jailed after stealing a scooter and leading police on a chase around Tortola.

Small stuff, unless you lived on an island.

I searched for Nigel Dean. The stories, all by staff writer R. L. Bunbury, emerged from the archives: the initial report of a suspicious death. Police ruling that it was a homicide. Investigation moving off the island and no continuing danger to the public. In other words, Nigel wasn't killed by a local serial killer. Everybody go back to sleep.

There was a phone number at the newspaper's offices on Tortola. I opened the desk drawer, took out a flip phone, one of two I'd picked up at a Walmart in Augusta. I flipped it open, then pulled up the *Miami Herald* on my laptop and clicked through to crime news. Crime reporter Alan Charles had a story about a heist of $1 million in electronics, the security guard tased and tied up. I dialed.

A man with a British Caribbean accent answered. I asked for Bunbury. The phone clicked and the call rang through.

"Bunbury," a woman said.

"Ms. Bunbury, this is Alan Charles," I said. "*Miami Herald*."

"Miss, and proud of it," Bunbury said. "*Miami Herald*. You're not calling about the scooter thief, I take it."

"No, actually it's about the Nigel Dean case," I said.

"What about him?"

She didn't sound surprised.

"I'm just wondering if there have been developments, stories I've missed. The one I read was two days after he was killed."

She didn't reply.

"Just curious. Any arrests?"

Bunbury paused. I waited again.

"Not that I know of," she said.

"And you would know, I'm assuming."

"Not necessarily. It's a very wide-ranging investigation."

"Like Miami? Any connection here? Your story said the investigation had moved out of BVI."

"Sorry, no Miami," she said. "What did you say your name is?"

I repeated it. I could hear Bunbury typing.

"Huh," she said. "You're in there, but how do I know you're this fellow? If I call this number back, will it ring in at the *Miami Herald*?"

"No," I said. "It'll ring my cell in my condo in Coral Way. I'm at home. They let us telecommute a couple of days a week. Helps with traffic congestion."

She didn't answer. I said, "Are you still there?"

"Yeah," she said.

"The Dean home invasion. Not local, then?"

"We don't believe these were ours."

"And not South Florida?"

I waited. Finally she said, "Maybe Russia, maybe London."

"Long way to go for a home invasion. So this wasn't some low-level thugs."

"Police would tell you they were very professional, the way they got into the villa, disabled the alarm system. And they were, how should I say, heartless in the way they conducted themselves."

"Torturing the guy, you mean."

She didn't reply. I counted to ten.

Finally, I said, "You still there, Miss Bunbury?"

"Yeah. Where did you hear Dean was tortured?"

"I thought I read that someplace."

"Not in my stories. Police say he was stabbed to death."

"Huh. We were talking about it here. Maybe somebody jumped to a conclusion. Taped to a chair and stabbed. Sounds pretty torturous."

"I said, 'tied,' not taped," Bunbury said.

"Which was it?" I said.

Another skip in the rhythm of the conversation.

"Investigators are withholding some details," she said.

"Are you?"

"We try to cooperate when we can. A life was taken, after all."

"I understand," I said. "Dean's girlfriend."

"Yes."

"She's lucky she wasn't killed."

"Yes. Very."

Something in the two words.

"What do you mean?"

"Just that," Bunbury said.

"She hid, right? In the wine cellar?"

"That's where I'm told they found her. The police, I mean."

"And she cooperated, right? I mean, she's not a person of interest, as they say."

I waited.

"What exactly is your interest, Mr. Charles?"

"I don't know. Sounded intriguing. World-class criminals target rich Englishman in his island villa. Kill him after extracting millions, or whatever it was. I thought I might grab a photographer and head over. We're gearing up on crime features. In print, there's a standing slot. Page one, below the fold. They're our top stories in terms of both click-throughs and time on the page. You know how metrics drive the content these days."

Again, no reply. I heard more typing. Probably trying to locate my phone number, at least the area code.

"I'm told Ms. Kovac spoke with police here," Bunbury said. "She was understandably distraught."

"Where is she now? Would I be able to speak with her, do you think?"

"They said she could leave the island, apparently. Word I got is that she went off the island to be with family. Flew out on a private charter. I tried to call her through the Dean family lawyer in London. I just got voice mail."

"Memorial service for Dean?"

"In England. The ancestral manse."

"Was she there?"

"You seem very interested in this woman."

"She's got the harrowing story to tell," I said. "Hiding in the cellar while the bad guys kill her boyfriend. Waiting for hours."

"That you'll have to get from the police," she said. "If you come to the island."

Emphasis on the *if*.

"If you're a reporter at all."

"Oh, I can assure you I am," I said, and I hung up. Powered the phone off and tossed it in the trash.

I sat in the study chair and ran through it. Marta had details that hadn't been released, which stood to reason. She was in the house. She was talking to the cops on the scene. Bunbury wasn't all that sympathetic to Marta—but why? No respect for the trophy girlfriend? Didn't know she'd been trapped there? Had Marta not seemed sufficiently distraught? If not, where did Bunbury get that from? The BVI cops, who she seemed cozy with?

And if Marta wasn't the grieving widow, what was she? The abuse victim released from her torment? The insider? Tipped off the bad guys to the money for a cut? If she'd done that, why was she here? Unless it was for a place to hide.

From whom? Maybe Marta Kovac, the ultimate survivor, had taken a cut that wasn't hers.

I took a deep breath. "There you go again," I said.

And my phone, my actual phone, buzzed.

I picked it up off the desk. Saw a Maine number I didn't recognize. "McMorrow," I said.

"I saw your story. The *New York Times*. How dare you write about my mother without speaking to me," a man said.

11

Orrington is just south of Riverport on the other side of the Penobscot River. Barrett Hines lived in a house that overlooked the river from the end of a looping sort of cul-de-sac. It was hard to find, even with GPS, and took me an hour and a quarter to get there. When I arrived, I saw Lindy Hines's SUV in the driveway. Barrett was standing inside the front door, the same dog bouncing up and down at his feet.

He held the door open for me and we shook hands. When we made eye contact I was looking up. The dog yipped at me and backed away, lunged in to nip at my boot.

"Harry," Barrett said. "Zip it."

The dog quieted, sniffing my boots instead of biting them. Barrett led the way to a big open room with a wall of windows that looked out on the river, which was frozen except for a dark snaking stream at the center. There was a gravel pit on the far shore, with yellow loaders and backhoes parked near brown scars on a backdrop of white. Toto, this wasn't Tortola.

"Much boat traffic in the summer?" I said.

"Some," he said. "Have a seat."

He gestured toward an easy chair. There were two of them facing the windows, matching overstuffed, in dark brown leather. I imagined one was for his husband. I sat, took out my notebook and a pen. He turned his chair and faced me.

Barrett was a big guy, six-two and rangy. Television handsome, short-cropped hair with a flip in the front, a stylish stubble, and his mother's intense light-blue eyes.

"I'm sorry if I seemed rude," he said.

"Not at all," I said. "It's a very difficult time, I'm sure."

"I just want you to know the real story. Of my mother."

"Me, too," I said.

"She was a wonderful person. Like, completely unselfish."

I started to write.

"I still can't believe she's gone," Barrett Hines said.

"I'm sure. It's crazy."

"We talked every day, especially since she moved over here from the island."

"She was getting divorced?" I said.

"Yeah. My stepfather, he's a contractor on MDI. He relied on her for all the financial stuff. They used to argue like crazy, him making her cut all these corners. Ha, I hope to hell the IRS shows up, nails the sleezeball."

I looked up at him.

"Sounds like it wasn't amicable," I said.

"Rod is an asshole," he said. "An egotistical, narcissistic philanderer. I blame him for my mother's death."

He looked at my notebook.

"Go ahead. Write that down," he said. "You can quote me."

I scribbled in shorthand, looked up at him.

"But your stepdad, he didn't attack your mother. Why do you blame—"

"That bastard. You don't know the story," Hines said.

"That's why I'm here," I said.

He crossed his legs, settled in. I waited.

"Okay. Rod and my mom got married right out of college. My mom had gotten pregnant in high school, then the guy went and got killed driving drunk."

"I'm sorry," I said.

"Whatever. Totally useless human being. Mom went to UMaine, lived at home with my grandmother. Rod played basketball, but he wasn't a starter. I mean, as much as he tries to tell everybody he was a big star. He was a high school star. Big deal. Mom was cute and smart, way too nice. He can turn it on, I'll give him that. He probably cheated on her there, too, I don't know."

At least one picture was emerging.

"Okay. Fast-forward. And you have to understand MDI. That's Mount Desert Island."

"Right."

"There's the big money on the island. New York, Philadelphia, hedge funders, Rockefellers, Martha Stewart. Then there's the tourists—Acadia and all that—and there's people who have the shops and galleries and restaurants and B-and-Bs. And then there's people like my mom and Rod who work for the wealthy summer folks. If you're good at it, and you get in with the right people, you can make serious money."

I wrote in my notebook.

"Am I going too fast?"

"No."

He stood up, seemed even taller. Started to pace.

"For a few years, when I'm a kid, my dad is small-time. Garages. Boat sheds. Decks. Additions for the locals. Then he gets a break, does a carriage house for these people from Delaware who have this sort of average mansion in Northeast Harbor. Then it's a bigger fancy addition in Seal Harbor, bigger money. Then up in Northeast, these people have a fire and my dad gets the rebuild. Like I said. He can talk."

He stopped pacing, looked down at me.

"You see how this is going, right?"

"Things take off."

"Right. I mean, all of a sudden, Spruce Rock is, like, big-time. My dad's hiring, buying new trucks and equipment, subs are knocking on his door for work."

"All good," I said.

He turned toward the river, then spun back and said, "And who do you think was a huge part of making that happen."

"Your mom."

"Exactly," Hines said, almost triumphantly.

"She was the brains?"

"The financial brains, for sure. She majored in accounting at UMaine, and this was her thing. She did the estimates, the bids, negotiating for materials, figured out the margins they needed, took in the payments. Hiring and payroll and all the government forms and the permits and on and on."

"What does your dad do?"

"Struts around like he's a big deal. Have you met him?"

I shook my head.

"Marlboro Man with a hammer. He's a big guy, my size. That was a coincidence. Pretty jacked, good-looking. Like a Carhartt ad. The wives up in Northeast—their husbands are gone most of the time, out making money to pay for all of it—Rod's like some porn fantasy come true."

"Did he take them up on it?"

"I don't know. But I think it planted the seed. 'Hey, these women think I'm pretty hot. Maybe I am.' "

"Started to believe his own act?" I said.

"You got it."

"That why he and your mother split up?"

Barrett sat down in the chair, leaned toward me.

"The gym," he said.

"Ah."

"How many fifty-year-old contractors need to go to the gym? I mean, he's lifting stuff, hauling a nail gun around. Maybe not as much as he used to. I figure he felt like he was looking old. He's vain as hell."

I had stopped taking notes. Barrett didn't seem to notice.

"So at the gym there's this fitness coach."

"Uh-huh."

"Her name is Silk."

"Uh-oh."

"Right. She's, like, maybe forty."

"Attractive?"

"In a too-old-for-that-ponytail sort of way. Built like you would expect for a fitness coach."

"I see."

"They hook up. And you can guess the rest."

"They're still together?" I said.

"My mom moved out. Silk moved in."

"Huh."

"She wanted a horse. Rod built her a horse barn."

"Who's doing the books now?"

"Rod hired an accountant."

I wrote that down.

"That's an expense," I said.

"Hey, he's making money hand over fist, at least on paper. Building like a six-thousand-square-foot guesthouse in Northeast right now. I heard it's some super design, all glass on the ocean side. Guy runs some freaking hedge fund. I don't think he even asked how much it would cost."

I scribbled a bit more. Shifted in my leather chair.

"Your stepdad tell you all of this?" I said.

"We don't speak," Barrett said. "I talk—or should I say, talked—to my mom. She was just a wonderful person."

"Did you not speak because—"

I hesitated.

"Me being gay?"

"Yeah."

"I embarrassed him. Let him down. He thought I was great when I was a kid, playing sports, doing what he expected Rod Blaine's stepson to do. But when I came out, he made sure he let me know I was a big disappointment."

"I'm sorry to hear that," I said.

"Hey, it's all about him. Textbook narcissist. A gay son? All these construction guys he works with?"

"What? Gay guys don't work construction?"

"Of course they do. But in rural Maine, they're just careful who they tell," Barrett said. "Make sure they don't date too close to home."

"Sad," I said.

"Reality," he said.

"How did your mom feel about the split?"

"Like you'd expect. Hurt. Betrayed. I mean, she was so nice, she always gave him the benefit of the doubt. And then she couldn't. And she knew she'd wasted twenty-five years of her life."

I hesitated, then said it.

"I met her."

Barrett froze in mid-stride.

"What? When—how?"

I told him. The two of us in the parking lot. Ten minutes later, people screaming.

He stared off as it sank in.

"How did she seem?" he asked.

"Happy," I said.

I didn't say she'd wanted to chat.

"She had the dog with her. She was friendly, smiling. She seemed like a good person."

"Oh, she was. Then you know. Why the hell did she have to be there at that minute? Why did this asshole have to be there? Why the fuck did he pick her out?"

His eyes filled and he wiped them with the back of his hand.

"I don't know," I said. "I'm trying to figure it out."

"If my dad hadn't decided to screw around, she'd be alive. Living on MDI, going about her business," Barrett said. "That's the bottom line."

He watched me and waited as I wrote down those two sentences.

"I want you to put that in the *New York Times*. I want the whole world to know that."

I nodded, said, "I understand."

Barrett stood again, walked to the window. I got up from the chair, slipped my notebook into my pocket. I walked over and stood beside him. He was crying silently. I waited and he wiped his eyes again, took a long, deep breath. On the river, a bald eagle was flapping its way downstream. I don't know that Barrett saw it.

"Can I ask you a crazy question?" he said.

"Sure."

"My mom and dad were separated."

"Right."

"Mom would be getting substantial alimony. She helped build the business over twenty years. She's entitled to half of that, I would think."

"Sounds right. But I assume that's what the lawyers would be negotiating."

I glanced at him and he said, "What happens now that she's gone?"

"I don't know. But I guess the whole thing ends. The divorce, I mean."

"You can't divorce a deceased person, right?" Barrett said. "And you can't pay alimony to one, either. You think it's occurred to them? The cops, I mean."

"If they're good."

"Are they?" Barrett said.

"I don't know," I said. "Too early to tell."

He stared straight ahead. I waited.

"This guy is schizophrenic or something, right?" Barrett said.

"Or something. He's pretty sick. Thinks comic books are real and he's living in one."

Barrett was thinking. I waited for him and finally gave up and said, "How did your parents get along lately? Did they argue?"

"Not anymore. It was all through lawyers."

We stood, still looking out at the Penobscot. Another eagle flew by, an immature one, mottled brown.

"I could ruin the fucker," Barrett said.

I kept my eyes on the river.

"How so?"

"I know stuff. About the business. Things he made my mother do."

"Like with the books?" I said.

"Yeah."

"He had a guy pay him, like, two hundred grand in cash for a job that cost sixty thousand."

"Money laundering?"

"Guy was some investment type from Manhattan."

"Your mom told you this," I said.

"Right. Just saying. That's off the record. I'm saving it for when I need it."

I nodded, almost imperceptibly. Gulls flew by, then a single raven, but no more eagles.

"You're sure about blaming your dad for your mom being in Riverport?" I said. "In the story, I mean."

"Yes. I want that in there," Barrett said. "If I decide to use the money stuff, I'll go straight to the cops."

"Okay," I said. We turned and I held out my hand and he shook it, a strong, firm grip. I said I was very sorry for what had happened and I appreciated him talking to me, that I'd be back in touch with any questions.

"Do my mother justice," Barrett said.

"I'll do my best," I said.

Too little, too late?

I started for the door and he followed. We stepped outside and I turned back and said, "I do have another question. What did your mom say about working for Loaves and Fishes?"

"Just that the books were a gigantic mess. Boxes of crap that the person who runs it, she brought over to the office. Some of it literally on napkins. Nothing in order. A lot of it in the head of the lady there."

"Harriet. More than your mom signed up for?"

"Mom said she'd straighten things out, but it was going to be a project."

"How did Harriet like that your mom was coming in?"

"Not very much. But my mom was a positive person. She said she'd win her over, bring the place into the twenty-first century."

Barrett paused.

"She never had a chance. It just totally sucks."

"Yes," I said. "It does."

12

⁓

I was back home in Prosperity at 6:15. Roxanne had dinner on the table: tuna melts and a salad with kale and almond slivers and dried cranberries. Sophie sat and began picking the berries out of her salad with her fingers.

"Fork, please," Roxanne said, and Sophie began spearing the berries, one by one.

Roxanne asked what I'd been doing, and I said I went up to a town called Orrington and saw two eagles flying down the river. Sophie asked if they had a lot of eagles in Orrington, and I said it appeared they had a few. She asked if I was writing a story about eagles and I said, no, but maybe I should.

Easier than writing about a woman who'd had her head split open.

There was chat about school, a boy named Jo-Jo who was new and his moms brought him to class. Sophie said they seemed really nice, and Jo-Jo was crying when they left.

And then it was bath time and I went upstairs and started the tub. They followed and Sophie climbed in and started making crazy hairdos with soapsuds. I laughed and Sophie did, too, and then my phone buzzed and I slipped it out and left the room and stood in the hall.

It was Clair. He said we should work in the woods in the morning.

"Is Louis coming?"

"I don't know, but we need to talk," he said.

"Yes," I said. "We do."

There was a story, *Mike Mulligan and His Steam Shovel*. It was reassuring, a world where a steam shovel had eyes and a big smile. As we were reading, I wondered if this was what Teak felt like when he left the real world for the one he'd made up. A world better than the one you were stuck in.

And then Sophie was tucked in and we turned off the lights and Roxanne and I went downstairs. In the kitchen, she started loading the dishwasher. I put food in containers and the containers in the refrigerator. When it was done, I went to the study and plunged in.

I rewrote my notes, circling the critical stuff, filling in missing words. How much of Barrett would I use? The embittered son lashing out at his stepfather? Was it really Rod Blaine's fault that his soon-to-be-ex had been murdered?

He cheated on her. I kept working.

After Barrett, I picked up a second notebook. Bunbury. Who said anything about torture? I underlined that, flipped the pages. Looked up at the screen and typed in *BVI police*. The website came up. There was a picture of a commissioner, an older guy in a too-tight uniform. There was a paragraph on the department's vision, two more on their mission, a list of values, mostly about being fair and impartial.

Nothing about a rich guy who was slashed to death in his fancy house, or a girlfriend who bolted before the—

A touch on my shoulder.

Roxanne. I hadn't heard her come into the room.

"You're throwing yourself into this story to keep your distance."

"When I'm reporting and writing, I can control that much," I said.

Roxanne squeezed my arm.

I turned to her. She leaned against me, kneaded my shoulder.

"Lindy Hines moved to Riverport because her husband of twenty-some years dumped her for a younger woman," I said. "His fitness coach. They were negotiating alimony, which would have been sizable."

"His lucky day?" Roxanne said.

"I'd say so," I said, and looked away.

She looked at me. "Am I losing you, Jack? You've got that look where you shut everything else out and then you're gone."

"Just a lot on my mind."

I stared at the screen, the cheesy BVI police department website. Roxanne waited. I sighed, turned to her.

"She wanted to talk," I said.

"Who?"

"Lindy Hines. When I met her in the parking lot this morning. She said something about us being early birds. You know how you throw something out to start a conversation?"

"Jack, don't," Roxanne said.

"I was in a hurry, wanted to stay on schedule. I pretended I didn't hear her. Kept going."

"No."

"If I'd just turned around, chatted with her some more. 'Hey, why are you here so early?' Walked into the store with her, even."

"Jack, it's not your fault."

"Maybe if she hadn't looked like she was there alone. Maybe he would have changed his mind, gotten this crazy idea out of his head."

"You couldn't have controlled this, Jack."

"But what if I had just—"

"Enough. Is that why you're doing this story? Because you feel guilty that you didn't escort this stranger through Home Department?"

"It might have helped."

"Or he might have killed you, too," Roxanne said.

"I'm not helpless Lindy Hines. So this story is like a headstone for her. It says this isn't normal. I owe her that much."

"Are you going to write that you feel you could have saved her?"

I hesitated.

"What? Some first-person sidebar? I don't know."

Roxanne gave me a last squeeze on the shoulder, then stepped back like we'd finished our good-byes.

"I can't stop you, I know," she said. "And I don't know how far you're going to take it. Just be careful."

I mustered a smile.

"People keep saying that. Worrywarts."

"I'm serious, Jack," Roxanne said, and she turned and walked into the living room. I heard her kick off her shoes, knew she'd settled on the couch with her laptop.

I was alone with my friendly demon, her smiling face, her blood pooling on a concrete floor.

Sitting at the desk, I tried to chase her away. I looked at the BVI police Facebook page: hurricane recovery, arrests for assault and possession of cannabis, a guy killed in a scooter accident. A long report on a drive-by shooting with two people killed, including a nine-year-old boy. A plea for information from the public so the detective inspector could bring to justice those who had "callously and heartlessly taken his life."

I kept scrolling until I hit Nigel Dean. One short paragraph. He'd succumbed to injuries sustained during a burglary gone wrong. No one had been apprehended. The investigation was continuing.

And now Dean's girlfriend was laying low, but waiting for what? For Louis to pop the question, so she could latch on to another millionaire? For the home invaders to be caught so she could sleep easy? For Louis to take them out?

I stared at the screen, the questions circling in my head like birds, never finding a place to light.

When I went to bed, Roxanne was still up working. I looked in on Sophie and she was snoring softly. I gave her a kiss on the forehead, and then I went to bed and stared at the gray outline of the sky beyond the window. Listened to the creak of frozen branches in the wind.

And I slept until an awful image crept in. Sophie's soft child's throat was bared to the night and people were around her bed, saying, "Where is Marta Kovac?" One of them had a black hatchet and he raised it high over his head.

No, take me! I screamed.

And I woke up with a gasp, my heart still pounding as I left the bedroom, crossed the hall, and eased Sophie's door open. She was still asleep, but her throat was bared, just like in the dream. I covered it with the blanket, watched her until my heart slowed.

And then I was back in bed, Roxanne still downstairs tapping on the keys. I shut my eyes and tried to will sleep to come, no dreams. And then it was morning, Roxanne beside me, bedclothes kicked off. I felt the warmth of her, touched the curve of her hip. And then I got up and crossed the hall again, eased Sophie's door open. She was asleep on her stomach, her dark curly hair strewn on the pillow.

I stepped closer, leaned down. Listened to her breath. Took a deep breath of my own.

On Monday morning we drove in silence north to Hyde, Clair's jaw clenched. I could tell when he was ready to talk and when he wasn't. I'd learned to just wait.

Turning off the potholed paved road, we skimmed through a snow-covered dirt path. Then I slowed and turned into the woods, slipped the truck into four wheel. The pickup lurched, snow flying in the glare of the headlights. I downshifted as we climbed the rises, braked as we eased our way down. The yard was a half-mile in and it was slow going, but still, we were there right on time, seven a.m.

Clair parked beside the skidder. Lifted the plow and shut off the motor.

"What time did you tell him?" I said.

"Seven-hundred fifteen hours."

"Sanctuary is another forty minutes away."

"Can't coddle the boy, just because he's got company."

I smiled, said, "You've had your coffee."

"Right."

"Don't want to intrude on your grumpy time."

"Not quite there yet. I'll just listen."

"Okay," I said. "Here it is. I don't trust her."

Clair reached for his mug, took another swallow.

"Longtime partner gets whacked in a pretty horrible way. Not four months later she's banging the bejesus out of her high school boyfriend."

"Thanks for cleaning it up for me," he said.

"You're welcome."

"People grieve in different ways," Clair said.

"She's madly in love with Louis? She hadn't seen him in eleven years, for God's sake."

"Flames get rekindled."

"What, you been reading romance novels?" I said.

"I have my sensitive side," Clair said.

"And what does your sensitive side tell you?"

"Her lifeboat sank. She swam for the next one and climbed on."

I looked out the window. A blue jay landed on top of a pile of brush and looked at the truck. I reached in my lunch pail and dug out a peanut butter sandwich, broke off a piece and rolled the window down. The jay fluttered close and scooped the bread up and flew off.

"I looked on the Virgin Islands police website. This murder gets a paragraph. There was half a page about some guy who stole a motorbike."

"Maybe they pulled the local police off this one."

"But why?" I said.

"Her ex was politically connected in England. Didn't trust the locals not to screw it up, trample the evidence?"

"I get that."

"Then what's bothering you?" Clair said.

"She knows way more than she's saying. She knows they were Russians. She knows how they knew her boyfriend had serious cash.

She knows how they knew they were alone in the house that night, with no servants."

The jay was back; at least it looked like the first one. I broke off another piece of sandwich and tossed it.

"If she knew all that, would she blab all of it to a couple of relative strangers?" Clair said. "And remember, she's gun-shy around men. Gotta be, after all she went through."

"Gun-shy or not, somebody's looking for her. The police. The bad guys. Somebody."

Clair didn't answer.

"So she's using Louis. Good place to hide out, in the boonies of Maine. Some serious firepower on hand, and he knows how to use it. Dragging him into bed is just a way of getting in the door and staying there."

He scratched his chin, pushed his hat back.

"Think about it, Clair," I said. "Why would somebody be hunting for her?"

"Witness to a murder."

"Or she grabbed something and ran, and that wasn't part of the original plan."

"Where would that something be?"

"Stashed someplace," I said.

"What? Jewelry? Cash?"

"A million dollars in hundreds only weighs sixty pounds," I said.

"How do you know that?"

"Story I did about drug money being smuggled north."

"She's in good shape," Clair said. "Sixty pounds is nothing."

He looked at me and smiled.

"Listen to us, Jack," he said.

And then there was a rumbling clatter on the tote road. I reached for my gloves, warming on the top of the dashboard. Clair took a last gulp of his coffee as Marta's Audi came out of the trees and slid to a halt beside the truck. Louis was driving and he shut the car off and Marta got out from the passenger side. She was wearing aviators and a black knit cap, jeans, and a black sweater, the same L.L.Bean boots. Opening the rear door, she leaned in and pulled out one of Louis's Marine Corps field jackets. Desert camo. Marta stretched her back, her hands on her buttocks.

"Fit as a fiddle," I said.

13

—ﬡ—

Louis climbed out of the car and Friend jumped out after him. Moving to the back of the Audi, Louis lifted the hatch. Clair opened the door and got out of the pickup and I did, too.

"I hope you guys don't mind," Marta said. "I told Louis I'd be careful. I've just never seen lumberjacks at work before."

"Not sure we're much to look at," Clair said, "but you're welcome to freeze your butt off."

Louis was still at the back of the Audi as we dropped the tailgate of the Tacoma, reached for saws and toolboxes and gas cans.

"Hey," Clair said.

Louis nodded.

Marta had moved to the front of the car and was calling to Friend, slapping her hands on the front of her thighs. He kept walking, stopped and peed on a bush.

"She'll stay out of the way," Louis said.

"She can drive the skidder for all I care," Clair said.

Louis took his saw out of the trunk and put it down on the snow, then his toolbox and helmet. He didn't answer and didn't make eye contact.

"As long as *you're* good with her being here," Clair said.

Louis plucked at his saw chain, peered at it closely.

"She's afraid to be left alone at the cabin," Louis said.

We ran fingers over saw teeth. Unscrewed caps and poured chain oil and gas. It was their conversation and it was running in slow motion. I waited.

"My impression is, she's isn't afraid of much," Clair said.

He dug in his pocket for the key to the skidder. Pulled it out and put his glove back on.

"She's had to be tough," Louis said.

"I know that," Clair said. "Question is, do you want to be the next chapter."

The dog was snuffling in the snow, probably smelling partridge, snowshoe hare, deer—last night's woods traffic. Marta wandered back from the far side of the Audi, stood beside Louis.

"This is all the gear, huh?" she said.

"Tools of the trade," Louis said. He turned to her and, I imagined, smiled.

"What can I do?"

He patted her on the shoulder, then pulled her closer and gave her a quick hug, his hand on her hip.

"Keep the dog from following us in," Louis said. "We're working just up that road."

Marta broke into a fast trot down the tote road and Friend followed. Sixty pounds was nothing.

The road was a gash in the underbrush made with the front blade of the skidder, then trampled by its chain-wrapped tires. I picked up my saw and Clair's, and Louis and I started walking as Clair started the skidder with a clack of metal and a puff of blue diesel smoke. The smoke hung and then drifted sideways through the trees.

All the noise drove the birds away, left the trees frozen in place like they'd been startled. We walked up a rise, boots sinking in the snow and sliding on the underlying ice. I glanced back, saw the skidder lurch forward, smoke belching. Behind it, Marta was covering her ears with her gloved hands. Friend was nowhere to be seen.

"Dog's gone," I said.

"Brain is in his nose," Louis said.

"She gonna get lost trying to follow him?"

"She can just turn around, follow her tracks right back."

I walked. We moved to the side as the big yellow machine rumbled up behind us. I gave Louis a sideways glance and he said, "Sometimes you choose a situation. Sometimes a situation chooses you. Either way, you have to do the right thing."

He gave me a look, like he was daring me to push it. I nodded.

"She's solid," he said. "Just has shit for luck."

And he walked ahead. I waited for Clair.

He stopped the skidder and shut it off, climbed down from the seat. I handed him his saw and we fanned out into the woods, eventually spreading a few hundred feet apart. The three of us were staring skyward, eyeing the canopy, considering which tree to cut first, the way it would fall. The sky was pale blue, a backdrop to the black bouquets of branches.

We were cutting hardwood for firewood. Clair's saw revved first as we moved into a stand of mostly maple, oak on the ridges, some ash on the edge of what sixty years ago had been pasture. I picked out a big maple and yanked my saw to life. Looked up again, picked the best direction for it to fall, but there was a squirrel nest in a crook at the top, a bundle of leaves and sticks. I pictured the squirrels working away all fall, constructing a winter home.

I moved to the maple thirty feet to the left.

And then we were in the rhythm of it, two cuts on the upside, one that let the tree drop. Crashing and splintering, then the trunk hitting the snow with a *whump*, like a giant had stepped into the forest. Then climbing through the tangle, cutting the big limbs, some more than a foot thick. Working your way down to limb each one. Saw in one hand, dragging the brush out of the way with the other. Waving to Clair, now in the skidder, to drive in and hook up the chains. The clumped wood leaving a dark gash in the snow.

This was old school—no heavy equipment, no mechanical claw snapping trees off three feet above the ground. Drop, cut, limb, haul. We moved deeper tree by tree, leaving the softwood and poplar. I took an ash down as Clair hauled a twitch of red oak back to the yard. I glanced over, then started taking the big limbs off. Heard a metallic whine, saw sparks, pulled the saw back.

In the cut I could see a glint of metal. A big square nail showed, deep in the wood. The tree had grown over it fifty years ago or more and my saw chain had found it. What were the chances? I looked at the teeth, dulled by the metal. I could file the chain or swap it out for a sharp one from my toolbox.

I walked back to the truck, weaving around stumps, stepping over branches. Clair and Louis kept working and the roar of the skidder and rip of the saw receded. The woodyard was quiet.

There was no sign of Marta or the dog. I lifted the tray from my toolbox, fished out a sharp chain. Loosened the bar and slipped the dulled chain off, looped the new one on. I'd bolted the bar back in place, adjusted the tension, when I looked over at the Audi. I thought of Lindy Hines, her SUV, the mail on the seat, clues to her identity.

Saw in hand, I walked to the back of the Audi. The hatch was up, Louis's toolbox sitting on a piece of green tarp. I looked down at the bumper. There was a small Hertz sticker. I was right about the rental. Wondered what they'd think when it came back smelling like dog and chain oil.

I circled the car. The butt of Louis's Sig Sauer stuck out of the map bin on the front passenger's door. Marta's side. Didn't feel safe in the cabin alone, and left the gun in the car?

There was nothing on the seats, which also seemed odd. She'd driven all the way to Maine, and the car was as clean as when she'd picked it up at the airport. I looked around the clearing again. Listened, scanned the woods, then leaned back in and shoved the toolbox forward.

There was a cargo lid under the tarp and I glanced around, then gave it a yank.

It was locked.

I walked around the car and looked in the passenger window.

No keys.

I hesitated, then opened the passenger door, then the glove box. I fished out the Hertz papers, scanned the agreement—the Audi rented to M. C. Kovac, an address in Longboat Key, Florida. I remembered it vaguely as some rich town near Sarasota. I reached back into the glove box, under the manuals. Felt a small folder. I pulled it out, opened it.

The emergency key.

I looked around again, then took the key out. It was plastic, no electronic buttons. I hurried to the back of the car, tried it in the cargo bin lock. It slipped in. I turned it, lifted the lid.

Newspapers on top: *USA Today* and the *Miami Herald*. August 18 for both. I pulled them aside.

Saw money.

Stacks of it, lined up in neat rows like the bin was a teller's drawer. Banded hundred-dollar bills, fourteen across, three rows. Forty-two bundles. I lifted one out. It was a couple of inches thick. I thumbed through—hundreds, top to bottom. I put the bundle back, arranged the newspapers on top, eased the lid down, and locked it.

"Each one is fifty thousand," Marta said, behind me. "A little over two million, if you do the math."

14

I turned. She was standing ten feet behind me. Her tracks showed she'd come from that direction, made a big loop.

"The dog got away," Marta said.

"Not the only one, huh?"

She smiled.

"I guess I made a run for it, too."

"Escaped with the shirt on your back?"

"Something like that."

We stood there for a moment, neither of us moving closer. We could hear the saw and skidder in the distance.

"You don't trust me," Marta said.

"Trying to figure you out."

"Louis says that's what you do. Study people."

"Sometimes."

"So you can write about them," she said. "Are you gonna write about me?"

"I don't write about friends or family."

"Am I a friend?" Marta said.

"No, but Louis is. You're safe."

She walked toward me, stopped four feet away. Her cheeks were flushed from the cold. Her eyes glittered with a sort of predatory excitement.

"You're not making me feel safe, Jack," she said. "You're making me feel very nervous."

"You don't seem nervous to me."

She glanced toward the car.

"If you were a cop, you'd need a warrant to do that."

"That's why I like being a reporter."

"License to pry into everybody's business?"

"Not everybody's," I said.

Another pause. I could hear a nuthatch in the trees to my left. Then titmice rasping, chickadees joining in. Closer, I could hear her breathing.

"Where was the key?"

"The back of the glove box. You're supposed to put it in your wallet in case you lock yourself out."

I held it out and she took it.

"Will it start the motor?"

"No. Just opens the doors."

"Good to know."

One chain saw shut off. Clair starting to twitch the wood out.

"It was my share," Marta said. "Nine years of my life with Nigel. I figure I must've earned at least three hundred thousand a year for being treated like shit. You know he made me weigh myself in front of him? He said he didn't want me to turn out like my mother."

"I thought your mother died when you were a child."

"I had a picture, from my uncle. She was heavy."

I waited for the rest.

"I had to make sure the coffee was ready. Make it myself if the cook was off. Steam the milk. Bring it to him in bed. If it wasn't right he handed it back and said one word. 'Again.' Sometimes he didn't even look up."

"Why didn't you leave?"

"He said if I took off he had a list of guys who could find me, bring me back. 'Like bounty hunters,' he said."

"A good relationship is built on trust," I said.

"Ha. Right. But I told myself, Pretend to take it. Know where the money is. When the opportunity comes, girl, you go."

"And it came?"

"When they came charging in and I ended up in the hidey-hole, saw the cash, I knew it was time."

"What was he—a money launderer? Most people don't turn investment profits into bundles of hundreds."

"Nigel wasn't most people. He thought that underneath it all, the world was still a war zone. 'There are times when you can't use credit cards,' he used to tell me. 'Yemen. Somalia. Nigeria. Nothing like American dollars.' "

"How'd you get it off the island?"

"Cash opens all the doors. Hire a boat. Charter a plane. Rent a car. Before you know it, you're in the middle of nowhere, Maine."

"A lot of money for a rainy day."

"Not really. You'd be amazed at how fast a million disappears. Flows through your hands like water."

I waited. She moved a half-step closer.

"So now what? You know all my secrets. Almost."

"I don't think I know the half of it," I said.

"Sometimes it's dangerous to know too much," Marta said. "Let me tell you."

"Sounds like Nigel learned that lesson the hard way."

"There's a whole world of people who play very rough."

"We can play rough, too."

"I know that. Why do you think I'm here?"

"I'm beginning to get it," I said.

Marta looked around the clearing. The skidder roared and the noise moved closer, blue smoke rising over the treetops. Crows hurried past over our heads, flapping toward some crow destination. I wondered what had happened to the dog.

"What do we do now?" Marta said.

"With the dead man's money?"

"You kidding me? I earned every penny. His sisters treated me like some slutty whore. His snooty parents, Lord and Lady Tight-Ass, ordered me around like I was the help."

"Is somebody looking for it?"

"No. My guess is they're diving deep, trying to cover their tracks," she said.

"Not worth coming all the way to backwoods Maine for a couple of million?"

"Probably not. Chump change, as they say. And if I'm wrong, I've got Louis."

"I wouldn't want him to survive Iraq and Afghanistan and get killed over a trunk load of dirty money," I said.

"It'll be fine. Really. I do care for him, Jack; I really do. When I said I loved him, I meant it."

"He know about this?"

"Of course. There are no secrets between us."

I laughed. She stared at me and waited. I stopped laughing and stared back.

"So what do you want?" she said. "Other than me leaving the way I came."

I didn't answer. She smiled.

"That ain't gonna happen, Jack. Problem for you guys is that Louis loves me back. He always did."

We worked until 11:30, the piles of shorn trees growing in the yard. It was all going to a firewood processor named Rupert who would send in a log truck, haul the trees to his yard in Freedom, run it through a machine that cut and split the wood. Our time and equipment was donated. Mrs. Hodding used the money to pay her husband's nursing home bill.

In this neck of Waldo County, Maine, it was how you rolled.

Louis and I sometimes talked about Mrs. Hodding as we worked—the changes she'd seen in the ninety years she'd lived in this very beautiful place. One time I made the mistake of calling the area "undiscovered," and she looked at me—silver hair tied back, wrinkled skin pulled taut—and said, "What are we here? Some aboriginal tribe?"

But Louis and I didn't talk that day. When I approached, he turned his back and went to find his next tree. When he was limbing, he seemed to always be on the far side of the trunk. Finally, Clair gave a wave, signaling this was the last load, our signal that it was time for dinner. We hurried back to the woodyard, and Louis stayed fifty feet ahead.

By the time I got to the truck, he was loading his saw into the back of the Audi, tossing his toolbox in behind it. The Audi was running. Marta was in the driver's seat, the dog in the back.

"I'm gonna have to bail a little early," Louis said. "Marta's getting cold. She's got this circulation thing with her hands. Once they get blue, she can't get them warmed back up."

"Sorry to hear that," I said.

"Yeah, well, what can you do. Wasn't a problem where she was before."

He reached up and pulled the hatch closed. I moved closer, stood between him and the passenger side of the car. He started to move around me and I stepped in front of him.

"Louis," I said.

He looked toward the woods. The skidder came over the rise, chains clanking, the blue diesel plume trailing behind it. Clair was half-turned in the seat, looking back at the load, logs grinding and snapping.

"There's two million in cash in the trunk," I said.

"I know that," Louis said. "What do you think? I don't know how to reconnoiter?"

"This thing on the island; these are dangerous people. If they come up here to hunt down the only witness—"

He looked away, didn't answer. We watched the approaching skidder as Clair dragged the load into place, backed up to put slack in the cable, shut off the motor.

"You sure this is your fight?" I said. "That's all I'm saying."

"Hell of a lot more than Iraq was."

"I know you and Marta go way back. I just don't want you to get hurt. Or played."

"Nobody's playing me, Jack."

He turned to me and smiled in that dark, melancholy, Louis-spiraling-downward way.

"I'm getting her out of a jam," he said, nodding toward the idling Audi. "And remember, they taped a guy to a chair and killed him slowly. For money. I'd kinda like them to come up here. Give me a chance to add a few more marks on the right side of the ledger."

He gave me a last look, then turned away and climbed into the car. Marta backed out, gave me a smile and a wave. Her fingers looked fine to me.

Clair had the cable unhitched and was back in the seat. He restarted the motor, wound the cable back onto the spool at the back of the skidder. Then he climbed back down, said, "We lose our help?"

I told him about Marta's fingers.

"She's got him wrapped around one of them," Clair said, and he walked to the truck and climbed in. I followed, climbed in beside him. He turned on the motor and the heat and we opened our lunchboxes. Mine had a note from Sophie, one for Clair, too, his name in careful cursive. I handed it to him.

He put down his sandwich and opened the paper. I did the same. Mine was a picture of our family, me and Roxanne, Sophie in the middle. She'd written "My Family" over our circle-shaped heads.

Clair showed his to me: it was Clair and Pokey, with Sophie in the saddle. It was entitled, "Pokey's Best Friends."

"Girl's got talent," Clair said. "Gets it from her mother."

We gave our pictures another glance, folded them and tucked them back in our lunch pails. We started to eat bites of sandwich, poured coffee and tea from our thermoses. The windshield was starting to fog when I said, "She's got two million in cash in the back of that car."

Clair chewed slowly and swallowed. Took another sip of coffee. Swallowed.

"Not surprised," he said.

My turn to bite and chew and sip.

"I just can't believe these bad guys would let her get away with that," I said.

Clair took another bite, turned on the defroster. Portholes began to appear at the base of the windshield. Through them we could see the dark trees, standing like a wooden army against the snow.

We finished our sandwiches and dug into the pails to see what to have next. I took out a bag of homemade granola. Clair polished an apple on the sleeve of his jacket. He took a bite and chewed and swallowed, then said, "I'm not worried that she stole that money. I'm more worried that she didn't."

"Her cut?" I said, picking out M&Ms and eating them.

"For setting the whole thing up," Clair said.

"Knowing what was going to happen to him?" I said. "She'd have to be a serious psycho. Or maybe not, if this was after years of being abused."

Clair took another bite of apple, turned it in his big hand and took another. I was waiting for his reply when my phone buzzed in my jacket pocket. I dug it out, saw a Maine number I didn't recognize.

"McMorrow."

"This the reporter?" a man's voice said.

Raspy. Smoker.

"Could be."

"Dude," he said. "We gotta friggin' talk."

15

There were voices in the background. Men and women. The guy on the phone said, "Shut the fuck up," and they quieted.

"Who is this?" I said.

"I'm a friend of Teak's."

He coughed, cleared his throat. Spat.

"What do you want to talk about?" I said.

"Teak, what else? Can you come over?"

"Over where?"

"Center Street."

"In Riverport?"

"Yeah," he said, like, where else would he be?

"What's your name?"

"Mutt. Like the dog."

Someone shouted in the background. Mutt said, "I ain't gonna tell you again."

I put the phone on speaker.

"I'm not in Riverport."

"When can you get here?"

"I don't know. I was planning on tomorrow morning."

"That's too late," Mutt said.

"Why? You have a busy schedule?"

"A few of us won't be here then."

"Where are you going?" I said.

"One guy has a warrant, has to turn himself in. Another guy has a warrant, he has to beat feet. This other guy, his old lady gets her check. He'll be all fucked up by then."

"Which one are you?"

"Don't matter. But we're all here now. Can you be here, like, in an hour?"

"An hour? No."

"Okay, how 'bout two?"

I looked at Clair.

He opened the window and tossed the apple core out. Nodded.

"Okay," I said. "What number Center Street?"

There was a clatter and I heard him say, "This shithole got a number?"

A clamor of muffled voices and then Mutt was back. "The number fell off. It's this house on the corner of Spring Street. It's green. There's a door on the back side, down the hill. Used to have a window but it got busted out and now it's plywood. We'll keep an eye out for ya."

And he was gone. I rang off, looked at Clair.

"Friends of the guy who killed the lady with the hatchet," I said. "They want to talk."

"How many?" Clair said.

"I don't know. Sounded like a bunch."

Clair looked at me, closed his lunch pail.

"Haven't been to Riverport in a coon's age," he said.

16

Center Street was a couple of blocks up the hill from the public library, which was convenient for people like Teak, especially in the winter. We drove past the library and took a right, found the house in question. It was a three-decker tenement with pale green siding that was peeling off, like a giant animal had tried to claw through the walls. There were porches on the front, toys and trash on the porches, junked cars on what had been a lawn.

We rolled past once, Clair in the passenger seat. We came back and I slowed, looked for the plywood window. It wasn't visible so I pulled around the corner and parked. We got out and I called Mutt's number, the phone in my lap, on speaker. It went to voice mail, a woman's voice saying, "Iggy ain't here to take your call."

I was about to leave a message when a guy came around the corner from the back of the building. He saw us, hesitated, then waved, turned back around the building and disappeared.

"Cleared to cross the perimeter," Clair said, and we walked down the sidewalk to a path trampled in the snow. We followed it single file, me first, following the path around the corner of the building. It led to the door with the plywood. There was graffiti and trash, plastic vodka jugs and beer cans, syringes and Nyquil bottles. The door had a hasp and padlock but the hasp had been ripped off the side of the house. I poked a finger into the crack at the doorjamb and pulled the door open. Stepped in.

It was a sort of walk-in basement, a dirt floor and more trash. Crushed beer cans, broken syringes, dirty squares of cellophane. Light showed from another doorway twenty feet in, and we crossed the room, stepped inside. A work lamp hung just inside the door from an orange extension cord. Our eyes adjusted and beyond the glare we saw two guys sitting on a plaid couch, three standing by a workbench. The two guys on the couch were drinking 40s. Colt 45. There were two more guys along the wall to our right. Arthur and Dolph.

Dolph nodded.

"Which one of you is Mutt?" I said.

Both of the guys on the couch put their beers on the floor and stood. One stepped forward. He was tall and stoop-shouldered, six-four before he hunched. His hair was wiry and going gray, his nose broken over a scruffy grown-out goatee. His army fatigue jacket was open, showing a stained Patriots sweatshirt underneath. He held out his hand. I could see crude tattoos on his wrist, like what you'd see carved on a restroom door.

"I'm Mutt," he said.

We shook and I could feel something hard and out of place, like an old broken bone.

"I'm Jack. This is Clair."

"Don't trust us? Had to bring your dad?" Mutt said.

He chuckled. Clair smiled.

"Clair works with me," I said.

"What? He take pictures?" Mutt said.

"No," I said. "He doesn't."

He looked Clair over again and stopped laughing. I took a quick glance around the room, felt Clair do the same. They were of varying sizes and shapes, all guys except for a woman in a hoodie in the back corner sitting in a lawn chair. A lanky kid at the workbench caught my eye, probably strong and nimble enough to do damage. Clair moved a couple of feet in his direction.

Reaching into my pocket, I slipped out a notebook and pen. Opened the notebook to a blank page.

"Whatcha got?" I said.

He looked at the notebook, then back at me.

"Teak," he said. "He ain't no murderer."

"A whole bunch of witnesses say otherwise."

"I mean, he ain't killed nobody before."

"No one's saying he's a serial killer."

"Right. But here's the fucking problem," Mutt said.

There was a challenge in his tone, like the problem was of my making.

"Teak, he worked at the shelter sometimes."

"So I've been told."

"And we all go there on and off. Sleep it off. Get out of the fucking cold. Miss H. is a wicked good shit."

There were grunts of affirmation around the room.

"Seems like it," I said.

"She said you came to talk to her. But she didn't kill nobody, you know what I'm saying?"

"Right."

"So I'm saying, lay off Miss H. and the shelter," Mutt said.

"Yeah, leave her the fuck alone," the young guy at the workbench said. "Fucking media, making shit up."

I waited long enough to seem to have considered it, then said, "I talk to a lot of people for a story. I'll talk to Teak's family. I'll talk to the cops. I'll talk to the family of the woman who got killed, who, by the way, was helping with the shelter's books. Connection number two. And I'm talking to you."

"They'll shut Loaves and Fishes down, you put some shit in the paper like Teak flipped out 'cause the shelter didn't give him his meds."

Interesting. I wrote that down.

"What are you doing?" Mutt said.

"Taking notes. It's what reporters do."

"I didn't say you could do that," he said.

"Then why did you ask me to meet you?"

"So's we could talk. I'm giving you a fucking message."

"From whom?" I said.

"From whom?" Mutt said, stretching the second word out so that somebody snickered. "From me. But I don't want to be in the fucking newspaper."

"You're saying this conversation is off the record?"

"Right. So stop writing and start listening."

"I can do both," I said, and I scribbled on the pad. "What's your real name?"

"None of your fucking business."

"Fuck off," the chubby guy said.

"Okay. I'll just say, 'A man who goes by the street name Mutt, who declined to give his real name.' "

"You ain't saying nothin', dude. Not about me. Not about the shelter. You get the shelter closed down, a lot of people are gonna be out in the fucking cold. Not just us. Families and little kids and domestically abused women and shit. This area has a large at-risk population."

"I'm not trying to shut anything down," I said. "I'm just saying what happened."

"Just 'cause some bitch gets killed, ain't no reason to fuck everything up for everybody."

"Lindy Hines wasn't 'some bitch,' " I said.

"Whatever. I don't know her from shit. Maybe she pissed Teak off. Maybe she disrespected him."

"I don't think so."

"You wasn't there," Mutt said.

"As a matter of fact, I was."

"You saw the bitch killed?"

"Watch your mouth," I said.

Mutt's eyes narrowed and he took a step toward me.

"Who you think you're talking to, reporter man."

He lunged and grabbed my arm, started to twist. I wrenched loose and he grabbed for my notebook and I hung on and we both pulled. As I staggered toward him, the big kid sprang from his place by the bench and Clair reached out, clotheslined him with his left arm. He went down and Mutt tripped over him, and a page ripped from the notebook as he sprawled on his back, knocking a beer can over.

Foam gushed, everybody shouting.

The big kid tried to get up and Clair booted him hard in the ribs and he grunted and rolled the other way. I landed on Mutt, tore the paper from his hands. He reached behind him for something and I punched him hard in the neck, and he gasped and I slid off of him and got to my feet.

The chubby guy had a piece of two-by-four, and he took a shuffle step and swung and I turned and caught a glancing blow on the shoulder. The follow-through turned him toward Clair and I saw his eyes widen as Clair stepped in, planted a boot on the guy's instep, and yanked the two-by-four out of his hands. He gave the chubby guy a forearm in the face and he fell backwards onto the couch, blood gushing from his nose.

Mutt was on his knees, a box knife in his right hand.

"Knife," I barked, and Clair swung the two-by-four, smashed Mutt's wrist. He bellowed and Clair turned to the big kid, shoved him back onto the floor, and hammered him in the knee.

The guy howled and Clair hit him again.

I picked my notebook up and we backed toward the door. Mutt was on his haunches, holding his broken hand, teeth clenched. The chubby guy was pinching his nose, trying to staunch the flow of blood like they told you to do in Boy Scouts. Dolph and Arthur were wide-eyed, frozen in place against the wall. The big kid was on the floor holding his leg. All eyes were on us, but nobody moved.

I nodded toward Clair and said, "I told you. He's not much of a photographer."

We sat in the truck for a minute, collecting our thoughts and making sure they knew we may have left but we hadn't run.

Dolph stuck his head around the corner, then ducked back.

"Way to deescalate," Clair said.

"You're the one broke his wrist in fifteen places."

"Could have done the other one," Clair said. "I was going easy."

He turned toward me.

"You sure you're okay? Seems like there's more going on here than just a story."

"She was a nice lady," I said.

"Yeah?" Clair said.

He waited. Clair was very good at waiting. Lying motionless in the jungle all night was good training for staring me down.

"She wanted to chat," I said. "I was in a hurry. Could have changed the timing. Could have been in the parking lot when Teak was looking to pick somebody out."

"This a guilt trip."

"I prefer to think of it as penance."

"Not your fault," Clair said. "Rationally, you know that. Emotionally, you're carrying the whole thing. Seeing it happen and all."

I didn't answer.

"I understand," he said. "I've carried a lot of stuff for a long time. Still do. But sometimes life puts you in places and you just have to deal with it, at the moment and later. Nobody said this was gonna be easy."

I considered it.

"Word of advice. Keep poking these folks, but be ready when they poke back."

I nodded.

" 'Cause that there," Clair said, "was just a bunch of drunk amateurs."

We came out by the library, took a left. Street kids were sitting on the bench at the bus stop out front, a few more across the street. Mutts in the making. One was looking at his phone, tapping, texting.

There was a crosswalk in front of the library, a flashing light and a sign that said STATE LAW—STOP FOR PEDESTRIANS. A couple of the kids stepped off the curb on our side and I slowed. More started sauntering across from the library side, and I stopped. They looked at us, and Clair said, "You might want to be ready to—"

They whirled at the truck, smashed the windshield in front of my face, the window by my head. Rocks and a brick. Clair's side, too. Two leapt into the bed and started bashing the rear window, and I threw the truck into reverse and floored it.

They fell against the cab, the kids at the front chasing after us. Cars were coming behind us and I steered for the breakdown lane, peering through shattered glass, caught a tire and bounced onto the sidewalk, over a wall of paving blocks and into a patch of shrubs.

Clair was out of the truck first. He reached into the bed and pulled one of the kids out and flung him over the side, into the bushes. The other kid was halfway out when I got him by the shoulders and heaved him to the sidewalk. He was skinny, all sinew and bones under his hoodie, and he hit hard and rolled. I heard footsteps, turned.

The rest of the bunch was bearing down, fists raised, rocks and bricks ready. I stepped behind the driver's door, reached to the back of the seat for a lug wrench. They slammed the door against me, and I slipped to one knee.

"Kill the motherfucker," one of them said, and they yanked the door back.

Three kids, arms poised.

Three shots—*boom, boom, boom.*

They froze and looked across the truck. I sprang to my feet with the wrench, but they'd turned and were sprinting away across a parking lot, the kid I'd thrown limping at the rear. I saw Clair slide his gun back under his jacket.

"Somebody made a phone call," he said.

"This is Iggy," I said. "Please leave a message."

17

We were leaning against the front of the truck when the first patrol SUV rolled up, siren and lights. A young guy came out of the driver's side, slid his gun out, and held it at his side. A woman came out on the passenger side, her gun drawn, too.

Hernandez. From Home Department.

The guy—short and stocky like he'd played DIII football—had his gun leveled now, and said, "Keep your hands where I can see them."

We did, and he came close and said, "Do you have a weapon?"

"No," I said. Clair said, "A handgun. Shoulder holster. Left side."

He ordered Clair to turn around, put his hands on the hood. Clair did. He told me to do the same and I did. He searched us while Hernandez covered us from the side. He took Clair's gun out and she stepped in and took it. He extracted our wallets and handed them to her.

"Okay," he said. "You can turn around."

We did. Cars were slowing so people could get a look at us, the truck with the smashed windows on the sidewalk.

"Okay, we got a report of an altercation and shots fired," the cop said.

"I know this guy," Hernandez said. "He's a reporter. He was at the murder scene."

"The hatchet thing?" her partner said.

"Yeah. I have his card."

She reached into her breast pocket and took it out and held it up.

"Jack McMorrow. *New York Times*."

"Okay, Mr. McMorrow," the other cop said. "Why don't you tell us what the hell is—"

There was a siren whoop and we turned to see an unmarked car squeezing past the line of cars, blue grille lights flashing. It pulled up beside the SUV and stopped. Detective Tingley got out, strode up to us, and looked the truck over. Hernandez showed him Clair's gun. Tingley shook his head, looked at us, and said, "Here we go again."

We told the story to the three of them. It was the first cop's incident, so he took notes. Halfway through, he asked to borrow Hernandez's notebook because his was full. When we finished, he scribbled for a full minute to catch up.

"Nobody got shot?" Tingley said.

"No," Clair said.

"But one kid may be injured."

"Yes," I said.

"And you think they were set on you by somebody at the squatter house up on Center."

"Yes," I said.

"Because you'd just come from an altercation there," Tingley said.

"Right," I said.

"Where some street folks were mad because you were asking about the shelter and Harriet."

"Yup," I said.

"Any of them hurt?"

I looked at Clair.

"Just one," he said.

"Who's that?"

"He goes by Mutt."

"We all know Mutt. What happened to him?"

"He had a knife and I had to disarm him," Clair said.

"And he was injured in the process?"

"Yeah. His right hand."

"What'd you do? Use jiu-jitsu?"

"A two-by-four," Clair said.

"Clair had just taken it off of one of them when Mutt pulled the knife," I said.

Tingley looked at me.

"Jesus," he said.

We all stood there on the sidewalk, the cars still slowing to have a look at us and my truck. The sun had fallen behind the hilltop houses to the west and it was cold on the pavement in the waning light.

"This is just like they were telling me, McMorrow," Tingley said. "No good comes of having you around a case."

"Good for whom?" I said.

"For whom?"

Why did that word irritate everybody?

"For me, who just wants to close this case. Open and shut. Guy goes off his meds, kills somebody in broad daylight in front of fifty people, and doesn't even run. Teak was caught literally red-handed. Sad all around, but shit happens," Tingley said.

"The story isn't who did it, it's why," I said.

"Why? 'Cause his brain is all scrambled, for whatever reason. Now we got shots fired in the downtown, kids smashing windows, you and your partner here wreaking havoc with the local shitheads."

"It was more like they were trying to wreak havoc with us," I said.

"He did it, we locked him up, he won't do it again. End of story."

"Not for me," I said.

"And you decide for the rest of us? Go plowing your way through our case, stirring people up?"

"I just want to get to the bottom of it."

"This *is* the bottom of it, Mr. McMorrow," Tingley said. "You stuck in Riverport with your truck stove up, lucky nobody got shot, all to satisfy your curiosity. You're a smart guy. Ever think of doing something constructive?"

He turned to the patrol cops and said, "They'll see if they can find your rock throwers. We'll see if Mutt files a complaint, but knowing him, I doubt it. In the meantime, let's give Mr. Varney his gun back."

Hernandez did—first the gun, then the clip.

"We gotta get this truck off the sidewalk, Mr. McMorrow," Tingley said. "It's a hindrance to public travel. If you're smart, you'll take what you got, go write your story, and move on. You're lucky it was me showed up here, not Detective Bates. She'd'a locked both your asses up."

I called Triple A and they sent a wrecker. A big shambling kid in overalls got out, looked the truck over, and said, "Piss somebody off or what?"

He hooked the truck up and winched it onto the ramp. There was a good glass place out on Hammond Street, he said, and I said that was fine. He gave us one last curious look and drove off, strobe lights illuminating my smashed Tacoma like it was something captured on the battlefield and dragged around the city by the victors.

"Well, then," Clair said.

"The shelter," I said. "I'll call a taxi."

"Surprised you didn't ask that cop for a ride."

"He was a little grumpy."

"Isn't slowing you down," Clair said.

"Full speed ahead," I said.

The shelter was busy, clients lined up on the sidewalk, filing in the side door. An old woman with wild white hair like an exotic chicken was pushing a shopping cart. A few young guys were gathered in a clump, smoking and shuffling their sneakers in the cold. There were women with children, some being carried, some led by the hand. One little girl was carrying a stuffed bear by the leg, its head dragging on the concrete, which seemed fitting.

I looked for the guys from the basement but didn't see them.

We stood at the end of the line and waited to reach the door. When we did, I could see Harriet standing behind a table. She was handing out bundles of bedding, plastic bags of what looked like toiletries. I could smell food cooking. Spaghetti sauce.

Harriet was talking to an old man in a frayed plaid jacket and yellow baseball cap.

"How much have you had to drink, Red?" she said.

"Nothing since three o'clock, Miss H.," the old man said.

"Well, okay, dear," Harriet said. "But you be good now."

The man took his bundle and went left. Families were going to the right. We stepped up and Harriet looked up at us with a big smile, said, "Oh, but you're—"

"Right," I said. "This is my colleague, Clair. Just here to talk, if you don't mind. See the operation."

"We're kind of busy," Harriet said.

"Then how 'bout we come around and help."

Before she could say no we circled the desk and stood beside her. There were other volunteers in the open room behind us, where paper was being unrolled on long tables. I could hear pots clanging, something hissing in a pan. A young couple came to the table. The guy had dreadlocks stuffed under a knit cap. The girl did, too, and she was carrying a baby wrapped in a stained pink blanket.

The girl smiled. The guy looked at me and I nodded. Harriet said, "Have you stayed with us before?"

They shook their heads. She handed them two bundles and asked me to reach under the counter, look for one marked INFANT. I did and found it, handed it to Harriet. She gave it a quick inspection, then gave it to the mom, along with a sheet of paper on a clipboard with a small yellow pencil tucked in. Then she touched the baby on the forehead, like she was a priest giving a blessing. I smiled as the little family headed for the stairs leading to the family rooms, then turned to Harriet.

"Call off your dogs, Miss H.," I said.

She looked startled.

"What?"

"Your clients. A bunch of them tried to convince me to drop the story because it would reflect badly on this place."

Harriet put a hand to her mouth.

"They did what? Oh my God. I hope you're okay."

"We're fine. A guy named Mutt, not so lucky."

"Oh, Mutt, he can get carried away. He doesn't mean—"

A guy with a Walmart bag full of something stepped up. Harriet turned over her shoulder and waved and a woman in a frayed straw cowboy hat came hurrying from the kitchen.

"Let's talk," she said, and the woman in the cowboy hat took her place.

Harriet walked behind the lines to the office, and we followed. She sat at the same desk and I closed the door. There were chairs but there was stuff piled on them. We stood.

"I'm very sorry," Harriet said. "They're just very protective of this place. Of Teak. And me, I guess."

"Like a family here?" I said, slipping my notebook out.

"Yes. Loaves and Fishes isn't like some shelters. We're all in it together."

"Why's that?"

Harriet looked at the notebook, said, "Is this for your story?"

"Maybe," I said.

She got up and circled around and moved bags off of two chairs and dragged the chairs in front of the desk. We sat and she went back behind the desk and did the same. My card was still on the desk in front of her from last time and she picked it up and glanced at it.

"Jack," she said. "And—"

"Clair," he said.

"Right. You have to understand that I'm not like most people who run a place like this."

"No?"

"You see, the people who come here for help know I was one of them once. I know what it's like to have no place to go. And it's cold and you're hungry. And you know that you're not like other people, the ones who have houses and beds and full refrigerators."

I wrote it down, then looked up. Harriet—red-faced, a little disheveled, hands scuffed by work—hesitated.

"I grew up in places like this, Jack and Clair," she said. "My father was an alcoholic, a drinker, they called it back then. Not a bad man, but it was his Achilles' heel. He was a smart guy, a talker, too. My mom used to say he could talk himself into jobs and he could drink himself out of them. The railroad. Paper mills. In Portland one time he even got hired to drive a city bus."

There was a knock on the door. It opened, and the woman with the cowboy hat said, "The portable crib?"

"Closet under the stairs," Harriet said.

She closed the door.

I was ready with a prompt but Harriet began. "There were just the three of us. My dad wouldn't just lose the job, though. He'd pretend he was still working and go off every morning to drink up whatever little money we had, until there was nothing for rent or groceries or the light bill."

"And you were evicted."

"I remember trudging down the street with everything I owned in this pink plastic suitcase. Walking into a town office, a city hall. Listening as my mother tried to persuade them to help us. And I remember the feeling of those people looking at us like we were trash and they didn't want us sitting on their chairs. Well, I can tell you. When someone comes here, I never make them feel like they're less than anyone else. I won't have some little girl carry that memory because of me."

Harriet looked away into the distance, like there was more audience somewhere behind us.

"I had to fight my way through it. Portland, Westbrook, Lewiston. I was the new kid. The poor kid. The homely kid with cooties, wearing clothes from a thrift store. For a while that was my nickname. 'Hey, Goodwill.' But you know what?"

I shook my head.

"My mother was tough and she taught me not to take any crap, so I didn't. When there was a beat-down, a bunch of them on me, I made sure they paid. This one time in Kennedy Park—five girls on me, and I put two of 'em in the hospital."

She smiled at the memory. I wondered what it was. An earring ripped through an earlobe? Teeth broken?

"Let's just say, I know what it's like on the street."

"I'm sure," I said.

"How'd you end up here?" Clair said.

"Finished up at Riverport High and then community college. Working fast food, cleaning offices, even did a month in a slaughterhouse. People bringing in their chickens and pigs. They'll raise 'em and eat 'em, but they won't kill 'em."

She shook her head.

"How'd you get into this line of work?" I said.

"After school I did admin work, mostly for nonprofits. Started here as a volunteer. I was good at it, 'cause I understood the people, you know? Then the place needed someone to keep it from going under. And I stepped up. I'm not bragging, but I think when I go to a group or the city or a foundation, and I tell my story, they know this is more than a job for me. And you know what?"

"What?" I said.

"The clients know that, too. The families. The old alcoholics. Mutt, and probably some of the other guys you saw today. I fight for them, and I guess they'll fight for me."

"And Teak?" I said. "Did he have your back?"

"When his illness was under control, sure."

"What role does this place play in him getting his meds?"

A flash of annoyance.

"We have a case manager three days a week. She's not here tonight."

"Did she see Teak in the past few days?"

"I can't talk about clients' medical records. I shouldn't say anything about Teak at all. Except he needs somebody to speak up for him. To say he isn't a monster."

"But the case manager would normally see somebody like Teak," I said.

"Clients with mental health issues do see someone."

"And they get their meds here?"

"Some, not all. Some go to the outpatient clinic. They have a State team that works with some of the homeless, looks for them on the street."

"Was that team working with Teak?"

"I can't say."

"What if he went home to Ledge Harbor. Was there somebody to look out for him there?"

"I don't know. I just knew him here."

"Did he stay in the house on Center Street?"

"I don't know."

"Ever see him go into such a psychotic state that he was a threat to other clients?"

She lifted her shoulders in a shrug. There was another knock on the door, and the lady with the cowboy hat poked her head in again.

"Miss H., are there any more number-three diapers?"

Harriet got up from her chair.

"There's nothing in the baby closet?"

"Only number-ones."

"Oh, gee. I know there's a box someplace."

She turned to us.

"I've got to run. No bigger emergency than a pooping baby."

I flipped my notebook shut. We got up and walked to the door, and she herded us out, all the way to the front entrance, where the line was down to a heavyset couple with three little kids. We stepped out onto the sidewalk, where a cab was pulled up. I leaned down and the driver lowered the window.

"Gotta get to Prosperity," I said.

"You and me both, brother," the driver said.

Riverport was a city that, unlike Portland to the south, hadn't papered over its past. We drove through downtown streets with storefront churches and head shops in buildings with nineteenth-century detail. Strip malls and car lots next to cannibalized Victorians, the cars rolled onto what had been lawns but were now scrapes of frozen mud. The once-grand mansions draped with crude fire escapes, tacked with rows of cheap mailboxes filled with mail for "Occupant." And it all looked out over the oil-black, ice-filled river.

Teak and Mutt, Lindy and Harriet. It was like they inhabited some postapocalyptic city that the sun had deserted, everyone scrounging in the snow and grit. I wondered if Teak had turned this place into his own ice planet, like in the comics. Does the psychosis transform reality? Or does the reality shape the psychosis? A question for someone.

We rode in silence until the driver hit the interstate and headed south. He reached over and turned the radio on, country-western loud enough for us to talk.

"Do you think you could be a narcissist and still run a homeless shelter?" I said.

"It was all about her, wasn't it?" Clair said.

"The story about cooties must get 'em to open up their wallets at the fund-raisers."

"Think she has a family?"

I took out my phone, went to the Loaves & Fishes website. Harriet's bio.

"Lives in Riverport with her cats, Mouser and Toodles. Has several nieces and nephews whom she loves dearly."

"So that place is her whole world," Clair said.

"A world that revolves around her," I said. "You noticed who she never mentioned? Lindy Hines."

"Hines wasn't homeless. She doesn't amplify Miss H.'s own story."

We rode down the highway, got off at Newburgh and cut over to Route 202. The taxi sped south between the black walls of woods, climbing the hills as we approached Dixmont. We were the only car in sight, and the driver, a skinny guy with a mullet and big eighties eyeglasses, watched the roadside warily, like we might be waylaid by desperadoes.

"You sure you guys got the cash for this?" he said. "It's gonna be, like, seventy bucks."

"We're good for it," I said.

"You live out this way?"

"That's right."

"Freakin' deserted, man. Give me a nice trailer park any day. Least if some maniac breaks in, I scream, somebody's gonna hear me."

I smiled.

"Speaking of that," I said. "You know this guy Teak?"

"The hatchet guy?"

"Yeah."

"That why you were at the shelter?"

"Yeah."

"You cops?"

"No."

"What are you?"

"I'm a reporter. He's my audio engineer."

"Like podcasts?" the guy said.

"Yeah."

Another long pause as he processed it. Talk? Not talk? They can't make you.

"You know the guy?"

"You don't need my name, do you?"

"No. Not at the moment."

" 'Cause I don't know what the owner would think. Me being in the paper."

"Fine, just background for now."

"Okay. Well, sure. You could say, according to somebody who drove the crazy bastard around."

"Right," I said.

"That whole crowd, nobody has a driver's license. They're either whacked out or on meds, or they're drunks and none of them can afford a car anyhow. They call us. Job security."

"Teak called a lot?"

"Sure. Guy was always dragging something around. Lumber. Tools. Some shit he found by the side of the road. One time he calls me to this spot way out on Union Street, practically in Levant."

"How would he call? He didn't have a cell phone."

"Sure he did. Flip phone like you buy in Walmart, with the minutes on it."

"Doesn't that require a credit card?"

"I don't know how it works," the driver said. "I never used one."

"Right."

"I get out there to East Bumfuck, he's standing there with this friggin' beam, like a twelve-foot eight-by-eight, pressure-treated. I say, 'I can't put that in this cab.' He says, 'How 'bout if I cut it in half?' And he takes out this little handsaw from someplace in his jacket—he had all kinds'a shit in there—and he starts sawing away. I wait, and he cuts the thing in half and we load it in the trunk, the ends sticking out."

"What did he want it for?"

"Who knows? Some hobo jungle project."

"Down under the bridge?" I said, an area I knew well.

"No, the City Forest off Stillwater. He was building some kinda fort. Guy may have been a wingnut, but he didn't sit on his ass all day. I'll say that for him."

"How did he pay for his rides?"

"Cash money, homey. Guy wasn't broke. They're all on some sort of disability, while the rest of us work for a living. I mean, it ain't like they got a lot of overhead."

We were coming down a long grade, the driver feathering the brakes. The taxi skidded slightly and he corrected. He looked back at me.

"What's your name?"

I told him. He looked more nervous than the road and the woods would warrant. He took a breath like he was shoring himself up and said, "Yeah, well, all of us knew him, driving cab. Going on about his freakin' comic books."

"He talked about all of that?"

"All kinds of crazy shit. Planet this and that, King such-and-such. Like it was all real. He thought he was one of them. That was his problem. I mean, at the end. From what they say. Killed the lady with the hatchet. Right out of the story."

"Right."

We were almost into Unity where we'd take a left, head southeast. There was more traffic now, mostly pickups, and the yellow taxi looked like it had escaped from New York City. I watched the guy, the way he was chewing his lower lip, his mind grinding on something. I said it almost as it came to me.

"You drove him that morning, didn't you?" I said.

He glanced back and I knew.

"Hey, he wasn't any more whacked-out than any other time. He goes, 'Hey, Dickie. Home Department. Gotta buy a tool.' And off we go."

"He wasn't angry or agitated?"

"Seemed fine, for him anyway. Kinda quiet. Sometimes he rambles."

"Where did you pick him up? At the shelter?"

"No, downtown. The bridge on Franklin Street," he said.

The Franklin Street bridge, which Lindy Hines's apartment looked out on. They would have had to have left almost at the same time.

"He was just standing there?" I said.

"Right there at the curb," the driver said, "like he was waiting for the bus."

18

It was seven miles from Unity to Prosperity, ten minutes to consider it. The driver wheeled into the dooryard at Clair's place, seemed reluctant when I told him to pull in as far as the barn. Somebody could get killed here, never be seen again.

Not this time.

The fare was $62. I tipped him $20, got a receipt for the *Times*. The guy pulled out fast and sped off.

We crossed to the barn, turned on the lights in the workshop, and went inside. Clair started crumpling newspaper for the stove, tossing it into the firebox. Some cedar kindling followed, then some small pieces of ash. He lit the paper and we stood and watched the flames as they illuminated the room.

"There's a little park down on the stream," I said. "People drink down there, shoot up."

"He could've slept there," Clair said.

"Might be one of his regular stops, looking for cans and bottles."

The fire crackled, a pocket of gas igniting and throwing sparks onto the floor. Clair stamped them out with his boot and closed the door. We watched the flames through the glass, the volume turned down.

"What if he didn't just pick Lindy Hines out that morning?" I said. "What if he was stalking her?"

"He didn't tell the cabbie to follow her," Clair said. "He said to go to the store."

"How would he know she was going there? Unless they were hanging out."

"No indication of that."

"No," I said.

"Harriet said Lindy hadn't even been to the shelter proper. And I can't picture Teak hanging around the administrative office, where she'd picked up the financial stuff."

"No."

Clair opened the door and put in a couple of pieces of maple.

"I don't know him well enough," I said. "Not to write about him."

"Go meet him at the jail," Clair said.

"I will, if he'll go for it," I said. "But friends and family first. Got the friends covered."

"Now the family."

"Right. You go into a conversation with somebody like Teak with maximum background so you can follow the twists and turns of the conversation, encourage him to keep talking, build on whatever he reveals."

"Interesting. I just thought you went around asking a bunch of questions, and when your hand was tired from all that scribbling, you wrote the story."

"That's the rule," I said. "This is the exception."

I walked out of the barn and into the darkness. It was cold and I tucked my hands in my pockets as I started across the dooryard, headed down the path to home. Clair tamped it down with a gravel roller towed behind a tractor, like the old-timers did in the days before they plowed snow. The path led between thickets of alder and blackberries, now bare whips with needle-sharp thorns. It was a moonless night, a damp wind out of the south coming in on my right. I followed the faint path—my boot prints, smaller ones for Sophie from our trips to feed Pokey. I'd have to come back, tuck him in. Unless Clair did it, in which case he'd call.

Clair's guard was never down, more than forty years after the war; the same rules protected him, and he protected us. A bunch of drunks in a basement. Gangbangers from the city. A vengeful mom sworn to take Roxanne out. A thief ready to burn our house down with us in it. An evil dad in our woods with a long gun, bent on vengeance. Clair had always had our back.

Nobody like him had been looking out for Lindy Hines, but, then again, how would that have been possible? Who could have had her back if the threat had come from nowhere, for reasons that couldn't be explained, like lightning from a clear blue sky?

The guilt that was becoming familiar trotted out the same refrain: Maybe if I'd stopped to chat. Maybe if I'd spent one extra minute, she would still be alive.

As I approached the house, I was still thinking. Something didn't fit. Lightning just doesn't come from a clear blue sky. Or is there more to life than dumb luck? If we take one in the back, is it because we couldn't see it coming—or because we neglected to look? I'd once thought that if I worked hard enough, I could keep Sophie safe, Roxanne safe. As long as I was on guard.

No more. We do the best we can, but sometimes we're still just squirrels crossing the road. Most of the time you're lucky. Other times, your luck runs out.

I came out of the trees, saw the lights on in the second-floor bathroom. Tub time. I turned for the end of the shed, started to cross the driveway and sensed something to my left.

I whirled, got an arm up.

"Jack, it's okay. It's me."

Marta was to my left and three feet to the rear, tucked into the wall of the shed. She hurried to me, took me by the arm. She was one of those people, like you were magnetized and she was metal.

"Hey," I said.

"I'm sorry to bother you like this. But we need to talk."

She started to guide me toward the road, her arm intertwined with mine.

"I didn't see your truck, so I waited," Marta said.

"It's out of action for a bit," I said.

"Accident?"

"Something like that."

We were down by the road and she turned left, started east. I was about to ask her where we were headed when I saw a glimmer of light on chrome. The Audi pulled off onto the roadside along the woods.

"You could have just knocked and visited," I said.

"She's got enough to do," Marta said. "Doesn't need me barging in."

We reached the truck and she circled around, scuffling through the snow and dry grass. She opened the door and the interior stayed dark. There was a click and the passenger door unlocked, and I climbed in. My jeans made a scrunching noise against the leather.

We sat. Marta turned toward me.

"What is it?" I said.

"Louis," she said. "I thought I understood him, what he's gone through, but he's gotten really distant. It's like he just disappears. Emotionally, I mean."

"He does that," I said.

"This past week, it was like we couldn't get enough of each other. And not just in bed."

I must have flinched.

"Too much information, I know. But we were really talking. Like we used to. Like nobody else understands us like we understand each other. But now it's like he's lost in his own head."

"Sometimes he just finds it hard to be happy," I said. "He feels guilty. After all he's seen—the wars, the people who didn't make it."

"Survivor's guilt?" Marta said. "Shouldn't I be the one feeling like that?"

I looked at her.

"Should you?"

"Maybe not," Marta said. "The survivor part, yes. The guilt? Not as much. I went through my own sort of hell with Nigel."

"Okay," I said. "But you weren't in a war. A really horrible, pointless war."

"They're all pointless," she said. "Nigel fought in the Falklands. I mean, really. You want to talk about pointless. But Louis, I say, 'Babe, you okay?' A couple of times he looked at me like he forgot I was even there."

"Louis has some very deep and dark places where he goes sometimes," I said. "When we first met, I was in Sanctuary for a story and he was pretty spooky. People in town were afraid of him."

Marta frowned, said, "But I'm here for him now. I mean, I'm here forever if he wants me to be."

"Are you?"

There was a rustle in the grass by the truck and Marta said, "What's that?"

I looked out at the dimly lit road, waited. It crossed the road fifty feet in front of the truck.

"A fox," I said.

"Christ. Snakes aren't looking so bad."

We sat some more, Marta waiting me out.

"I think you're hazardous," I said.

"Me?"

"The people around you. The people who might be following you."

"They won't," Marta said.

"What if they do?"

"You guys can handle it."

"What if we don't want to handle it. I have a seven-year-old and a wife. They don't carry guns."

"You do."

"But I don't like it."

"Clair does," she said.

"He's different."

"Louis does."

"He's different in the same way," I said.

There was a pause in the conversation. Then Marta, facing the windshield, said, "What's your real problem with me?"

I looked out at the road, which was deserted, for now. Considered how candid to be with her. But if Louis was pulling away . . .

"I don't trust you," I said. "I can't help it. I don't believe your story about the money or the robbery."

"It was in the news," Marta said.

I shook my head. "Story was full of holes. And I talk to people for a living. I figure your story is about sixty percent true."

"Which part do you think isn't?" Marta said.

"An important part. I think somebody's hunting for you and that money."

"What you don't get, Jack, is that for some people, that's not much money at all."

"My guess is that for these people, it's not the amount. It's the principle."

She suddenly smiled, patted my arm.

"I understand. But Louis said you and Clair have his back. If I stay here, I just need for you to have mine, too. Me and Louis, we're a package."

I didn't answer, and after a moment she reached for the key, started the motor. Digital screens came alive across the dash, bathing us in a green alien glow. I popped the door, slipped out into the road. Without looking at me, Marta put the car in gear and it moved away slowly, the exhaust emitting a barely audible throb, the red lights receding.

Half the package had spoken.

We were sitting on the couch, a Chardonnay and a Ballantine ale on our respective laps. Roxanne's bare feet were tucked under my legs for warmth, her brown eyes glittering in the candlelight like onyx.

"At least this guy with the comic books, it's obvious," I said. "He's sick. She's dangerous."

"As opposed to a guy who cuts people's heads open with a hatchet?"

"Yeah. Arriving here totally out of nowhere, running away from some heinous crime. Dragging around all this money, stolen at least once."

We both drank.

"I think Louis feels responsible for her," Roxanne said. "Him leaving for the war is part of the reason she ended up where she did. And the abuse from this guy."

"I don't know. I just think if she was trying to pick my brain about how Louis ticks, it was for her sake, not his."

We sat. She took another sip of wine and watched the woodstove. A log collapsed into a mound of fiery coals. The heated metal ticked.

"There was something more," Roxanne said. "You away tomorrow?"

"Yeah. MDI and Ledge Harbor. I've got to nail this story down before somebody else gets it."

Roxanne watched as I got up, opened the stove door, slipped another log in.

"I know you hate guns," I said. "But these guys, Russians or whatever—you'd hate them more."

She looked at me.

"The Mossberg pump is in the safe, in the closet. There are two handguns. The Glock nine-millimeter and that old twenty-two long-barrel. That's the one with the hard trigger pull. It's in the back of the mudroom cabinet, up high."

Roxanne hesitated, finally said, "Okay."

"All that money. She's got to be hiding out. Waiting for things to cool down. But these guys, they have long memories."

"Or it's like this," she said. "In this horrible way, Marta escapes a very bad abusive relationship. Then she reunites with Louis, her one true love. The money is like her divorce settlement. And besides, why leave it behind for murderers? Maybe this new life for Marta is the only good thing to come of all of it."

I took it all in.

"Maybe," I said, "and maybe not. I'll put a full clip in the twenty-two."

Sophie called out and Roxanne went up. I could hear the water running, Roxanne pouring a glass of water. It was a stall for Sophie, an attempt to put off the inevitable of sleep.

It reminded me of Marta's behavior in the car. A distraction to put me off. I had this sudden flash of a female bird dragging its wing as it scurried away, luring me away from its nest. Killdeers did it. Plovers. What did they call it? Injury-feigning display.

What was Marta afraid of? That I'd persuade Louis she was a phony? Convince him to tell her to hit the road? Where would she go with her car full of cash?

I went to the study, flipped the laptop open, and searched for a few folders. I found an old list of contacts, scrolled through it to find K.D. Carlisle Looked at my watch. It was 7:40. At the *Times* the afternoon news meeting was long over, editors and reporters dug in.

I called.

"Foreign," a woman answered. "Carlisle."

"McMorrow," I said.

"Jack," she said. "Good to hear your voice. Like old times. You pushing the envelope, me reining you in."

"Now I'm Vanessa's cross to bear."

"I count her gray hairs."

"She'll miss me when I'm gone," I said.

"I miss you now. Everyone's so damn professional."

"Life's too short, Carlisle. Stir things up a little."

"We do. We just don't get a shot at doing it."

"Maybe I can change that for you. Who do you have in London?"

"Three reporters who were in grade school when you were on Metro," Carlisle said.

I told her about Nigel Dean. His untimely death. The dearth of information online.

"What do you care about BVI?" Carlisle said.

"I don't," I said. "I just care about my buddy, whose old girlfriend was shacked up with Dean, survived the home invasion, and arrived here with a trunk load of cash."

"Inside job, got her payoff?"

"Or maybe she just got lucky."

"I don't believe in luck, and you don't either," Carlisle said. "This one reporter, Janie Brockway, she's got good sources at Scotland Yard."

"Listen to you, Mrs. Bond," I said. "I never got north of Washington Heights."

"Heights is all gentrified now," Carlisle said. "Mott Haven, Hunts Point—you might still feel at home there."

"No, I feel at home here, actually."

"And still cranking out the crime. I remember what Jim Dwyer said about you. Send McMorrow for coffee, he comes back with three good stories and five guys who want to kick his ass."

"It's a gift," I said. "You have Brockway's email?"

"On its way, McMorrow. Tell her I sent you."

There was a murmur as she covered the phone.

"Sorry," Carlisle said. "What are you working on for us?"

I told her.

"The woman's dead?"

"At the scene."

"Jeez," Carlisle said. "I remember something you said to me once. You were doing that story on the woman who was walking naked through Central Park because she was Eve and there were no clothes in the Garden of Eden. Before the cops came, you walked with her for about a mile, had a chat. You got back, you said, 'Crazy people make perfect sense. They just use a different starting point.' "

"I'm going to the jail tomorrow, try to see him."

"Think he'll be lucid?" Carlisle said.

I pictured Teak, the hatchet, the blood.

"I don't know," I said. "In his own way he seems to think he's making perfect sense, too."

"The dark angel," she said. "These stories always have an evil sibling banished to the dark side."

Siblings? Almost two days in, I had no idea. First stop, before the jail, Down East.

Carlisle said she had to go, then jumped back in. "Another thing you said, McMorrow. 'Dig deep enough, nothing is random.' "

"Cocky little pontificator, wasn't I."

"I used to write them down," Carlisle said.

"Slow days in the newsroom, no doubt," I said, and we parted. The phone was still in my hand when it buzzed.

"Mr. McMorrow."

It took me a second.

"Barrett."

"You've got to get down here. The bastards—they wrecked my mother's apartment."

19

I was outside of the building in an hour. There were a couple of marked cruisers out front, a police Malibu double-parked. I parked Roxanne's Subaru up the block on the bridge, walked back. The door to the foyer was locked, so I texted Barrett. He came down and let me in.

"It's sick," Barrett said. "Who would do this?"

We got in the elevator.

"They trashed it. Pissed on the family photos. That's why I came by after school. I'm starting to plan the funeral, the photos for the display. The frames are smashed, the photos all torn up. They smashed the glasses and plates. Poured everything from the refrigerator out on the bed."

"God," I said.

"I know," Barrett said, his voice cracking. "I mean, how low can you go?"

We were out of the elevator, walking down the corridor. I could hear voices, saw a photo flash at the end of the hallway.

"Hear about a murder victim on TV and break into their apartment? I mean, really. There's a special place in hell."

"Despicable. Did they steal anything?"

"Hard to say, but her jewelry at least. My mom used to buy herself stuff, when they started making money. Rod wasn't gonna buy her anything."

"It's all gone?"

"The whole box. It was in the bottom drawer of the dresser."

"You told the police?"

"Yeah. The cop, Hernandez, said they'd keep an eye out at pawnshops."

"Did your mom have any photos of her jewelry?" I said.

"I don't know."

We paused at the door, stepped inside.

Tingley looked up.

"Jesus, look what the cat dragged in."

"I called him," Barrett said. "I wanted him to see this. Let the world know what scum there is in Riverport, Maine."

I followed him into the room, stepping over broken glass and scattered books. I stood next to Tingley as he watched an evidence tech dust the slider.

"That's how they got in?"

"Off the record?"

"Why?"

"There's some specifics we don't want released."

"Like what?" I said.

"Nope," Tingley said.

"I can just ask Barrett. He'll tell me. Or I can make it seem like you're in charge."

He looked away, shook his head in disgust.

"Okay," Tingley said. "Climbed up on the veranda and broke the slider."

"Nobody heard anything?"

"They lathered up a towel with grease. I'd like to keep that out. You know, grease, like for a car. They pressed the towel to the glass and hit it with a rubber mallet."

"So they thought this out."

"It's sick. I mean, I'm not a violent person, but if I got ahold of these punks, I'd beat the shit out of them. Can you believe this mess?"

I could, because I was looking at it. There were newspapers and magazines strewn on the floor. Papers scattered and trampled, yellow with urine stains.

"Footprints, huh?" I said.

"I'm requesting you leave that out," Tingley said. "We don't want them to read that and toss their shoes."

I nodded, looked down at the stuff, saw the logo of the shelter, the bread and the fish.

"This is the stuff from the shelter?"

"And everything else," Barrett said. "The kitchen drawers. The lady's underwear, the eggs from the refrigerator. Ketchup and mustard and pickles. And the stuff from the shelter. It was on the dining room table. They . . . I don't know how to say this, but one of them defecated on my mom's couch and used the papers from the shelter to, you know, wipe."

"Yuck," I said, looking at the couch, the ripped upholstery, the smear of brown on the pale gray fabric.

"She loved that couch. I helped her pick it out. We went all over the city."

I turned to Tingley.

"I've heard of people hitting the houses of deceased people during funerals. I hadn't heard of it specifically for homicide victims."

"Yeah, I know," he said. "Talk about kicking somebody when they're down. Pretty ballsy, too, considering it's connected to a murder investigation and police, they're gonna be paying extra attention. It's like rubbing your nose in it."

"Jewelry worth a lot?"

"I don't know," Barrett said. "Under ten thousand? That's including the stuff that was passed down to my mom by her mom."

"We'd prefer that not be given out to the public. These scrotes might pawn it for a hundred bucks."

"Or sell it to be melted down," I said. "Spent a long time in here."

"Middle of the day, most people at work," Tingley said. "Had the place to themselves."

"Still, adds to the risk."

"Yup."

"For what?"

"Get their jollies," he said. "I figure it for kids. Addicts aren't gonna hang around to trash the place. They'd be across town in twenty minutes turning the jewelry into cash, jamming shit into their arms."

"Shitting on the couch?"

"I know. Pretty twisted."

"Why would anybody do that?" I said.

Tingley eyed the wreckage, shook his head. "Off the record, why would anybody hurt the lady in the first place?"

"There's an explanation for that," I said. "Teak's sick. But this?"

"Some people are crazy. Some people are assholes," he said. "What can I say?"

He looked at me.

"I know. That's not for the paper."

I stood and viewed the carnage, and when Tingley's back was turned, slipped my phone out and shot a few photos. I was putting the phone away when another guy walked in, and he and Barrett embraced.

The new guy said, "I'm sorry."

They separated and Barrett turned to me and said, "This is Jack McMorrow. From the *New York Times*."

"Travis Chenard," the man said. "Barrett's husband."

We shook hands. He was a big guy, sandy-haired, ruddy cheeks, like an Aussie footballer. They were a very handsome couple.

"Good to meet you," I said. "Unfortunate circumstances."

"It's totally unfair. Lindy never hurt a fly. And then it's like the whole world turned against her. I mean, pick on somebody else, you know? One time, that's just crazy, but stuff happens. But twice?"

He was right. This was cosmic overkill. If the first attack was madness, this was over the top. Made to seem senseless. Reckless. So much so that there had to be a reason for it, beyond picking on a murder victim. The murder itself was twisted. This was over the top.

I looked around once more. Cash, unaccounted for? The jewelry? Maybe it belonged to her ex's family, and Rod wanted it back. Maybe there was something in here he wanted back more than Aunt Beulah's pearls. Maybe there was something here that he'd lifted out of a house, working for the wealthy MDI set? Something that gave Lindy leverage in the divorce negotiations.

Barrett was walking toward the door, shaking a garbage bag open. I touched his arm, nodded toward the hallway. He followed.

"A question. Could there have been something in here that Rod really wanted? And he had to cover that up by wrecking the place?"

I looked into the wreckage.

"Like her laptop, for example. Photos? Where's your mom's laptop?"

He looked the wreckage over, too. "Gone," Barrett said. "I figured somebody would just try to sell it,"

"Or not," I said. "You tell the detective there that there's a laptop missing?"

"Yeah."

"Why don't you tell him what that laptop might have contained. Like the company's books, the taxes or the overpayments."

"I don't know if I'm ready for that," he said.

"Goddamn, Barrett," I said. "Look around. It's time to take off the gloves."

When I left he was talking to Tingley, who looked interested. Maybe he was a real detective after all.

I went down the hallway, let myself out. It was dark and cold and the street was deserted, so my footsteps crackled. I walked past the cruisers, the unmarked Impala, and out onto the bridge. The water was running under the ice somewhere in the darkness below, the gurgle echoing under the bridge. Was it the River Styx that carried souls into Hell? College had been a long time ago, but bits of knowledge, stuck to brain matter like lint, surfaced at times like this. The ferryman Charon taking souls down the river to the afterlife.

I peered over the railing, saw the pale gray ice reflecting the streetlights. Maybe Hell wasn't an inferno, but a frozen wasteland where people wandered naked and shivering. Did Teak belong there? Maybe not. How could you have all of this horror and mayhem and not hold someone responsible?

Jesus. Just give me a bad guy. Just give me a target, something to chase. Don't let this stand.

As I pondered it, I took my keys out. Skirted the back of the car and leaned down.

Saw a broken passenger window. The dent in the driver's door, the print of a boot. The cracked windshield, the glass etched with lines like lightning bolts. The message scrawled on the hood.

GO AWAY, ASSHOLE

"You bastards," I said.

I looked closer. The letters were drawn in something thick, like paste. Lipstick. I wondered if Lindy's makeup bag was accounted for. I turned around, went back inside the building, told my story to Hernandez. She came downstairs, looked the car over, took a few photos with her phone. Called up and asked Tingley to come down.

He did, circled the car.

"So much for random kids," I said.

"Yeah," he said. "Question now is, what are you doing that's pissing people off?"

"My job," I said, and I got in the car and drove off, squinting through the cracks. "Go away?" I said. "Fat friggin' chance."

20

Roxanne wanted to know if the *Times* would cover the deductible on our insurance. I said I'd ask. She said she needed to get to school with Sophie in the morning. I said the car was drivable, if you looked out between the cracks.

"Is New York filled with reporters' spouses driving cars with smashed windshields?" she said.

"No," I said. "In New York they take taxis."

The next morning she dropped me at the Prosperity Garage on the way to school. Phil, the proprietor, was sitting behind a wooden desk covered with greasy receipts and parts catalogs. He looked up, pushed his hat back, and said, "McMorrow. What is it now?"

I told him I needed a loaner, told him why.

"Rocks," he said. "Last time it was bullet holes. You drop down to the B league or what?"

He grinned.

"I loan you something, it gonna come back blown all to hell?"

"Kid gloves, Phil," I said.

He snorted, looked at the wooden board with keys hanging on hooks. "Older F-150 out there. Black. Has brush bars on the front, in case you need to push your way out of trouble."

"Perfect," I said.

Phil got up, hitched his trousers, went over and took the key off the hook and tossed it to me.

"Only reason I do this for you, McMorrow, is I need stories for my memoir," he said.

"Doing my best," I said, and I saluted and walked out the door.

The truck was at the side of the gravel lot, half plowed in. It was ten years old, maybe more, lifted up over big tires. I climbed the snowbank, popped the door, climbed onto the running board, and hoisted myself in. The truck smelled like cigarettes. There were empty Budweiser cans strewn on the passenger-side floor, most of them crushed. I started the motor and it roared to life through loud exhaust. I put it in four-wheel drive, then in gear. It climbed the snowbank like it was a ripple in the pavement, thumped down on the other side.

There'd be no sneaking up in this thing. It was made for full frontal assault.

"Good," I said. "Bring it on."

Clair had a tractor apart in his barn, the small Kubota he used to clean Pokey's paddock. His plan was to call Louis, maybe stop by with a few beers. I told him I'd be fine, just going to talk to Teak's family Down East, see if I could find Rod on MDI. I figured the family would want to talk about Teak's better qualities. The contractor guy would say a few dutiful things about the tragedy, maybe talk about how she was a good person, always eager to help out. Besides, it would be midday, broad daylight. What could happen?

As I drove toward Belfast, I looked around the truck, reached down under the driver's seat. There was a lug wrench there and a foot-long length of pipe. The Glock under my jacket.

The tools of my trade.

I jumped on Route 1 and headed north, watched the towns tick by. Searsport, Stockton Springs, Prospect. It was a gray day and everything looked drab and ragged under the snow. These weren't tourist towns, and the efforts to snare the summer folk were halfhearted. Inns that you would only blunder in to. Restaurants where rich New Yorkers would get a long stare from the locals. Gift shops that had been out of business for years, junk gathering dust and dead flies in the storefront windows.

I made time on the flats below Verona, crossed the bridge and looked out at the bay, another advantage of the big truck. There was ice along the shoreline, empty white-capped waters to the south. As I approached Ellsworth, I could feel my game face coming on. I stopped and filled the truck with gas, climbed back in, and rumbled on.

I swung northeast on Route 1 and soon the place began to change, like I'd entered a different, darker, and more serious country. The spruce woods were closer. The vehicles were pickups and tractor-trailer rigs. I passed a marine supply store, then a crumbling ice-cream shop with plywood over the windows, the word CLOSED sprayed in orange paint like a warning.

Teak was from Ledge Harbor, at the tip of one of the peninsulas that made up the coastline from here into Canada. I swung off Route 1, followed the next pickup south. Along the way there were glimpses of coves where the tides had lifted the ice and broken it into silvery plates that were piled on the weed-covered rocks. There were tidal bays, the ice laid out on the mudflats like puzzle pieces. The occasional farmhouse, trucks and cars parked haphazardly, most of them snow-covered.

And then I was on the outskirts of a village, with stacks of lobster traps at most houses, everything looking out on a harbor where the lobster boats were on their moorings, all pointed east, in formation. Piers and floats and small boats turned hull-up, idled lobster boats propped up on metal stands. There was a store with gas pumps, a Budweiser sign glowing, three pickups out front. I pulled in.

I undid my jacket and the holster and put the Glock under the driver's seat. Grabbed a notebook off the passenger seat, patted my jacket pocket to make sure I had a pen. Swung out and down and walked to the front door and opened it. Stepped in and waited for my eyes to adjust to the dim light.

There were four guys sitting at a counter to the left of the door, a woman behind the counter. She was pouring coffee when she looked up. The four guys turned almost in unison and looked at me over broad shoulders.

"How you doin'," I said, in the way that doesn't require a reply. The guys looked at me, the four of them all red-faced beneath their baseball caps, ruddy streaks along their cheekbones.

One of them nodded, the guy on the end. I walked to the empty stools to his left and sat down, two over. The woman—small and ageless, hair in a gray-blonde ponytail she'd probably worn since high school—held out the pot.

"Coffee?"

"Please," I said.

The guys had turned forward, then away. They began talking among themselves, and the woman came and put a mug down in front of me, then a paper napkin and a spoon. She poured coffee and I smiled and said, "Thanks." She reached over and took a bowl of creamers in plastic cups from in front of the four guys and put it closer to me.

I reached for one, peeled the foil off, and poured it into my coffee. Stirred. The guys were talking quietly, something about Canada and government and someone who was a son of a bitch. The woman came back and said, "Anything else?"

"Yes," I said. "Maybe directions."

The guys turned my way and waited.

"I'm looking for Teak Barney's family. I understand they live in the village here."

She looked at them. They looked at her and then back at me. Their faces were expressionless, all five of them. I smiled at the nearest guy and said, "You all know Teak, right?"

Still no response. I waited. After a long moment, the closest guy, who was bigger and a little older than the others, and seemed to carry some sort of authority, said, "Who's askin'?"

"I'm Jack McMorrow. I'm a newspaper reporter."

I could see them harden, around the eyes.

"Don't know that we need to talk to any reporter," the guy said.

"You don't. Only if you want to let people know who Teak is, really," I said. "Other than an accused murderer."

The three guys beyond the leader looked away, sipped their coffee. The woman swung away and put the pot down, reached for a rag.

"We know who Teak is," the guy said.

"The rest of the world doesn't," I said.

"Don't care what other people know or don't know."

I sipped my coffee, looked back at him.

"I get that," I said. "But if there's a good side to Teak, and I figure there is, then don't you think people should know that?"

"Why?"

"Out of respect for him. His family. What they've been through with his illness. It's not easy."

The guy listened.

"Otherwise he's just a murderer. I know it's a lot more complicated than that."

He looked at me, then raised his mug and drank. The woman picked up the pot and topped them off. The pot was empty and she put it back down. There was another full pot on the burner but she didn't offer any to me.

"Who are you again?" the guy said.

I told him.

"What paper you from?"

"The *New York Times*."

He looked at me, then glanced out the window.

"That truck don't look like it's from New York," he said.

"It's not. I live in Waldo County."

"Why you writing for some paper in New York, then?" he said.

"More money in it," I said.

He considered that. The others had turned back and were staring at me hard but with more curiosity than hostility. I was breaking through.

"I'm trying to tell the whole story of Teak," I said, "not just part of it. TV'll make him out to be a monster. Local press doesn't seem to be interested in anything but what the cops say."

Another long pause. I waited them out. After a minute, the closest guy swiveled his stool toward me.

I took my notebook, said, "Do you mind?"

He shrugged.

"Don't get all excited," he said. "Ain't said nothing yet."

"And your name is?"

He hesitated, then said, "Pete."

I held out my hand and he reached over and we shook. He could have broken bones but he didn't.

"Pete what?"

"Don't matter."

The others listened to their spokesman. The proprietor had found something to scrub.

"You don't know the Barneys," Pete said.

I shook my head. "Nope. Looking forward to it. Where do I find them?"

"Don't know that I want to be the person set a reporter on them," he said.

"I'll find them eventually," I said. "Somebody will have some backbone."

His jaw clenched. His buddies tensed, leaned forward like dogs waiting for the signal, which would be something like, "How 'bout we step outside."

I pushed away from the counter and slid off the stool. Nodded and said, "You have a good day."

Nobody nodded back. I walked out the door, across the lot to the truck. I heaved myself up and in and started the motor. It rumbled, the noise echoing off the side of the restaurant. I leaned down and took the wrench out from under the seat and put it on the floor, the sharp end sticking up. I left the Glock where it was. Wrote in my notebook, describing the scene, the guys and their attitude. Their weathered cheeks and broad backs. Waited some more.

And they came out.

Three of the guys headed toward two pickups. Pete got into a third, a big Dodge, silver over black, with bait barrels and fuel tanks in the bed and a sticker in the back window pledging allegiance to Dale Earnhardt, Number 3. The other two trucks backed up, spun their tires as they sped by me and out onto the road. Pete backed the Dodge out slowly, came around to put his driver's side along mine.

I buzzed the window down. He did the same. When he spoke it was without looking at me.

"Shit has a way of flying around in a town like this," Pete said.

"I'm sure," I said.

"If you were to go outta here, take a left, go right at the first fork, half-mile down, you'd see a double-wide. Shit piled up everywhere, a boat and some traps. Look for a silver convertible with a tarp over it. One of Timmy's projects ain't ever gonna get done."

I nodded. "Thanks."

"Between us, they ain't the town's finest. Decent-enough people once, but that was a while ago. Teak may be a murderer, but some might say he's the best of the bunch."

I considered it.

"None of that's for the paper, and I don't want my name in there nowhere," Pete said.

"I understand."

"Your word?" he said.

"My word," I said.

He nodded. "Good enough," he said, and he drove away.

The double-wide was light blue, set in a space bulldozed out of the spruce and birch woods. The tarp on the convertible had collapsed under the snow. The car was surrounded by boat trailers, lobster traps piled six high, a couple of four-wheelers, a riding mower with the cowl removed, a couple of chest freezers, a gas grill, tires, rusting bicycles. To the left of the door there was a dumpster overflowing with trash bags with a giant cardboard TV box on top. A pile of sawed-up hardwood was scattered in the gravel and an old Chevy pickup was backed up to the front door.

I drove on, pulled off the road onto the shoulder, waited for a car to pass. I reached under the seat for the Glock, slipped it in the holster, and clipped it fast. Then I made a U-turn, drove back to the house, and pulled in and parked beside the Chevy. Shut off the motor and got out and walked to the front door. Knocked. The aluminum storm door rattled. Dogs barked, more than one, and something crashed into the door from the inside. I waited. A man cursed and said, "Git the fuck back."

The inner door swung open. A man stared at me, squinting into the light. He had a gray-brown beard, sunken cheeks, wild eyebrows. He was holding an aluminum cane like a club.

I smiled. He pushed the door open six inches. Dogs were darting around his legs, growling and snapping. He whacked at them with the cane and they backed off. When the barking diminished, I could hear a television playing inside.

"Yeah."

"Mr. Barney," I said.

"Who are you?"

"I'm Jack McMorrow. I'm a reporter. I'm writing about Teak."

He scowled, raised the cane.

"Jesus Christ. Already hung up on Fox. 'How does it feel to be the father of a murderer?' How the fuck do you think it feels? How many of you fake-news bastards are there?"

"I don't know. You tell me. Who else you chased off?"

"That's it so far."

Good, I thought. Nobody sniffing around my story up here.

"Where the hell you from?"

"The *New York Times*."

"The *New York Times*?" he said, like it was a particularly egregious insult. "What the hell does the *New York Times* want to know about Teak?"

The dogs were back, three of them, all mutts. He swung the cane again and one of them yelped.

"It's an important story," I said. "About Teak and mental illness and the ways we help or don't help the people who have it."

"What makes you think I give a shit about you and your story? My boy's locked up. He ain't never coming home."

"I know. It's a sad story all around. I want to make sure that Teak is represented fully, not made out to just be some crazy person."

"Well, he ain't just that," Tim Barney said.

"But what he did—"

"Hey, I'm wicked sorry about that lady," Tim Barney said. "I'll give you that."

"Lindy Hines."

"Right. I mean, she ain't done nothin' and she's gone. Just like that. It's fucked up. You can tell her folks I said so. I'm sorry this happened to her. To Teak, too. 'Cause he's done, sure as shit."

"Right," I said.

He gathered himself up. I waited.

"Thing is, Teak done this bad thing, but when he was a kid, he was as sane as you and me."

"I'm sure," I said, feeling an opening. "And I do want to talk about what he was like before he got sick."

He looked at me hard, squinting and scowling. And then he said, "I blame the goddamn comic books. Started reading that shit, was never the same."

"Can we talk about that then?" I said.

He wavered, gave the dogs another whack.

"It won't take long."

He looked at my truck.

"Come all the way from New York, huh?" he said.

I smiled.

"It's important."

"Well, git in here, then," he said, turned and moved deeper into the house. I followed.

21

The place was full of stuff. Stacks of car magazines. Trash bags full of clothes. A piece of plywood on sawhorses, engine parts spread out on the board. The room reeked of solvent.

There were two recliners, one occupied by a grizzled gray cat. The chairs smelled new and faced a massive TV that occupied most of the end wall. A talk show was playing, two larger-than-life women screaming at each other about someone cheating. Barney made no move to turn it off, or the volume down.

He whacked at the cat with his cane and it snarled and leapt stiffly off the chair and slunk away. The dogs were all around me, one of them sniffing my crotch.

"Git away from there, you slut," Barney said, whacking the dog, too.

"Set," he said, and I did. He sat in the other chair, held the cane across his lap like a rifle. In the time I'd been there, it hadn't touched the floor.

I took out my notebook. Barney looked at it and said, "You one of those places that pay?"

I looked at him, taking a second to get it.

"Pay for interviews?" I said. "No. Sorry."

He shrugged.

"Teak," I said. "When did he start to get sick?"

"Jesus," Barney said. "Eighteen? Nineteen? He was outta school, working sternman for me. Hard worker, the boy was. Strong as a bastard, go all day, too. I mean, Teak, he always gave a hundred percent. Played basketball up to the school there, and the coach said it. 'Teak, he lays it all out.' Come home from games, knees and elbows all scraped up. He'd just throw himself after that ball."

He paused.

"I didn't raise him to be no murderer. You make sure you put that in there. I did the best I could by him. After his mother died, for a while it was just me and the kids. Ain't easy, lobsterin', trying to keep track of where the hell they are, who they're with."

"I'm sure," I said. I flipped the page on my notebook.

"Him and his brother, night and day. Jason, he was always looking for the easy way. Ask him to do something, he'd try to sweet-talk his way out of it. Pay him, he'd hire Teak for cheap, pocket the difference."

"I see."

"And another thing. Teak, he's a stand-up guy. His girlfriend Tawny, after he knocked her up, he was right there for little T. K., changing diapers and shit, feeding the kid bottles, whatever."

Ah, Teak as a dad. The story had just gotten exponentially sadder.

"How old is T. K.?"

"He's six, maybe seven. I can't keep track. Teak started getting sick, got to the point it weren't good for him to be around the boy. Weren't sure what he'd do, all this comic-book Hakata crap going on in his head. Him and his secret missions."

Barney paused.

"So when did it start swirling around?"

"Right outta high school, when it got really bad. Like I'd lost him. Didn't know where his head was at, and wherever it was, I couldn't go there."

I nodded, kept writing.

"Broke him right up, not being able to support his family. 'Cause Teak, he ain't sick all the time. He comes out of it, he knows his life is fucked up, that little boy growing up without a daddy."

I was writing fast and hard. He waited for me. I wondered if he thought it would get him that payment.

"Tawny with somebody else?" I said.

"Oh, here and there. Nothing that's stuck. She hangs around with Jason some these days. Don't get me started on that twisted shit. But hell, she's got her own—"

He hesitated, looked around the room for the right word.

"—issues, as they say. Anyway, it all got worse for Teak when I went away."

I knew that euphemism, said, "How long were you gone?"

"Four to six."

"Months or years?"

"Months," he said. "Shit, I ain't no hardened criminal. Receiving stolen property, buncha bullshit. Like I told the fucking DA there, how was I supposed to know where the goddamn snow machines come from? Just figured it was a good deal."

The dogs looked up from the floor.

"Right," I said.

"But like I say, I blame them comics. My brother, he goes to live with his girlfriend in Gouldsboro, cleans out his trailer. Gives Teak his comics. Called it a collection, but really it was just a lot of crap in a box. Right from the get-go, Teak couldn't keep his nose out of the things. I'd say, 'Teak. Go watch the friggin' TV.' No, he'd sit on his bunk and just read those things for hours. I'd say, 'Teak. It's just a bunch of made-up horseshit.' "

"So are a lot of things."

"Not around here. You make stuff up, people notice."

"That right."

"You know what guys were calling Teak?"

I shook my head.

"Lobsterman. Like Superman. 'Hey, Lobsterman. Can you fly? Hey, Lobsterman, flip that boat over.' "

"I get it," I said. "And all of this seemed real to him?"

"Like this thing with the hatchet and Lindy Hines?"

"Yeah."

"Well, sure. He was still working for me, before I hurt my back. Thing is, he read all this crap and then he made up his own. Crazy stuff. His hero or whatever was Finnish, like from the country there. I'd say he was a Viking, and Teak, he'd go, 'Finnish, Pa. The Vikings were scared shitless of the Finnish.' "

He looked at me, shook his head.

"Vikings? Finnish? I mean, what the fuck?"

"His hero have a name?" I said.

"Yeah," Tim Barney said. "That's Hakata, like I said."

He drew the word out. *Ha-ka-ta.*

"Means 'ax' in Finnish. So I guess it was like Ax Man. Teak drew these pictures of the guy in his costume. I go, 'Teak, what the hell, boy? It's like you're playing with friggin' paper dolls.' "

"Right," I said.

"And then it hits me. I go, 'Jesus, he thinks this stuff is real.' It was like the rest of us were the ones who were clueless. I remember I said one time, 'Teak, it's all made up. There ain't no Hakata or any of the rest of 'em.' He smiles at me in that way he has, this little thing he does with his eyes. He goes, 'Nobody's ever seen Jesus, neither.' "

I wrote that down. The women were still screaming on the giant TV.

"So you got hurt and couldn't fish," I said. "And Teak took off?"

"Even before that, every coupla months he'd just disappear. I mean, you can't have a sternman doesn't show up."

"Where did he go?"

"I don't know. Riverport, mostly, I think. Wanted to be in the big city. He'd be gone a coupla weeks. Come back like he'd been on some secret mission. Sometimes he'd kinda let it slip that Hakata had asked him to go do something."

"Really. Were they violent things?"

"I don't know," Barney said. "I mean, you don't want to think the worst about your boy. This thing with this lady. Your own flesh and blood doing what he did? Jesus God almighty."

He started to tear up, and I wondered what Brock at the diner had been warning me about. I'd met worse.

Wiping at his eyes, he heaved himself out of the chair, again without using the cane. I wondered if it turned into a sword.

"Gotta use the head," he said, and walked across the room and through a door by the kitchen. I heard a door close and I got up, walked to the counter, the dogs padding behind me. There was a half-empty jug of coffee brandy, a joint stubbed out in a clamshell, a dirty dish towel in the sink. A spot of blood. There was a needle protruding from under the towel. I poked at it and the syringe slipped out, blood in the barrel. I lifted the towel, saw the burnt spoon.

Back injury. Opioids. In this part of Maine, Barney was the rule, not the exception.

I went back near my chair and stood. There was a copy of *Cousin Harold's Weekly* on the table. I looked closer, saw that it was open to Trucks: Light Duty. One was circled: *2007 Chevy Silverado. Sharp, red. Low miles. No rust. Never plowed. $10,000. Cash only. Eastport.*

I heard someone pull in and turned, hurried to the door and looked out. There it was, the sharp red Chevy. A man and woman slid out. More of the clan. I crossed to the chair and sat, notebook on my lap.

The door rattled open and they stepped in, the woman first, the guy behind her. I figured them for Jason and Tawny. Both gaunt, sunken eyes and gray shadows. Meth sores around their mouths. Tweakers. The woman was carrying a pizza box. The dogs jumped and yipped, tails wagging. The woman said "Git away" as the guy closed the door behind him. They looked at me.

"Hi there," I said.

"Who are you?" the guy said.

"Jack McMorrow."

"Where's my dad?"

"Bathroom."

"Whatcha doing here?"

They looked at the notebook. Eyes dilated. Wired. They'd smoked up.

"I'm a reporter. I work for the *New York Times*. I'm talking to Tim about Teak."

"Jesus Christ," the woman said.

"Are you Tawny?" I said. I turned to the guy. "And you're Jason?"

The woman said, "What the fuck?" Which I took for confirmation. The guy stepped in front of me and said, "Out," jerking his thumb toward the door.

The dogs joined in, barking and circling like dervishes.

"Easy, Jason," I said. "I'm just doing a story. Tim and I were having a talk."

"Out," he shouted, boozy breath in my face.

I didn't move. "Tim was right in the middle of his story," I said.

"I don't care what he was in the middle of. Get the fuck out."

The woman—skinny as a skeleton, draped with a blaze-orange sweatshirt—hurried out of the room toward the bathroom, tossed the pizza on the counter on the way. I heard her call out "Timmy, are you out of your mind?"

The guy—my size, beard, camo parka, hat that advertised ammunition—said, "We ain't talking to no fake news."

"You related to Teak?"

"I'm his brother, and I speak for this family; me and Tawny, we got no fucking comment."

I smiled, trying to go easy, not set him off. I didn't want to wrestle with a meth head. If I did, I wanted to be ready. Last one I'd seen had fought four cops to a standstill, took a Taser like it was a tap on the arm.

"You don't have to comment, that's fine," I said.

"You bet your fucking ass it's fine," he said.

He grabbed for my notebook and I yanked it back. He missed the notebook, grabbed me hard by the upper arm. I wrenched loose and backed away, dogs darting for my legs, snarling and snapping.

Tawny and Barney came back into the room.

"Jason," Barney said. "What the hell you doin'?"

"We told you to go," Tawny said to me.

The dogs were lunging and I heard my jeans rip, felt teeth slash my thigh. Jason pulled a knife off a sheath on his belt. I reached under my jacket, pulled the Glock out, and pointed it at his face.

They all froze, except for the dogs.

"Back off," I said to Jason.

"He's fucking DEA," Tawny said.

The dogs were nipping at the tear in my jeans, smelling the blood. I looked away to kick at them. When I looked back, Jason was a half-step closer, the point of the knife blade making small circles in the air.

I shifted the Glock, fired a round into the wall behind him, just to the right of his head.

"Fuck," he said, and ducked. Tawny shouted, "Tim," and Barney hurried from the room, probably to get his own gun. Tawny was screaming, "Jason, get him." The dogs were snarling and snapping as I moved toward the door, Tawny and Jason pivoting with me. I reached behind me, opened the door, and yanked it open. Kicked the storm door and backed out.

I ran to the truck, started it, slammed it into reverse, and spun my way back out onto the road. As I threw the truck into gear, I saw Jason fling himself out of the house, run for the pickup. His own gun. I stopped, reversed, buzzed the passenger window down.

Fired two shots at the right front tire.

The first round hit the fender. The second blew the tire and the truck sagged, Jason throwing himself between the truck and the house. I hit the gas, put the gun on the passenger seat, thought, *That was the $10,000 truck in the ad. The big TV. The chairs.*

Where'd this crew get cash?

22

I sped north, passed the store, and headed for Route 1, checking the rearview mirror. A mile up the road, I saw a pickup in the distance, but closing. Older Chevy. Jason in his dad's truck? Tawny riding shotgun?

I sped north, the big Ford roaring. The Chevy was a quarter-mile back, heeling through the curves, straddling the center line on the straightaways. I could outrun them until I hit some sort of traffic, and then they'd be on my back bumper.

Jason the tweaker had lost face. He wouldn't let that stand.

I sped up on a straight, went airborne over the next rise. The truck landed heavily, bounced a couple of times as I wrestled it down the road. There was a sharp left-hand turn, a frozen cove. I floored it, then jammed on the brakes, slid off the road and along the side of a boat shed. At the end of the shed there was a loading dock, and I yanked the wheel, slid up to the dock, and stopped.

Took my foot off the brake to turn off the brake lights. Sat with the Glock in my hand. Watched the rearview.

Saw the Chevy speed past, bound for the intersection with Route 1.

They'd be back, once they saw I wasn't in sight in either direction. I drove out onto the road, headed north for a hundred yards, and turned into the yard of a lobster co-op, a long, barn-like building, the water end on pilings.

I circled, backed along the south side, out of sight of the road from the north, but with a view of the road as it continued south. I waited. Fingered the Glock. Watched the road.

A refrigerator truck pulled out from the other side of the shed, crossed the lot, and turned north. I considered following it out, staying snug on its rear bumper. Decided to stay put.

Waited another five minutes. Maybe they were staking out the main road, figured there was only one way off the peninsula. Sitting in the truck and snorting whatever, getting good and riled.

I counted off four more minutes.

Saw them pass.

The Chevy was headed south, Jason behind the wheel, Tawny in the passenger seat. I watched until they disappeared behind the next bend, then drove slowly out of my hiding place, crossed to the north side of the building, and exited the lot. Hit the gas and caught up to the lobster truck a quarter-mile from the intersection. I waited for a short straight, punched the throttle, and passed the truck, hoped it would run interference behind me on the bends leading up to Route 1.

There was a stop sign. I rolled through it, headed west. I was sagging back into the seat when my phone buzzed. I dug it out.

"Yeah."

"Hey," Clair said. "How's it going?"

"Well, let's see. Bit by a dog, chased out of a house by a couple of meth heads. Had to fire a warning shot, put a round into the guy's tire. I guess those are the highlights."

"Glad to hear everything's under control," Clair said.

"Smooth sailing. Family makes Teak seem downright productive. Unemployed drug users, except seem like they recently came into some money."

"What kind of money?"

"New old truck, recliners, and a big TV."

"Bigger than a scratch ticket, short of the lottery. Rob their dealer?"

"I'm thinking more like a windfall. Not sure they have the organizational skills for a successful robbery."

I heard Clair's truck start, a metallic hum as he hit the switch that lifted the plow.

"Where you headed now?" he said.

"Renys in Ellsworth, buy some jeans. Dog ripped my pants."

"That's the way they're wearing them," he said. "All torn up."

"There's a little blood, too."

"Don't know if that's caught on," Clair said.

"Next stop is MDI, find the ex," I said. "If your ex-wife dies after you dump her for a younger woman, are you still a widower?"

"No, just a jerk."

"Teak saved him a pile of dough."

"There's always a silver lining," Clair said.

"Thank you, Pollyanna," I said. "Still, I don't think he's going to be glad to see me."

"What goes around, comes around," Clair said.

"That's the idea. Find the bastards, ruin their days."

"Jack."

"What?"

"I know. The woman killed right in front of you. It's hard up close. First time I saw a man killed was a kid from Hatch, New Mexico. Place is famous for chili peppers. Name was Gino. He flunked out of college and got drafted. Real funny guy, thought the whole thing was absurd, him being a soldier. Which it was, but not the best attitude to take into combat. Anyway, Gino stepped on a mine and it blew his bottom half right off. I was two guys in front."

He paused. I waited.

"I thought it was my fault somehow. Should have reminded him one more time, him not being a natural at this sort of thing. But people kept dying, and I figured if we carried that around with us, it was only gonna make our job harder and get even more people killed. It was self-indulgent, you know? People get killed. And a lot of times somebody's standing next to them. That doesn't mean—"

"I get it," I said. "I'm fine."

There was a long pause, Clair's way of saying he knew I wasn't.

"Speaking of robberies," he said.

"Yes."

"On the Louis front."

"What?"

"Marta called and told Mary the woods were weirding her out."

"And?"

"And Mary said, 'Come up here, dear. We have this big empty house.' "

"Huh. You talk to Louis?"

"Yeah. He said she won't be alone. Follows him closer than the dog."

"They found her," I said. "And somehow she knows."

"Louis asked her that and she said no. She's just going stir-crazy."

"I don't like it."

"Too late," Clair said. "They're on their way."

"I don't want her near my house," I said. "I don't trust her."

"A lot of half-truths, for sure."

"As in, she's lying her ass off."

"I'll deal with her. And he's my problem, not yours."

"Semper Fi?" I said.

"That's right."

"I don't know, Clair. There's a time and a place for all this loyalty stuff. My gut says this isn't one."

23

Renys was in a strip mall in Ellsworth, behind fast-food joints, next to a movie theater. I walked in, located the jeans, flipped through the piles and found my size. I checked to see if they were skinny jeans. They weren't, so I went and bought them.

The high school girl at the register said they didn't carry Band-Aids, glanced at the rip in my jeans, and held my money with two fingers like she might catch something. I stuffed my bloody jeans into the trash can outside the dressing room. A woman on her way into the dressing room looked at the bloodstains and then at me.

"Nothing to see here, folks," I said. She stepped into the room and slammed the louvered door shut.

I smiled. It was just the send-off I needed.

The ride to Mount Desert Island was a straight shot east. There were deserted motels, a petting zoo that was closed for the season, ice-cream shops boarded up like a hurricane was bearing down.

In ten minutes a cove appeared on the left, more planks of ice tossed topsy-turvy onto seaweed-covered rocks. Then there was another bigger cove on the right, and I was onto the island. The road forked, the left lane going to Bar Harbor. I took the right, figured Rod Blaine's headquarters would be on the backside of the island. He might be making money, but it wasn't old enough to get him into Northeast Harbor.

I pulled into the lot of an antique barn, closed for the winter, the old stuff in the window getting older by the minute. On my phone I found Spruce Rock Construction in West Tremont, on the southwestern edge of the island. I pulled out and continued south, the road leading to the village of Somesville, all green shutters and white clapboards. A few disoriented tourists were wandering the deserted street like tropical birds blown off course.

I kept driving, reached Southwest Harbor, more shops, snow-covered B&Bs, a single sailboat on a mooring by the marina. The road swung southeast and I followed it, the carefully picturesque houses giving way to trailers, an abandoned farm, a couple of ranch houses with lobster traps stacked by the driveway.

There was a sign for Tremont and I turned right, followed a road that kept the shoreline at a safe distance. There were houses tucked into the woods on the inland side, driveways through the trees. Then the landscape opened up and there was pasture flanked by spruce and fir. After a crest in the road, there was a spread with a new house on the right, a horse barn on the left, the property bounded by a long split-rail fence.

I remembered Barrett talking about Silk—that Rod had built her a barn and bought her horses.

I slowed and turned in.

The house was two stories and oversized, three dormers on the second floor facing the road, and a separate two-story garage with truck-sized doors and a workshop on the side. There was a black Land Cruiser parked in the pull-off in front of the garage, and I pulled between it and the house and got out. The drive and paths were neatly cleared, showing a bed of pea-sized white stone, everything lined by cobbles.

Not cheap.

I walked to the front door of the house and pushed the bell. A dog answered, a small one, yipping excitedly, then another coming in late, same bark. They scratched at the other side of the door for a few minutes, barked louder when I rang the bell again.

But no one came.

I turned and looked out across the road to the barn. There was a new Toyota pickup parked there, also black. A matching set. I walked down the drive and across, fifty yards to the barn. The door was closed but I could hear music playing. Some sort of New Age chiming. I knocked once, slid the door open, and stepped inside.

It was a big open space that smelled of raw wood and horses. There was tack hanging on the walls, a saddle on a stand, like you'd put a quarter in and your kid could go for a ride. I said, "Hello," and heard a woman's voice, but she wasn't talking to me.

I walked in that direction, went through a doorway and saw a long passage, box stalls on the left side. The voice was coming from the second stall and I approached and looked in.

A woman was brushing a big horse. The horse was dark brown with a white blaze and looked fit and sleek and expensive. The woman had blonde hair pulled back in a ponytail that protruded from under a black knit cap. She was wearing a black down vest over a red fleece sweater, tall rubber boots, and leggings. She looked sleek and expensive, too.

"Hi, there," I called, and she looked up and flinched, put a hand on her chest.

"Oh my God, you scared me," she said.

"I'm sorry," I said. "The music."

The horse snorted and waggled his head. She patted him.

"I'm Jack McMorrow," I said. "I'm looking for Rod Blaine. I'm from the *New York Times*."

She smiled, said, "Oh, great. We were hoping we'd hear from you."

At last, a warm welcome for the press.

She led the horse to the far end of the stall, put a scoop of grain in a bin on the wall. The horse lowered his head and started to eat. She put the brush on a shelf and hurried to the gate, opened and stepped out, and shook my hand.

"I'm Silk Salsbury," she said. "Rod's partner. He's on a job site, but I can tell you where to find him."

Huh, I thought. Maybe not the monsters Barrett Hines had described.

We walked to the big room and crossed to some sort of separate office. There were photographs of horses on the wall, some with Silk, too. She was less pretty in person but still very attractive. Very different from the sturdy, fifty-something, sensible-shoed Lindy Hines.

There was a framed map of the island on the wall with the horse pictures, and Silk stepped up to it, tapped the glass with her finger.

"Rod's at the job in Seal Harbor," she said, like I should know about it. "Do you know the island?"

"I can GPS it," I said.

"It's easy. All the way back to Somesville, right on Route 3, and stay on that all the way past Northeast, then, like, two and half miles to Seal. There's a Spruce Rock sign by the road. You take that right and it's like a quarter-mile down to the point. You'll see our trucks."

"Okay," I said.

I was about to ask her thoughts on Lindy's death when there was a booming sound from the stalls, a young woman's voice saying, "Silk. Are you there?"

Silk turned, said, "Oh, Minotaur. He's having a bad day. I gotta go. But listen, do you have Rod's cell?"

She was headed for the door, snatched a business card off the desk and handed it to me. "In case you get lost," Silk said.

And then she trotted off. I glanced at the card. Rod Blaine was president of Spruce Rock Construction, LLC. Silk Salsbury was VP. Both of their cell numbers were listed.

They hadn't wasted time consolidating.

I left the barn, walked up to the house and got into the truck. It started with a rumble and I backed up, headed out. From the top of the rise, through a gap in the trees, you could see a glimmer of shimmering ocean. It was quite a spread, a far cry from the Riverport condo.

It was almost twenty miles up and around the island, and I had time to think about Lindy in this new light. Had she been bitter, leaving her marriage, and business, just as the latter was taking off? How would Rod Blaine justify jettisoning his wife for a newer model? Did he feel any responsibility for her death? Was he eager to talk to me because he wanted to get something off his chest?

I drove north on the coast road, passed a place called Pretty Marsh, which was pretty, but I couldn't see the marsh from the truck. Then I backtracked through Somesville, started down the east side of the sound. This was old-money territory, discreet signs at the top of long driveways down to the ocean, names for the houses that dated back to a time when people did that. Naming your McMansion was pretentious; here, back in the days when the Rockefellers moved in, it had been de rigueur.

I skirted the village of Northeast Harbor, another village of shops and galleries, understated as the preppie clothes in the windows. The ocean, big and gray and empty, was on my right as I drove the last couple of miles to Seal Harbor. I watched for the Spruce Rock sign, and finally spotted it. The logo of tree and mountain from the card.

I stopped too late, backed up, and drove slowly down a steep gravel driveway through dark, dense woods. And then the woods opened up, and there was big shingled manse, pickups parked off to the left. Beyond the pickups was a massive carriage house, with raw new shingles, rising three stories. I parked by a new Ford pickup, the gold Spruce Rock logo on the door. It was a $60,000 truck, all the bells and whistles. Rod's ride.

I collected my tools, pen and notebook, and got out and went to the door. I could hear compressors running, nail guns banging, guys shouting over the noise. Stepping in, I smelled propane heaters and varnish and, when my eyes adjusted, saw the ocean through the glass rear wall of the place. The glass wall gave way to a vast veranda where workers were cutting what looked like mahogany or some other exotic wood. I pushed a glass door open and walked out. Scanned the deck and picked him out.

Rod was tall and lanky, narrow hips and broad shoulders. He was wearing a brown canvas jacket, a baseball hat, and work boots. He was dressing down a young guy, saying, "Can't you read a blueprint?"

I waited as they looked down over the railing, Rod pointing to some mistake. When he straightened and turned, I was there. I said, "Rod Blaine?"

He looked down at me dismissively, like I'd come to ask for a job. "Who's asking?" he said.

"Jack McMorrow. I write for the *New York Times*."

His face broke into a grin and he held out his hand eagerly, took mine and shook it vigorously.

"Jack," he said. "Glad you could make it up. What do you think?"

He gestured toward the building behind us, the spread of the deck.

"Beautiful," I said. "It's not what it seems from the other side."

"That's the magic. The reveal. You think it's going to be a place for the cars, maybe a few rooms for the help. But you get in here and you're right over the ocean. I mean, look at that view. With the original building that was here before, that was wasted. We're removing the barrier that exists between us and the majesty of nature in a location like this. This is full immersion design, but still in keeping with the aesthetic tradition of these grand cottages."

"Beautiful," I said again.

"Want to do the whole tour? Is your photographer coming in?"

I looked at him.

"I'm thinking there's some misunderstanding," I said.

He stopped.

"What? You're from the *New York Times*, right? You've been talking with Millicent?"

I smiled.

"The architect?" he said.

"I write for the *Times*, but I don't write about houses."

"Then what *do* you write about?"

"At the moment I'm reporting a story about the murder of your estranged wife, Lindy Hines."

His smile dissolved, his face drained, ruddy to gray.

"I can't talk about that. I mean, it's horrible. I still can't believe it happened. Me and Lindy, things didn't work out, but she didn't deserve that."

"I know. So can you tell me more about her? What she was like as—"

"This has got nothing to do with me," he said. "Nothing."

Blaine looked around, grabbed me by the upper arm, and pulled me across the deck and through the door. He shut it, still holding me by the arm.

"Listen. We've been separated for two years. I'm with another woman now."

"I know," I said. "I met Silk. She gave me directions."

"You told her you were writing about Lindy?"

"We never got that far. She did seem oddly happy to see me."

Blaine looked away, then back.

"Jesus Christ," he said. "What did you say your name was?"

I told him. He took a breath and regrouped.

"Jack, I can't be in your story. I mean, I'm trying to put all of that behind me."

I looked at him. "I don't quite understand. I'm writing about Lindy, who she was. Your marriage may have ended, but you were a big part of her life. And your stepson's."

"Barrett? Is that who set you on me?"

"I didn't need any setting," I said.

"I don't know what he said about me, but if you print any of it, I'll sue you."

I shrugged.

"Hey, if you can get some local lawyer to take the case, go for it. It's your money."

We stared at each other for a few long seconds.

"Okay. Let's back up. It's like this. Between us, I've got a deal in the works. A very big deal. Investors who want to take this, what you see here, and go national. Design-build on spec. The Northwest. Florida. North Carolina. These private equity guys are right at that tipping point, you know? And putting me right in the middle of a story about some crazy homeless guy who happens to kill my soon-to-be ex-wife—it's not what I need right now."

I didn't answer.

"You get it, right? They see that, think, 'What? Who is this guy from Maine? What else in his life is messed up?' And they take their money elsewhere."

I still didn't answer.

"So no," Blaine said, getting in my face.

"No comment?"

"No—as in, I don't want my name in your story at all. I'm not with her. Hey, we grew apart. It happens. We were only talking through lawyers. What's she got to do with me?"

A guy came through the door with a sheet of blueprint. Blaine waved him away.

"Still," I said, "my job is to write about Lindy, explain who she was as a person. You were a part of who she was."

"Was. As in past tense. Not anymore."

"So you don't want to talk to me? Don't want to hear my questions?"

"I told you. This crap has nothing to do with me. I mean, it's too bad, sure."

Too bad. Lindy's head split open. It was all I needed.

"Your stepson told me for the record that he blames you, partly. He said that if you and Lindy had stayed married, she wouldn't have been living on her own in Riverport, and she never would have crossed paths with Teak Barney."

His face went red, jaw snapped shut. He leaned in and said, "You put that in your paper, I won't sue you. I'll beat the living shit of you."

"You know this conversation is on the record," I said.

"Fuck you and your record," Blaine said. He leaned in and I didn't budge. And then he fell back.

"Okay. Sorry. I'm just upset. I mean, I thought a lot of Lindy. Shit, I loved her for a while. I still can't wrap my head around this thing. It's nuts. And she didn't deserve that. We had our problems at the end but she was a good person."

I waited.

"Anyway, there's just a lot going on in my life even before this craziness."

I nodded.

"How 'bout this? I should get word on this deal in, like, six weeks. How 'bout you wait on this story until after the deal's done?"

I shook my head. "The news is the murder. This is the follow. No way can I wait six weeks. Or six days. Or six hours."

He started to boil over again, fought it back.

"Okay. How much they pay you to write this? You on salary?"

I hesitated.

"Freelance."

"So, what? A couple of thousand bucks?"

"Something like that."

"I'll pay you twenty grand, cash. Go sit on your hands for a couple of months. Go on vacation. You married?"

I didn't answer.

"Take the wife to Barbados. Sit on the beach and drink rum. Fuckin' A. I got friends here with hardware. As in private jets. I will have you flown down in a friggin' Citation."

I took out my notebook.

"What was she like? I'm told she was a hard worker with a great head for numbers."

He looked at me, his mouth open.

"Get off this property," Blaine said.

I shut my notebook, slipped it into the back pocket of my new jeans.

"Out," he said, and pointed toward the door to the driveway. "And if one word of this conversation appears in print, my lawyer will be on you so fast it'll make your head spin."

"Looking forward to it," I said. "Good luck with your deal."

Two guys came into the room, tool belts clinking. They looked at Blaine, then at me, and one said to him, "Everything all right here?"

"Just escort this guy outta here," Blaine said. "He's trespassing on private property."

They turned to me.

"Put him in his vehicle," Blaine said. "See him up to the road."

One of the guys reached for me.

"You heard him," he said.

"Back off," I said, and shrugged his hand away.

"You're gone, buddy," the other guy said, stepping in to grab me, hoist me up. I brought my arm down hard, the point of the elbow banging his forearm hard.

"Fuckin' A," he said, holding his arm to his belly, reaching for the hammer on his belt. Thought better.

"Remember what I said," Blaine said.

"Every word," I said.

They watched as I climbed up into the big Ford, started the motor. I assumed they were still there as I drove up the drive to the main road. But I'd moved on—was wondering why Lindy Hines was dead and somebody like Rod Blaine skated.

Time to take a stand.

24

I was somewhere above Stockton Springs when my phone beeped for the tenth time since MDI. Email. I pulled over, picked up my phone.

> *Vanessa at the* Times: *How is it going with the homeless guy murder? Let me know. Photos?*
>
> *Newsletter from Prosperity Primary School: The Parents Group will meet Monday at seven p.m. The agenda includes organizing of volunteers to build the new playground.*
>
> *Google Alert: Lindy Hines, Riverport, Maine, murder: the Riverport PD will hold a press conference at nine a.m. at the Police Department to announce resolution of the murder of Linda "Lindy" Hines.*

Resolution? I didn't think so.

I tossed the phone onto the seat, pulled the truck back out onto the highway. The exhaust blared and the tires rumbled. I stewed all the way to Belfast where I rolled over the bridge, looked out from high above the harbor. The bay was gray ice water, deadly as burning oil. The harbor was empty but for a couple of lobster boats, bows pointed into the offshore wind. The view brought me no comfort, no soothing calm at the sight of the island of Islesboro, Castine somewhere in the haze on the far shore.

The tourists could turn the Maine coast into a fantasy. Thanks to Teak's dad and brother Jason, and drugged-out Tawny, I knew better. Thanks to Rod Blaine, the phony, self-centered coward, I saw through it. On this day, for me the Maine coast was a rockbound place of drug-addict scuffles and shameless shiny greed.

Sell your soul for a slag of meth or the prospect of a new Range Rover. Trample the good folks in your desperate need for either. And who were the good ones?

Maybe Teak, before he got sick. Eager to please. Put me in, Coach; I'm ready.

Certainly Lindy Hines, kind and gentle, blindsided by her husband's ambition and lust, then bludgeoned by bad luck.

I turned west at Belfast, drove up into the hills, thinking that was the story, even if nobody wanted me to tell it. Screw them.

Clair's news loomed like black clouds drifting in from the west. The light falling with the sun, I came down the ridge into Prosperity, passed the Dump Road, drove another three miles, and turned off to come in from the other side. I did, and slowed as I passed Clair's big house, slowed more as I passed the drive up to the barn. There was no sign of Marta's Audi or Louis's Jeep.

Change of plan?

I drove up the road, pulled into the dooryard, and parked by the shed. I put the Glock under the seat in its holster, locked the truck. Roxanne's Subaru was there, the window still broken, the boot-shaped dent in the door. As I walked into the house I wondered how she'd explained that to Sophie.

There are bad people in the world. Your daddy hates their guts, and the feeling is mutual.

When I walked in, I heard Sophie and Roxanne in the kitchen. I came around the corner, saw Sophie standing on a stool, wearing an apron.

"Hey, Dad," she said, and she hopped down and came over and gave me a hug. Her mouth was rimmed with cookie dough.

"We're making cookies. They're for school, but Mom says you can have a couple."

"Great," I said. "Perfect with my tea."

"We'll have them with juice, but Mrs. P. will have coffee. She drinks coffee all day long."

"That's not good for you," I said.

"Jonathan told her that, and she said she had to go somehow."

"True," I said. A caffeine overdose beat a hatchet to the head.

I crossed the room, gave Roxanne a kiss on the cheek. She was stirring batter with a wooden spoon and her face was flushed from exertion and the wood fire.

Sophie came back and hopped up on her stool and started stirring again.

I smiled. Kissed her again. She turned to Sophie, said, "Let's start rolling it into balls."

A conversation postponed.

I asked Roxanne how her day was and she said it was fine. She'd been tutoring a kid named Brant who was six and didn't know all his letters. "We can't all be geniuses," I said.

"He doesn't know his colors, either," she said.

"What does he know?"

"The F-word," Roxanne said.

"Ah," I said. "That will come in very handy."

She and Sophie rolled the dough into balls and lined them up on a cookie sheet. Sophie's were smaller and misshapen. They'd taste the same.

"Any visitors today?" I said, taking a Ballantine out of the refrigerator.

"Not since we've been home. Who were you expecting?"

I took a swallow of ale and said, "Nobody in particular."

That got a sideways glance, and then the cookies were headed for the oven. I opened the door, stepped aside. Said, "I'll be right back. Have to check something with Clair."

I brought the beer with me, walked down the path to Clair's barn. Dusk was deepening and the woods were dark on both sides. Something fluttered in the cherry trees; a roosting winter robin? Then a scurry and the snap of a branch. I stopped. Listened. Peered into the gloom. Felt for the Glock but it wasn't there.

I continued on, wondering why I was jumpy here on my home turf, which I knew by heart. The answer was easy: The woman who was supposed to arrive, who I didn't know at all.

With a last listen, I kept walking, my boots crunching in the crusty snow. Forty yards on, I saw the lights in Clair's barn, smelled smoke from the stove. I kept going, opened the workshop door and stepped in. Music was playing—Vivaldi, Schubert, Beethoven?—and I called out. Clair didn't answer.

I walked down the passage to Pokey's stall and he turned and snorted, came over to the gate. I patted his head, and he looked at me with his big wise eyes, snuffled my hand to see if I had a treat. I didn't, and he turned away. I walked out the way I had come, crossed the dooryard to the house.

The Audi was parked alongside the back door, out of sight of the road.

I climbed the steps, knocked once, and opened the door and stepped in. I smelled roast chicken and heard voices. Walked into the kitchen and saw Marta leaning against the kitchen table, holding a glass of wine. Mary was at the stove, lifting a pan out and up. Clair was quietly setting the table.

"Jack," Marta said. "I'm glad you came by. I was afraid I'd miss you."

She took three steps, gave me a quick Euro cheek rub. There was a muscular leanness to her, something lithe and feral.

"Nice to see you, too," I said.

"Marta came to get a little bit of civilization," Mary said. "Sometimes the woods can get to you. Don't I know."

"Yeah," I said. "Even if you come a long way to find them."

I looked at Marta.

"Maybe I'm losing it, but I just started to get the willies, hearing things," Marta said. "I know I was driving Louis crazy, tagging after him."

"Oh, I understand, dear," Mary said. "These two, off on their adventures, who knows where. We have seventy acres out back and that butts onto somebody else's hundred. You're lucky you have Louis's big dog. I've been telling Clair we need another dog, but he's still grieving for Lady, our dear old beagle, twenty years later."

Clair smiled. "Which is a respectable mourning period for a good dog," he said.

He glanced at Marta, who had gone somber, perhaps thinking of Nigel, duct-taped to a chair.

"Jack, are you eating?" Mary said.

"Thanks, but I'm dining with my girls," I said.

I drank more of the Ballantine, said I really should be going—just wanted to say hi. Marta mustered a disappointed smile as Mary told me to give Sophie a big hug for her and an extra good-night kiss. I turned and stepped outside.

Listened. Heard Clair say something about potatoes. I went down the steps, walked to the Audi, felt the hood. It was cold. Marta had been visiting a while. I walked to the back of the car, reached for the latch. The hatch popped open. With a glance at the door, I lifted the door, leaned in and pulled the cargo lid.

It was unlocked. The compartment was empty.

"If you need a loan, just say so," Marta said, standing ten feet behind me, in the dooryard.

"I didn't hear you," I said.

"Hey, I can see how you'd be curious."

"Like to know what's being brought into my backyard."

She was beside me now, sidling up. There was something physically familiar about her, like she wanted to be close to get you under her control.

"It's not your backyard," Marta said.

"Close enough," I said. "My pony, my daughter, my wife."

"I think Roxanne and I, we could be friends. Why not you and me?"

"Nothing personal. You're just a very unknown quantity with a disturbing back story."

She smiled, exhaled into the air, her breath turning to vapor in the cold air.

"I Googled you," she said. "It's a trail of bodies in your stories. So don't get all sanctimonious on me, Jack McMorrow."

I turned to look at her. She was pretty and hard, like a jewel.

"Where's the money now?" I said.

"I put it in the bank. A savings account. Two percent."

I laughed.

"Because somebody's coming for it?"

"Because it made me nervous, all that cash. And you know what?"

"What?" I said.

"If I told you where it was, I'd have to kill you."

I didn't answer.

"It's a joke, Jack," Marta said.

"I know jokes," I said.

"Tell me one."

"Knock, knock."

"Who's there?"

"On the run from," I said.

"On the run from who?"

"Russians? Cops? Maybe both. I haven't figured it out."

She smiled.

"Good one," she said. She raised the glass of wine to her lips. I drank from the can of Ballantine. The night was suddenly very quiet, the air chill.

"I'm a survivor, Jack. It's what I do."

"Nice work if you can get it."

"It's not by choice," Marta said. "My parents, my uncle. Nigel, the way he turned out to be. I didn't ask for any of that, but I play the cards I'm given."

"Evidently," I said.

She tipped the glass up and drained the wine like it was vodka and we were in her old country. She moved a step closer and our eyes locked.

"I like you, Jack," she said, "so I'm going to tell you this. This is my big chance, to start my own life. So I get that you don't like me. Whatever. But don't get in my way. I guarantee it wouldn't end well."

With that she turned and walked away. The real Marta Kovac.

25

When I got back to the house, they'd started without me—homemade vegetable soup and a baguette.

"We were hungry," Sophie said. "You were dawdling." She lifted her spoon to her mouth and slurped.

"Sophie," Roxanne said. "That's bad manners."

Sophie took a silent sip, swallowed, and said, "Do you think Louis and Marta will get married?"

"Depends on if they fall in love," I said.

"How will they know?" Sophie said.

"They'll know if one day they realize there's nobody else on the entire planet Earth they want to be with," Roxanne said.

"Like you and Daddy?"

"Yes," I said.

"But what if the other person doesn't love you back?"

Then somebody ties you to a chair and cuts you with a knife, I thought, and your girlfriend takes off with the money.

"You find somebody else," I said.

After dinner was tub time. The cookies were in the oven, and Roxanne called down for me to check them. I did, decided they looked done. I took out the cookie sheet and laid it on top of the stove, took a cookie from the center, and blew on it to help it cool. I poured a glass of milk and went to the study and opened my laptop. I typed in the search box: "Who hunts for international fugitives in the US?"

The list filtered in. At the top: US Marshals Service.

I scrolled and read. But did they hunt for suspects? Persons of interest? Missing witnesses? What was Marta, anyway?

As Sophie clattered down the stairs, I closed the browser. She came into the study in her zebra-print pajamas and said, "How are they?"

I took a bite.

"Delicious. Best ever."

She said, "Don't eat any more." Ran to the kitchen, where she was rummaging through the drawer of bags and wrappers when Roxanne came down to help. The cookies went on a plate, two saved out. Sophie ate hers with milk, too, said she was going upstairs to read her book. *Pippi Longstocking.*

I had a smart daughter. Took after her mother.

After five minutes, Roxanne came into the study with her rationed cookie and a mug of coffee for her, tea for me. She put the mug down on the edge of my desk and sat down on the couch. Taking a bite, she sipped the coffee and chewed.

"Marta is at the Varneys'," I said. "She said Louis's place was giving her the willies. The woods, the dark."

"The dark house and dark Louis," Roxanne said.

She took a bite of cookie, took another sip of coffee. There was melted chocolate on her lip.

"Where's he?" she said.

"At the compound? He's not there. And the money isn't in her car."

"Where do you think she put it?"

"Told me she put it in the bank. But hidden in the woods would be my guess. Where she can get it fast."

Roxanne sipped and then said, "Does that mean she thinks somebody is coming for it?"

I shrugged. "I don't know. She told me she's a survivor, that this is her big chance for a new life. She warned me not to get in her way."

Roxanne finished her cookie, washed it down with coffee.

"Too late," she said, and she turned and went back upstairs to Sophie.

I went outside and got the Glock from the truck, the magazines, too. I was strapping the holster on when I heard a *swoosh* of a branch behind me, the thump of falling snow. I whirled, hand on the gun butt. Clair was standing there in the spruces to the side of the dooryard, the bough he'd plucked still swaying.

"We on red alert?" he said.

"More like yellow," I said.

"Who? The street kids from Riverport?"

"Your houseguest. She bugs me. Something about her."

"Serious bugging, a Glock forty."

"Marta's serious," I said.

I told her what she'd said about not getting in her way, the money gone from the back of the car. Clair had no comment, so we just stood in the cold, stared up at the sky. The clouds had thinned and Venus was flickering like a candle behind a gauzy curtain.

Still looking up, I said, "You ought to be honest with Louis. His girlfriend is trouble. Have you talked to him?"

"A couple of hours ago."

"And?"

"He just said she was getting cabin fever."

"Could have gone to New York or Chicago or LA," I said. "She has a couple of million bucks."

Clair didn't answer. We stood and stared skyward for another minute. Finally he said, in a quiet voice, "You have to remember, he's a Marine. He'd die for me."

"And you have to remember, last time she left someplace in a hurry, somebody was taped to a chair with his blood draining out onto the floor."

Clair took a deep breath, touched the bill of his John Deere hat, and left the way he'd come.

Roxanne was in bed, Sophie in the middle, snoring softly. I crossed the room, put the Glock on the top shelf in the closet. Roxanne watched me over her book, then looked back down. I sat on the edge of the bed, pulled my shirt over my head, unlaced my boots, and took off my jeans and socks. Then I slid under the covers, felt Sophie's skinny arms, her feet coming to my thighs. I was listening to her breathing when I fell asleep.

I woke up to the tire drum of a passing car, headed east. I looked at my watch. It was 4:08. Early even for the locals.

The regulars began at a little after 4:30. A guy down the road who drove a milk truck, picked his rig up in Albion at 5:00. A couple who worked at the hospital in Riverport. Every other week, three twelves, six to six. A kid who was a welder at Bath Iron Works and drove a big Chevy pickup with loud exhaust, 4:48 every morning. You could set your watch.

And then the Dump Road rush hour was over. I listened to Sophie breathing, Roxanne turning over, easing back to sleep. Sophie kicked me in the hip, said something in her sleep, and then she was quiet.

I was starting to doze off when I heard it. A car or truck rolling slowly past the house, engine idling. And then it stopped, the motor purring softly. I was awake now, heard another vehicle roll up. It stopped. The motor idled.

I got up and pulled on my jeans and shirt and socks, went to the closet and slipped the Glock off the shelf. I padded past the bed, reached down and snagged my boots. I put the boots and gun on in the kitchen, grabbed a black jacket and knit hat off the hooks, and eased out of the door and through the shed.

The wooden door creaked on its rollers. I stepped outside and the snow crunched under my boot. I froze. I waited for my eyes and ears to adjust.

The sound of idling vehicles was coming from somewhere between my place and Clair's. I walked down the drive and then cut in along the line of spruce and fir. Eased up to the edge of the road and looked right.

There were two of them, dark SUVs parked back to back, lights out. I took a step, then another, creeping toward them against the black backdrop of the trees. There was movement and I froze. Peered into the darkness. There were two figures in the closest SUV, unknown number in the other. Gun held low against my leg, I was about to take another step when two doors popped open. The rear vehicle. Two more, the one in front.

Four figures materialized, equipment creaking and clinking.

Cops.

I slipped the gun back under my jacket.

They gathered in a clump and then one of them said, "Let's go," and they did, walking two by two toward Clair's house. I heard the snap of a slide, a cartridge being dropped into a chamber. They receded into the darkness and I followed slowly, passing the still-idling SUVs, hearing the soft hiss of police radios.

And then there was the sound of boots running on snow-covered pavement, pounding on a door.

"US marshals," a man's voice shouted. "Open the door."

Marta.

They called twice more and then there were voices, lower. I heard Clair say, "Do what you have to do," and then they were inside. I walked slowly along the edge of the trees, saw one of them posted out front, the other presumably watching the back in case Marta went out a window.

They were too late. Marta had left at 4:08.

A sound behind me. I turned as a flashlight beam blinded me, a guy said, "Hands on top of your head."

The cop from the rear of the house had circled back.

I put my hands on my head, said, "I'm a neighbor. I came out to see what was going on."

He was a wiry guy with a glint in his eyes that said he loved the chase. His partner approached, too, gun out, pointed at my chest. They both had on flak vests with U.S. MARSHAL in white letters. The first guy said, "Keep your hands right there, sir," and he reached in and patted me down.

He ripped my jacket open and yanked out the Glock.

"You expecting trouble?" the other marshal said.

"If it comes, it's usually about this time," I said.

"What's your name?"

I told them. If it rang a bell, they didn't let on.

"Where do you live?" the second cop said. He was older, the spokesman.

I told him that, too. Said my wife and daughter were asleep in the house.

"What's her name?"

"Roxanne."

"Your daughter?"

"Sophie."

"How long have you lived here?"

"About fifteen years."

"So you know your neighbor, Mr. Varney?"

"Oh, yeah."

"Know a woman named Marta Kovac?"

"Yes," I said, "but not as well."

26

We stood with them in Clair's kitchen: me, Clair, and Mary. He was dressed. She was in pajamas and slippers and a pale blue fleece jacket. The other cops had US MARSHAL on the backs of their jackets in big letters, too. In the cozy kitchen, it seemed like overkill.

One of them was a woman—Latina, short hair, strong like she did CrossFit. Her name was Ruiz and she was a deputy US marshal in charge of this fugitive task force team, she said. She had a phone in her hand, and she asked if we minded if she recorded the conversation.

We shook our heads.

"Marta Kovac was here at the residence," she said.

"Yes," Clair said.

"When did you last see her?"

"When we went to bed. Around ten."

"Did you hear her leave the house?"

I looked at Clair. He could hear a crow's wing flap, a fox yipping on the ridge a mile away, a hummingbird approaching the feeder.

"No," he said.

"But she had a vehicle?"

"Yes."

"Where was it parked?"

"Behind the house."

"Could you describe the vehicle for us, Mr. Varney."

"An orangish, brownish SUV sort of thing," Clair said. "Foreign, I think, but maybe not. They all kind of look the same."

"You don't know the make or model? The plate number?"

He shook his head.

"How do you know Ms. Kovac?" Ruiz said.

"Met her a couple of times. She's an old friend of a friend of ours. Louis Longfellow. He lives in Sanctuary. That's about twenty miles south of here. Just east of Union."

"An old friend, but you only met her twice?"

"She's his friend, not mine. From high school. She just came up to visit us here."

"Why?"

"She said the woods where Louis lives were making her nervous. She's a city girl, was my impression."

Ruiz looked to me.

"When did you first see her?"

"A couple of days ago," I said.

"Did she tell you where she was living before she came to Maine?"

"Some island in the Caribbean. I didn't catch the name. Didn't mean anything to me. She said her boyfriend was killed in a home invasion."

They exchanged glances.

"Did she say where she might go from here?"

Clair shook his head. Ruiz looked at me and I shook my head, too. Mary said, "Are you sure you don't want coffee? It's no trouble."

Ruiz declined for the team. And then she asked Clair, "Was Ms. Kovac carrying anything? On her person or in the vehicle?"

"Like what?" Clair said.

"Let's say something like a sizable amount of cash."

Clair glanced at me, shrugged.

"Not on her person, that I could tell. She was pretty slim, you could see that. You know how they wear those legging things and tight tops now. I never was in her car, so I can't say."

Ruiz looked at me. The other three did, too.

"She had a small bag when we saw her at Louis's place," I said. "I assumed it was her clothes."

Ruiz nodded to the kid and he took my gun from his jacket pocket and handed it to me, butt first. Then he handed me the magazine. Ruiz reached in her back pocket, took out a couple of cards, and handed them to both of us. They had her name and contacts and the Marshals Service seal.

"If you think of where she may have gone," she said.

"What's she supposed to have done?" I said.

"Let's just say that people down in the Caribbean want to talk to her. She was at the scene of a crime and fled before she could be questioned."

"A person of interest, then," I said.

"Yes. A person of a lot of interest," Ruiz said. "Or we wouldn't be here."

They left with much clomping of boots and creaking of equipment.

Mary said, "Marta seems like a nice girl. I hope she hasn't gotten in with the wrong crowd." And then she said she was going back to bed, and did.

I looked at Clair.

"It's an Audi Q7 with Vermont plates," I said.

"Right," he said.

"As of a couple of days ago, she had a couple of million in cash in the back."

"Yup."

"Some of the time she was packing a handgun."

"Some of the time," Clair said.

I waited.

"What can I say?" he said. "Louis asked me to look out for her."

I was up when Sophie came scampering down the stairs.

"Morning, sweetness," I said, but she ran past me to the kitchen counter and hoisted herself up.

"They're still there," she said, looking at the platter of cookies.

"Where did you think they would go?"

"I thought you'd eat them," Sophie said. "Where did you go? I heard you go outside in the middle of the night."

"Actually, it was morning."

"Where did you go?"

"There were some people outside I needed to talk to."

"Who were they?"

"Just some police officers," I said.

"What did they want?" Sophie said.

"They were looking for somebody."

"Did they find him?"

"No," I said. "They didn't."

"Is he hiding in the woods?"

"No," I said.

"How do you know?"

"I checked," I said. "Don't you worry."

Roxanne came down a minute later and started the coffee. Watching her move—nightshirt, black Patagonia, bare feet—made me feel human again. I made Sophie two pieces of peanut-butter toast. Cut up a banana and arranged the slices around the edge of the plate. She picked up a slice of toast and licked at the peanut butter. Moved her chair so she could see the cookies, then looked at me.

"I won't eat them," I said.

I had another cup of tea. Roxanne drank her coffee and looked at the news on her laptop. I'd read the *Riverport Broadcast*, the front-page story about Teak's first court appearance that morning at ten. There was a blurry photo of him with his long hair disheveled, standing on a downtown street. I turned the paper over because of Sophie, but she didn't seem to notice the newspaper at all.

She snatched a slice of banana and ate it, chomped a piece of toast. Then she slid down and ran for the stairs. Roxanne came over to the table and sat.

"Well?" she said.

"US marshals," I said. "Looking for Marta."

"Did they find her?"

"She'd left."

"At what time?"

"A few minutes after four."

Roxanne sipped her coffee, closed her laptop, and said, "Where are they now?"

"I don't know. Tracking down the next lead? Trying to locate her car?"

"Where is she?"

"No idea. Gone."

Roxanne said, "When I was a kid we played hide-and-seek. I always waited for the seeker to search a place and when they'd moved on, that's where I'd hide."

I smiled.

"You'd make a good fugitive."

She drank some coffee, reached over and picked a banana slice off of Sophie's plate. Ate it and took another. Ate that one, too.

"Where are you going today?" she said.

"Back up to Riverport. A few stops for this story."

"We'll be home at three-thirty," Roxanne said.

"I'll be here," I said.

We left together at 7:25, Roxanne's Subaru in the lead, Sophie in the backseat. It was crisp and dry, full sun from the eastern sky, snow glittering in the trees. At the main road, they turned right. I beeped and Sophie turned around and waved. With a pang I went left.

Hide-and-seek.

I drove west to Unity, caught the Riverport Road, joined a line of cars trailing a slow-moving pickup. I pictured an old couple headed up to Riverport to do some shopping. No hurry. Dunkin'. Walmart. Home Department and home.

The lucky ones.

Even at this speed I'd be there by 8:45. I figured I'd go to the arraignment early, get the lay of the land, snag his court-appointed lawyer for comment. Still a half-hour to kill.

I drove past fields, woods, frozen bogs with black streams showing like giant snakes. Muskrats and beavers holed up for the winter. Then the truck-stop fringes of Riverport began to show, and I took the first exit and a left, headed up the south end of Main Street. There were gas stations, used-car lots, storefront businesses, some still surviving, some with windows boarded up like coffins. I passed the city's only casino, drove another mile and slowed, watched the street numbers dwindle, waited for the sign for River City Comic Cave. Spotted it, hand-painted and peeling, and pulled over.

I parked across the street, got out, and crossed to the door. There were superheroes arranged in the window—faded posters, dusty action figures frozen in midflight. I tried the door and it was locked. I cupped my hands around my temples, felt the bruise from Mutt and friends, peered in.

Someone was moving, toward the back. I knocked on the glass. The figure disappeared. I knocked again, louder. I heard a man's voice, then the figure reappeared and he started toward me.

From the other side of the door he said, "Fifteen minutes."

I held up my *New York Times* ID like a badge.

He flipped the deadbolt, then turned his back and walked away. I opened the door and a bell jingled over my head. I stepped in and it smelled musty, like a box full of damp books.

By the time I got to him he was standing behind a tall counter like Scrooge in the counting house. He was sixty, maybe, big but chubby, wearing a T-shirt with a faded image of Captain America. His khaki trousers were cinched tight just underneath a roll of flab. His hair was thinning and streaked with gray, pulled back into a ponytail. He had both hands on the counter as he said, "I figured one of you would find me eventually."

I introduced myself.

"Thought you were a cop."

"Common mistake," I said. "What's your name?"

He hesitated.

"Reggie," he said.

"Reggie what?"

"Just Reggie."

"Like Madonna?" I said.

"And Bono," he said.

I took out my notebook. Wrote "Reggie" in big letters and looked up and said, "So you know him."

He nodded.

"A frequent customer?"

"Only shop in town. People go to the Internet now, but you don't get the same—"

He gestured toward the poster-covered walls. Wonder Woman was soaring just behind his head.

"Atmosphere?" I said.

"Community," he said.

"Right."

I wrote that down. *Community.*

"Teak reads all of this?"

"Devours it. Thor, Superman, Spider-Man, Green Lantern, Captain America, Flash, Wonder Woman, Plastic Man. Teak's very knowledgeable."

"I'm sure," I said. "What's Hakata?"

"That's his own superhero. The one he invented. Hakata, the Finnish god warrior."

"Why Finnish?"

Reggie shrugged. "Same as why Thor? A lot of this is based on mythology. When I met him he already had done all this research on

Finland, had a whole world all figured out. All these Finnish gods, and they come back to save us."

"And Hakata is one of them?"

"Right. Wears this black hood and mask. Red H on a chain around his neck. Carries an ax with special powers. Kind of like Thor's hammer. Sent to Earth to save us from the forces of evil."

I was writing. He waited, then said, "You know he's nuts."

"I'm aware of his illness."

"Nothing against it. We're all crazy in our own way," he said.

"So what does Hakata do?" I said, steering him back.

"Fights demons, enemy kings. Teak's thing is that the evildoers can inhabit anyone's body. So Hakata is always trying to sniff out who's real and who's an evil creature in a person's body. Hakata's ax has the power to detect an impostor."

"And then he kills them."

"About the only thing you can do with an ax," Reggie said.

He nodded to the wall of comics. "It's all allegory, you know. I mean, the Bible isn't literally true, but it still sets out a code of behavior."

I looked at them. "But he believes all of this was real."

"Pretty much. Especially when he's, you know—" He twirled his finger beside his ear.

"And how often is that?"

"Not all the time. Not even most of the time. He goes seriously off his rocker every two or three months. He told me the meds make him feel like a zombie and he had too much to do. I guess the lady at the shelter had to keep on him to take his pills. So I started nagging him, too. If he came in and he seemed all agitated."

"Was he violent at those times?"

"Not exactly; not in here. Sometimes kind of manic, talking about Hakata, and that he had a mission to go on. Other times he was just real quiet, but you could tell stuff was whirling around inside his head. That was the only time he seemed scary. Because even though you didn't know what he was thinking, you knew it was some crazy shit."

Reggie reached under the counter like this was a holdup and he was grabbing for a gun. He came up with a stack of papers, laid it on the counter. There was a handwritten title page, HAKATA, SON OF THE THUNDER GOD. Below the title was a crudely drawn picture of a guy with a hood and mask and the red H on his chest.

The outfit from the store.

"Like I said, I figured somebody would show up."

"I'd love copies of any of this," I said.

"Sure," he said. "From what I saw on TV, he's not getting out anytime soon."

"Probably not. Cops been in?"

"No, you're the first. But I'm telling you what I'll tell them."

The guy motioned to the walls, the covers, then pointed to the picture of Hakata with his ax.

"You know what they're doing in all of these?" Reggie said.

"What?" I said.

"Good," he said. "Superheroes save people. Cities. Whole planets. They don't hurt anybody, unless that being is evil. There's a strict code of conduct. Morals."

"Teak thought Lindy Hines wasn't really Lindy Hines?"

"It's the only explanation I can think of. I mean, when Teak is feeling okay, he'd help an old lady cross the street. He'd carry somebody's groceries to the car."

I nodded, wrote that down.

"Funny thing is, he'd come in here, me stuck behind this counter, captive audience. You get to know a guy. Between us, it really kills him, being sick. Being on the street, not being able to support his family."

"Yeah. I met some of them."

"Down East. Fishermen, right?"

"His dad was a lobsterman."

"Right. Well, I'm no shrink, but I think that's what Teak's all about. When Teak's down, he feels like he's failed his kid, his mom and dad and brother, his girlfriend. Tears him up."

"He told you this."

"Right. So he'd have to be really off his rocker to kill somebody like that. I mean, way beyond anything I ever saw. He'd come in, talking about Hakata—how he'd been to his castle and Hakata had given him his orders. I mean, Okay, Teak. Whatever you say."

"Uh-huh."

"Another thing," Reggie said.

He tapped the counter with his forefinger.

"Teak or Hakata—they wouldn't hit somebody from behind. They'd challenge them, face-to-face. Mano a mano."

"Right," I said.

"All this stuff is very chivalric. Honor is very important. Integrity."

"Got it."

"So if Teak thought somebody was really sent here to do evil, he'd say it to their face. Challenge them to battle. The Teak I know wouldn't sucker-punch anybody. No way."

"Or ax them from behind."

"Can't believe it. I mean, he has a tattoo. *W-W-H-D*. And a question mark. It's on the inside of his left arm, up high."

"What would—?"

"Hakata do. Thing is, if it was an evil god inside her body, he'd challenge it to do battle and defeat it. Hakata, and Teak, they don't need to sneak up on anybody. It's beneath them."

The door rattled open and the bell jingled. I looked over my shoulder and saw a young guy start to sift through the stacks in a bin. I turned back.

"How much is this pile here?"

"These aren't much. All beat-up. How 'bout thirty bucks."

"How 'bout a few pages of *Hakata*? Including the cover."

He considered it.

"Will I get them back?"

"Sure."

After the story was out and nobody else had it. The cover was gold.

"Then how 'bout another fifty, like a deposit."

"Deal," I said. I took bills out of my pocket, handed them over. He took a roll of cash out of his pocket, added mine.

I turned to the door, the papers under my arm, then turned back.

"What's *Hakata* mean anyway?" I said. "In Finnish. Someone told me it was 'ax.' "

"Close but not quite. It means 'hack,' " he said. "Like it sounds. Hacking away at something."

"This was just one big swing."

"And Teak is one strong son of a bitch," Reggie said. "That lady, she didn't have a chance."

"No," I said. "Not a fair fight. Not a fight at all."

27

The hearing was at the Penobscot County Judicial Center, a new complex downtown on Exchange Street a couple of blocks from the river. I parked and went in the front doors, stopped for the deputy just inside. I told her who I was and what I was there for. She directed me to the courtroom on the second floor, and I proceeded through the metal detector, waited while other deputies gave me the electronic pat-down. The corridor outside the courtroom was filled with cops and lawyers and family members hoping to bail somebody, or at least wave from the front row.

I stood and surveyed the group, listened to their murmuring. There were stories here, I knew, but I was only after one. I walked inside, asked a court deputy, an older man with a hearing aid, if the hearing for Teak Barney was still on. He said it was, as far as he knew. I asked if Teak would appear or be arraigned by video, and the deputy gave me an inspecting look and then a shrug that said he knew but wouldn't say. I turned away.

The courtroom was all blond wood and blue carpet. The seats were partly filled, tattered people waiting to find a way out of some sort of scrape. Fancy building, same scuffed-up lives.

I found a seat in the front row, settled in. An assistant district attorney, a young guy in a tight dark suit, was reciting the charges against a scraggly-haired kid in an orange jumpsuit. Aggravated DWI, failure to stop for a police officer, driving to endanger, driving after suspension, speeding thirty over.

All a good idea at the time.

The judge, a brisk woman with silver hair and an efficient manner, set bail at $1,000 cash, which might as well have been a million. The deputy led the kid away and a bailiff came over to the bench and bent down and whispered something to the judge. She said, "Okay," and the ADA picked up her folders and made way for a woman in a gray suit.

I figured her for an assistant attorney general up from Augusta, called in for the homicide. Her name was Wagner: fifty, blonde hair, horn-rimmed glasses, all business. When she turned to the rear of the court, I did, too, saw Bates and Tingley, both in their courtroom outfits: gray slacks, blue blazers, blue shirts. They walked up to the front of the room and stepped through the gate, took their place by the prosecutor.

They were followed by the defense lawyer for the day, a schlumpy-looking guy wearing a tan sport coat, a black shirt, and purple floral tie. Maybe it was a look. Maybe he was color-blind. Maybe the judge would feel sorry for him and cut Teak a deal.

He put a briefcase on the defense desk, took a folder from the briefcase. The judge nodded to the bailiff, who nodded to the deputy, who opened a blue door to the far right of the bench.

And Teak stepped in.

He was wearing an orange jumpsuit. His hands were cuffed to a belt around his waist and shackles jingled at his ankles. There were deputies on either side of him. He looked around the room and smiled.

It was a benevolent sort of gaze, like a king surveying his assembled subjects from the balcony of his castle. The deputies gave a pull and led him to the defense desk, where the schlumpy lawyer nodded and pointed to the place beside him. Teak stood at attention and smiled at the judge.

A deputy said "All rise," and I heard a rustle behind me as the group reluctantly stood.

"Are we ready?" the judge asked the lawyers.

"I am ready, m'lady," Teak said. And smiled.

The judge glanced at him, said, "Good, Mr. Barney. Then let's begin by reading the charge, the reason you're here."

She picked up an open folder and said. "Mr. Barney, you are charged with homicide, namely causing the death of one Lindy Hines, on Dec. 6, in the city of—"

"That was the name she had taken here on your planet but she was not of Earth, m'lady," Teak said. He spoke in a radio voice with a sort of ye olde English accent, like somebody in an old movie about knights and damsels.

"Mr. Barney, you will have an opportunity to speak but—" the judge said.

"She was sent here by Perkele. He turned her into a *piru*, m'lady. A demon. The *piru*, they can take over the body of a mere mortal person. Like it's nothing. You don't know, m'lady, the *piru*, they're walking the streets of your cities and towns. They're like invisible to you because—"

The defense lawyer leaned over and grabbed Teak by the arm, muttered, "Not now."

"Mr. Barney," the judge said, louder but still in control. "You will have a chance to present your side of this. Now is not the time, sir."

"I'm sorry, m'lady," Teak said. "I do not know all of your earthly rules. When Ukko asked me to help him, he said there would be times when I would be tangled up in earthling customs. I understand."

There was a twitter of laughter in the courtroom. Somebody behind me said, "He's fucking whacked."

"Mr. Graves," the judge said, "please control your client, or we'll have to do this by video."

The lawyer leaned closer to Teak and whispered something. Teak nodded, then looked back to the judge.

"You remind me of Ku, m'lady. The goddess of the moon."

There was louder laughter. Teak smiled, shook his head. "If they knew Ku," he said, "they would not laugh easily. She can summon Akka and she has unlimited power."

The judge slammed her gavel down, said, "That's it, sir. It's your turn to listen. Can you do that?"

Teak made a broad sweeping bow, like one of the Three Musketeers.

"Yes, m'lady. I'll listen. It could be interesting, the goings-on in your humble court."

The gavel slammed down again and the judge said, "Last warning, Mr. Barney. If you can't sit down and shut up, we'll do this by video from the jail."

Teak gave the regal smile again, looked around the courtroom, then raised his arms until the chains at his waist stopped him. "Remember," he said. "Gods walk among us."

People snickered and giggled.

I quickly scribbled on a piece of notebook paper, ground the pen into the lines over and over. Teak was turning to see the back of the courtroom and the deputies moved a step closer. As he started to turn back to the judge, I held up my notebook. He stopped short, looked at the notebook, then at me.

"Hakata," he said, reading the name.

Then he nodded, gave me some sort of salute, a clenched fist held out to the side. The judge looked my way just as I slipped the notebook back onto my lap.

"We will meet again, my friend," Teak said, in a deep, wise voice.

"Mr. Barney," the judge said. "If you could give us just some of your attention."

He turned to her. The lawyers stood and waited, glancing at Teak, waiting for the next eruption. The judge started again, reading the part about Teak causing Lindy Hines's death. Teak nodded, like the judge had it about right. She asked the lawyers if they had anything to say, and Graves said he hadn't had the opportunity to talk to his client. Wagner, the prosecutor, said the State had nothing more. Teak smiled at her, too.

The judge said Mr. Barney would be held without bail. He nodded gratefully, like she'd conferred an honor, said, "Very wise, m'lady."

She took a quick exasperated breath, then asked Teak if he understood, and he said, "Yes, m'lady. And I thank you for your hospitality. When someone visited from another galaxy or dimension, Ukko always—"

She pounded the gavel as the deputies swooped in, pulled Teak out from behind the table, and started leading him toward the blue door. Halfway there, he turned, searched for me in the crowd, and our eyes met.

And then he was gone.

I felt a tap on my back.

Tingley.

"McMorrow," he said. "The lobby."

He turned and I followed, eyed by defendants and their lawyers, the ones in jackets and ties. When I pushed through the door, he and Bates were standing off to the side. They glared. I walked over to them, holding my notebook.

Tingley said, "What the fuck?"

"I don't think they allow that sort of language here," I said. "Not from the cops."

"Frig that," Tingley said. "If I want to—"

"What did you say to him?" Bates said.

"None of your business," I said.

"It's my business if you're tampering with the defendant in a homicide," she said.

"I think he's pretty tamper-proof."

"You could tamper yourself all the way to a jail cell, McMorrow," Tingley said.

"I'm just trying to figure the guy out."

"What'd you say?" Bates said.

"Just let him know I want to talk to him."

"Wait for the trial," Bates said.

"Yeah, right," I said.

"Guy's whacked, kills somebody in cold blood in front of twenty witnesses," Bates said. "I don't see much to talk about."

"Why you're a detective and not an editor."

"We'd prefer that this trial not be moved because of some inflammatory jailhouse interview," Tingley said.

"Not my problem," I said. "With all due respect."

"It will be your problem, if the judge—"

He paused and pulled his radio out of a holder on his belt. Tingley did, too. They held them up to their ears.

"Holy shit," Tingley said.

"My God," Bates said. "The son?"

"Whose son?" I said.

"Damn," Tingley said.

They wheeled around and started for the door in that accelerating lumber that cops have when they're in a big hurry but don't want anyone to know. I was right behind them, out the door, across the parking lot, and onto the street. They had blue lights flashing.

I stayed with them through the downtown, weaving through traffic, running red lights.

All the way to Orrington.

28

There were three sheriff's cruisers out front, crime-scene tape across the entire front yard of the house. An ambulance idled behind the cruisers and cops milled around the front door. The door was open and I could see Barrett Hines body on the floor, at least his feet.

Bates and Tingley went under the tape but a deputy stopped me. I asked her if the S.O. did homicides and she said no, state police. But S.O. had secured the scene. "How did it come in?" I said.

She hesitated.

She looked around.

"I know Barrett," I said.

"Okay, but you didn't hear this from me."

"Right."

"And it isn't pretty."

"Gunshot?"

She said, "I can't talk to the press."

I smiled, said I understood. I didn't go away.

"This is horrible," I said. "His mom was the one—"

"I know," the deputy said.

"What, somebody knocked on the front door, when he opened it they popped him?"

The cop looked around.

"Listen, it all has to come from somebody way above my pay grade."

And then she looked around one more time, turned back to me and stabbed her chest with a forefinger.

"My God," I said. "Tell them I think I know what it might have been about."

She looked at me.

"What's your name?"

I told her.

"Will they know who you are?" the deputy said.

"Oh, yeah," I said. "We go way back."

"Stay right here," she said, as if that would be a problem.

I stood in the cold, joined by the reporter from the *Riverport Broadcast*. His name was Trevor something, the same guy from the Home Department scene. He said he had an in with the local cops.

"They give me the releases first," he said. "Doesn't that piss the TV guys off." He grinned, very pleased with himself.

I looked at Barrett's feet, the dutiful son, dead on the floor. Why was this guy grinning? Trying to be tough?

Trevor asked who I wrote for and I told him. He looked at me with a knowing smile, like I'd slept my way to the top. He said, "That's a sweet gig. How could I get to write for the *New York Times*?"

I looked back at him, made sure he was looking me in the eye. "Die and come back to life as a reporter," I said.

He waited for me to smile, but I didn't. We were standing in an awkward silence when Tingley came over, ignored Trevor, and, with a jerk of his head, led me away.

We stood by his car amid the flashing lights, radio chatter, and idling motors. Steam billowed up from car exhaust and it had started to snow, fine flakes falling straight down like frozen drizzle. Tingley wiped snow from his glasses, then said, "Get in."

He sat in the driver's seat. After he cleared away some papers and an iPad, I sat beside him. The car was hot as a sauna, and he said, "Jesus Christ," and flipped the heat and fan off. Wiped his glasses again and put them back on. Looked at me and said, "What?"

"Barrett Hines," I said.

"What about him, other than he's dead?" Tingley said.

"You know he blamed his stepdad for his mom's murder."

"Yeah, you told us that. Seemed like a reach."

"Well, he told me later that his mom knew of some shady financial stuff involving his dad's business. He said Rod made Lindy cheat on taxes, that sort of thing."

"Huh," Tingley said.

"He said, 'I have something on him.' Words to that effect."

"You're saying the stepdad, the guy with the construction company, could have driven over here and stabbed his own stepson in the chest? He goes down and the stepdad gives him another one in the neck?"

I said that's what I believed had happened.

"Jesus, that's cold," Tingley said.

"Worse things are done for money," I said.

"Did Barrett say he was going to confront his stepdad with this information?"

"He was very angry, as you know. It was like this was his secret weapon."

"To do what?"

"Get even, maybe," I said.

Tingley took off his glasses again and reached over my leg to the glove box. He clicked it open and took out a napkin. From Subway. He wiped his glasses and balled the napkin up and stuffed it in a compartment in the console.

"He threatens the stepdad, maybe tries to blackmail him?" Tingley said.

"Rod has some big deal he's trying to finalize. Investors to take his company to the next level, more regional than local. He didn't like me coming around, I'll tell you. Tried to bribe me to kill the story, or at least hold off for a month."

"And you said—"

"No way."

"Good to know you're an equal-opportunity pain in the ass," Tingley said.

He smiled. I smiled back.

"I'll bet you say that to all the reporters," I said.

"No," he said. "I don't."

We sat for a minute while he mulled what I'd said. Finally, he said, "Whole families don't get taken out—not coincidentally."

"No."

"If it hadn't been for the mom, it could have been a lovers' spat. Maybe there was another guy, somebody got jilted when these two got married."

"Maybe the mom's murder was cover," I said.

We both thought about it, then shook our heads in unison.

"His husband found him?" I said.

"Yeah. Barrett Hines doesn't show up for school and doesn't call in, which is something he never does—loves the kids, and they love him. Guy was dependable, responsible, never sick, et cetera, et cetera. The principal can't reach him, she calls the husband—his name's Travis Chenard—who's at work. Some computer thing. Travis calls and gets no answer and hurries home. You know, thinking Barrett had slipped in the shower and broke his leg or something."

"And found this," I said.

"Yeah," Tingley said.

"A lot of blood."

"Again."

"Mother and son. Why we're here at all. This one's actually a State Police case."

"Murdered two days apart," I said. "What are the chances?"

Tingley looked at me. "Of lightning striking twice? Slim to none."

"Where's Travis now?"

"Upstairs. There's like an office. Talking to Bates."

"How long had Barrett been dead?"

"Off the record? Totally?"

"Yes."

"Not long. Blood was still sticky. I mean, an hour and a half, maybe. Travis said he left at 4:45 because he had some project deadline today. His whole team went in early."

"You think it could have been him?"

Tingley looked at me.

"This is all way off the record," he said. "Anything official, you have to get from SP."

"Right," I said.

"Guy's totally devastated. Stuck in the chest, the neck. and all that. A wicked mess. He freaked. Still may need to go to the hospital, get sedated."

"So no."

"Nobody's in or out this soon, but I'd say he's a very strong no."

We sat. The snow melted on contact with the still-warm windshield.

"Four forty-five," I said. "Still dark."

"Very," Tingley said.

"They'll be doing the door-to-door."

"Already started."

"Even if it was dark, maybe somebody saw something," I said. "A car parked."

Tingley looked at me. "Do I tell you how to write a story?"

"No," I said. "I just want this person caught."

"You and me both."

"He seemed like a good guy," I said. "Loved his mother."

"No doubt," Tingley said. "Doesn't keep horrible things from happening. Sometimes I think it increases the odds. The mom's a case in point."

"Yup."

"Even if she did help the husband cook the books."

"Maybe he made her do it. Maybe she was trying to make amends, doing this volunteer thing."

I paused.

"They gonna call him?" I said. "Rod, I mean. Is an estranged spouse considered next of kin?"

He looked at me. His glasses were still fogged up. He swiped them with his forefinger, one lens, then the other.

"Like I said before, McMorrow."

"Who's the lead?"

"Guy named Scalabrini."

"Ah."

"He's the one told me he knows you," Tingley said.

"The Sanctuary arsons," I said. "He wasn't a bad guy."

Pudgy, reddish hair, smarter than he looked, more reasonable than I'd expected. And he knew Louis.

"SP spokesman as usual?"

"He's on his way up. There'll be a press conference."

Waste of time. Trevor and the TV guy asking obvious questions, pretending to be listening intently to the obvious answers.

"You think Barrett could have been blowing smoke?" Tingley said.

"I don't think so," I said.

"But you can't be sure."

"What?" I said. "You think you're the only one who knows bullshit when they hear it?"

29

A State Police crime-scene van rolled up as I walked to my truck. I shot a few photos with my phone: the van, the cops, the tape, the house. Then I got in the truck and watched as evidence techs got out, started unloading equipment. I got back out, took a few more pics, climbed back up and in. A TV car pulled in, a Subaru with the station logo on the doors.

I got on the phone.

Vanessa answered. She listened to my twenty-second version, said, "Five hundred words. When will I have it?"

"Twenty minutes," I said. "I'll text you."

Turned out to be twenty-three. Damned tiny keyboard and my old stiff fingers. Lead was straight news:

> ORRINGTON, MAINE—*The son of a woman murdered in a brutal daytime assault by an ax-wielding assailant was murdered himself two days later when an unknown assailant went to the man's home here before dawn and stabbed him when he answered the door.*
>
> *Barrett Hines, 32, was found in a pool of blood in the entryway of his home by his husband, who had been alerted*

> *when the elementary school teacher didn't show up for school.*
>   *One investigator, asked what the chances were of two members of the same family being targeted in unrelated attacks, said, "Slim to none."*

I followed with a recounting of Lindy's killing, Teak's arrest, a couple of grafs about Teak himself. Known to police. Longtime mainstay of the street community in Riverport, drifted to the city from a small fishing community in Down East Maine after beginning to suffer from mental illness in his teens. Fixated on comic books.

> *Lindy Hines also moved to Bangor from the coast, leaving her home on Mount Desert Island in October partly to be near her son. "I just worked here and she was a tenant, but she was real nice," said the manager of her condo building, Leroy Larkin. "Always had a smile."*

I reread the story, corrected the typos. Couldn't fix the underlying situation: lives ended, horrifically. The world going to hell.

I drove north on the River Road, the Penobscot off through the woods to my left. I thought of watching the eagles through Barrett's window, his big frame, handsome and confident on the outside, inside, seething with anguish and resentment.

And now he was dead, the life drained out of him as he stared at whoever it was who had attacked him. Not because he was an evil alien posing as a high school teacher. Not because he was in the wrong place at the wrong time. Not because the guy in the parking lot walked on by.

Who would have thought that it would be Lindy's murder that would make the most sense?

I left the countryside behind for what we take as civilization. Convenience stores. A chiropractor's office. Fast food and fast coffee. I pulled in to a Dunkin', ordered a tea at the drive-through, had it handed to me by a cheerful young woman with a ring in her eyebrow and another in her nose. For the rest of the world, life went on.

I was driving so I could think, the truck's white-noise rumble the backdrop as I ran through it all. Barrett and Lindy, Rod and Silk. Louis and Marta, Harriet and Teak. The little bastards who smashed up my truck.

Was the world really going to hell, our civilization coming apart? Not entirely, not if I could make some small part of it make sense.

Back in town I circled up by the library, turned, and drove past Lindy Hines's condo building. It was quiet, no clue to the mayhem that had gone on inside. The love-torn super would have had the place cleaned up. With Barrett gone, who would sell it? And where would the money go?

I snaked my way through the downtown, saw the little park on my right, Arthur and Dolph on the bench. They had umbrellas open. I swerved to the curb, shut off the truck, and got out.

Their eyes flashed as they recognized me, then went quickly back to know-nothing mode.

I strode up, said, "Morning, boys."

Dolph looked away. Arthur said, "Hey."

The umbrellas had the University of Maine logo—donations to Loaves & Fishes? The two of them looked like something out of a British sitcom.

"Where's Mutt today?"

They hesitated, then shrugged, first Arthur, then Dolph following his lead.

"How's his hand?" I said.

"Got a cast," Arthur said.

"Good for him. He's lucky he didn't get both hands broken. My friend, he doesn't screw around."

They looked at me, nothing moving but the eyes. The snow ticked on the fabric of the umbrellas.

"Miss H. around?" I said.

"Closed until one," Arthur said. "She's sick."

"That's too bad. Doesn't she have a backup?"

More shrugs.

I started to walk off, then turned back. "Hey, I saw your friend Teak today. In court."

"Huh," Arthur said, brightening. News he could spread on the street.

"I was going to tell Miss H. about it. I know they were close."

"Best buds," Dolph said.

"Really. Miss H. look out for him? Like his mother or something?"

"Miss H. looks out for everybody," Arthur said.

"But Teak needed a little extra?"

"Miss H. kept him from going totally fucking bonkers," Dolph said.

"How'd she do that?"

"Like, if he was giving somebody shit, starting a fight, she'd go, 'Teak, dude. Calm down,' " Arthur said.

"It's like, 'Teak—you take your freakin' pills?' " Dolph said. "She kept some meds in the desk for him."

I looked at him.

"Really. She did that for clients? Like an emergency stash?"

"Just Teak," Dolph said.

"Miss H., she had Teak's back, you know what I'm saying?" Arthur said.

I looked at them, said, "I think she took her eye off the ball."

They shrugged in unison.

"Shit happens," Dolph said.

Arthur nodded, and they got up from the bench and shuffled off, their umbrellas speckled with snow.

The note taped to the inside of the window on the shelter's side door said "Back by 1 p.m." It was a little after eleven. I hesitated, looked around. There was mail sticking out of the box to the right of the door, the envelopes wet on top. I started to stuff them down and out of the weather, looked around, and pulled one out.

It was from some nonprofit, addressed to Harriet. An address had been crossed out and c/o LOAVES & FISHES SHELTER written over it. I looked at the address—49 Swing Street, Riverport—then stuffed it back in with the rest.

My phone showed Swing Street off Hammond, maybe a mile away. I rumbled my way there, past numbered cross streets. Third, Fifth. Swing was two blocks off Seventh. Harriet's house was two blocks up Swing.

It was a small bungalow set on a narrow lot between bigger houses, like it had been slid into place off a truck. There was a tiny deck out front, an American flag beside the front door. There was no garage but there was a driveway. The driveway was full, with three vehicles parked end to end. The van I'd seen at the shelter, closest to the house, then a newish orange Jeep, the kind with the removable top, and a red Mitsubishi sports car. The Mitsubishi had blacked-out windows and an oversize exhaust.

I parked in the street and walked up the drive. As I climbed the front steps, the door banged open and a kid backed out. He was saying, "See ya, Auntie. Thanks."

As he turned I could see him stuffing cash in the front of his jeans. He looked at me and said, "Hey."

I said, "Hi there. Harriet home?"

He was seventeen, eighteen, boy-band cute, his blond-streaked hair flipped up in the front. His jeans were tucked into unlaced boots, and he was wearing a Boston Bruins game jersey with BERGERON on the back.

"Yeah, she's in there with my sister."

I came up the steps and he moved aside, said, "Have a good one," and bounded off the porch and trotted to the Mitsubishi. He climbed in, revved it once, and wheeled backwards into the street and sped off.

As I started for the door a girl appeared. Her back was to me, too, and she was saying, "Auntie, I'll call you. Love you."

When she turned she gave a start, put her hand over her chest, and said, "Oh, you scared me."

She wasn't scared. She was very pretty, though, with long blonde hair and a carefully made-up face, like she was pretending to be a grown-up. Her jacket said RIVERPORT FIELD HOCKEY and NIKKI. Her jeans were strategically shredded up to her thighs.

"Sorry. Looking for Harriet."

"She's here. You work with my aunt?"

"I'm a reporter. She's in a story I'm doing."

"Awesome," she said. "Your story should say Auntie H. is awesome. I mean, she's, like, the greatest person. Do you want to interview me?"

She smiled like it was something she bestowed on boys and men alike, knowing it would make their day.

"Maybe," I said. "Let me get back to you."

Nikki turned back to the open door. "Auntie," she called. "Someone here to see you." Then she turned and gave me another smile and said, "See ya."

She moved by me and I turned to the door, which was still open. There was a shuffle and Harriet appeared. She was holding a paper plate of brownies and she called, "Nikki! You forgot."

Nikki slid out of the Jeep and ran over and up, grabbed the plate, and ran back. Harriet smiled at her, then turned to me.

"Kids," she said, and then, "Mr. McMorrow, what can I do for you?"

She stepped back into the room and I scuffed my boots on the mat and followed.

Harriet was wearing gray warm-up pants, a bulky green sweater, and slippers. She stood in the middle of the room and I said, "Sorry to bother you at home. I saw the note at the shelter. I have to leave town pretty soon, so I thought I'd catch you."

"Oh, that's fine. I'm a little under the weather. Some respiratory thing. You get this stuff in my business. The kids stopped by to check on me."

She sniffled.

"I won't bother you. Just a quick question."

Harriet turned and started scooping stuff off the couch. A bundle of paper towels. A plastic bag overflowing with socks. A pile of men's parkas.

"People drop stuff here all the time, too," she said. "Sit."

I did, taking the place in.

A very small room, very full of stuff. Framed photos of her niece and nephew on the end tables, more on the wall by the door. One was a collage, snapshots overlapping, their tilted faces frozen in mid-smile.

Harriet shoved a pile of sheets and towels off of an easy chair and sat. She looked at me and smiled.

"Your niece and nephew?" I said.

"Yes, Nikki and Shane. He's a senior, Nikki, she's a year younger. They just stopped because they're going on a school trip. Washington, DC. See the museums and the White House and all that."

"Good for them."

"Oh, yeah. They're great kids. I don't have children of my own."

"They seemed very nice. Good-looking, too."

"Oh, yes. My little sister, their mom, was the pretty one. Still is."

"And what were you?"

She wasn't flustered by the question.

"Me? Oh, I guess I was the do-gooder. You know, food baskets at Thanksgiving. Looking in on the old people on the block, see if they needed anything. Did I tell you that we stayed in shelters ourselves when I was young?"

"Yes, you did."

"Yeah, well, when we got on our feet, I felt like I had to pay everything back."

"Good of you," I said. "Most kids wouldn't think of it."

There was an awkward pause, and then I said, "Your niece and nephew—do they live nearby?"

"My sister lives on Fifth. It's, like, two minutes away."

"Nice."

Fifth Street, I thought. What I'd seen was pretty modest. Small houses on postage-stamp lots. Those two, with the cars and looks, must be the cool kids on the block.

"Nancy's divorced. She's a secretary for the DMV. Her second husband, he found another woman, younger by the way, dumped Nancy and the kids and ran off to Florida."

"That's too bad," I said.

"Her first husband—he wasn't much use, either," Harriet said. "Wicked bad drunk. Anyway, I just try to help out. Give them some more family."

"They seem close to you."

"Oh, they are," she said.

Another pause, and I said, "I saw Teak this morning."

That stopped her.

"Oh, my goodness. Did they let him out?"

"No, he was in court. His initial appearance. They read the charges. It's the first thing that happens—in public, I mean."

"Oh, God. It's all so horrible."

"Yeah," I said. "Nothing good about it."

"How was he? In court, I mean. Is he feeling better? Are they giving him his meds? I had to remind him all the time, 'Teak, did you take your pills?' I kept some at the shelter for him. I could tell when he was going off."

"That's good of you, Harriet. So it's more than handing out blankets."

"We like to say we shelter the whole person," Harriet said. "He's a good man. They all are. They're just sick."

She smiled benevolently, the shepherd of a ragged flock.

"So was he okay?" she asked.

"Not really, no. He was pretty out there. Talking his superhero stuff to the judge."

"Oh dear."

"Yeah. But he actually seemed pretty cheerful. I think he truly believes he did the right thing."

Harriet seemed to consider that for a moment.

"That's the thing about Teak," she said. "He really means well. He's always trying to help. Even when we had problems at the shelter with him, it was usually because he was defending someone or taking offense at someone for picking on somebody. A client would swear in front of a child or something, or push their way into line in front of a family."

"But that was when he was doing well?" I said.

"Right."

"And when he wasn't?"

"He usually wouldn't stay. When he was feeling symptoms, he seemed to need to be alone. That's when he'd go to the woods or wherever he was camping out. He'd just take off. Walk for twenty miles."

We sat for a moment. The place smelled of laundry detergent. The donated sheets and towels.

"When he goes off his meds, how long does it take to start to show?"

"Oh, gee. I'm not sure. A couple of days, maybe? Not long. I can tell when he isn't doing well. You can see something in his eyes."

"And the last time you saw him?"

"I've been thinking about that, since it all happened. I mean, I thought he was okay."

"So you actually keep some meds for him at the shelter?"

"Well, yeah. Sometimes he forgets. Or loses track of time."

"Had he forgotten lately?"

"I didn't think so. But it had been two or three days. He was off someplace. Like I said."

I considered it. Teak off by himself, his illness kicking in big-time.

"Funny thing is, he seems to be doing okay now. In court, he seemed pretty pleased with himself, but calm, too. Talking about this Hakata, but he wasn't raving. It was like he wanted to educate the judge on all of it."

"The meds kicking in, maybe," Harriet said. "Or he just got over it. Afterwards it's like he's just floating along."

"How long does that take to happen?"

"Depends," she said. "Sometimes he peaks and just crashes. When he's going on about the Hakata stuff, that's usually on the way up or the way down."

"You know that *Hakata* means 'hack' in Finnish."

"I knew it was 'chop' or something."

"And the ax has special powers."

"Right," she said.

"But I was told that Hakata only fights bad guys. And he does it on the field of honor. Not sneaking up and whacking them."

"In Teak's head, Lindy Hines must have been an evil person or a demon or whatever," Harriet said.

"But had he ever threatened anyone with an ax before, that you know of?"

"No, not the ax. I mean, he would get in people's faces, punch somebody. Once he knocked this guy's teeth out. The guy made an inappropriate comment to a girl."

"But not an ax or a stabbing or a gun?"

"No, nothing like this. It's like something inside him snapped."

I wrote that down, looked around the cramped room with its family pictures and shelter supplies. I felt like there was something just out of reach, but maybe I was mistaken to think Harriet was the one who held the answer. She wasn't a shrink; she just handed out blankets and beef stew.

I glanced at the pictures of the niece and nephew, smiling like they were models on a fashion shoot. And I said, "Speaking of parents and kids—"

Harriet wiped her nose with a tissue that she produced from somewhere in her sleeve, like a magician.

"Barrett Hines, Lindy's son."

"Right. He's good-looking; she showed me a picture."

He's dead," I said.

Harriet's face froze in a weird half-smile.

"What? But that can't be—"

"Somebody knocked on his door early this morning and stabbed him, stuck him in the neck."

"Oh my God," Harriet said, gasping. "Oh my God."

"Yeah. Pretty horrible. His husband found him."

She was looking at me like she was hearing things.

"But he was fine. I talked to him," Harriet said. "Yesterday."

"You did?"

"He called. I said how sorry I was about his mom. He said it hadn't sunk in."

"What did he want?"

"He said his mom had a box of papers from the shelter. They were from when she was helping us out. They were in her car."

"Which he had," I said.

"Yes. He said the police had returned it to him."

She replayed the conversation.

"He said he'd drop the box off. I said, 'Oh, God, don't worry about that—with all you have to deal with.' He said he had to go to town anyway. Talk to a funeral home about a service. I said, 'Really, this is not important.'"

"What was in the carton?" I said.

"Just a lot of paperwork. Forms we have to file with the federal government showing how many clients we've served, what we did for them. Forms for donations, so people can get their deduction. All of our expenses, which we have to declare. It can take longer to fill out the paperwork than it does to actually help people."

"Do you need all that?"

"Not right away," Harriet said. "I mean, it's not like I'm keeping track of all this stuff very well anyway. I said, 'Don't worry about it. Do what you have to do. Think of yourself.'"

She paused.

"She was really close to him—Lindy. I mean, when we met, she said, 'I'm going to have dinner with my son.' She was excited about it. She said one of the good things about moving to Riverport was that she'd see her son more often. I mean, it's like me and Shane and Nikki. It just makes my day, even if it's just for a few minutes."

"I guess having been close to your mom isn't much of a defense when somebody with a knife shows up at your front door."

"But why? And after Lindy?"

She wrung her hands, shook her head.

"That was the whole family," I said. "There's the ex-husband, but he wasn't Barrett's dad. It's like somebody wiped out the last of the Hineses."

She was dabbing the tissue at her lips like she expected tears to run from her mouth.

"What's happening to this world, Mr. McMorrow?"

"Nothing good," I said.

"It's like things don't make sense anymore," Harriet said. "All these shootings—killing people in churches and stores, and that concert in Las Vegas where that guy just mowed people down. And we have Teak doing this awful thing, and he's a nice guy. Otherwise, I mean. Now this, to Lindy's son."

She paused, looked unseeingly at the mounds of clutter, then back at me.

"But if Teak is in jail."

Harriet trailed off, her mind starting down the trail.

"Why would somebody else kill somebody from the same family? Especially if Teak, he didn't really know what he was doing. It's not like he even knew who she was. I mean, who she really was. Not whatever he was thinking she was."

"An alien," I said. "Who had taken over a woman's body."

"Jeezum," Harriet said.

"Yes. Jeezum."

Harriet had her hands clenched on her lap, the tissue protruding from her right fist. She was staring in the direction of the pictures of Shane and Nikki, but seeing nothing.

"I'm sorry to bring bad news," I said.

She looked at me.

"What if . . . ," Harriet began, then faltered. "What if it was the shelter? What if Teak saw Lindy Hines at the admin office somehow? I don't know that he ever went there, but what if he did? And what if somehow that got tangled up in his mind? And then he saw her at Home Department, and all that tangled-up stuff went even more haywire."

"Something did," I said.

"But if she hadn't tried to help us, would she be alive today? And her son. What if . . ."

She trailed off again. I stood.

"They'll figure it out," I said. "You can't just walk up to somebody's front door in Riverport, Maine, and stab them to death and get away with it. They're working their butts off as we speak."

"I hope they find the person," Harriet said. "The homeless population, they'll bear the brunt of this, you know. There's a saying: One goes astray, the rest pay."

Astray? That meant a cow jumping a fence, not someone getting their head split open.

I turned to leave. Harriet got up and followed me, wiping her nose. To the left of the door there was another photo of Nikki and Shane. They were with Harriet at Disney World. Nikki, Shane, Harriet, and Mickey Mouse. Left to right.

I turned back to Harriet and said, "You're the fun aunt."

"I'm the only aunt," she said. "I have no choice."

I smiled, put my hand on the latch of the storm door.

"I'm going to ask Teak if he knew Barrett," I said. "I think he'll tell me. I don't think he really knows how to lie."

She was close beside me. I could smell mint, like toothpaste. She dabbed at her nose with the tissue. Her hands were red and gnarled, like she worked on a farm or a fishing boat. Scrubbing dishes at the shelter.

"How can you talk to him?" she said. "Isn't he in jail?"

"Doesn't matter. They can't hold him incommunicado. It's his decision. Lawyer, when he gets a permanent one, will tell him not to, but I don't think Teak likes being told what to do."

"No," Harriet said.

"Do you want me to say hello for you?"

She didn't answer for a moment, then turned to me.

"Sorry. This cold has me all fogged up. But sure. Tell him Harriet sends her best. Tell him even with all this, I'm still with him. Every step of the way."

30

I drove through the city, the drab streets lined with nondescript houses, boulevards of businesses that were either doomed or deceased. It was all bleak, and I felt my mood plummeting.

I'd seen so much death over the years, people killed for money, for power, for someone else's survival. But it was the random killings, the lives taken for no reason at all, that bothered me most.

We aren't flies to be swatted, mosquitoes to be slapped. We all deserve a fighting chance. Goodness shouldn't be its only reward.

I ran through the conversation, starting with Nikki and Shane, oblivious and spoiled rotten. Life was a party paid for by their maiden aunt, who makes her living helping the least fortunate.

And was generous to a fault. If cleaving somebody's skull didn't bump you out of Harriet's inner circle, what did?

I drove south, past the casino, the used-car lots, the snow plowed into dirty piles. I followed the river south, then turned off. The road passed driveways slashed into the woods, houses huddling in the distance like army camps, everyone hiding behind walls, guns cocked and ready.

And then I swung onto the cul-de-sac, saw that some of the cops had left, but the TV trucks had taken their places. There were only two other houses on the circle and there were reporters at the doors of both of them, a young woman and a young guy holding microphones to the neighbors' faces. *Did you know Barrett Hines? . . . Just to say hello to. . . . Do you know why anyone would want to kill him? . . . No, he seemed like a nice man . . . Talk to him much? No, but him and his friend, they always waved. . . . How does this make you feel? . . . I never thought this would happen here. I guess we'll start locking our doors.*

I parked just past Barrett's house and got out. The door was closed and the ambulance was gone, which meant the body had been hauled off for autopsy. I skirted the crime tape and walked past the front of the house, turned at the other side of the driveway. I was trudging along the path in the snow when Bates and Tingley ducked under the half-open garage door and stepped out.

They looked up and Bates shook her head. I stopped, waited for them to come to me.

"Any comment comes from the spokesman," Bates said. She brushed by. Tingley stopped. We waited for her to get in their car.

"I came to give you something," I said. "About Barrett."

Tingley backtracked, stopped under the eaves of the garage. Brushed snow out of his hair.

"Shoot," he said.

"I was just talking to Harriet, who runs the shelter. She said Barrett called her, said he wanted to bring back a box of stuff. Records that his mom was looking at."

"In the back of the car," Tingley said.

"Right."

"But he never did," I said. "If the stuff's still in the car."

"Okay," Tingley said, waiting for more.

"Seems weird that he'd care about that two days after his mother is murdered. Who cares if there's junk in a car, one that he'll probably never bring himself to drive? Why is he cleaning up loose ends like papers from a place his mother barely worked. Why does he care?"

"I don't know," Bates said. "Trying to stay busy, take his mind off the tragedy or whatever. It happens. I remember telling this guy his wife had been killed in a car accident. What's he do? Doesn't say a word. Just walks over to the woodpile, starts splitting wood. Musta gone through half a cord while I was standing there."

"I still think it's odd," I said.

We stood. It wasn't much of an eave and a puff of wind spattered us with snowflakes. Tingley brushed them off the shoulder of his jacket like dandruff.

"You're right," he said.

"Happens," I said.

"Scalabrini said you're a nuisance but you've got good instincts."

"Should I blush?"

He smiled.

"Okay, one for you, McMorrow," Tingley said. "SP case, like I said, so don't say you heard it from us."

I nodded.

"Heard toxicology came back on our friend Teak," he said.

I waited.

"He'd been taking his meds, all right. Head full of methamphetamine."

"Whoa."

"Yup. Would ramp his symptoms up to a whole new level."

"Would explain why he'd suddenly take an ax to somebody," I said.

"In broad daylight," Tingley said. "In front of the Christmas wreaths."

"Delusions would have been in technicolor."

"I guess. Ever try wrestling with a tweaker?"

As a matter of fact, I had.

"One for you," I said. "Teak's brother Down East, Jason, is a serious meth head. Teak's ex, Tawny, too."

"Would give him access," Tingley said.

"Brother has a new truck. New to him. When I went up there I saw indications of an influx of cash. TV. Furniture."

"Maybe Teak was dealing for him."

I pictured Mutt and friends.

"Or just gave Jason an in, access to a new market?"

We mulled it. The snow fell. At the street, Bates was sitting in the car, bathed in the blue-gray glow from her laptop. She was talking on the phone. I took mine out, searched for effects of meth.

"Delirium, panic, psychosis," I said. "For a guy who already has hallucinations and delusions and is manic."

"Just what the doctor ordered," Tingley said.

Bates flashed the headlights. Tingley gave me a last nod, and a tap on the shoulder. Said, "We'll talk." We were best friends.

I rolled out of the cul-de-sac, the truck rumbling and crunching. They were in the Malibu, Bates on the phone. At the house across the street, an older guy was talking to Trevor from the *News*. The real story wasn't idle chatter from the neighbors.

Teak on meth. He'd be a loaded gun with a hair trigger. Who knows what he would have been seeing as he followed Lindy Hines into the Christmas department. His comic-book world come to life. A middle-aged woman clearly possessed by the devil.

But did a tweaker kill Barrett Hines? Had Teak somehow passed on his delusions to someone over a meth pipe? The mother was the devil. The son was her spawn.

I pulled out onto the main road, running through the other possibilities. Was his stepfather capable of it? Had the police talked to Rod? His ex-wife murdered, saving him a bundle of money, and now his stepson gone. A potential rat erased.

And so it went, out of Orrington and south along the river, which was what they told lost explorers to do. Follow the river and it will lead you out of the wilderness. I sure as hell hoped so.

I tracked the Penobscot to Bucksport, a scrappy little town that had once boasted a paper mill. The mill was closed now and the town was struggling. The word made me think of Barrett—whether he went down right away or grappled. The position of the body would suggest that he'd fallen right over after he got stuck. Were his eyes open, staring at the person who bent down and jabbed his neck? Were his last breaths spent trying to make sense of it all? Or did it make perfect sense to him, just as his mother's murder had not?

I crossed the Verona Bridge, and then I was on the west bank, a long straight stretch of two-lane road. It was 2:15, and I was still forty-five minutes from home, wanted to be there when Roxanne and Sophie got back.

I hit the gas on a long upgrade where the road slashed through stone on the west side, the river glimmering far below on the right. It was widening into the head of Penobscot Bay when my phone buzzed. I picked it up off the seat.

"McMorrow," I said.

"Hey," Clair said.

He'd send smoke signals before he'd call.

"What's the matter?" I said.

"Where are you?"

"Route One, almost to Stockton Springs. Headed home."

"Get to Belfast, head north up to Jackson."

"Why?"

"Marta," Clair said.

"What about her?"

"They found her car," Clair said.

"Yeah?"

"In a gravel pit. Burned."

"Whoa," I said. "How'd you find out?"

"Ruiz, the US marshal. She called."

"Why you?" I said.

"They were looking for Louis but he wasn't around."

I swallowed.

"Looking for Louis to do what?" I said.

"To try to make an ID."

"Of what? A body?"

"They wanted me to look at a boot," Clair said. "There were woman's clothes outside the car."

I had an hour to think about it, all dark thoughts. Through Searsport, skirting Belfast, north to the tiny crossroad town of Waldo, the bigger crossroad town of Brooks. And then I was into Jackson, where a few roads twisted their way through the woods, skirting steep wooded ridges where trailers were tucked back into the trees.

Clair had said the car was found in an abandoned gravel pit off the Bog Road, which ran all the way to Monroe. I asked where on the Bog Road this was, and he said he didn't know, but figured he'd just follow the cops.

He did, from the west, and I did, coming from the south. My cop was a Waldo County sheriff's deputy in a marked pickup. I stayed back a hundred yards, tracked the truck up Route 7, the Moosehead Trail. There were woods on both sides, dark and dense, an occasional trailer, a rotting farmhouse surrounded by rusting vehicles, everything succumbing to the irresistible forces of decay.

This was rough country—made Louis's Sanctuary look like the Hamptons. I wondered what Marta had made of it, if she'd been alive this far and not stuffed in the back of the Audi like a road-killed deer. But she must have been alive, if they'd taken her clothes off, I thought. Or maybe not. It was a sick world.

The pickup slowed and I spotted another truck, civilian with a flashing red light on the dash, marking the road in. I sped up, got close to the deputy's truck, and swung in behind it when it turned. I waved to the local and he waved back. I was on official business. I'd seen Marta's sweater and vest, her L.L.Bean boots.

It was a logging road, unplowed and streaked with tire tracks. I put the Ford in four-wheel and followed the deputy into a clearing, with mounds of snow-covered slash that looked like beaver lodges in a frozen bog. And then we were across the clearing and into another road that swung to the left and up a rise, then straightened out and down. Fifty yards in there was another pickup, local fire department, the guy standing in front of it. He waved the deputy on and I followed like I belonged there, and we went deeper into the cut-over forest, the trees stripped away on both sides, everything but occasional clumps of birch and poplar.

There were lights up ahead, red and blue, and then a fire truck, a bunch of guys standing around it. They were looking at a pile of twisted and blackened metal, roped off by crime tape like it was an art exhibit: Do not touch.

Beyond the fire truck there were unmarked SUVs, State Police, marked SUVs, Waldo County Sheriff's Office. And a crime-lab van. And people in evidence tech suits peering at the blackened mound. And a couple of K-9 tracking teams, one woman officer and her dog headed toward the woods.

And Clair's big Ford.

I pulled in and parked and got out of the truck. I saw a couple of guys with US marshal jackets standing by a black Ford Explorer. I walked up to them, recognized them from Clair's kitchen. I said, "Hey. Jack McMorrow. Where's Officer Ruiz?"

They gave me a long stare, then one of them pointed to the burnt car. Ruiz came around from the other side, saw me, and started over. Clair was behind her. He was looking at the wreckage and then he shook his head and looked up. Saw me and joined us.

We stood in a circle and looked at what was left of the Audi. It was a gray-black hulk squatting on wheels with the tires burned off. The snow was melted away for forty feet around. The acrid smell of burnt rubber and foam hung over the clearing.

"You want to take a look at the clothes?" Ruiz said. "Mr. Varney already has, but two opinions are better than one."

I nodded and she turned and led the way around the car and away from the tote road. The crime tape encircled more of the clearing, and there were clothes on the ground in the enclosure. We walked to the tape and peered in.

Jeans. The green vest. The cream-colored sweater. The L.L.Bean boots. Underpants and bra, black with tiny pink flowers. The clothes were strewn like they'd been tossed. The ground was trampled, and there was an outline of scuffed snow in the vague imprint of a human body. And a small spatter of blood.

"Christ," I said.

"They look familiar?" Ruiz said.

"What she was wearing when she and Louis came over to my place," I said. "I don't know about the underwear."

Clair nodded.

"You're sure," Ruiz said.

"Yeah," I said. I looked toward the remains of the SUV, the blue tarp.

"I guess you caught your fugitive," I said.

"It would appear so," she said.

"Looks like somebody else caught her first," Clair said.

The vision of what had likely happened swirled through our minds. Abduct the pretty woman from out of state, drive the Audi back into the woods. Assault her in some horrific way. Torch the car.

But where was Marta? Abducted? Dumped in the woods?

"Somebody called it in," Ruiz said. "Locals figured it was somebody burning brush and didn't exactly hustle to get out here. By the time they did arrive, the vehicle was pretty much what you see."

"Nobody inside?"

She shook her head.

"And no sign of her," Clair said.

"Tracks to the edge of the woods. Another set of tire tracks going out."

"Cold to be without clothes," I said.

Chickadees flew over the hulk and chattered their way into the woods. I could hear nuthatches and titmice, too. Then the whistle of a brown creeper.

Life goes on.

Ruiz lifted the tape and led us away.

"Thanks," she said by the trucks. "We'll be talking."

We nodded and she walked back toward the huddle of cops. The State Police evidence techs were taking photos. The woman and the dog were coming back. She looked at Ruiz and shook her head.

The dog looked disappointed.

"Dead end," I said.

"Looks like it," Clair said.

We stood amid the flashing lights, the huddled cops, the burned wreck.

"Louis," I said. "You reach him?"

"Not yet," Clair said.

"We should go there," I said.

"Police are looking for him, too."

"Probably not thinking this was some random act."

"Never their first guess," Clair said. "Boyfriend, husband—always the first suspect."

"We always hurt the ones we love," I said. "We'll probably find him first."

"If he wants to be found," Clair said.

Multiple texts on the way south. To Louis, saying we needed to talk. From Vanessa at the *Times*, just checking in. To Roxanne, saying I'd be later than 3:30. From Roxanne:

> —IS CLAIR AROUND?
> HE'S WITH ME.
> —WHAT'S GOING ON?

I tapped the phone.

> THEY FOUND MARTA'S CAR. BURNED IN A GRAVEL PIT.
> —WHERE IS SHE?

THEY DON'T KNOW.
—OK.
—I'LL TAKE SOPHIE FOR A RIDE AND A HOT CHOCOLATE.
COME HOME WHEN YOU'RE HERE.
PROBABLY NOT NECESSARY.

I paused.

BUT CAN'T HURT.

And then we were driving, as far as the Prosperity General Store, where Clair parked the Ford and plow and climbed in with me. We zigzagged our way toward Sanctuary, there being no direct route. The woods and fields rolled past, the occasional house, the remnant of a settlement, Budweiser signs glowing in the store windows like flares warning of an accident.

I was silent, my jaw clamped. Clair was the same, more his natural state. We were on Route 131 outside of Searsmont, fifteen miles from Prosperity, when he finally spoke.

"I screwed up," he said. "I should have turned her in."

I could have said, "Yeah. You screwed up, and now she's probably dead." Instead I said, "Maybe she changed her clothes and torched the car. Covering her tracks."

"Who was in the other vehicle?"

"Accomplices."

He looked skeptical.

"That looked like a violent crime scene to me," he said. "If I'd told them what I knew this morning, marshals might have grabbed her. She'd be in jail. Somebody figuring out how to get her down to those islands," Clair said.

And not abducted or killed in a lonely gravel pit in Jackson, Maine—the last place Marta Kovac would choose to die.

I drove, downshifting, upshifting, the truck slinging its way over the rises.

"A hitchhiker?" I said. "Somebody jumps her when she's pumping gas? She was armed, smart, knew how to protect herself. Some local lowlife did what Russian mobsters couldn't?"

"Or they found her first. If the marshals tracked her this far, the bad guys could have, too."

"And they somehow get in her car, force her to drive into that pit, assault her, then burn it? Why take her with them?"

"Get more information out of her," Clair said.

I was tracking the curves, banging over the unavoidable potholes.

"She told me she was a survivor," I said. "Warned me not to get in her way."

"Road's probably littered with people who wrote that girl off."

"Yes," I said, thinking Marta's nine lives had most probably run out.

We passed the turnoff to North Appleton, continued toward Appleton proper. The sun dropped behind the ridge to the west and a cold dusk began to settle. Soon it was dark, like Clair's mood, a heavy shadow settling over him and the stone-walled pastures. We'd driven this route a hundred times, looked at the map to see Stover's Corner and Pitman's Corner, Gushee's Corner and Sherman's Mill.

I'd make some comment about who Gushee was and Clair would say, the guy who lived at the corner.

Not today.

We rode in silence all the way to Sanctuary, skirted the village and continued on to the Ridge Road, which led to the Pond Road. I slowed for Louis's driveway, turned in, and saw that the cable was up, a piece of red surveyor's tape hanging from the center. The truck's headlights showed tire tracks where vehicles had pulled up to the gate, stopped, and backed out. I stopped the truck and we got out, leaving the lights on and motor running. We saw footprints in the half-frozen puddle, circling the cable. Fresher footprints in the snow, coming back out.

"Guess they went in to try to find him," Clair said.

"Good luck with that," I said, "if Louis doesn't want to be found."

Clair took his keys out of his jacket, walked to the padlocked cable. I got back in the truck while he unlocked the cable and dragged it aside. He climbed in and we drove down the driveway, the cops' tracks leading the way.

The Jeep was parked in the yard, a dusting of snow on the roof and hood, no tire tracks going to or from. The cops' tracks stopped at the front door, then reversed. Made a loop around the Jeep and then went back up the drive.

We went up the steps and onto the porch and Clair knocked hard and loud, and we waited, and then Clair said, "I know where he is."

I followed him around the house and past the woodshed and into the woods. There was a path cut into the brush but no footprints in the snow. I was about to point this out when Clair said, "He likes to come in from different directions." I nodded and followed.

We walked for twenty minutes, traversing some of Louis's three hundred acres. At one point we crossed a marsh, stepping from hummock to hummock, walking gingerly on the ice, crunching through dead cattails. And then we were on dryer, higher ground, with big hemlocks blocking the light. The path disappeared, but Clair knew the way, and he walked in his steady, unstoppable way, through the big woods, and into a bramble of birches and spruce.

And then I smelled smoke as we slipped down an embankment, then up the other side of the trough, where exposed roots made for steps. Ahead of us there was a boulder the size of a garage, and Clair went to the right of it, came around the other side, and called, "Hey, Marine."

There was a camo tent pitched tight to the rock, gray and green and white like dappled snow on trees. A campfire was burning in a ring of stones, and there was something cooking on a spit over a bed of glowing coals.

Rabbit.

We walked closer.

"Hey, Marine," Clair called again.

We stood and waited and there was a soft brushing sound behind us. We turned and the dog was there, woofing softly and coming in to sniff us out. Then Louis came out of the spruces, the branches whipping backwards as he passed. He was carrying another snowshoe hare by the back legs. The hare was white with blotches of brown. Louis was dressed in the same camo as the tent.

"Gentlemen," he said. "Just in time for lunch."

He walked over and laid the hare down on the snow near the fire. The dog watched in case it was faking and might make a run for it.

"Didn't hear a shot," I said.

"Snare," Louis said. "No need to wake up the whole neighborhood."

He almost smiled, calm and relaxed in his hideaway. I was thinking it was too bad to spoil his mood when Clair said, "Louis. It's Marta."

Louis straightened, didn't look at Clair or at me.

"What?" he said.

"Found her car in a pit in Jackson. Her clothes strewn around, the whole thing burned."

Clair paused to let that sink in, but only for a few seconds.

"Police couldn't find you so they called me. To ID the clothes."

"The vest?" Louis said.

"Yup. The boots and the sweater."

"L.L.Bean?"

"Yeah."

"Underwear?"

"Black with pink flowers," Clair said.

Louis was still turned away from us. The rabbit was on the ground, staring up like it was listening.

"I thought you said everything was burnt," Louis said.

"Clothes were a little distance away," Clair said.

Another long pause. A woodpecker tapping in the distance. A deep drumming. A pileated.

"The Sig?" Louis said.

"They didn't mention a gun."

"How many bad guys?"

Clair shrugged. "Hard to say. Scene was pretty messed up. Dog found one track leading out, but it ended at the woods. Another vehicle came and went."

Louis bent down and slipped his knife from his belt. He gutted the rabbit, then skinned it. Three practiced cuts. Then he stepped close to the fire and picked up the spit that lay on the ground beside it. Skewered the rabbit and put it over the flames.

We all watched. Eventually grease dripped and there was a hissing flare in the coals. The dog moved close.

Louis turned to us. Shook his head.

"She's not dead," Louis said. "I never met anybody like her, always a step ahead. It's like this sixth sense."

I thought of her car rolling by, 4:08 a.m.

"She did tell me she's first and foremost a survivor," I said.

"She knows what's coming, and she has plan B, C, D ready in case she's wrong," Louis said. "Even in the Marine Corps, all the battle planning, I never saw anything quite like her. She was like that when we were kids. Had to be, because nobody else was planning for her."

"Marshals were hot on her trail," I said.

"Dodged them by an hour," Clair said.

"If they were tracking her, maybe the bad guys from that island were, too," I said.

"Run her off the road, drive the car into that pit," Clair said.

"She'd find a way out of it," Louis said.

"Maybe not this time," Clair said, a little more gently.

"Did she walk out of there naked?"

"Maybe had clothes with her," Louis said. "Burned the car, changed her clothes, and left."

"There was blood," I said. "Not a lot."

He turned and crouched by the spit. He turned the rabbit and more grease dripped. The dog had scooched forward, his eyes locked on the cooking meat. Still looking away, Louis said, "What about the money?"

"It wasn't in the car," I said. "Not last night."

"Seems like two million, even burnt up, would leave something. A pile of money-shaped ashes," Clair said.

"Then if it's here, she'll be back," Louis said.

He bent over the cooking rabbit and sliced the breast open. The knife, his Marine-issue KA-BAR, was like a razor. I thought of Barrett.

"You boys want a taste?" Louis said.

We shook our heads. He tossed a piece to the dog, who caught it in midair, swallowed.

"Police want to talk to you," Clair said.

"I'll call them," Louis said. "After I eat."

We stood and he still crouched. He sliced off a piece of meat and popped it into his mouth. Chewed slowly.

So he really didn't believe she was dead, and maybe he was right.

I paused. A thin column of smoke rose from the fire, sifted into the treetops, and slipped away. Just like Marta.

"So let's say you're right," I said. "She left there of her own accord. So who's with her? And where is she now? Canada? Laying low until the marshals move on and she can come collect her money? And what are we? A smokescreen? If she didn't have the money with her, will they come to collect it? And what happens if she won't talk. Will they come looking to squeeze it out of you? Out of us?"

I paused, added, "She's trouble, Louis. She brought this mess with her."

Louis stood, tossed the hare carcass to the dog, who took it and walked ten feet and dropped it and started licking. Louis wiped his knife on his jeans and slipped it back into its sheath. Turned to me.

"My problem, Jack," he said.

"All of our problem now," I said. "You, Clair, me. Mary and Roxanne and Sophie. She dragged us into it."

I turned and started back, following our tracks. I walked quickly, striding across the high ground, jumping from hummock to hummock in the bog. These woods seemed deeper and darker now, something dangerous I needed to escape. For whatever reason—lust, love, loyalty—Louis had sold his soul.

I emerged from the woods, glanced back and didn't see Clair. Sitting in the silent truck cab, I stared at nothing, ran through it. The money. The gun. Marta's warning. Had someone else gotten in her way?

I started the motor, looked to the woods. There was a ripple of motion behind the trees and then I could see Clair coming out and toward me. He got into the truck and shut the door.

And headlights flickered from the trees.

Coming fast down the driveway, sliding into the clearing, boxing the truck in.

An SUV. A Malibu. Ruiz slung herself out of the SUV, started over. The door of the Impala opened and a guy got out, another cop. The hair. The stance. The walk.

Scalabrini from CID. Jack McMorrow, this is your life.

I buzzed the passenger window down as Scalabrini walked up. He looked at me and smiled. "Jack McMorrow. Long time no see."

"I'd like to say it's good to see you, but it isn't," I said.

"What's it been? Two years? And now another fire."

"Right."

"So how's our friend Louis?" he said.

"Been better," I said.

"Ruiz filled me in," Scalabrini said. "Thought he was smarter than this."

"Yeah, well, love is blind sometimes," I said.

Clair opened his window and Ruiz leaned in and said, "Where is he?"

"In the woods," Clair said. "Just cooked a rabbit."

"Is he armed?" Ruiz said.

"Usually," Clair said.

"Now?"

"Didn't see anything, but if I had to guess . . ."

"Are you?"

"Yes."

"McMorrow?"

I nodded.

"Mind leaving the firearms in the truck?" Scalabrini said.

We hesitated, slipped the guns from under our jackets, placed them on the truck floor.

Scalabrini said. "Think he's gonna run?"

We both shook our heads.

"Nothing to run from," Clair said.

"Will he resist?" Ruiz said.

"No," we said in unison.

"Will he want to talk?" Scalabrini said.

"As much as he ever does," Clair said.

He led the way down what was now a path. We walked single file, Ruiz and Scalabrini behind me, the cops shining their lights ahead of our group. The light was blue on the snow and our boots crunched in unison, like soldiers on a march. After a while, we saw the fire through the trees, flames now, Louis tossing on wood.

As we approached, Ruiz said, "Call out to him. So he knows it's you."

"He'll know," Clair said.

"How?" Ruiz said.

"The sound," he said.

"What about us?"

"He knows you're coming," I said.

As we entered the clearing, Louis got up from his crouch by the fire. He turned to us, wiped his hands on a camo rag. The dog stood beside him and faced the police. A united front.

"Louis," Scalabrini said. "How ya been?"

Louis gave him a long look and said, "Busy."

Scalabrini glanced at the dog, whose eyes were locked on him. Louis said, "It's okay," and Friend moved a few feet away and crouched.

Louis and Scalabrini shook hands. Ruiz stood back, like one of us might bolt. Louis looked at her.

"Ruiz. Marshals service."

"Who you hunting?" Louis said.

"Marta Kovac," Ruiz said.

He gave her a cold look, said, "Is that right?"

Scalabrini nodded to Ruiz and she looked to me and Clair, said, "Come with me, gentlemen."

She moved to the far side of the clearing, maybe fifty feet, out of earshot. We followed her, stood in the snow. Ruiz stayed between us and the woods, out of habit. Scalabrini punched at his phone, started recording. Then they started talking, he and Louis huddled shoulder to shoulder.

I caught a few words here and there.

"And that was what time? . . . Didn't argue? . . . Tell me again where you were at . . ."

And then there was quieter talk, Scalabrini doing most of it.

Finally we heard his voice raised, angry now, "Who would want to hurt her, then? Somebody did it. Or did she rip her clothes off and torch her own vehicle?"

The dog edged closer. Louis and Scalabrini were turned toward us, the dog pivoting with them.

"I don't know," Louis said.

"You must have some idea, Louis," Scalabrini said. "Did she tell you who she was running from? Where'd this fucking money come from?"

"She said it was hers," Louis said.

"Where is it now?"

Louis shrugged.

"If I didn't know you, I'd think maybe you killed her and took it," Scalabrini said.

"I don't need her money," Louis said.

"No? Well, you don't seem too surprised by any of this."

Louis stared, didn't reply.

"Stay in town," Scalabrini said.

"Mostly do," Louis said. "If I have a choice."

Scalabrini walked over to us, looked at Ruiz, and said, "Let's go."

She looked at us with a sort of regret, like she'd wanted the chance to release us into the woods and then run us down. Another time.

They left, followed their own tracks out. We walked over to the fire and Louis and the dog, now crunching the rabbit bones.

"What about the Russians?" Clair said. "Didn't she tell you where she was going?"

Louis stared at the smoldering fire.

"You don't want them looking for her," I said. "You want the trail to end right there in that pit."

He crouched and stirred the fire with a stick.

"Did the two of you set this up?" I said. "If they think she's dead, they stop looking?"

He turned and reached for a dead limb, snapped it under his boot, and threw both pieces onto the fire. The coals sparked.

"A lot of bad people out there, Jack," Louis said. "Very bad people."

And then he dropped to a crouch, his back to us. I could see the shape of the gun butt at his waistband.

We turned and walked out of the clearing and down the path. When we reached the yard, the house was dark. The cops were gone. We climbed in the truck, picked the guns up from the floor. We looked around at the trees, the deepening shadows.

"Think she's dead?" I said.

"Fifty-fifty," Clair said.

"There's a lot we don't know about her."

"Barely scratched the surface," he said.

31

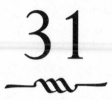

We were back in Prosperity in forty minutes, a quiet ride. Roxanne's car wasn't in the driveway. The lights were on, all of them. I texted Roxanne and she replied.

—2 MINUTES

"I'll take watch until the morning," Clair said.

"I'll see the girls off at the school."

He looked away, peering into the skeletons of lilacs by the driveway. Then he looked back at me.

"I mean what I said. About being wrong," Clair said.

"Happens," I said.

"Shouldn't," he said, and he turned and walked off into the darkness.

I turned and went into the house, hung up my jacket and my gun. Then I put a log in the woodstove, heard Roxanne's car pull in. I went to the window and Sophie saw me and waved as she ran up the walk. She met me at the door and I hugged her even longer and harder than usual.

Roxanne followed Sophie in. She was carrying a grocery bag and she unloaded it on the counter. Fresh salmon. White wine on the counter, but it was for cooking. I opened the refrigerator and closed it, leaving the Ballantine on the shelf.

"Sophie, honey," Roxanne said. "Go get the story you did at school. Show Daddy."

Sophie tore down the hallway and scrambled up the stairs.

"It's on the news," Roxanne said. "You think someone kidnapped her?"

"Looks like it. But Louis doesn't think so."

We could hear Sophie's footsteps crossing the hallway upstairs, then starting down the stairs.

"Either way, somebody's loose out there," Roxanne said.

"But only one knows where we live," I said.

"God, Jack," she said. "I thought we were done with all of this."

"We didn't ask for any of it this time. It came to us."

We were quiet after Sophie went to bed, Roxanne watching political shows on television in the living room, me sitting for ten minutes, then making a loop around the house. The study was dark. The second-floor bathroom, too. The front-side vantage point was our bedroom. I came down after loop number three and Roxanne said, "She wouldn't come here. Not now. What would it get her?"

"The money," I said.

"You think she left it behind?"

"I don't know. She wouldn't want to lose it all if the cops picked her up. Even if they hauled her back to the islands for questioning, the money would be waiting. All these abandoned houses and fallen-in barns around here . . . but she'd leave tracks in the snow."

"She needed to put it in a place where tracks wouldn't attract attention," Roxanne said.

"Under our noses," I said.

I got a flashlight and the Glock and went out to the shed. Peered behind the woodpile, opened the chest freezer. I pulled sleds and snowshoes aside and flicked the light up into the rafters. Then I went to the staircase and walked slowly and silently upward. I emerged in the loft, flashed the light around. Nothing had changed. Everything was in its place.

Marta hadn't been there.

I came back down, went outside. It was a dark night, full clouds, and I circled the house, crunching over the crust. I left shallow tracks. The only ones around the house were my own.

I was standing in the dooryard when I heard someone exhale behind me.

"Hey," I said.

"Hey, yourself," Clair said.

He stepped out of the shadows and stood beside me. He was dressed in black, from his boots to his gun.

"I was checking to see if she might have stashed the money here somewhere."

"I checked, too," Clair said.

"And?"

He shook his head.

"Same," I said.

We stood. I heard a barred owl in the distance, thought of Clair pretending that he never heard Marta leave.

"Heard her going down the stairs," he said. "In her socks."

"Hear her going around the yard?"

"No."

"Was she alone here?" I said.

"Sitting on the step when we got back from getting groceries," Clair said.

"The barn."

"I looked."

"I'd look again."

We stood, bearing the weight of our collective guilt.

"You could have turned her in," I said. "I could have chatted with the dog lady."

"Think we're slipping?" Clair said.

"Don't know. But I figured if we did, Louis would take up the slack."

"Boy's head isn't screwed on straight these days. Like he was on a very delicate balance, and when she got here, it threw him right off."

"Yeah," I said. "We're on our own."

"Like old times," Clair said.

We were quiet and I heard the owl again. *Who cooks for you?*

"What's your real guess?" I said. "If you had to make one."

"I think she's coming back," Clair said.

"Be good if it's her alone."

"Maybe," Clair said.

When I got back to the house, Roxanne was standing in the doorway. I brushed the snow off my boots and stepped inside.

"All quiet. Clair's out and about."

I took off my jacket and hung it on the hook, put the flashlight and gun on the counter.

"I was worried," Roxanne said.

"She's probably long gone," I said. "Or dead."

"If she's not and we see her, we'll know she's alive. She won't be able to disappear as easily then. She can't let that happen."

"Odds are slim."

"But not none," she said.

I made another cup of tea, poured the cold one into the sink. Then I went to the table and bobbed the new tea bag up and down in the water, watched the tea leaves darken the water like blood.

Roxanne pulled out a chair but didn't sit.

"You know how you go online and it seems like everything's just gone crazy?" she said.

"Yeah."

"Insane awful murders and leaders with not even a pretense of morals and good people getting swept away by the worst storms ever and crushed by earthquakes and burned up in forest fires and everything turned upside down."

I waited.

"I feel like we've turned into that," Roxanne said. "Like we can't get away from it. An ax murderer in Home Department, and Lindy and her son killed, and Ukraine and Russians and Marta and some friggin' island and millions of dollars."

She put her hand on my shoulder. "It used to be somewhere else, far away. But now it's right here."

"The walls have been breached," I said.

"What kind of world is this?"

"One where you don't really know anyone, and nothing is what it seems."

"I know you," Roxanne said.

"And I know you."

"And Clair and Mary."

"Yes."

I tried to think of something else reassuring to say. Nothing came to mind.

32

We went to bed early, lay there in the quiet. Listening.

And then, after a long time, I heard Roxanne's breathing settle into a gentle rhythm and I looked over and she was asleep, as beautiful as ever. It seemed an eternity since we'd made love with abandon, like Teak and Marta had somehow stolen that innocence away. I watched her for a minute, then got up and went downstairs, gun in my waistband.

In the study, I stood in the dark and looked out at the backyard and the edge of the woods. The moon had risen and the snow was bathed in a pale blue light. Clair had good visibility.

I drew the curtains and went to the desk, tapped at the keyboard. Kovac and car accident and death and Ukraine.

Stories popped up, but they were in Russian and Ukrainian, except for one on the English-language site of Interfax, the Ukrainian news agency. It was from the archives, dated August 6, 2004: Jaromir and Dasha Kovac had died when their car was sideswiped on a mountain road. They were on their way home from a holiday in a place called Bukovel. Their daughter Marta was injured and trapped in the wrecked car for three days before it was spotted by passersby. Marta survived on a bottle of juice and a packet of almonds. Finally, fearful of dying of thirst, she resorted to dropping lighted matches out of the broken car window and lighting the meadow grass on fire.

A hiker saw the smoke and alerted authorities. "The wind was favorable and blew the fire away from the vehicle," said a spokesman for the National Police. "She is very fortunate."

Had Marta's luck finally run out in Jackson, Maine? Or had she been "very fortunate" once again?

I still came down on the side of my gut. She'd be back.

It was after eleven when I switched gears, filled out an email request to see Teak in the jail. The website said regular visitation was Sunday, Tuesday, Thursday, and Saturday afternoons, limited to one session per day. Professional visits ("Attorneys, clergy, etc.") were anytime between eight a.m. and nine p.m.

I was professional, most of the time. I hit SUBMIT, was watching the whirling ball when I heard Sophie bounce out of bed, then her footsteps on the stairs. She came into the study, leaned against me.

"I heard you typing," she said.

"Lots of work to do," I said.

"Like what?"

Figuring out whether the nice lady in our kitchen was the killer or the killee. Getting inside the head of an ax murderer. Hoping to make sense of it so I could sleep at night.

"Just stories," I said. "Let's go to bed."

The jail was part of a compound of county offices on Hammond Street, just down the road from Lindy Hines's condo. I made a loop up to the library and back, looked at Lindy's windows overlooking the stream. The slider was papered over with cardboard. I wondered if the lovesick super had cleaned up the mess.

A trail of tragedy, and I needed to finally talk to the guy who had started it all.

The public entrance was on the ground floor, a gabled doorway with the stone and brick jail on top of it. I parked and walked over, notebook conspicuously in one hand, ID in the other. The door opened to what was an empty foyer with one-way glass on the far end, a buzzer button beside it. I walked up, knowing there was a corrections officer on the other side, and pushed the button. The speaker hissed and a man said, in that neutral cop tone that is somewhere between polite and threatening, "Can I help you?"

"Yes," I said. "I'd like to see Teak Barney."

"Visiting hours are . . ." He recited the days and times, said, "You can find the visitation procedure on our website."

"I've read it," I said. "I'm a professional visitor. I sent in a request."

"You a lawyer?"

"A reporter. Jack McMorrow. *New York Times*."

The speaker went silent.

I waited. Flashed a smile for the invisible guy behind the glass. Waited some more. The door rattled and an inmate came out. He was wearing jail-orange and carrying a black trash bag. He looked at me and said, "You have to push the button."

A trusty. He was mid-twenties and slight, hair in a ponytail, missing a front tooth.

"Thanks," I said.

"They helping you?"

"I think so," I said.

296 · GERRY BOYLE

He pulled out the bag from the trash can. Coffee must have spilled, because the odor filled the room. He put the new bag in. I turned away from the microphone and said, "You know Teak Barney?"

The guy looked at me, startled, then wary.

"A little."

"How's he doing?"

"You family?"

"No," I said.

He waited for more but I didn't offer. Then he glanced at the window, turned his back to it, and said softly, "He's doing fine, except he's batshit crazy."

"Making sense?"

"To himself," the guy said, and then he went to the speaker, pushed the button. The metal door buzzed and he pulled it open.

I said, "You see Teak, tell him a friend of Hakata is here."

He nodded and stepped through the door. It clanged shut the way jail doors always do.

I stepped back to my place in front of the window. Waited. Rocked on my heels and forward onto the balls of my feet. I was about to start whistling when the door rattled open and a woman in a brown uniform stepped out. She turned to me and put her hands on her belt.

"Captain Townsend," she said.

"Jack McMorrow," I said.

She was fortyish, with short sandy hair, a square jaw. Her blue eyes didn't seem to blink, and in a place where sun didn't shine, she was incongruously tanned.

"You're from the press."

"That's right." I held up my notebook. She pointed to my other hand, the one holding the ID. I handed it over: driver's license and *Times* credential. She looked at the photos on both and then at my face.

"You want to see Teak Barney."

"That's right. I saw him in court and I need to follow up. I sent in the request from your website."

"We don't process those every day," Captain Townsend said. "Besides, I don't know if that's possible. I don't know you. *New York Times*? Buncha made-up bullshit."

"I understand. But a question for you: Is Mr. Barney in the medical unit? Incapacitated? If not, if he's just incarcerated; you can't hold him incommunicado. If he wants to see me, it has to be permitted."

The jaw clenched and her eyes narrowed.

"According to who?"

"The law. I'm sure you're vaguely familiar with it."

"What if I don't see it that way?"

"I hope you do. But if you don't, then the *Times* gets a fancy lawyer, I see him anyway, and I write in my story that jail administrators tried unsuccessfully to violate his civil rights. And I look into whether that's standard practice at this correctional facility."

I smiled.

She looked at my ID again, running through the scenario. Her name in the newspaper. The whole thing possibly blowing up, ACLU and every other pinko outfit jumping in. When all she had was another year and then out, that double-wide waiting in the park in Zephyr Hills, Florida.

"What makes you think he'll want to see you?"

"He will," I said. "Guaranteed."

She looked at me, then took a deep breath. Her name tag rose and fell and then she said, "Wait here. It may be a while."

"I have time," I said. "I appreciate your help."

Captain Townsend put her hand on the door and it buzzed and she went back inside, the door snapping shut behind her.

There was a bench along the wall and I went and sat down. Opened my notebook and started writing out my questions for Teak. They were all in my head, but I wanted to let the people behind the glass know I considered the interview a foregone conclusion.

Why Lindy Hines?

Had you seen her before?

Do you regret killing her?

What made you do this? Why then? Why there?

What role does Hakata play in your life?

What about your family? Were you worried this would hurt them?

Do they understand comics? Hakata?

Are you getting meds in jail?

Had you taken your meds in the days leading up to the killing?

Do you get your meds at the shelter?

Harriet says you're a good guy. Do you think that's true? Are you still?

You could get forty years for this. Was it worth it?

Did you know Lindy Hines had a son? Did you know he was killed too?

The outside door opened and a guy came in carrying a carton. He looked at me and nodded and stepped up to the window and pushed the button. The same jailer answered. The guy said he had books to donate to the jail library. The jailer told him to leave them on the floor by the bench.

The guy did, dumping the carton on the tile with a thud. Reminded me of Arthur and Dolph and the boxes at the shelter. Then the guy left. I looked down at the titles. Paperbacks, murder mysteries. The one thing this murder wasn't, unless it was the mystery of the human brain.

I waited. Scrawled some more—Marta and Barrett, lists of unanswered questions. Why Barrett? Did he really have something on Rod? Enough to kill for? If Marta was dead, was that the end of the story? What if they never could prove it either way?

I folded the notebook closed. Got up and read the notices on the board beside me. AA. Narcotics Anonymous. How to put money on an inmate's account. (Bring cash.) A four-day waiting period for inmates transferred in. Children under five on a visitor's lap didn't count toward the two-person limit.

I wondered if Tawny would ever bring their son in, if little T. K. would ever meet his dad, the guy who killed the lady with the—

The door banged open. The captain stepped out, holding a clipboard. She dropped it on the counter. I stepped up and filled in my name and address, the date and time. She jerked her head toward the door and said, "This way."

I followed her down a beige-walled corridor, took a left and a right. Townsend coded through another metal door and a corrections deputy met us—young, high-and-tight cop haircut, very bulked up. There was another turn and another door. That led to a cubicle of a room with a chair, a counter, and a Plexiglas window looking into an identical cubicle. There was a phone on the wall to the left of the chair.

"Non-contact?" I said.

"Don't push it," Townsend said.

She said she'd see me when I was done. The thick-necked deputy said he'd be on the other side of the door, that I was to knock when I was ready to go. He slammed the door and there was a moment when the metallic clang echoed. And then there was silence.

I sat.

Took out my notebook and pen.

Waited.

33

One minute. Two. All the way to five when I heard voices from the other side. And then the opposite door opened and a deputy held it and Teak stepped in. The deputy exited and the door closed.

Teak stood with his arms folded across his chest, his legs slightly apart. His long hair was pushed back so it fell behind his ears and onto the shoulders of his orange jumpsuit.

He looked at me, an intense stare like a cat in a cage. Stepped to the counter and sat.

He reached for his phone receiver and I did the same. His brown eyes were open wide and unblinking.

"You know Hakata, my friend?"

It was the voice from the courtroom, deep and knowing, a benevolent king speaking to a vassal. I touched the record button on my phone, held it to the receiver.

"I know of him," I said.

"And your name on this planet?"

"Jack McMorrow. I'm a reporter."

"Yes. I was informed of this by my keepers. Who has sent you to me?"

I thought for a second.

"My editors in New York."

He smiled. "Ah. New York. I have known it."

I doubted that Teak had been as far as New Hampshire, except in his head.

"How are you doing in here, Teak?" I said. "Are you being treated okay?"

Small talk to warm up, except he got right to the point.

"It is good," he said. "Ukko has a plan. I will stay until he dispatches me again."

"I see. And you await your orders?"

"I do his bidding," Teak said.

"Did Ukko send you to Home Department?"

He flinched, just in the eyes. Recovered and gave me the patronizing smile.

"He cannot be everywhere. There was something that needed to be done and I was summoned."

"Killing Lindy Hines?"

He gave a snort.

"Alas, he had assumed the poor woman's form, absorbing her life energy. He had been to Tuonela, land of the dead, and the evil ones had divulged the secret of transformation."

"Who?" I said. "Who had assumed the form of Lindy Hines?"

"Perkele," Teak said. "The devil god."

"When you killed Lindy Hines, did you kill Perkele as well?"

"Perkele was forced to flee the woman's body and retreat. He will return. It is only a matter of time."

He looked at me calmly. Waiting for the next obvious earthling question.

"Teak, you're a guy from Down East, Maine. Grew up in Ledge Harbor. I went there. I met your dad and your brother and your ex. I didn't meet your son." The smile fell away and there was a flash of alarm in his eyes, then a new wariness. He tried for the regal pose again, but couldn't hold it.

"The young one stays with the mother of his mother," Teak said. "He is safe there."

"Safe from what? From Tawny and Jason and the drugs? From you?"

Anger this time, maybe panic. A quick pant. His eyes darting to the corners of the room.

"From the world. It is a dangerous place."

"That it is, Teak," I said. "Lindy Hines found that out."

"She was a caught in the vortex."

"And you don't want T.K. to be caught in the vortex?"

"He can't be caught," Teak snapped. "He can't be part of this. He must grow up in peace."

His breathing was coming hard and fast. I waited.

"And not a lot of that around here," I said.

Teak looked at me. Took a deep breath. Said nothing.

"Your dad told me about you as a kid. He said you were a hard worker, and then you got sick. And you don't go back there much anymore."

"My father is of this planet," Teak said, mustering the smile again. "He is a good man."

"Yeah, and he's worried about you."

"I'm sorry my calling led me away from the ancestral village on the great ocean."

"Your calling?"

"Ukko needed assistance on Earth. I answered his call. I had no choice."

He was falling back into it. I had to jar him loose again.

"You had no choice when you killed Lindy Hines?"

"It had to be done. To prevent Perkele from carrying out his plan."

"I have to say that Lindy Hines was a very nice lady. She had just moved to Riverport after she split up with her husband. He's a jerk. She moved here to be close to her son, who was a very nice guy. A schoolteacher. She had a little dog that she doted on."

He leaned toward the glass.

"She was doomed. When Perkele leaves a mortal body, he sucks it of life. She would have died within hours. In this universe, it is often the innocent who pay the price when evildoers roam free. There would be more innocent victims if we did not keep evil at bay."

"A murder for the greater good?"

Teak nodded. "Thus it must be."

"Lindy Hines was an accountant. She'd volunteered to help the shelter with their books. The finances and all that. Did you know that?"

He didn't reply or shake his head.

"Miss H. knew her. Miss H. is a close friend of yours, right?"

Teak smiled, held the phone to his ear. "Miss H. is a strong person."

"You helped her out there, she said. Fixing stuff."

"She has no one who can assist her."

"And she reminded you to take your medication. Is that right?"

He nodded.

"Did she remind you lately? Had you been taking your meds?"

"There are times when I need all my powers."

"And the meds drag you down?"

"Hakata, the divine one. When he calls, I must be ready."

"Like you were ready for Lindy Hines."

"Perkele."

"The meds make you unready to help Hakata? But you were ready this time?"

"I was fully ready to carry out my mission," Teak said.

"Why? How did you get ready?"

"The sacred elixir," he said. "It comes from the gods."

"How do they get it to you?"

"They have their ways," Teak said. "They are all-powerful."

He gave me the benevolent smile, McMorrow the mere mortal.

"Is your sacred elixir also known as crystal meth?" I said.

He looked puzzled, shook his head.

"I know this poison. It has ruined many a good man and woman."

"So you wouldn't take it?"

Teak shook his head again.

"But it was in you, Teak," I said. "In your blood."

"No."

"I was told that the blood test showed meth in your system."

"No."

"What is your elixir, then?"

"It is not of this world."

"Where do you get it? From Jason? How do you take it? Do you drink it?"

He looked at the wall above the window and scowled. His held the phone receiver tightly, clenching and unclenching his hand so that his biceps flexed. I waited, then said, "I met your buddies from the shelter. Arthur and Dolph. And Mutt. They send their regards. Miss H. does, too. She said to make sure I told you she's still with you, no matter what."

He looked at me more closely.

"You have spent a lot of time on me, Mr. McMorrow," Teak said.

I leaned closer to the window, got more of his attention.

"There's another reason, Teak," I said. "I was there at the store when you killed Lindy Hines. I saw you standing over her with the hatchet. What do they call it? A tomahawk?"

He was staring hard, listening intently.

"Did quite a number on her head. Blood all over the place."

He stared at me like he was waiting for the point.

"You know her dog was in the car? Very loyal little guy. I'm sure the dog wondered where his mistress had gone. Cops ended up giving him to her son. And then you know what happened?"

Still the stare, but the first traces of a scowl, his mind whirring to get it all to fit.

"The son, Barrett was his name, somebody killed him, too. Stabbed him at his apartment. That wasn't something Ukko needed done, was it? I mean, you're in here. Are there other people like you around here, helping Ukko out?"

"No," Teak said. "No one else hears Ukko. But other gods issue decrees. Vedenemo, god of the waters. Tapio, god of the waters. They may have sent their own emissaries."

"Okay. Then did Ukko recruit you? I'm just trying to understand all of this."

"It was Ukko," Teak said. "He sent the message to me in the stories. Through his messenger vessel, my uncle."

"Okay. I see. Then how 'bout this? Could this Perkele devil guy have jumped from Lindy Hines to her son? If he needed another earthling form?"

Teak looked rattled, like he was still trying to process, fit it into his Hakata world. He let the phone receiver fall away, then pressed it to his head. "It is not known to me," he said.

"Okay, Teak. Another question. And I appreciate you taking the time."

He nodded, tried to put the benevolent smile back on, but came up way short.

"Everyone I talk to says you're a good guy. You help out whenever you're needed. Hang drywall. Fix the steps. Do a little plumbing, electrical work. Protect the weaker people at the shelter if somebody's picking on them."

"It's what I do," Teak said. "It's what Hakata would do."

He held up his forearm, showed me the tattoo. *W-W-H-D?*

"Exactly," I said. "Here's my question, then. Why would a good guy like you, or Hakata, kill a nice lady like Lindy Hines?"

"I told you. She wasn't—"

"Yeah, I know. Some devil had taken her form. But she didn't know that. I met her, and she was just nice Lindy Hines, trying to make the world a better place, you know? She didn't have to help out with the shelter. She could have just stayed home and watched TV, hung out with her dog. She didn't know anything about any of this. She was just out getting Christmas decorations, and wham. You whack her with your hatchet and kill her dead. Do you see anything wrong with that?"

Teak folded one arm across his chest.

"It's like, what kind of god would do that to the poor lady? Does that bother you?"

Teak took a quick breath, looked away from me for the first time. His eyes darted from side to side and then he closed them, started massaging his temples.

"It had to be done," he said, not in his Hakata voice, and not to me, more to himself. "She was gonna hurt a lot of people."

We were slipping out of ye olde English.

"How, Teak?" I said. "How was she going to hurt anyone? This nice lady?"

He leaned closer. His eyes were wilder, darting, frantic.

"She wasn't nice," he shouted. "She was evil. Perkele had possessed her. He was going to use her."

He dropped the phone to the counter and came out of his seat and started pacing around and around the cubicle. He had his hands on top of his head and he was muttering, the words muffled by the glass.

And then he stopped in front of the window, leaned toward me, and shouted, "You don't understand! You are blind. You don't have the power."

That I could hear. Then he leaned in, shook his fist at me, and shouted, "Oh, yes. Now I see you. You are blind! Perkele, be gone."

The door rattled open on his side and two deputies hustled in. Teak turned, and as they came for him he swung, caught one on the side of the head. The guy staggered and recovered and then plunged back in. They piled on and took him by both arms, started dragging him out. He fought back, thrashing with his elbows so one deputy lost his grip. Teak spun and hit the other with his free fist, and the second guy jumped on his back, tried to get his wrist.

Teak was bellowing, "Unhand me, unhand me," when the first deputy wrenched loose and they both rode Teak to the floor, jammed his arm up his back. He was writhing and shouting when the door on my side opened and the thick-necked deputy came in, took me by the upper arm, and pulled me out of the chair. He was between me and the window and he pushed me out the door where Captain Townsend was just arriving.

"We're going to have to ask you to leave," she said, and they each got on a side of me and started hustling me down the hall. Through one door, then another, and then I was back out in the foyer. The thick-necked deputy hurried back inside.

Holding the door open, Townsend said, "Asked around about you. They say you're nothing but trouble, and they're right."

"Is he getting his meds?" I said, and she turned and stepped through the door, slammed it behind her.

I stuck my phone and notebook in my pocket, stepped outside into the glare. Took a deep breath, kept seeing Teak on the floor, guards on top of him. Hakata had forsaken him.

I sat in the truck, went through my notes. Underlining quotes. Putting stars next to the strongest. Then I did a search on my phone: Finnish mythology. And there they all were, on a homemade website put up by a college professor at the University of Helsinki. Ukko, Perkele, Tuonela. Teak had taken their land of the dead and brought it home.

So what had I learned, face-to-face with Teak Barney?

That Teak was, indeed, batshit crazy?

He was that, stuck in a fantasy world that he'd transferred from his comic book to become his reality. Teak Barney was no ordinary mortal. Ukko and Hakata had tapped him for a higher purpose.

But I had broken through at the end and he'd snapped. Even Teak was having trouble reconciling Lindy Hines inhabited by an evil alien with the mortal one, a nice lady going about her business. And reconciling Teak, the helpful, good-hearted guy, with the Teak who cut a woman's head open with an ax. At the end of the conversation, they'd collided.

But there was one thing Teak hadn't done. When I'd told him that Lindy Hines worked for the shelter, even indirectly, he hadn't seemed particularly taken aback or even surprised. Had he really picked her out at random? Had he seen her somewhere and fixated on her for some reason? Had their meeting at the store really been a coincidence, or had he been stalking her? The cab had picked him up just up the street from her building.

Very good of her to help Harriet, he'd said, very calmly, and the conversation had gone on. And then, in minutes, he'd wigged out. What exactly was wrong with him? And what was the magic elixir?

It went dark in the parking lot along the jail wall, clouds racing overhead and shadows tracking them. Then it started to sleet, hard bits that ticked off the hood.

I started the truck and let it warm up for a minute, then put it in gear. I was about to pull out when a red minivan turned onto the narrow street. It looked familiar and I waited, saw the driver as it passed.

Miss H., coming to visit Teak.

Good luck with that.

34

〜〜〜

Harriet parked a few spaces down. I got out and walked over, tapped the passenger-side window. She looked at me, startled, then smiled and motioned for me to get in. I did, tossing a roll of paper towels and a bundle of diapers into the back.

The van smelled like her house—laundry detergent, disinfectant. There was a picture of her niece and nephew stuck to the dashboard. They looked like they were at some sort of dance, Nikki in a short dress and Shane in a white shirt and jeans.

Harriet was gussied up, too, right there, not in a picture. Black leggings, a red faux leather jacket, and flat-heeled black boots. Dressed up for a jail visit.

She turned to me and said, "Are you here to see him?"

"Already did."

Her face seemed to fall. Did she want to be the first, the bestest friend?

"How's he doing?"

"Okay at first, then he got pretty agitated."

"Oh, I'm sorry," Harriet said, and she seemed to mean it, like he was more than just a client. Was she in love with him? Some weird homeless-shelter crush? Had she slept with him, now knew that she probably never would again?

"I was hoping, you know, that with his meds and all, he'd be better."

"I don't know that becoming unpsychotic is going to help him," I said. "Maybe he's better off staying in his made-up world."

Harriet frowned. "Then what? Just let him stay crazy?"

I shrugged. "I don't know. The guy I just talked to wouldn't be found competent to stand trial, I don't think. He calls the guards his 'keepers.' He thinks he can leave the place when somebody named Ukko says it's time."

"Oh, Teak," Harriet said.

"But one thing started to come out," I said.

"Oh?"

"I think he's got doubts creeping in about whether he did the right thing."

"Hurting Lindy Hines."

Hurting. The ax had delivered one big hurt.

"Yeah. I was telling him about Lindy helping you out, what a nice person she was. He said she was evil, the devil—he used a different name—but it was like he was having a little trouble believing it—like he was trying to keep the whole thing from falling apart."

"Huh. In some ways, that's worse," Harriet said. "For him, I mean."

"I don't know. Do you leave him in fantasyland? Or do you make him better so he has to face the reality of what he's done? He'll go for a head defense and—"

"What's that?"

"NGRI—not guilty by reason of insanity. That works, and he goes to the hospital and they treat his illness. Maybe someday he gets out."

She looked away, maybe pondering the notion of *someday*. Then back to me.

"I can't see him?"

"It's not friends and family time. And I seriously doubt he'll be up for a visitor. They had to subdue him. It got kind of ugly."

"Oh, no," Harriet said.

"I'm going to give him a day or so before I go back," I said.

She looked at me. "You're going to see him again?"

"Sure," I said. "I have to know him for the story. Also, I think he wanted to tell me something."

We sat for a minute, not talking. It was still sleeting, with gusts of cold, wet wind. Inside the van it was warm as a clothes dryer, and Nikki and Shane stared at me from the dash, smiling like TV stars.

"He said he took an elixir to get ready to take on Lindy, who was really Perkele, the devil from Finland or wherever. And I've got it from a reliable source that toxicology showed meth in his system. I wonder what that elixir was. Did he take drugs?"

"Teak? I don't know. I don't think so. I mean, he was already—"

"Sick. I know," I said. "But what about Mutt and those guys? Or his little brother and his ex, Down East? They were total meth heads. Did they come down to Riverport?"

"I don't know. You have to remember, I'd see him maybe four hours a week. I didn't know where he was the rest of the time, who he was with. He knew Mutt and the rest of them, but did they hang out? I don't think so, but I don't know for sure."

I looked out the window as sleet spattered the roof, melted as it hit the warm windows. Harriet reached for the door latch, said, "I guess I'll go and give it a try."

"He's probably in isolation now, if he isn't in restraints."

"Then I'll leave him a note," Harriet said.

She got out of the van and I did, too. She came around to the street, stopped, and said, "He needs to know he still has friends."

"You may be the only one at this point."

She seemed to brighten at the thought, a martyr who thrived on being needed.

"I don't give up on people. Most folks, if you have faith in them, they come through in the end."

"I don't know, Harriet. I wonder what Lindy Hines had faith in," I said. "The innate goodness in people? See where that got her. And her son, too."

Harriet looked distressed.

"Yeah, well, it was just one of those freak things. You can't give up on somebody just because—"

"One freak thing, maybe, Harriet," I said. "Not two."

It was 10:10; already seemed like a long day.

I pulled out, gave the jail a last look as I drove away. The shadowy windows. The razor wire keeping inmates in the yard. The single basketball hoop. Would Teak be out shooting baskets with the boys, hustling for rebounds just like he did back in the day? Or would he see the game as a strange practice of us mere mortals? Strange and sad, how things sometimes turned out.

I pulled over and picked up my phone. Searched for NGRI, Maine, murders. Pulled up stories on defendants in this part of Maine who had gone for it. A guy who killed his landlords and said in court they were shooting microwaves into his brain through the walls. He was found guilty, got forty-five years. Another guy, in his twenties, chopped his father into small pieces and scattered them around Ashville, way up north. He was found not guilty.

The state forensic psychologist was named Penelope Bainer, who, in the testimony I'd read, was smart and direct. Her office was at Great Woods Hospital in Riverport, on the waterfront.

I pulled out, started wending my way through the city, and in fifteen minutes was standing in front of another window, this one with two-way glass.

There was a guy on the other side, big for a receptionist, but I assumed that came in handy in a hospital full of Teaks. I told him my name, who I wanted to see. He asked if I had an appointment and I said no. He asked the nature of my business and I said, "*New York Times*. Writing about Teak Barney.*"

He looked at me harder, slid the window shut.

I went and sat, notebook on my lap. Glanced at the magazines on the table: *Good Housekeeping, National Geo*. I waited as ten minutes went by. That meant she was there and she'd see me. The brush-off would have come sooner, and besides, I had her pegged as bright and curious, somebody who would want to know what I was writing about one of her soon-to-be cases.

A door clicked open to my left. Dr. Bainer came out, strode confidently over. I got up. She was in her early sixties, attractive, with a thick mane of highlighted reddish hair, wearing dangly green earrings that matched her oversized cardigan.

"Mr. McMorrow," she said, as we shook hands. "You know I can't talk about pending cases."

"Right."

"Including the one that's going on right now."

"I know. What about mental illness and culpability. In general terms."

She considered it for a moment, said, "We can try."

Her office was filled with books and journals and case files, filling the shelves, stacked on the desk. The window looked out on the half-frozen river. There were three chairs, and we sat. I opened my notebook.

"Schizoaffective disorder," I said.

"Yes."

"The symptoms are—"

"Hallucinations, delusions, disorganized thinking. Jumping from subject to subject in a way that doesn't make sense. There are different types. If the person has the manic type, they'll have euphoria, risky behaviors, mania."

"Like believing you're living in a comic book?"

"No comment."

"A person with this manic version could be physically strong?"

"Could be."

"Flights of grandeur?"

"Sometimes."

"Inflated notion of their importance?"

"In their world, sure."

"Treatable with medication?"

"Sure. Zyprexa. Risperidone."

"Is that effective?"

"It varies. But most of the time, yes. People can break through the meds, but it's the exception."

"And off the meds?"

"It's hard to say. Not much could happen. Or the symptoms could be full blown, at that time of the cycle. Think of it as extreme hyper versions of our moods. Sometimes you're up. Sometimes you're very down."

"And the delusions—they might be up or down, based on triggers that aren't real."

"They're real to them," Bainer said.

I paused, looked up from my notebook.

"What would make someone with this illness suddenly take their delusions to a new level?"

"And kill someone?" She shook her head. "Can't go there."

"Okay. Do the symptoms of the illness typically worsen over time?"

"They can. Delusions can intensify. Same for manic or depressive behavior. Our brains aren't like static organs; they're changing all the time as we age. People with mental illness, they're no different."

She stopped. Waited.

"What's the ramp-up to something like that? If someone is okay one day, can they totally wig out the next?"

Bainer hesitated, dabbed at the corner of her mouth. Her finger came away with lipstick. A pale pink.

"Typically, that person would begin to show symptoms that would grow more pronounced over time. Two or three days. Maybe more. Everyone's different."

"Can you see it coming?"

"If you know someone well, yes, sometimes you can."

She looked at me, said, "Off the record?"

"Yes, you can. "

"Are you trying to establish that the Hines murder could have been prevented?"

"I'm trying to figure out how people can say, 'He was fine. I just talked to him yesterday,' and now he goes and does this. My question is, was there a switch in Teak Barney's mind that got thrown? Like, *click*—from helpful handyman to ax murderer."

"Again, off the record? Can I trust you?"

"Yes, you can."

She looked at me more closely, an expert sort of inspection. I passed.

"The brain usually doesn't work that way. It's affected by chemicals, and those take time to take hold. It's not like they're normal and they go into their crazy room and come out a minute later in full-blown psychosis."

I considered it, my pen still.

"Crystal meth," I said.

She froze.

"I have it from a reliable source that Teak had meth in his system."

Bainer shook her head. "No comment."

"Okay, hypothetically, what would a drug like that do to a patient with schizoaffective disorder?"

She hesitated, said, "Hypothetically."

"Yes. We're speaking of all patients with this disease."

She hesitated again.

"All of that person's symptoms would be elevated. Delusions. Paranoia. Manic energy."

"Physical strength?"

"Could be."

"A schizoaffective person on steroids," I said.

"Yes," Bainer said. "Speaking in the vernacular, not the medical. Meth isn't a steroid."

"So if somebody like Teak is kicking around the streets, ends up with a bunch of tweakers, that could be a dangerous thing."

"You think?" she said.

I drove up the hill away from the river and the hospital, took a right on Main Street, passed the Irish pubs, Indian restaurants, a German beer house. The sleet had turned to fine snow and the mostly empty sidewalk was sugared white.

I drove south, saw the police station on my left, Tingley and Bates in there somewhere, maybe working the phones on the Barrett Hines case. Who wanted him dead?

On the right was the park. I slowed and parked by the monument to war dead, figured they'd need another monument soon—to people killed in the Queen City. I shut off the motor and sat. The truck smelled like cigarettes and motor oil, definitely not a do-gooder's vehicle. More like a battering ram, knocking down doors, exposing the naked underbelly of Riverport. Bar Harbor. Sanctuary.

Somebody had to do it.

I sat and the snow dropped onto the warm windshield, melted and slid down. I hit the wipers, looked out. Saw two familiar figures crossing the park's diagonal sidewalk, carrying what looked like grocery bags, headed for the neighborhood behind the shelter. Arthur and Dolph.

Maybe they'd like an update on their good friend Teak.

I got out, walked to the corner, and turned up the street. I could see them through the trees, sauntering in what seemed the only speed they had. I turned down the path, met them head-on.

They looked up, then down onto the path. See no evil.

"Hey, boys," I called.

They saw me and stopped. I kept coming. They would have turned and gone the other way if there had been time, but there wasn't.

"Arthur, Dolph," I said. "How's it going?"

They looked at me, then at each other, waiting for a spokesman to step up. It was Dolph this time. He said, "Okay."

"Glad to hear it. Listen, I just saw Teak at the jail."

Holding their shopping bags, they looked at me warily, like this was veering too close to trouble.

"He's doing all right. Still talking about his comic-book stuff. I don't think they know what to make of him in there."

I waited for a response. Waited some more.

"Yeah," Dolph said.

"Listen, I have a question for you. It's important."

They listened, clutched their bags of stuff. There was snow in their hair but they didn't brush it away.

"Teak says Lindy Hines, the lady at Home Department, she'd been invaded by Perkele, who is like the devil. He can take over people's bodies."

Arthur nodded.

"Did he ever tell you that? That he knew a woman around here who'd been taken over by this alien thing? Or anyone else, for that matter? I'm just wondering how long he'd been thinking like this."

"Teak, he can be way out there," Dolph said.

"Crazy dude," Arthur said.

"Yeah, I know. Seriously nuts, thinking all this stuff is real."

"Yeah, that lady, she was real nice," Dolph said. "She weren't no alien, you ask me."

I smiled at him.

"You knew her?"

"Brought her the boxes," Dolph said.

"You brought her what boxes?"

"Miss H.'s boxes," he said. "So's she could help us out."

"Oh, the records and stuff."

"Yup. She was real nice," Dolph said. "Gave us sandwiches and these wicked good homemade cookies."

Arthur nodded in agreement. "Still warm."

They both smiled. Lindy Hines had known the way to their hearts.

"You delivered the cartons and had lunch? Who was driving?"

"Cowgirl—her other name is Sadie. She used to come to the shelter. Now she's got her own place, but she helps out when Miss H. is right out straight."

I remembered her. The diapers.

"Cranked the tunes," Dolph said.

"Country," Arthur said.

I grinned. "With that hat, Sadie must be a country fan."

"She's from Alabama," Dolph said. "Or Kentucky. Someplace like that."

"Good times," I said.

"Miss H. was some ugly when we got back," Dolph said.

"Why's that?"

"We didn't tell her before we went. We just grabbed the stuff and left. Sadie looked up the lady's address. Thought we was helping out."

"I'm sure you were," I said.

"She was some pissed," Dolph said. "Told Arthur to get his head out of his ass."

Arthur nodded.

"Well," I said, "everybody has a bad day."

They suddenly stopped talking, looked back into the park. A cluster of people had come off the sidewalk. Two uniformed cops were walking up to them. They must have asked for ID, because the people started fishing in their pockets.

"We gotta go," Dolph said.

"Yeah," Arthur said.

"One more question," I said, and moved closer.

"Did Teak do drugs? I mean, meth or coke or whatever?"

They looked at each other, then at me. Shook their heads in unison like twins.

"Teak, he don't do that shit," Dolph said.

"He's whacked enough," Arthur said.

"Any tweakers in the basement that day? Mutt?"

They shook their heads again.

"The woman with the hoodie?"

That got a shrug, which was as good as a yes.

"Teak know her? What's her name?" I said.

They looked at each other. This time Dolph shook his head first. Arthur followed his cue. When they turned to me, their mouths were clamped shut. They turned and hurried away, across the street into a parking lot, winding their way between the cars.

I turned and left the park the way I had come, made my way back to the truck. Climbed up and in, started the motor, slid back out and scraped the snow from the windshield. Got back in and waited for the heater to kick in.

And thought, There were tweakers at the shelter, and I doubted the woman in the hoodie was the only one.

And the divine Miss H. had a temper.

35

I headed south, out of the city and along the river, the black current flowing along beside me. And then I swung west, up into the hills where the two-lane road was slick with sleet and snow. I slowed and put the truck into four-wheel drive, heard a *thunk* up front, hit the gas. The motor roared and I sped up hills that for a hundred years had kept people in their settlements for the entire winter.

Hitch up the wagon, go three miles down the road. Get back to feed the horse and milk the cows.

The mayhem of modern times. Money launderers and drug dealers and crazy guys with hatchets. Somebody with a knife—probably not crazy at all.

It was the one that made the situation inexplicable. Teak? It all made sense. Marta? A different kind of sense, but all about money, clear as the water around Virgin Gorda. Barrett? That's where it all went off the rails.

I mulled it over as I drove. There were crimes of passion, crimes of greed, crimes of psychosis. But which one was Barrett's murder? Mother and son. What did they have in common, other than a box of receipts in the back of a car. And what of Rod? He didn't kill his ex, much as it made a problem go away. Could Rod have known Teak? How could the up-and-coming contractor be part of Teak's world? Rod was on the fast track up. Teak had bottomed out. He was gum on the bottom of Rod's boot.

The miles ticked past, the hills shrouded in the midday dusk that fell in December. No view from the ridgetop in Dixmont. The woods closing in on the road in Troy. I hit the brakes as I came into Unity, watching for Amish buggies as I turned off and headed southeast toward home.

Farmhouses like lighthouses on hilltops, shorn cornfields showing like tidal flats. Everything gray-white and dead and still, and then I was coming off Knox Ridge, headed down into the valley. I turned off on the Dump Road, black woods on both sides, thinking I'd be settled when Roxanne and Sophie got home. A fire going, all of us sitting in the warm kitchen, them talking about their days.

Talk to Clair, figure out who had the next shift.

I was getting out of the truck in the dooryard when I sensed him and turned. He'd approached my blind side, as always, was standing there like he'd known I was coming.

"How was the day?" I said.

"Quiet. Nobody showing, woods or the road.

He held a short-barreled shotgun, pointed at the ground by his right leg.

"Gotta go," Clair said. "Mary has an eye appointment, for four. The dilation thing; I'm driving. Then we're going out to dinner, Darby's in Belfast. You see if you can keep out of trouble."

"Try," I said. "New gun?"

"Mossberg five-ninety. Nice tactical shotgun. Louis borrowed the Benelli."

"Talk to him?"

"Yeah. Still says it isn't her; she'll have changed cars and clothes, and she'll be back."

I thought of Lindy, the pool of blood under her head. Barrett, his own pool in the hallway. In that string of events, Marta's clothes on the ground, the car burnt black—it all carried the odor of death.

"Awful lot of dying," I said. "You think it's over?"

Clair took two shells from his pocket, fed them into the chamber.

"No," he said. "Bet you two million dollars."

And he turned and walked away.

I leaned back into the cab for my notebooks and gun. Walked to the side door, unlocked it, and let myself in.

I'd beaten them home. One mission accomplished.

I went to the kitchen, took out a Ballantine. Thought of Marta and put the beer back. I put the kettle on. Dug out a Barry's tea bag from the cupboard and put it in a mug. I waited for the water to boil, looked at my watch; 2:45. I had time.

The tea poured and steeped, I added some milk and sipped. Thought of Teak locked in a cell, his mind soaring through the galaxy. Harriet coming to comfort him, a man who had split an innocent woman's skull, slicing Lindy Hines's head like a hard-boiled egg.

And Marta, her underwear scattered on the snow like strewn hothouse flowers. If she was dead, assaulted in some heinous way in her last moments, I owed her a serious apology.

Listen to you, McMorrow.

Taking the tea to the mudroom, I put my jacket and gun back on, the Glock reassuring on my chest. I took a last swallow and went outside. It was dark, clouds sneaking in from the east. I surveyed the yard, walked to the road, and looked up and down.

Nothing and nobody showing. I walked back to the house, followed the path past the shed and into the backyard. The path merged with the trail to Clair's barn, and I walked between the scrubby cherry trees, the field pines elbowing in. The snow was hard and weathered, the tracks indistinct. I thought I could see the shape of Sophie's small boot. A frozen deer print. A couple of big paw prints. Fresher.

Louis's dog.

I looked ahead and then down at the ground, kept it up until the barn was in sight. The tracks were occasional and blurred, until the dog had come upon a rabbit trail and ranged off the path. Then the tracks were plain. Louis hadn't left a trace.

The tracks showed the dog had come out of the woods just short of the barn, then continued on the trodden path, where the tracks faded out. I kept walking, past the dooryard side of the barn, over to the door.

I tried the door and it opened. I was about to step in when a voice behind me said, "Jack."

36

It was Louis. He was standing at the corner of the barn, like he'd come around and stopped. He was alone, and then the dog bounded from behind the barn and circled me, sniffed my boots.

"Smells something," Louis said.

"Jail," I said.

He came a couple of steps closer.

"Went down to the house to find you but you weren't there."

"Just got back. Went to see Teak."

"How's he doing?"

"Fine, for an ax murderer."

"Probably helps that he's crazy," Louis said.

"Both a boon and a bane," I said.

Louis nodded, barely, looked away. Friend continued to sniff my boots, the scent of fresh dirtbags.

"What did you want?" I said.

"Wanted to explain," he said. "Still do."

"Explain what?"

"Explain Marta."

"What about her?" I said.

"Why I'm acting the way I'm acting."

I waited. Even the dog, flopped on the snow, crooked his head and seemed to be listening.

"I'm in love with her," Louis said. "Always have been."

I felt like I'd been hit with a shovel.

I said, "Huh. I thought you bailed, joined the Marines and left her high and dry."

"No," Louis said. "We were eighteen. I proposed. Had a ring and everything. Had a big ruby in it. Belonged to my grandmother."

"She said no?"

"Said we were too young."

"So you ran off to the war?"

"Didn't have a plan B," Louis said. "Had to find one quick."

"Iraq, Afghanistan."

"Sure took my mind off her."

"But not really?" I said.

"No," Louis said.

"All this time I thought you were just moody."

He smiled.

"Is she here?" I said.

He shook his head.

"Was she?"

He shrugged.

"Did you come looking for Marta or the money?" I said.

"Same thing," Louis said. "Follow the money, that's where she'll show up."

"Unless," I said.

He shook his head.

"Pretty woman, they think she's helpless, she turns the tables. Marta's very good at pivoting."

"Pivoting?"

"Turning an obstacle into an opportunity—it's the way Marta works," Louis said. "It's instinct."

"Why?" I said. "You've known her since she was a kid. What's her deal?"

Louis looked away. He had me talking like she was alive.

"Always had to fend for herself," Louis said.

"After the car accident."

Louis smiled.

"It was no accident," he said. "Father was ex-military turned mobster. Sold off Soviet military hardware in the nineties. Had a falling out with the group, so the gang ran them off the road, left them to die."

"But she lit the field on fire," I said.

He was startled, but only for a moment.

"You looked it up."

"Basic research," I said.

"See what I mean?" Louis said. "She's resourceful. Tough. Smart."

I thought about it.

"Yeah, and the apple doesn't fall very far," I said. "She ends up with some shady money launderer?"

"She didn't love him," Louis said. "It's all about survival."

"Until it isn't," I said.

We stood. The dog got up and gave me another sniff.

"Why would she cover her tracks if she's innocent?" I said.

"They're gonna try to pin the Virgin Gorda murder on her. Can't touch the Russian mob, bought off everybody in London, so they need somebody to take the fall."

330 • GERRY BOYLE

"Had her boyfriend tied up and tortured until he gave up the money?"

"She wouldn't do that," Louis said.

I hesitated, said, "Maybe she would, Louis. If she thought he was going to dump her. If she thought she was going to end up with no money, maybe she'd do that in a second."

The dog perked up. Lifted his head, then put it back down. Louis shook his head.

"Love is blind, Louis," I said. "You're a good man, but this is where we part. She comes back, I call the cops. Fair warning."

Louis looked at me and there was a coldness in his eyes, like I was no longer Jack his friend but an adversary in the lethal game he played very well. It was the look I imagined he had in combat before he pulled the trigger.

He turned and walked across the dooryard to his Jeep, held the back door open for the dog. The dog leapt up and in, and Louis got in, too, started the truck, and pulled out. He backed a full half-circle so the driver's door was facing me. Buzzed the window down.

"That would be a big mistake, Jack," he said, and put the Jeep in gear and pulled away. The dog watched me intently from the backseat, the way he did when someone or something was a potential enemy, target, prey.

I stared right back.

After the Jeep had gone down the road, I gave an audible ten-count and, with a last glance at the house, stepped into the barn workshop, closed the door behind me.

The room was quiet and shadowed, the light coming in from the west where the stalls were, with a few small windows. I walked the perimeter of the shop, leaned down to look under benches, behind motor stands. There were cabinets for tools and I opened those, saw wrenches and screwdrivers and nothing else. I leaned close to the wall to look behind the cabinets, saw nothing but rough-hewn boards covered in decades of dust and dirt.

That led me to the doorway and I went left, started down the long corridor, stalls on the left. Pokey stirred at my footsteps and poked his head through the slats of the gate. There were apples in a burlap bag hanging on a nail and I fished one out, held it up. Pokey took a bite, bared his teeth as he reached for more. Three bites and the apple was gone, and he chewed and chewed, looking to me to see if there was more.

"Anybody been in here, buddy?" I said. "Pretty woman, dark hair?"

He gave my hand a last nuzzle and snort and turned away.

I walked down the passageway, eyeing the empty box stalls. Nothing inside but old hay, leather straps hanging from the wooden walls. And then I was at the staircase. I went up.

The loft was mostly full, bales stacked up to the rafters. It smelled like hay and the air was dusty. I got out my phone, turned on the light, walked slowly along the front of the bales. There was a third-floor loft reached by a ladder, and I climbed it, stood on the catwalk. The walls were bare, light showing through the cracks between the gable end doors.

A second ladder led to the cupola and I climbed that, too, found a swallow's nest, a few initials carved into the boards. None were "MK."

I climbed back down to the main loft, made my way slowly to the rear of the space, facing the field and woods. There was lumber stacked, a horse weather vane acquired but never installed. Some furniture piled along the wall, evicted from the house but not dispatched to the kindling pile. I shone the light into the tangle of chairs and tables, saw nothing. I swiped my finger along the chair arms and seats and came away with a gray smudge of dust.

Nothing had been recently moved.

I headed for the stairs, figuring I'd go to the open-ended cellar. There were old horse-drawn mowers and harrows, rusting away in place. It was dark, and there might be a place where a bag could be stuffed up over the stone foundation, dark enough that Clair hadn't noticed. This was where Pokey's stall was swept down through a trapdoor, the manure and straw shoveled out with the loader on the front of Clair's small John Deere. Hay and grain in; manure and straw out.

The grain was stored in a big wooden bin and funneled down to the boxes through a wooden chute. Grain was dumped into the bin out of burlap bags, Clair running them up through the loft door with the conveyor. Pokey ate a lot of grain in a winter, and the bin was almost full in early December.

I stopped and leaned over the rim. Put a hand down and ran it through the grain, cool and smooth as coarse sand.

I put the light on it. There was a rise at one side, whereas usually the grain rose to a sort of peak in the center, like sand piled from an hourglass. I moved around the bin, leaned over, and swept at the grain. It fell back into the indentation and I swept it aside again.

Dug deeper.

Felt nothing but the cool kernels.

Another sweep.

Felt something hard.

I climbed up on the side of the bin and peered in. There was a dark streak six inches beneath the surface of the grain. I climbed over and in and scooped the grain away with two hands, like I was digging for buried treasure.

Which I was.

It was a gray canvas duffel. I yanked it out by the straps on top and wrestled it to the surface. It said PATAGONIA in big letters on the side. The zipper was on top and I brushed it off, pulled it open.

I knew what was in it, but still I had to lift the flap.

And there they were.

The stacks of $100 bills. I felt an urge to look behind me, like if the money was there, Marta would be, too.

And maybe this was why Louis had been at the barn. Searching? Checking to make sure the stash was safe? That things were going according to plan?

I zipped the bag closed, slid it back down into the hole in the grain. It didn't go as deep as it had been, and I pulled the bag back out, dug the hole wider, scraped the bottom. I lifted the bag and dropped it straight down in and it fit better. Sweeping the grain back into the hole, I covered the bag, then kept shoveling with my hands until the hole was a faint mound. I climbed out of the bin and leaned back inside and tried to give it the same contour I'd found. And then I walked to the stairs and started down. Every two steps I stopped and listened.

Pokey clumping in his stall. Crows calling. The rattle of a loose windowpane.

I walked quickly and quietly past the stalls and into the workshop, went to the door. Looked out the window and it was darker, the gray dusk falling fast.

Nobody showing.

I opened the door and stepped out. Closed it behind me. Looked around again and then walked across the dooryard to the entrance to the path, kept walking.

It was darker in the woods, the brambles and branches trembling in the wind. I looked left and right, peering into the shadows, seeing only more shadows behind them. Ahead I could see a trail, a snaking opening, paler shade of gray. I thought I saw someone, but it was a bent tree trunk, part of a dying apple from the days when this was all farm.

I kept walking, a steady pace, then stopped suddenly. Looked left and right and back. Listened. Started walking again, telling myself Marta might not be back for months. She might not be back ever, cremated not once, but twice.

I stopped again.

And then I picked up the pace, and the house was in sight. There were lights on in the kitchen, Roxanne and Sophie home from school. Alone.

I crossed the yard, circled the garage, went in the shed door. Let myself into the mudroom, then the kitchen. Roxanne was putting Sophie's lunch containers into the dishwasher. She looked up at me and said, "Jack, are you okay?"

I moved closer, whispered, "The money. I found it."

Sophie came running into the kitchen, said, "Daddy. You're all covered with dirt."

37

Dinner. Tub. Bedtime. Books. Anticipation.

We went to the study, sat on the couch. I started at the beginning, which seemed long ago. Teak at the jail, Harriet there, too. Dr. Bainer. Louis and his new gun.

Louis at the barn, looking to explain himself. I walked her through it, told her about the love part.

"Now it makes sense," Roxanne said.

"It does?"

"He isn't thinking straight. He's smitten, seeing only what he wants to see."

"Or she's someone who killed somebody, burned them to cinders," I said. "It's like it doesn't matter. He's still on her side. He pretty much warned me to leave her alone."

We mulled that over for a moment—Louis as adversary; Louis picking sides.

"The money," Roxanne said.

I told her. The bin. The grain. The bag.

"Maybe Louis left it there, for Marta to pick up."

"Or the other way around," I said.

"Either way, safer than keeping it at his house, with all the cops around."

We sat again, staring straight ahead, our minds whirring. And then it was Roxanne who said, "We should leave it right where it is. If it's there, she'll take it and leave. She comes back and it's gone, she's going to come looking, or someone else will, who's been told where it is."

That scenario wasn't a pleasant one.

We were quiet.

"You protect your own," Roxanne said.

"Yes," I said.

There was a thump from upstairs and then Sophie's footsteps. She called down the stairs, "Can somebody get me a drink?"

"I'll do it," Roxanne said.

"I have to tell Clair," I said.

"Don't be gone long. Or far," she said. "We'll go to school in the morning, but I want you here tonight."

It was a dark night, low clouds and no moon. I stood and listened to the crackle of the woods, peered into the darkness. There was no one in sight on the road, east or west. The spruces across the way were a wall of black.

I heard a boot step, turned.

"Thought I was gonna have to smack you upside the head, get your attention," Clair said.

"I heard you," I said. "Was playing possum."

He smiled, said, "What do you got?"

"Two million in cash," I said. "Give or take."

"Where?"

"Buried in the grain bin in the barn," I said. "A waterproof duffel."

"Stashed it and ran."

"If she does come back, it's trouble. If someone else comes, it's even more trouble."

We stood. A coyote yipped from deep in the woods, then another, even deeper.

"Louis said her dad was some sort of criminal in Ukraine, selling weapons after the Soviet Union collapsed. Both parents got killed by mobsters."

"Not entirely surprised," Clair said. "She's got this sort of amorality to her. Almost feral. In a very attractive way."

I nodded. The night was quiet around us.

"I saw Louis here. He said he's in love with her."

"I figured that. Head over heels."

"Not necessarily on our side," I said.

"No," Clair said. "Not this time."

When I went back into the house, Roxanne was going up to bed. I heard the bedsprings squeak, a sound that on another night might have meant something very different. Then the bedroom TV came on, cable news. I went to the kitchen and made a pot of tea, poured it into an insulated mug. Then I turned the lights out on the first floor, put on my parka, and went to the sliding door to the deck. I opened it and stepped out, circled the house on the cleared path. Each step was like walking on broken glass, the crunching sounds crackling into the woods.

It would be a night to sit and listen.

338 • GERRY BOYLE

I walked around to the big black Ford, unlocked the door, and
reached the Glock out from under the seat. I slipped it out of its
holster, slid the gun and an extra magazine into the right-side pocket
of my parka.

The metal was cold to the touch. I warmed it with my hand,
thought of John Lennon, his song about happiness. Then I walked
around the house again, and climbed the steps. I opened the slider
and went inside and took a kitchen chair from the dining room and
set it on the deck.

Sat. Sipped my tea. The woods rattled like the trees were on the
march. I watched. Listened. Ran through the day in my head, kept
sticking at the same places. Was Harriet romantically involved with
Teak? What triggered his explosion? Did Barrett really have something
incriminating on Rod? How would we feel if the body in the car did
turn out to be Marta.

Manning the barricades, afraid of a dead person.

Barred owls again, their calls echoing through the frozen woods.
A branch snapped. I stood and made my way down the steps. Froze
in the shadow of the house and listened.

Another crack.

Gun out, I waited and listened, straining to hear a footstep, a
cough or a sniffle.

Nothing.

Fifteen minutes went by and still nothing. My feet were cold, my
gun hand, too. I circled the house slowly, froze in the driveway as a
truck approached from the east. I eased behind Roxanne's car as the
truck slowed, the headlights slashing the darkness.

I heard music. Country-western blaring behind closed windows

The truck passed, an old Chevy pickup, two people showing. It sped up as it passed Clair's house, continued on down the road. And then it was quiet again. Dark again. Silent for a moment, and then the woods noise.

Snap. Crackle.

I walked the rest of the way around the house, stopped at the deck. Listened again. Heard only the whisper of the woods. Walked up the steps, grabbed my mug, and slipped back inside.

From the base of the stairs, I saw that Roxanne had turned off the TV and the light. Moving to the living room, I stood in the front window, looked out at the road and the driveway and the hard-crusted snow. I looked at my phone. It was almost ten. I checked my email, flipped through the queue.

One email stopped me, from the day before.

From: Jane.Brockway@NYT.com
Subject: Nigel Dean

> *Hey Jack. Janie here. We met, but you probably don't remember it. I was an intern. You were the hard-ass metro reporter in a beat-up leather jacket. I had a crush on you. Now I said it. True confession.*
>
> *K. D. Carlisle says you want to know about Nigel Dean. Very tough guy. Guess the people who killed him were tougher.*
>
> *Word on the street only: Dean was a money launderer. He'd "invest" in companies, when in reality the dirty money was flowing the other way. He buys and sells, makes paper profits, the dirty money gets reinvested and comes out clean. Then it goes back where it came from, minus his cut. I'm thinking he got greedy. Russian mob, they don't fool around. They're also very connected here. If it had been a home invasion by some locals, they'd be sitting in a Caribbean jail by now.*
>
> *After 2 here. Gotta work tomorrow.*

Cheers.
  PS: What are you working on? Owe me one now,
McMorrow. Nigel Dean have ties to Maine?

I wrote back.

Thanks. Be in touch.

And a white lie.

  I remember you as an intern. I knew you'd make good.

Nigel Dean was very dirty. Marta was with him for years and would have sniffed it out in minutes. Maybe it was luck that she got away with $2 million. I didn't think so.

She had a plan. Launder herself. Disappear Marta Kovac, resurrect herself as someone else—with money to live on until she set up the next guy. What went wrong? Her old boyfriend's buddies weren't the Maine rubes she'd expected? One of them asked a lot of questions?

And this place in Maine, it wasn't as close to the ends of the earth as she thought. Marshals tracked her down. And if they could do it . . .

I closed the laptop and the room went dark. Then I went back outside, sat in my chair, the Glock on my lap. Listened. Watched. Walked around the house. Listened and watched some more.

At midnight I came inside, locked the slider behind me. Sat on the couch and watched the yard through the glass. Made a circuit around the house, stopping at windows that provided vantage points in each direction. Told myself I should sleep, and sat on the couch again.

It could be days. Weeks. Life had to go on, even with the boatload of money in the barn. But still, I tried to get into Marta's head. Watch the house, wait until everybody's gone. Move in fast, grab the bag, and go. A last hurdle before the new life begins.

I'm Marta Kovac and I'm missing, presumed dead. If I tell you otherwise, I'll have to kill you.

At two a.m. I was still on the couch, thinking, listening. Three. Four. And then I woke up and Roxanne was shaking me, saying, "Jack. It's quarter to seven. We're getting ready to go."

It was snowing, fat white flakes that floated down like autumn leaves. I scanned the yard, the road, the woods on both sides. No tracks.

There was an inch of snow on the car and I cleaned Roxanne's windows, then took a swipe at mine. Got in the truck, put the gun on the seat. Roxanne pulled out first and Sophie waved from the backseat. I followed, saw them into the school, and backtracked home.

I circled the yard, saw only the remnants of my own trail circling the house. Then I went inside, put the kettle on, and made another cup of tea. Then I sat and looked through my notes: My first visit to the shelter with Harriet and Dolph and Arthur. Mutt and the boys in the basement. Teak's dad, still proud of his son—or at least, the son he once knew. His brother, who had no comment.

I flipped through the pages, underlining key points, scrawling stars next to the best quotes. Barrett: "Rod is an egotistical, narcissistic philanderer. I blame him for my mother's death."

A complicated story, but weren't they all. I visualized a headline in the *Times*: MURDERS OF MAINE MOTHER AND SON: ONE RANDOM, ONE UNSOLVED.

And then another: FLEEING CARIBBEAN MURDER AND RUSSIAN MOB, WOMAN SUFFERS VIOLENT DEATH IN RURAL MAINE.

That story I couldn't write. Yet.

I went back to Teak. Something not quite right about that headline. Yes, two murders. But was Lindy's killing totally random? Not quite. I tried another subhead: "Volunteer killed by a client of the agency she wanted to serve."

Leaned back in the chair and stared at the screen. It was true. Teak had killed Lindy. She had volunteered at Loaves & Fishes. Barrett was her son, but he had no connection to the shelter.

But yes, he did. The papers in the apartment. The cartons in the car. The boxes delivered. Harriet angry and upset. What had they said? "Miss H. was some ugly."

I got up from the chair and went to the window to think.

Yeah, Barrett hated his stepfather. Yeah, he had information that could ruin Rod, maybe get him in trouble with the IRS. And Lindy had that, too. She was an accomplice to whatever minor tax fraud they'd committed. Fudging the books. Trimming the profits.

But that hadn't gotten Lindy killed. Teak had killed Lindy, but he was sitting in the earthlings' jail when Barrett had been stabbed. Did he have someone else he'd recruited to the cause? One of the guys from the basement crew?

"No," I said aloud. "They all knew Teak was nuts."

There was a knock at the door from the shed. I took the Glock off the desk and went through the kitchen to the window. No vehicle in the driveway. Tracks leading not from the road, but from the side of the garage. From the direction of the barn.

Marta.

I racked a cartridge into the chamber.

Four knocks, louder than the first. Clair?

I was walking back into the kitchen when it struck me. The boxes. Lindy had the cartons of shelter stuff when she was killed. Barrett had the same records, sitting in Lindy's car. Where were they now?

More knocks. Marta not going away?

I put a hand on the latch. Lifted.

Pulled the door back.

Harriet. Red knit hat, puffy dark green parka, L.L.Bean insignia.

"Hi, Mr. McMorrow," Harriet said. "Hey. Sorry to bother you. I actually went to your neighbor's house first. I thought the lady at the store said it was the white house with the big barn, right? So I went there, but nobody was home, and then I said, 'Harriet, maybe she said the house *before* the barn.' "

She looked down and saw the gun at my side and her eyes bugged out.

"Whoa. I guess you don't like visitors."

"No, it's fine," I said. "There's been some stuff going on."

I slipped the Glock inside my jacket pocket. She took a step closer and I backed inside the room. Harriet said, "Could I come in? Just for a few minutes?"

But she was already in.

"I don't want to bother you. Your wife and daughter, I mean. If you're—"

"They went to school," I said. "What brings you down—"

She lunged, the glint of a blade coming at my chest. I leapt back, flung my arm up too late, felt the hot sting, the point prick just below my throat. The knife arm jabbing, the left hand clutching at me, my jacket, my shirt. I scrambled backwards, hit the wall, spun to my right, the knife in my left upper arm, stuck right in.

I shouted, sidestepped, Harriet following close like we were dancing. The knife stayed in my arm—white-hot pain, a black grip—and she lost her hold on it, and I backpedaled down the hall as she grabbed for the knife, missed, grabbed, missed.

She was strong, quick, her jaw clenched and her eyes intense, fixed on the knife. I tried to get my gun out but the jacket was swinging behind me like a cape, and then she had the handle and yanked it out and away from me. I shouted in pain as she fell two steps back.

Lunged again.

I had hold of the gun in my pocket but the butt caught. I whirled like a bullfighter, went for her knife hand with my left. She slashed up and I felt the blade slice my palm, the hand going hot and numb.

I screamed and she charged at me, tried to pin me to the wall with her left arm, the right going back to thrust. Another burn in my chest, Harriet pulling back for another jab. I let go of the gun, locked my right arm around her left, spun hard, and flung her against the wall. She hit hard, her head snapping back, and I bulled forward, got inside the knife arm, jammed my forearm against her neck. She was slashing at my back, my side, and I felt the blade slicing above my belt, more burning, and I pushed hard with my forearm, bulled forward, legs scrabbling on the floor, slipping on my blood.

I stayed with her as she slashed, got my left elbow up and jammed it into her face. Blood spurted from her nose and I pressed her to the wall, felt her shifting her grip on the knife, trying to stab, not slice, get the knife in deep.

For Barrett, the heart. For me, kidneys, spleen.

"Drop it," I said, hollering into her face, and I let off her neck, took a half-step back, grabbed for her knife hand and missed.

Pulled my arm back just out of reach of a slash, and leaned in to kick her hard in the shin, jumped on her instep. She howled and it turned into a shriek, and I jammed my forearm back across her throat, pressed her into the wall like she'd go through it.

She got another jab in, stuck me in the butt. Her mouth gaped and her eyes bulged. The knife arm waved, the blade scraping my bare back at my waist. I pressed her throat harder, said, "Drop it," but she didn't. I kept pressing, shouting again and again, and she was gagging.

And her right arm went limp.

The knife fell to the floor.

I glanced down, kicked it down the hall. Let off on her throat and she fell back against the wall, gasping and coughing. I shoved her sideways to the floor, rolled her onto her back.

Harriet was breathing hard, chest heaving. Blood was running from her nose, down her cheek. I picked up the knife. It had a long narrow symmetrical blade, made for stabbing. The grip was leather, slippery with blood, hers and mine.

I bent to the bottom drawer and took out a roll of duct tape, stuck Harriet's knife in with the plastic bags and aluminum foil. Took a knife from the block and ripped the sleeve of my shirt open. The cut in my upper arm was a two-inch gap showing pink inner flesh like raw tuna. I tore a length of tape off, wrapped it around my bicep and over the cut.

My palm was bleeding, dripping horror-movie splotches onto the counter. I wiped my hand with a kitchen towel, tore off another length of tape, and wrapped my palm. My fingers were stiffening and my thumb was numb. I took the gun from my pocket, put it in my left hand. Taped it in place, my finger inside the trigger guard.

Harriet had stopped coughing and had turned over, was on all fours. I walked toward her, and she staggered to her feet. I put my right arm around her neck and dragged her to the kitchen. Yanked a chair out and shoved her down into it. Slapped her on the side of the head hard enough to stun her, then quickly stooped to wrap her in tape at the waist, around and around the chair.

She was shaking her head and saying, "She started it. She did."

"And we're going to end it, Harriet," I said. "End it right here."

All of my cuts burned. I grimaced, went to the sink and poured her a glass of water. Plunked it down on the table in front of her. Went back to the counter for a box of tissues. I plunked those in front of her, too. I moved to the chair opposite her and sat, my taped gun hand on the table.

She pulled a tissue out and pressed it to her nose. Looked at it and it was crimson. I took my phone from my pocket, tapped it once, then again to open the recorder. Hit the red button and put the phone at the center of the table.

"The police," she said, her voice husky, larynx bruised. "Aren't you going to call them?"

"No police," I said. "This is an interview. Start talking."

She looked at me.

"Go to hell," she said.

"Not going anywhere," I said. "You aren't either."

38

We sat face-to-face, silent except for her ragged breathing.

The graph on my phone recorder was flat, like a monitor hooked up to a dead person.

"Why Lindy?"

She pressed her lips shut.

"Why Barrett?"

No response.

"His DNA will be on the knife," I said. "I don't care how much you tried to wash it. Leather grip was a mistake."

I waited, then said, "You'll get fifty, minimum. Nikki and Shane will be collecting Social Security."

Her lips parted, then closed.

"Think of this as your chance to sway public opinion, maybe influence a jury."

She looked at me, trying to adjust to this new reality.

"It was for them, wasn't it?" I said. "The cars, the trips, the clothes. None of it was for you, was it?"

I could see something building, and then it burst through.

"Of course it wasn't for me," Harriet snapped, like she was insulted. "It was all for them."

"So they could have the life you never had."

"They deserve it. Not their fault their mother married a piece of crap."

"So it started small. And then things just got out of your control. Is that right?"

Harriet looked at the bloody tissue again. Balled it up and placed it on the table and took another one.

"I didn't mean to hurt anyone, I really didn't," she said. "You know me. I help people. It's what I do."

I didn't know her. I wondered if I truly knew anyone.

The graph on the recorder was flat-lined. Harriet looked at it and said, "I had no choice. Lindy. She was going to bring the whole place down. I could tell, the way she looked around, the way she asked questions. 'Who pays for these workers? Do you pay their Social Security? What systems do you have in place?' "

She looked at me and her mouth formed a sneer.

"Systems. I don't have *systems*. I just find the money to feed these people. To put them up so they don't freeze to death. Walk a few miles in my shoes, you know? Alcoholics and drug addicts and people who are mentally ill and people who are all three. And I'm all they have, between freezing to death or drinking themselves to death or sleeping in the gutter. Miss H. will help them out."

She crumpled the red-splotched tissue and put it on the table in front of her. Her nose was crusted with coagulating blood.

"How much, Harriet?" I said.

She wiped her eyes, folded the tissue into a square and wiped her eyes again.

"I don't know," she said. "What, you think I kept track?"

"A lot?" I said.

Harriet nodded.

"I was going to pay it back."

She looked at me for a reaction. I gave her none.

"What was the first time?"

"A couple of hundred. Nikki wanted to go on this school trip to Boston. Museums and two nights in a hotel. My sister told her no, it wasn't in the budget. Telling that poor girl she'd have to stay home while all of her friends went. That's just wrong."

"I suppose it is," I said.

"Because then they all know she's the poor kid, she doesn't belong. And they talk down to her. Stop inviting her to things. I know, believe me. Because I was the poor kid. I told you about that. And I wasn't going to let that happen to my Nikki. Not to Shane either."

"The cars," I said. "The clothes. The spending money. Trips to Florida, Disney World."

"They needed me. It was like the clients. They didn't have anybody else."

"A hundred thousand?"

Harriet dabbed at her nose, didn't answer. I waited.

"I don't know," she said. "Maybe."

"And Lindy Hines was going to see it, plain as day. Skimming the donations; is that how you did it? Had to be more than bake sales and donation jars."

She hid behind the tissue.

"You're very smart, Harriet," I said. "What did you come up with?"

The recorder twitched away. My gun hand throbbed. I couldn't feel my trigger finger. She looked at the gun and I lifted it off the table, pointed it in her direction.

"Don't even think of it."

"Do you have the safety on?" Harriet said. "It's making me nervous."

"Glocks don't have safeties," I said.

I let that hang, said, "My finger is twitchy. From the cut."

She looked at the gun, then at me.

"People work around the holidays. Thanksgiving and Christmas are wicked busy months. Then I lay them off in February."

"But keep paying them," I said. "And the money goes into an account that you control."

"I mean, I wasn't taking donations," Harriet said. "A lot of it's from grants."

I nodded.

"Teak," I said.

She took a breath, looked around the room. When she looked back I was still staring at her.

"He was always talking about vanquishing evil," I said. "What did you do? Give him an assignment?"

"I just told him about this evil thing that might happen."

"That was all it took?"

She shrugged.

"It was like his comic-book life was coming true, I guess," she said.

"What was the elixir? I'm thinking meth. Mix it with juice? Put it in a silver chalice?"

She looked at me. I lifted the gun.

"I won't shoot you in the head. I'll start with your hands."

She swallowed, looked away from me as she said, "It was warm cider. A water bottle."

"Where did you get the meth?"

Harriet shrugged.

"Our clientele, lots of ways."

I considered it. Teak's family. Recliners and a new TV.

"He never killed anybody before, not to make Hakata come to life," I said. "I'm thinking it took more than the meth."

I waited a beat and said, "How much?"

Harriet tried to look puzzled. "How much what?"

"How much did you pay him?"

She looked at me more closely. "What did he tell you?"

I didn't answer. She opened her mouth, then closed it.

"This is the way I see it, Harriet. It was an emergency. Teak was on the fence about taking Lindy out, the galactic warrior idea not quite doing it. You had to give him more motivation. Send money home, Teak. Be a hero. And vanquish some evil at the same time."

Harriet looked at me, lips pursed.

"Ten grand? Twenty?"

I lifted the gun and aimed it at her elbow, let the barrel make a small circle. Harriet looked at it, then back at me.

"Ten up front. Ten when it was done. Ten when he gets out."

"Insanity plea," I said.

"If he isn't nuts, who is?" Harriet said.

"The money will kill that angle. You go down, he goes down."

She looked pensive, mulling it over, then looked at me and said, "Okay, then. Just shoot me. Kill me right now. Self-defense."

I considered it. "What? You have a life insurance policy that pays out to the kids? But if you sit in jail for forty years, they get jack?"

"Do it, Mr. McMorrow. Just end it. Please."

I shook my head. She took a long, resigned breath.

And dove across the table for the gun. I yanked it back, one of her hands on the barrel. She twisted my wrist, had the gun pointed at her cheek, was digging into the tape to get her finger on the trigger. I punched her hand and she hung on and I twisted her arm, slammed it on the table. She squirmed loose.

Her finger was digging in, she had the trigger guard. I pulled her arm toward me and the gun trained on my belly, her finger still picking through the tape. I raised her arm and slammed it back down on the table, elbow first.

She gasped. Her hand went slack. I shoved her back into the chair, pointed the gun at her face.

She was panting. The blood had started to run from her nose again.

"Okay, Harriet," I said. "Here's the deal. You tell me about Barrett, I'll give you the gun."

She looked startled.

"Really?"

"I'll leave the gun outside. One round in the magazine. I'll go for a ride down the road and back. I have another gun in the truck."

She brightened.

"You'd do that for me?"

"Sure. You want to die, fine. Beats sitting in a cell for fifty years."

She almost smiled. Settled back into the chair. The recorder was still on.

"Well, okay. Barrett. He was the same. Asking me what his mother had found out. Said he was going to look through the boxes himself. I couldn't let that happen."

"A slippery slope," I said. "What did it feel like to kill somebody? Yourself, I mean."

She looked away, like she was trying to remember.

"I thought it would be, like, way harder, but it was just like meat, like when I was working at the slaughterhouse. Same fat and muscle and stringy stuff."

"Barrett Hines wasn't a chicken," I said.

"I know. I'm just saying, the knife, it just went right in."

"Did he say anything?"

"He just looked at me, very surprised, and then there was blood. He reached down and felt it, then tried to grab the knife. But it was too late. He fell down and then he took a few breaths and then he just stopped."

"Breathing."

"Right. He just went still. Like on television. That was good. I didn't want him to suffer or anything. His mom didn't suffer. Somebody said she was dead before she hit the floor."

She smiled at me hopefully, like this showed she wasn't such a bad person after all.

"Third time wasn't a charm," I said.

"No, you moved faster."

"Should have parked out front," I said. "Come in and gotten settled, waited until I turned my back to make you tea or something."

"Right. Well, too late now. A lot of things are like that. If you knew then what you know now."

Harriet looked at me, mustered a weird smile, and said, "Can I do it now?"

I picked up the phone, turned off the recorder.

"I changed my mind," I said, tapped the numbers.

9-1-1.

39

There were the usual sirens and flashing lights, Prosperity Volunteer Rescue first on the scene, and in fifteen minutes the driveway and road filled up. The low point of the next hour was Roxanne and Sophie rolling up to the scene, Roxanne running wide-eyed into the house, breaking into tears when she saw me safe, talking to a deputy at the table.

"I tried to call," I said.

"My phone died," she said.

"I'm sorry. Tell Sophie I'm fine."

Roxanne turned and hurried back out.

The local paramedics sliced the tape off my hand, a woman named Richie I'd seen at the store saying I needed to get the palm stitched up. She said they'd probably use glue on the cut on my arm, that they'd transport me to the hospital in Belfast. I said I needed to wait.

It was an hour before Tingley and Bates rolled up. Harriet was somewhere outside, I figured, cuffed in the back of a cruiser. They came to me first, Bates sitting at the table so she could take notes, Tingley standing at the counter. I told them the story. The knock at the door, Harriet there, the knife coming out, the facts that emerged.

"All this to be the favorite aunt?" Tingley said.

"Everybody wants to be loved by somebody," I said.

They took Harriet to jail, probably for life. I went to the hospital in an ambulance, and only had to stay two hours. Roxanne left Sophie with Mary and Clair and picked me up at the entrance to the ER. She hugged me in the car and it hurt my arm. I winced, but only inwardly.

I turned in the passenger seat of the Subaru, with its broken window, and held her right hand with mine. She squeezed my hand hard and held on, not wiping the tears that trickled down her cheeks. We were five miles out of town before she spoke.

"Is this it?" Roxanne said.

I looked at her.

"Is this the worst thing," she said, "and now we can just live our lives—be happy?" she said.

"I am happy," I said.

"You could have died, Jack. If she'd gotten you in the heart or cut an artery. I mean, she almost got your wrist. The artery there—"

"The ulna," I said. "But she didn't."

"And all because you were there in the store when that woman was killed."

"Yes."

"And decided that you had to write that story," Roxanne said.

"It's a good story."

"But how can you write it now? With everything that's happened?"

"With one hand tied behind my back," I said.

40

Teak had his day in court. I was there, along with his dad. And Barrett's husband Travis. The reporter from Riverport, Trevor-something, and a couple of talking heads from TV. And Rod Blaine, sitting in the row behind Travis. I walked by him and he nodded. I stopped and said, "How you doing?"

He looked back at me and said, "Sorry. I was an ass."

And then the room filled up, and the odd bits of family were interspersed with cops and lawyers and docs and a few members of the public who were sick of watching television.

Compared to his last appearance, Teak was subdued and looked smaller, like a superhero who had lost his powers. He was wearing shackles and a white collared shirt and khaki trousers. He sat beside his lawyer, a young guy who did defense work, including cases that were high-profile but total losers. Get your name in the paper, brings in the drunk drivers and divorces.

After Harriet's arrest and murder charges, this one was hopeless through and through. We all listened as Penelope Bainer was questioned by the state prosecutor She said she'd examined lots of supposedly crazy people who had killed people. A few of them had Teak's illness, schizoaffective disorder, as she'd explained it to me earlier. Symptoms generally include hallucinations, delusions, disorganized thinking, depression, and manic behavior, she told the court.

Teak Barney? Check, check, check, check, and check.

But Bainer said she didn't find Teak particularly threatening in their one interaction.

"As a matter of fact," she said, "he can be quite engaging."

She walked through the hours after Teak's arrest. When Teak first went to the hospital ER, they shot him full of Haldol to subdue him. Then he was given Zyprexa, his antipsychotic, and the regular dosage knocked him for a loop. He slept for two days and was groggy for another after he came to.

"But this was his regular medication," Gaddis said. "Why did it affect him this way now? He'd functioned quite well on Zyprexa in the past."

"It was too much," Bainer said. "It was essentially a double dose."

"How could that be?"

"Because Mr. Barney hadn't gone off his meds," Bainer said. "He'd ingested crystal methamphetamine."

The courtroom perked up.

"It's not a given that the murder was committed while Mr. Barney was truly psychotic," Bainer said.

"Then what was he?" she was asked.

"Very wired," Bainer said. "Intense. Probably paranoid and delusional. But still able to focus. To carry out the plan."

For Teak, it went downhill from there. Bainer said it was clear to her that Teak was trying to mimic his delusional symptoms when he was speaking to her. The problem was that in real life, Teak was by most definitions crazy. But he wasn't *that* crazy. There was also the matter of the ten-grand down payment.

Teak went back to jail. His lawyers had their work cut out.

I wrote in my notebook: *35 years.*

The story ran on page one, below the fold. We had a photo of Teak being led from the courtroom, holding his head up in some attempt at dignity, like a captured king. Matched it with a shot of Harriet at the shelter, ladling out beef stew. The headline said, FROM A HARDSCRABBLE HOMELESS SHELTER, A LETHAL PLOT EMERGED.

I reread the story online at breakfast: Harriet held without bail, the woman they called Cowgirl stepping up to keep the shelter going. Teak's dad saying his boy always wanted to do good, and even in killing "that lady," his son thought he was doing the right thing.

It was 6:10. Dark and cold. I was on my second cup of tea and there was a knock on the door. I got up and opened it. Clair stepped in.

"What?" I said.

"Marta. Ruiz said they spotted her."

"Where?"

"Toronto."

"Alive?"

"Partly," Clair said. "They think she's been trafficked."

A sinking feeling came over me, like black mud.

"Jesus."

"Yes."

"They talk to Louis?"

"Ruiz was looking for him."

"You?"

"Tried calling. Not answering."

"Let's go."

"Follow the money," Clair said.

"Always," I said.

We walked down the path to the barn, walked through the shop, and climbed the stairs to the loft. I used my phone to light my way. Clair knew each tread by heart.

We approached the grain bin side by side, peered over the edge and down. Where there had been a mound of grain, there was a duffel-sized hole.

We rolled up to the driveway. This time the cable was up.

"Didn't we just do this?" I said.

"Time flies."

"When the world is going all to hell," I said.

I parked the Ford in the snowbank and we got out and zipped our jackets and started walking. There were fresh tire tracks, in and out. We trudged on, down the road between the trees, boots scuffing the hard snow. The closer we got to the house, the heavier the sense of foreboding grew.

And then we saw lights, smelled smoke from the woodstove. Louis was alive. Recently.

We climbed the porch, and Clair knocked on the big front door. Then he tried the latch and the door swung open. The dog was waiting, standing in front of us, not wagging but not growling either.

Clair said, "Where's Louis?" and the dog turned, paws clicking, and started in the direction of the bedroom. We followed and walked through the door. Stopped. Stared.

"Hey," Clair said.

"Hey," Louis said back. "You too, Jack."

He was leaning over the bed. It was covered in guns, arranged on an old sheet. Shotguns, handguns, a short-barreled rifle with a metal stock. Boxes and clips of ammo. A couple of scopes. Gun cases on the floor.

"Taking inventory?" Clair said.

Louis didn't answer. Picked up a long magazine and snapped it into the short-barreled rifle.

"Didn't know you had an H and K," Clair said.

"A lot of things about me you don't know," Louis said.

"You going looking for her?" Clair said.

"Yeah. She sent me a text. Must've gotten hold of a john's phone."

"Where?" Clair said.

"Toronto," Louis said.

He picked a case up off the floor and laid it on the bed. Flipped it open and put the rifle inside, snapped the lid shut.

"How you going to get this stuff through the border?" I said.

"Hire a fisherman to take me in. Coastline is a sieve. Buy a car and I'm off. Like Marta said, you have cash, you can go anywhere."

"You have hers?" I said. "From the barn?"

"What do they call it? Poetic justice?" Louis said.

He started putting ammo into a plastic box.

"You might not win this one," Clair said.

"Doesn't matter."

Louis snapped the ammo box shut and laid two handguns in a single case. Turned back to us.

"Face it, guys. We're the warrior class. You too, Jack. Your stories, the two of us stepping in—that's not about news. Don't kid yourself.

It's about beating back the bad guys, you know? Keeping them at bay. Giving good people a fighting chance. There have to be consequences."

It was the most I'd ever heard Louis say in one chunk. I thought of Harriet and Teak, sitting in jail. Barrett and his mom, dead and gone. Marta suffering a worse fate.

Bad guys were up by one. Maybe Louis would make it even. In this not nearly perfect world, it was the most we could hope for.

"Good luck," I said.

"Take care, Marine," Clair said.

We walked out of the room. The dog watched us go.

ACKNOWLEDGMENTS

Several people were remarkably generous in helping me as I wrote this story. Heartfelt thanks goes to Leo Pando, for insightfully leading me into the universe of comics and comic-book heroes; Dr. Debra Baeder, for guiding me as I ventured into the fascinating world of forensic psychology; Dr. Louisa Barnhart, for her insight into the mind and medication; and Dr. Michael Klein, who shared his experience dealing with emergencies like the one that begins this novel. I only regret that I could implement a tiny fraction of their vast knowledge, and that for this story I did frequently break out my poetic license.

Also, I greatly appreciate the counsel of my editor, Genevieve Morgan, and the vote of confidence of Islandport Press publisher Dean Lunt, who has rounded up all the McMorrow novels and presented them handsomely. And a shout-out goes to copy editor Melissa Hayes for reading *Random Act* so very carefully.

Lastly, for my family, who patiently listened as I used them as sounding boards yet again. Now I will leave you alone. But not for long.

—Gerry Boyle, June 2019

READER'S GUIDE

We hope you've enjoyed *Random Act*, the twelfth novel in the Jack McMorrow mystery series. Many readers race through the pages of a McMorrow novel, so we are including these discussion questions in the hope that you take time to reflect on the story and characters and talk about your reactions with other Boyle fans.

Early on in the novel, Jack is at the scene of a brutal crime. The murder of Lindy Hines drives Jack to report on the crime and understand Teak's motivation. Why do you think Jack can't let go? Do you think this obsessive characteristic is good for Jack? Is it a characteristic necessary in a journalist?

McMorrow novels are populated by authentic Maine characters. In Random Act, *Boyle introduces Marta to the mix. She is from a very different world from Sanctuary or Prosperity, Maine, or even Bangor. What did you think of Marta? Intriguing? Unsettling?*

Speaking of Marta, this story reveals more of Louis's past, and clues to his present life. How do you relate to Louis? How does the introduction of his love interest change the dynamic between Jack, Clair, and Louis?

The friendship between Jack and Clair is one of the most enduring relationships Jack has. How does this friendship impact Jack's success? Would Jack be able to do what he does without Clair?

While many readers enjoy spending time with Jack, others love Clair. If you could meet either character for coffee in real life, which one would it be?

In Random Act, *Boyle and McMorrow explore the world of mental illness and homelessness. Did that strike you as a realistic portrayal?*

Lindy Hines is clearly the victim in Random Act. *But are there others? Who?*

Boyle's mysteries are about serious stuff but they also have elements of humor. Were there moments in Random Act *that made you laugh?*

Boyle has said that there have been times when he thought he might have written novels with McMorrow's friend Clair as the protagonist. And for one movie project, he wrote a screenplay that featured Roxanne as the heroine and McMorrow was barely in the story. Who would you like to see in the spotlight in the next McMorrow novel?

McMorrow has been chasing down stories for many years now. What kind of challenges do you think an author faces writing a long series? How has the world changed? How has the role of newspapers changed?